WRITTEN IN THE Deep

Written in the Deep

By E.L.Irwin

www.elirwin.com

ISBN979-8-9911671-3-0

Cover Design by Jena Brignola

To those unafraid to dream, the ones who see possibility over every horizon.

May you never steal, lie, or cheat. But if you must steal, then steal away my
sorrows. If you must lie, then lie with me all the nights of my life. And if
you must cheat, then please cheat death, because I could never live a day
without you.

--An Irish Blessing

Contents

CHAPTER ONE

Unexpected

Bethany-

My phone buzzed dragging my eyes from the figures in front of me to see an incoming text from my longtime boyfriend, Garrett. Mouth lifting in a tired grin, I swiped up and read:

We need to talk. It's important.

That sounds ominous. Pushing back from the desk, taking a welcome break from going over the ranch books, I rubbed my eyes and stretched. *He'd better not be bailing on me to go rodeo somewhere; he promised.* Taking a drink of my lemon water, then a deep breath, I replied:

You want to come over?

I certainly couldn't leave right now. New guests were scheduled the day after tomorrow and I had a hundred and one things to tend to beforehand. *He knows this.* Waiting for his response, my mind made lists, organizing the tasks, trying not to forget anything. My phone buzzed:

No.

I waited, brows raised, *no?* That was it? Irritated and about to reply, bubbles indicating he was responding came up.

Look, I'm sorry, Bethany...

My heart squeezed sharply in my chest, as tension sank its teeth into my gut. *Sorry for what?* And why did this sorry somehow feel...different? His message continued:

I'm sorry to do this by text. But I can't face you, or your parents, right now. And maybe that makes me a coward—but I guess I just don't care. Better a coward and alive, than brave and dead.

My pulse beat slow and painful as my hands started to shake, making it almost impossible to text back:

What are you trying to say, Garrett? Are you...what are you trying to say?

I held my breath, waiting for his reply, fighting to keep the panic at bay.

You know we've been floundering for a while now. I just can't, in good faith, allow this to go on any longer. You deserve better. I deserve better. So, this is it. I'm ending things between us.

With trembling fingers, I typed:

What are you even talking about? We've been fine, at least I thought so.

With each passing second, my heart thudded, raw and achy in my chest. Rubbing at it, I waited.

You'll always have a place in my heart, but I don't love you any longer—I haven't for some time now. I thought maybe that spark, that fire would light again, but it hasn't and I can't go on living a lie. So...this is it. We're done. I'm sorry.

Pain, sharp and stabbing, lanced through me. My breath stuttered as I blinked the moisture from my eyes.

Garrett, no. Just come over. Please.

Please, just come over. I knew if we could simply talk about this, we could work things out and get back on track. He didn't reply for several long moments, then:

Do you want your stuff back? Or no? I can leave your things with my sister if you want them. Though, if it's not too much to ask, I do need my Navy ballcap back. Undamaged, please.

I stared at my phone, my heart shattering in my chest. Was he for real?

I can't believe you're breaking up with me...

His text ignored my pain, made it irrelevant in his world:

Should I give your things to Delaney, or not?

He definitely wasn't interested in working anything out. The acute pain brought anger:

This is it? After all this time together, you're just ending it, no reason, just we're over, BY TEXT??

He didn't reply. After three minutes, in which I vacillated between heartbreak and anger, I sent:

I don't want my things back. I'll make sure Delaney gets your hat.

He sent a thumbs up emoji and that was it. We were over.

Five years together and now nothing. He didn't love me anymore. Didn't want me. I sat in shock for several minutes, feeling my heart crumble more with each painful breath I took. It felt as though my lungs had forgotten how to work. He'd called himself a coward, and obviously, he was one, however, there was also some truth to his claim. And I needed to be in control of myself before going to face my parents. Because there was a strong likelihood that they would sincerely want to kill him. Or, at the very least maim him.

Garrett and I had begun seeing each other our sophomore year of high school, continuing well past graduation. We had talked of marriage and a future together, like every other normal couple had done. It hadn't always been perfect. What, with him doing rodeo, and his talk of joining the Navy, we'd had our moments. But those had been few and far between and we'd stuck with it, both of us committed to *us*, to making things last for the long haul. Or so I'd thought. Never in a million years could I have imagined Garrett and I might break up. We were *it*. Voted cutest couple all three years we were together in high school.

We had so much in common. We both loved country living: horses, riding, the quiet life. He'd been a nice boyfriend. I mean, there were times I'd wanted to hold him under water until all the bubbles stopped, but who didn't feel exasperated with their significant other at times? And, my parents had even seemed to like him, or at the very least, they hadn't killed him or threatened to kill him—that I knew of any way. Nor had any of my adopted aunts or uncles.

I say adopted, because they weren't blood family—simply people we were extremely close to and had been my entire life. My aunts and uncles had all been close friends of my parents long before I was born. Mom's best friends: Calvin, Gina, Candi, and the twins, Deken and Derek, who now lived in Montana, she'd known since she was a small child. Calvin had known Mom the longest, having been raised by my grandparents—Mom's parents—Granny and Papa, after Uncle Cal's dad had passed away.

Calvin and Gina had married not long before I was born. Mom's other friend, my Native American aunt, Candi, had married Dad's close friend Cory when I was three; I'd been a flower girl in their wedding. She and Uncle Cory lived down in Southern California. Aunt Candi is a dress designer and has been since designing my mother's wedding dress and her business had taken off. Dad's other best friend, the one he was closest to, Samuel, had married Tiffany. Tiffy, we all called her, had been a ranch guest before falling in love with the area, my family, and Uncle Samuel. All of them had been the best family I could have asked for and none of them had seemed to mind my boyfriend.

Garrett...had been perfect for me. At least, I'd thought so. He was taller than me, which is a plus—and a must—because I'm tall: five foot ten and a half. I blame my dad for that. Garrett was strong and a hard worker. And he was a good kisser. His arms had made me feel safe, cherished.

I understood his need to avoid my parents, though. My dad was intimidating even when being friendly. Dad was...well, not former military, per se; he'd never enlisted. But through a private contractor he was employed for, he'd had all the training. The scary kind. He used to do government undercover stuff; I don't know much about it—my parents are tightlipped about that part of Dad's past. But I do know that he was, and still is, known as someone you don't mess with. And he knows people. People who can make other people disappear. Permanently. My mother isn't too far off. Not former military or anything, but she's been known to be confrontational. Though, I'm told she's mellowed quite a lot over the years. Not to say that my parents are mean or cruel. Not at all. They'd literally give you the shirt off their backs. They were just, shall we say, protective of their only child. As well as each other, and basically everyone they loved.

I took a deep breath, holding it until my chest burned, before slowly letting it out. Then repeated the exercise five more times. When I felt strong enough, I found Mom in the arena brushing her horse, Red. She didn't ride him anymore; he was just too old, but she brushed and walked him daily. Like Red, she'd trained her new saddlehorse, Rhys, from a colt as well. From outside the fence, I studied her a moment, making certain my emotions were in check. We share our blond hair and green eyes. Though where Mom was tall and curvy, I was more willowy. I have curves, they're just not as pronounced as hers, and mine tend to get a little overlooked on my taller and thinner frame. Most people who meet us think we're sisters. I guess that means I've got good genes and should, hopefully, age well, because she still looks fantastic. Not that I needed to worry about that any time soon. I was only twenty years old, after all, and wouldn't be twenty-one for a couple more months.

"Hey." I opened the gate and moved towards her.

"Hey, sweetie." Mom finished what she was doing before turning to face me. By that time, I was standing beside Red, finger-combing his mane. She got one good look at my face, which apparently wasn't as controlled as I'd hoped, and gently gripped my shoulder. "Baby, *what's wrong?* What happened?"

I couldn't hold back the tears. My lip trembled as I tried to find my voice, and had to swallow several times to get the lump out of my throat. When I'd finally managed to get the whole story out, she pulled me into her embrace and the tears really started. Mom held me, letting me get all the emotion out, rubbing my back in soothing, circular motions. When my emotion was spent and I'd calmed down, she softly snarled, "I'll kill him."

Pulling back, I shook my head and tried to wipe the moisture from my face. "No, Mom. Just let it be. It's over. *We're* over."

"He *hurt* you."

"I know he did, but...just let it be. Please?"

Her gaze searched mine, before nodding silently. "What do you need? What can I do?"

"Would you let Dad know, and make sure he doesn't go after Garrett? I'm going for a ride—I need some time to think, okay?"

"I will." Mom hugged me again, just a quick squeeze, before pulling back and giving me space. "It'll be okay. *You'll* be okay. I promise. You're strong and wise beyond your years. You'll come through this stronger than you were. I love you, baby."

"I love you, too, Mom, and thanks. I'll finish the guest-prep when I get back." Turning, I headed for the barn. My horse, a big silver-black Appaloosa gelding whinnied from his stall, bobbing his head up and down in anticipation. I greeted Wick, named for the character John Wick, with a chuckle, a sniff, and a bit of carrot I'd swiped from the crisper in the fridge. I let him out of the stall and scratched Mom's gelding, Rhys, before turning towards the tack room, knowing Wick would follow me. I took the time to brush out his coat before saddling him. Letting those actions and his nearness soothe me. The whisk of the coarse bristles over his soft coat. The calming scent of *horse*. I inhaled deeply, taking him in, held it, then slowly let it out as I lay my head against his neck and leaned into his sturdy frame.

Wick stands just shy of sixteen hands. His coat was a mottled dark grey, with a black mane, tail, and socks. Across his rump was a white blanket sprinkled with black and grey spots of various sizes and shapes. In short, he was beautiful, and I loved him. Like Mom had with both of her horses, I'd trained him myself and have had him since he was six months old.

Ten minutes later, Wick and I were headed for the hills. Sundown was still several hours off, so we had plenty of time. Hitting the trail, I surrendered to the horse, the saddle, and the mountain, letting everything else fade away.

I arrived back at the Jump Off—which was what we called the location where all the ranch trails began—as the sun was beginning to set. I pulled Wick to a stop as we reached the low ridge where it overlooked the house and barn. Further on, up in the trees, the roofline for the house I'd been born in could be seen. We'd lived there the first five years of my life, until Granny and Papa had approached Mom and Dad with the idea of swapping houses. They'd said they were feeling too old to be running the ranch and wanted to slow down. Mom and Dad took over the management of The Blues Avenue and my grandparents had started travelling. Now, I resided in the room that had been my mother's when she was growing up. It was the house my parents had courted in. A lot of history lay here, and I found this view of the ranch one of the most beautiful sights around.

As my eyes took in the rugged and beautiful landscape, my mind inevitably turned back to the events of the last several hours. Garrett and I had intended to live here and build our lives together. Eventually, we'd intended to take over the running of the ranch, as my parents had done before me. My throat closed up again as in my mind, I reread his text. As I relived those crushing moments. Rejection, no matter the form it comes in, is a bitter pill to swallow. Logically, I knew I'd get through this. It would be hard and painful, but I would make it. Knowing that made what I was currently feeling only the smallest amount better. Still, I guess, it was better than nothing. My heart would need time to heal. I knew this. *One day at a time, Bethany.*

My phone had been vibrating with notifications nearly nonstop for the last hour or so. I'd ignored all of it, waiting until I'd taken care of Wick and the other horses for the night before pulling it out of my pocket.

Seventy-three notifications waited.

Several were from Delaney, Garrett's sister, and my best friend. Several more from Jack, my best guy friend. Jack was Aunt Gina and Uncle Cal's oldest, named Jack after my mom's dad, Papa Jackson. And then there were the texts from the rest of the aunts and uncles: Calvin, Gina, Cory, Candi, Samuel, Tiffy, Deken, and Derek.

They were all basically the same message in various forms. Was I okay? They were sorry. Should they kill him? And Delaney had added that her brother was the most colossally stupid person she knew. Delaney wanted to come over, but I wasn't ready for company yet. I needed to see my dad first and make sure all was fine there.

Taking a deep breath, I stepped into the house. He was waiting for me, leaning against the kitchen counter. In addition to being former intelligence, Dad was a former Hollywood heartthrob, and actor—it had been his cover and was the means to how he'd met Mom. The studio he'd worked for, at the time, had hired Mom to train Dad for a role in a movie he'd been contracted for. And, though he's now in his fifties, Dad still looks good. Was still tall and muscled. Still intimidating. His stunning blue eyes rested gently on me and though it had been hours since everything had happened, to my chagrin, I felt my mouth tremble and my eyes prick. Dad moved away from the counter, taking me in his arms. He didn't say anything, simply held me tightly, chin resting on my head, as I fell to pieces again.

After I'd quieted down and lifted my head from his chest, Dad wiped my face with the kitchen towel, then tenderly placed a kiss on my forehead, and sighed. "You know I want to kill him, right? Or maybe just make him cry for a good long while?"

I nodded, another tear falling, even as I sniffed in mild humor. "Don't. Don't do anything, Dad. Okay?"

"I won't, kitten." He'd given me the nickname on the day of my birth when I'd entered the world screaming like a Banshee, and he'd said I'd been adorable, like a cute, chubby, angry kitten. "But I'd *really* like to."

"I know." I acknowledged.

"You all right?"

I inhaled. "I will be."

"That's right," he nudged the underside of my chin with a knuckle "you will. He's not worth it. Not worth your time, energy, nor tears. He never was."

My voice trembled. "It just hurts. I thought he was the one, you know?"

"I know. And I know it hurts. That's *why* I'd like to kill him."

"But you won't," I stated as firmly as I was able. "And you won't have anyone else do it for you either, right?"

"Maybe just a little killing?" Dad pinched his fingers together. Then at my silent stare, he studied me in seeming contemplation. Finally, he relented on a longsuffering sigh. "Right. Scout's honor."

Seriously, I had the best parents ever. "Thanks. I'm going to shower, then plan to head to bed. I need to be up early as I've still got things to get done before the next guests arrive. I love you, guys."

Before hitting the shower, I called Delaney. "Bethany! I am *so* sorry. So, so sorry. What was my brother *thinking?* Are you okay?"

"It's all right, Del." I tried to instill life into my voice, but I was drained and struggling. "Not gonna lie and say this doesn't hurt, because it does. But I'm fine. Really."

She seemed to absorb that, then asked, "What did your parents say? Are they going to kill my brother?"

"No one is killing anyone. We're over." I shrugged to myself, knowing she couldn't see me. "That's it. Life moves on."

"Why did he have to ruin everything?" Her voice trembled and came out breathy.

"Del, don't be angry with him. He's your brother. As much as I'm angry and hurt by this, I don't want you guys to be at odds."

"I know. I love him. I do. But I'm furious with him. I can't even look at him right now."

"Well, I'm okay. I will *be* okay. It'll take me a little time, but I'll heal." My head was beginning to throb, probably from all the tears, and exhaustion was creeping in. "I need to shower and get to bed; I've got a crap ton still to do tomorrow to get guest-ready. Love you."

"Love you, too. And I'm coming over tomorrow to help, and I'm bringing brownies."

That made me smile. "Sounds like a plan, thanks. Goodnight."

"'Night."

I hung up, then sent a text off to Jack, letting him know I was fine and would talk with him tomorrow. I figured Mom or Dad would let the uncles know. I wondered if Granny and Papa had been told yet. They were somewhere in the Mediterranean on a cruise. Sighing, I grabbed clean PJ's and headed for the shower.

Jack-

   Call me.

Jack read the text as he turned the bacon in the skillet. Delaney had called in tears over two hours ago, telling him the news of Bethany's and Garrett's breakup. He couldn't say he was saddened by the news; he'd never really liked the guy. Had more tolerated him on account of Bethany and Delaney. How Del and he were siblings was anyone's guess. They were two completely different people. Delaney was kind, warm, and thoughtful. Not to mention gorgeous. She wasn't tall. Average height. But she made up for any shortage with personality. Happy. Joyful. Bringing a smile to those around her.

Not so with Garrett. Punk was a good word for him. Dirtbag was another. Always complaining. Finding something to criticize in those around him. Both Delaney and Bethany were accomplished riders, but he'd find a way to critique and pick apart everything they did. How Bethany had always seen it as Garrett just trying to help was beyond him. Now, the jerk had broken both Bethany's and Delaney's hearts, and for that alone was Jack sorry over the news. He hated seeing either of the girls in pain. Turning the stove off, Jack dialed Del's number.

"Jack." When she answered, he could tell she'd been crying again. Her voice sounded thick. Despite that, he felt the velvet in it brush over him, causing his heart to stumble.

"Hey." He leaned against the counter, hating the anguish in her voice.

"I spoke with her."

"How's Bethy doing?" From his early years, when he'd struggled to pronounce Bethany, saying it more like Bethaminny, he'd given up and had just called her Bethy. This simplified rendering of her name had stuck, and years later, that was what he still called her. "She texted back a bit ago, but I haven't spoken with her yet."

"She's in pain." Delaney sniffed. "She sounded wounded and exhausted."

"That's to be expected."

"I know. I just don't understand." Her breath stuttered. "Why would Garrett do this? *Why?*"

"You know he's always danced to his own tune."

Delaney was silent a moment. "You never really liked him, did you?"

Jack blew out a breath. "I tolerated him, for your sakes."

"They could have had everything, Jack. The house, kids, white picket fence, *everything*."

"Some guys are just never satisfied. And that's a deficiency in them, not those around them."

"I'm going to the ranch tomorrow, to help her get things ready. And I'm making brownies."

Jack smiled to himself. Delaney could cook. "I'm in. What time?"

"Probably between ten and eleven."

"See you then."

Callie-

Callie Fitzpatrick and Olivia Gunn had met at university and become fast friends, their relationship lasting for decades on end. Though Callie lived in Ireland and Olivia in Scotland, they remained close and devoted to each other. They'd even stood up in each other's weddings. It had been a dream of theirs, a whimsical idea more or less, that when their grandchildren had been born, first Liam to the Gunn's, then six years later Bethany to the Fitzpatrick's, the two friends had laughingly joked amidst the congratulations, that Bethany and Liam be promised to each other. Years had gone by, and though the two of them talked about the idea frequently, there'd never seemed to be an opportunity.

Now, Callie hung up the phone, just as the sun rose, and stared into the distance. Her youngest, Asher, had called, as he was inclined to do—they spoke each week, same day, same time. Today he'd seemed off. Callie, being the mother she was, heard the difference in the tenor of his voice and questioned him. She'd learned of Bethany's recent heartache and her own heart had gone out to her granddaughter. As she'd done several times before, Callie had extended an invitation for Bethany to come visit. As a family, Asher, Kate, and Bethany had been to Ireland to see them many times, but Bethany had never had a chance to come by herself. Maybe now would be a good time. Asher said he'd see and keep that option open.

On a whim, Callie went to her computer and fired it up. Then she opened her email and composed a new letter:

Dearest Olivia,

I hope to find you and Harold doing well. A development has occurred that may or may not bring about something you and I have long hoped for. Bethany, might, I repeat, might be coming for an extended visit. Should that prove to be the case, what is Liam up to these days? Think he'd fancy coming? Let me know.

Your friend,

Callie

The reply came early the following morning.

Dearest Callie,

I think Tiernan should have an injury of some sort. Liam wouldn't bat an eye about coming to help you run things while Tiernan recuperates. He'd never suspect a thing. It may just work.

Olivia

Bethany-

"Bethany, you know your mother and I, we love you." Dad began, nearly six weeks later. I was in the barn rubbing down the horse I'd been working. Another project I'd taken on to keep my mind off, well, everything. Largely succeeding, there were still times when it all came rushing back. Then my heart would crack again and the tears would come. Though, mostly it was anger that came now. I'd thought I was getting better at dealing with it, or at the least, hiding it. Guess I wasn't doing that good a job, as Dad was now looking quite concerned. I was proud of him, of Dad. He hadn't gone after Garrett, had just held me as my tears fell and told me I'd be okay. "But, kitten," he continued, "this has got to stop. You can't keep hiding out here on the ranch. You can't keep avoiding people in town." Dad leaned his big frame down, lowering his head, making sure our eyes met, so I'd know this was serious.

To be honest, he was right. I had been hiding out and avoiding people, though I didn't like admitting it. It was simply me avoiding hearing from anyone attempting to commiserate or sympathize. Offering condolences. *Ugh.* My feelings were scattered, embarrassed, and pathetic, and didn't require a witness. Scattered, because a part of me still ached over what might have been, what I'd put my hope in. Embarrassed, because I'd so thoroughly trusted in Garrett and our relationship, and pathetic for crying over him for as long as I had. Cody, Wyoming isn't that big of a town. Running into him was bound to happen. Avoiding that likelihood was the goal. Not because I was weak and thought I'd cry, but rather because I wasn't entirely sure I'd be able to refrain from saying or doing something that might require bail money afterwards. Garrett's ending things had ripped the blinders off. My hindsight was 20/20, allowing me to clearly see him for who he was. An unhappy, unsatisfied man-child, discontented with the world around him.

And *none* of that had been my fault. I'd tried appeasing him and his need for perfection. But it wasn't me he was truly unhappy with; it was himself.

"We've spoken with your grandparents," Mom said without preamble as she came to stand beside Dad, taking his hand in hers. "You're going to stay with them for a few months this summer."

I blinked. "Um, Mom, that's great, but you know they only live about a hundred yards away, right? And besides, they're still gone."

"Not those grandparents, kitten." Dad's tone called me out even as his voice firmed. "You're going to stay with Grandma Callie and Grandpa Tiernan."

"I'm going to Ireland?" I said deadpanned.

"Just for a few months, to give you a change of scenery. Your grandparents are looking forward to having you to themselves for a while." Mom slipped her arms around me. "*Go.* Learn to breathe again, baby. We'll hold things down here."

"But, I...I can't! I've got...horses to ride. Responsibilities."

"You can." Dad placed a hand on my shoulder, no give in his demeanor. "Jack and your mother are going to finish up those horses you took on. Your uncles are close and will pitch in where we need help. We've taken care of everything. You leave in two weeks. Besides, your grandparents could really use your help right now. They're both getting on in age and are slowing down. Your grandpa seems to have twisted his ankle and, well, I think this works out the whole way around."

"Two *weeks!*" My voice hit a higher octave. It wasn't that I was entirely opposed to going to see my grandparents. Actually, going to Ireland sounded amazing. It was more that my parents hadn't consulted me when they'd made these plans. Then again, I'd have most likely fought them on the idea—I had a stubborn streak a mile wide. That I'd inherited from both of my parents, I might add. "I...I just can't...is Granda all right?"

"He's fine." Dad dismissed my concern. "Just some discomfort and swelling. He's got a couple local lads coming to lend a hand with the heavier stuff. They fixed up that attic space, making it a third story, with two bedrooms and a bathroom now. You'll be able to stay there and have some privacy when they have guests."

My grandparents ran a small Bed and Breakfast, just three rooms, from their little farm in Kealkill, Bantry, Ireland. I was quite familiar with the area from our numerous trips to visit them over the years, and loved it there. Loved my grandparents, too. Maybe this would be a good thing. I'd have to see. Though, I was still annoyed I hadn't been consulted at all about these plans. Was annoyed with Jack—the traitor—for going behind my back like he had and conspiring with my parents. He'd be hearing from me soon enough. "What about my birthday?" I whined.

"You'll celebrate it there." Mom grinned. "Where better to celebrate your twenty-first than in Ireland?"

Jack-

She's going to kill you when she finds out you did this.

Jack muted the TV and grinned at Del's text, giving her his full attention. Smothering his smile, he responded:

She'll be fine. Bethy needs to go.

Delaney's response came swiftly:

Oh, I'm not arguing that, but she's still gonna be furious.

Jack scratched at his chin as an idea took root. Testing the waters, he sent:

If she hurts me, you can kiss it and make it better.

She responded with a laughing face emoji and:

In your dreams.

Lately, yes. Jack ran a thoughtful thumb over his lower lip. He needed to keep a lid on his growing feelings for Delaney. Now wasn't the time to complicate things. He'd need to wait and proceed with caution. He definitely didn't want to lose his friendship with her, even if what he wanted was to be more than friends.

Callie-

Callie hung up the phone and tried to contain her hopeful glee. Bethany was coming. Barely containing her excitement, she opened her email and sent her friend this letter:

Dearest Olivia,

Bethany is coming here! She arrives in about two weeks and will stay for the summer, well through August. We told Asher that Tiernan twisted his ankle and could use the help. See what you can do to get Liam here.

Callie

CHAPTER TWO

A Conundrum

Bethany-

As I entered the barn, Jack was coming from the tack room, saddle and bridle in hand. Not hesitating, I walked right up and poked him sharply in the chest.

"Ouch, Bethy!" He flinched back. "What'd'ya do that for?"

"You know why, you little traitor!" I hissed, striving to keep my voice down. "How could you side with them?"

Sighing deeply, Jack set the items he was carrying down, then put his hands on my shoulders, holding me in place. "Because you needed to go. You know you need this, you're just too stubborn to admit it. Besides, you'd have done the same for me and you know it."

"Could have given me a heads-up, though."

"Would that have made any difference?" He shook his head. "You'd have fought it then, like you're doing now."

"I'm not fighting it."

"So, you're pleased to go then?" he challenged.

"I'm not angry about going; I'm angry the decision wasn't mine to make, that you all made the choice for me."

"Semantics, Bethy." Jack carefully jerked me forward, pulling me into his chest, holding me close. "Not much to do about it now, except go. Stop fighting it."

My breath escaped my chest and I slumped against him. Jack was not only taller than me by several inches, but he was stronger, which had always irritated me. Right now, though, I appreciated those aspects about him. "I'm not fighting it, Jack. I'm not. I'm just…"

"I know." He squeezed me gently. "Which is why you need to go. You need to get him out of your system, out of your heart, and out of your head. He was never worth your time. Take this opportunity to rediscover you."

"How'd you get to be so wise?" I grumbled good-naturedly as I pressed my forehead against his chest.

"I've got a great younger cousin," he squeezed me again, "who gave me similar advice once. I took notes."

Chuckling, I pulled back, took a breath, kissed his cheek, then headed to the tack room to gather my own gear for the horses I'd ride today.

Liam-

Liam Gunn pushed away from the table and stretched his tall, work-hardened frame, before settling back in his seat. Though educated as a lawyer, his heart hadn't been in it. Sun, soil, and livestock were in his blood and called to him. Something that displeased his father greatly, though his grandparents had always supported him in his endeavors. His gaze now searched that of his grandmother and grandfather, going from one to the other. He loved them deeply; they'd been strong, constructive roles in his often-turbulent home life, and he would be eternally grateful for them and their calming influence.

Around them and their table flowed the pub noises. Conversations, laughter, the tinkle of ice in glasses, the rattle of silverware, the crackle of flames in the hearth. He scratched at the whickers on his chin. "Yer sayin' I'm to go Ireland for the summer? And who's to be helpin' the two of ye whilst I'm away?"

"We've got that covered as young Eoin will be available. And Callie and Tiernan really need the help," Harold, his grandfather, said. "They're booked solid, and even with their granddaughter coming, they'll need a hand. Tiernan has sprained his ankle somethin' fierce."

"Aye." He thought over what they'd just proposed. Namely, that he'd go to Ireland for the summer months to help their longtime family friends as they ran their Bed and Breakfast and farm. He wasn't averse to going. Had been many times over the years. Was quite familiar with the area and families—it wouldn't be a hardship. And though he'd had plans to start dating the new lass in the bakery down the lane, he was glad to go. Something they said though... "Ye said the granddaughter...which granddaughter would that be?" If he was to play nanny to some little preteen, he'd maybe think twice about that idea.

"The American one," Olivia, his grandmother, casually said as she took a sip from her pint.

That brought him up short. The American granddaughter. Aye, but which one? Echoing his thoughts, he said, "As I recall, they've three of them. Care to narrow it down?"

"Sorry, love. It'll be Bethany. Ye remember her."

"Aye." Bethany. Liam's heart struck a furious pace in his chest, and it took him a moment to catch his breath. From the first time he'd seen her he'd been ensnared. Even at three years old, she was the bonniest wee thing around. Like an angel, all golden and lovely with those green eyes. He'd followed her like a faithful hound, making sure she was safe and no harm came to her. As the years went by, as both of their families visited in Ireland, he accompanying his grandparents as they called on their close friends, and she as she came with her parents to see her own grandparents, the both of them growing, he'd still found her to be the bonniest wee lass.

Each time he saw her it was like a punch to the gut. She literally stole his breath. She'd had a boyfriend the last time the Fitzpatricks had come. A serious one from what he'd gathered. He'd known it was only a matter of time—lasses like her didn't stay single for long. Still, he'd felt his heart sink as it looked as though his unrealized dreams had come to an end. He'd watched her from afar that last summer, keeping his distance, knowing she was taken; though, the longing never quite left him. Was always there, beneath the surface. Though, he'd tried his best to ignore it and stamp it down. He'd dated other girls over the years, but his gaze always seemed drawn back to her. His thoughts never far from her. He'd never indicated to anyone how he'd felt, keeping his cards close, as he did even now.

Asher, Bethany's father, a man of astute understanding and far reach, had somehow taken note of his regard however. He'd pulled Liam aside and explained in no uncertain terms that was he to ever cross lines, he'd end up in a world of hurt. Though Liam had been young and full of fire, he had believed the man. Still did.

Scratching again at the short, yet thick beard he wore, his thoughts on the blond lass, he asked, as nonchalant as possible, "If the Fitzpatricks are coming, are ye sure I'm needed there? Seems Asher should be able to handle most anything."

"Oh, it's just the granddaughter coming. Not Asher and Kate this time," his grandmother said. "Are ye not wanting to go, then?"

Not the parents. Not Asher. Or Kate. Just Bethany. He hoped his face was blank, giving away none of the rioting thoughts in his head. He wondered how much she'd changed. If she'd still recognize him. If she'd still be oblivious to his attraction. If she'd still have her boyfriend, or worse, if she were married. "Nae. Nae, I'm fine to go. When, ah, when would they need me?"

"She's due to arrive in a couple weeks, just before the season kicks off, so I'd say around that time," Olivia said as they stood from the table.

Harold waved to Seamus, their server, then turned to Liam and clapped him on the back. "Well, lad, are ye able to go?"

Liam held the door for his grandmother, then followed his grandfather out after her. "Sure." He nodded a smile at them. "Sure, and I'll be there." He sat in his lorry for a moment, after they'd driven away, letting the engine warm up a bit before he put it in gear. As he drove home, his thoughts had once more returned to Bethany. There was a lass he could spend the rest of his life with, raise some bairns with. Liam blew out a breath of longing as he parked in front of his loft over the bakery.

Olivia-

Olivia Gunn opened her email as soon as she and Harold arrived home. Her heart pounded, giddy, brimming in excitement and possibility. Things were lining up. Could it work? Would their dreams and prayers be answered? She flexed her fingers over the keyboard, took a deep breath, then typed out a quick message to Callie.

Callie!

We're all set here. Liam's coming. I don't think he suspects a thing and should arrive around the time Bethany comes. I confess, my heart is pounding just thinking on how this may work. You'll have to keep me posted on the progress. I can hardly stand to sit still. Oh, I hope this works as we've dreamed.

Olivia

Liam-

About a week after dinner with his grandparents, as Liam unlocked his door, his cellphone rang. He'd answered without looking, his phone wedged against his shoulder, as he wrangled the key from the lock. "This's Liam."

"Liam, this is Asher Fitzpatrick."

Liam's heart stalled in his chest, and he had to clear his throat. "Aye, what can I do for ye, Mr. Fitzpatrick?"

"Dad said you were coming for the summer to help with the farm. I appreciate that and wanted to ask a favor of you."

"Go on." His throat was dry, and he found himself desperate for a drink. Any drink. Something to settle his nerves.

"You might have heard, Bethany's coming to stay and I wanted to ask you to keep an eye on her. She's recently had her heart broken and doesn't need to have it broken again."

"Aye." Frowning, Liam rubbed at his lip and considered the man who'd been foolish enough to break her heart and let her go. *What a bleedin' idiot.* "Aye, I will."

"I'm depending on you, Liam. Don't let me down."

"Nae sir, I willna."

"Much obliged." Asher hung up and Liam collapsed on the sofa, waiting for his heart to restart.

Asher-

Kate watched him, her eyes sparkling. "Well?" she asked as he set his cellphone down on the dresser. "What did he say?"

Asher approached his wife where she lay in their bed, waiting for him, his pulse already racing. "He said he'd keep an eye on her." His gaze travelled up her leg, taking a deep breath as he took her in.

"Do you think he suspects anything?"

"I do not." Asher knelt on the bed, his knee brushing her thigh as he leaned over her. "It's all set. He's going, and he'll keep an eye on our kitten." He kissed her, his mouth lingering against hers. "Now that that's settled, I don't want to talk about any other men while in this bed with you."

Kate grinned up at him even as he stole her breath. He heard the prayer she offered up, that Bethany would be healed and made stronger from this fire she was walking through. Then, he made sure she didn't think about anything else as he clicked the light off and loved her thoroughly.

CHAPTER THREE

Meant to Be

Bethany-

In the end, it didn't matter what I'd said, or even that I was an adult capable of making my own decisions. I was going and that was that. Final. One might have thought being twenty, almost twenty-one, might have made some difference; one would have been mistaken. So, it was that two weeks later, Dad was hugging me tightly, silver lining his eyes. "I love you, kitten. Be safe. Have fun. We'll see you in August."

Mom pulled me close as well, wrapping me tightly in her arms. "Don't be too mad at us. It was this, or we killed him. I figured you'd prefer this to us going to prison."

That made me laugh. "I love you, Mom. Thanks for always knowing what to say and what I need. You guys are the best. Truly."

Mom let me go, then with passport and boarding pass in hand, I stepped into line. Looking back, I noted several people taking pictures and pointing at my parents, then me. It was something we'd gotten used to over the years—Dad's movie star status. Then he met Mom and walked away from it all. And though he had a touch of silver now in his brown hair, he was still good-looking and got quite a bit of attention wherever he went. Dad was still fit, still a presence no matter where he was or what he was doing. And Mom, though in her early forties, was still beautiful, and still drew admiring glances. Only from a distance, though; no one was stupid enough to provoke my father.

I studied them as I stood in line. Their love was the stuff of fairy tales. Legend even. I wanted, desperately wanted, what they had. That kind of love and devotion. The love they have for one another...their passion...that's what I'd hoped to have someday. I'd thought I'd found that in Garrett. Familiar angry heat laced through me. No. I wouldn't dwell on that now. This was a new start, and *he* was history.

I waved as I reached the security checkpoint, and saw Dad place a gentle kiss against Mom's brow, each comforting the other at my leaving. Taking a deep breath, I turned to the security officer and handed over my documents.

My flight took me from Cody to Salt Lake City, where I caught my connection to Dublin. I found my seat and saw the one next to mine was already taken. A young woman, probably close to my age, was in the window seat. She offered a shy smile as I stowed my bag in the overhead compartment. "Hi." I smiled back as I sat beside her.

"Hello," she responded. She turned away then and faced the window. I leaned back and adjusted the seatbelt, getting comfortable. Flight attendants made their way up and down the aisles, helping everyone prepare for takeoff. From the corner of my eye, I noted my seatmate's hands grip the armrests, turning white as she squeezed tightly. "Nervous?" I asked.

Swallowing, she nodded.

"First time flying?"

Again, she nodded.

"There's not much to it; really. Bit of a rumble at takeoff and landing, but otherwise, it's smooth sailing. Or, flying, I guess."

"Thanks." Her voice was barely more than a whisper. The inflight passenger announcements began, and the girl beside me focused unerringly on them, as if her life depended on it. Which, I supposed, it might, God forbid. Not wanting to distract her, I remained silent, having heard it several times before. I wondered what her story was, where she was going. Maybe she was off to school or starting a new job. There were so many possibilities. Maybe she was travelling to get over a broken heart, like I was. Either way, it was her business, not mine. My heart went out to her, though; she looked so forlorn. Often, I've wondered at the people we meet in life. Why they were put there in the first place. Maybe I was seated beside this girl to simply offer her comfort as she obviously faced her fear or anxieties of flying.

Once the cabin crew were all seated and the plane began taxiing down the runway, hoping to take the girl's mind off our impending takeoff, and hopefully easing some of her concerns, I asked, "Where are you headed?"

Taking a deep breath, she replied, "Ireland."

"So am I! My name's Bethany, by the way. What part of Ireland?"

"Ivy," she smiled. "Mainly Cork and Clare."

"Oh, nice! Are you going by yourself? Or are you meeting someone there?"

"Just me."

"Wow, that's awesome. Wish I'd taken the time, or been brave enough, to go on my own before. I've been several times with my parents—my grandparents live just north of Kealkill in County Cork—so we visit them quite regularly. But I've never been on my own. What brings you to the Emerald Island?"

"To be quite honest, I'm...not sure really. I simply wanted to go. It seemed like a good idea...so here I am."

We continued talking well into the flight. I learned she was from a town called Sequim, pronounced skwim, in Washington state. She worked at a bookstore there and I thought that was pretty cool. We shared more as the flight went on, just talking. She seemed to calm down, which I was grateful for. Then after dinner was served, we each retreated into our own activities. She turned on a movie and I reached for a book. At some point I must have fallen asleep, because the next thing I knew, breakfast was being served. I hoped Ivy had been able to rest and didn't feel I'd abandoned her. Not long after that we began our descent as the plane made its way over Ireland. Ivy leaned closer to the window to get a better view. I couldn't blame her; it was beautiful. So many different shades of green surrounded by the deep blue of the ocean.

Ivy and I made the short exchange in Dublin to catch the next flight on to Cork. That one seemed to take only a handful of minutes. No sooner had we lifted off, it felt like we were touching down again. Ivy and I hadn't sat beside each other this time, but she was just two seats in front of me and I was able to keep an eye on her. She appeared fine, and the flight was so short I didn't overly worry.

Once the seatbelt light turned off, I stood and stretched as I gathered my things from the overhead. "Ivy, it was really great to meet you. Here's my number, in case you need anything, even if it's just a face you happen to know." I handed her my business card.

"Thank you so much. I appreciate that and may take you up on your offer."

"Do; I look forward to it." We were exiting the plane by then and I looked for my grandparents. With Dad being so tall, nearly six feet, five inches, you'd think my grandparents would be tall. They're not. Well, Granda is right at six feet, but Nana is closer to five feet. She was so short I had to bend over to hug her. And did so, as I reached them where they waited, hand in hand, a little way past the exit terminal. Bright smiles had lit their faces as soon as they'd spotted me. Once all the hugs and happy tears of greetings were out of the way, we got my luggage and were quickly on the road.

With a new, more grownup outlook, my eyes took in the scenery as we traversed the roadways. Granda drove and Nana had me sit in the front while she took the back. We reached the R585, headed toward Kealkill, and of course, everything was green. Literally every shade of green as far as the eye could see. Mosses of various kind grew on every surface it seemed: the rock fences, brick and wood structures, trees. The air held a rich, earthy scent. Clean, damp, and refreshing. We crossed and recrossed small rivers and streams as we made our way. Trees, glens, and houses peaked at us through the low cloud cover and mist. Occasionally, we'd see a cow, or horse, or a random sheep or two. I'd never want to give up the freedoms

I enjoy living in the US, but there was definitely something magical about this place. Something that spoke to the soul.

"Well, Bethany love, yer da's told us the sad news. It's sorry, yer nana and I am, that you've been hurt by the eejit."

"Thanks, Granda. Yeah...I guess we just weren't meant to be."

Nana patted my shoulder from the back, then squeezed it gently. "Sure, and there's someone out there just for you, pet."

Smiling, I looked at her over my shoulder. "Mom told me the same thing."

"And right she was. You never know. Maybe you'll meet yer lad while here with us?"

"Sure, and Liam'll be along Friday next, to lend us a hand for the summer. He can show you about town and get you a nice fella," Granda stated.

From the corner of my eye, I saw Nana shoot her husband an exasperated look and wondered at its meaning. Maybe Nana was simply irritated Granda was pushing the idea of dating. Either way, the mention of Liam had my heart kicking up. He'd been my secret crush pretty much from the time I understood there was a difference between boys and girls. And though I was recouping from a broken heart, I couldn't deny my heart seemed well enough healed at the moment. Then my head got to thinking and I wondered if he was no longer available. "Liam's coming? And how's he doing? It's been years since I've seen him. He's probably married with a couple kids by now..."

"He is not," Granda stated, taking a firmer grip on the steering wheel. "That's a lad can't seem to settle down. Shame, too, as he's grown into a strapping figure of a man. Tall. Though, not as tall as yer da, now. Oh, but handsome, he is. Has all the lasses sighing over him."

"Oh, there's truth in that," Nana said, a dreamy quality to her voice. "If I were younger, and not married, of course. There's a lad I'd throw my hat at."

"Well, ye are married." Granda threw a good-natured scowl over his shoulder. "So, just you keep yer hat."

"Are we picking him up at the airport, then?" I inhaled long and deep, still trying to convince my heart to settle down.

"No, Sean'll run up to get him. You remember Sean?"

I did. Sean and Liam had been best friends. Where one was, the other was sure to be. "Yeah, I remember him."

"As yer probably tired from the flight, we'll take you on back to the house tonight. We'll go to Collins tomorrow," Nana said as we drove past the pub in question. Collins Bar was the local meeting place in town. When visiting, we ate there at least once per week. It had a wonderful homey and cheery vibe to it. From what I remembered, they poured a great pint, too.

"That's fine; thanks." As I was in Ireland, I was legal to drink, and that pint sounded wonderful. Not that my age would matter much longer as I turned twenty-one next week. I was sure we'd be back at Collins to celebrate my special day. A handful of minutes later, we pulled up to their house. For a moment, I sat and took it all in. Remembering the many fun times I'd had here. The bright, lemon-yellow double swing hanging from the oak tree, where Nana snuck cookies, or biscuits as they were called here, out to me when Mom wasn't looking. The green barn in need of a new coat of paint where I'd first realized I was in love with Liam. He'd taken my little hand in his giant one and led me out to see the newborn calves in the field. I'd thought he was my knight in shining armor, as he'd carried me on his shoulders and kept me safe from all the large cows.

The various buckets and tubs of flowers scattered around lent a splash of color to the already vibrant landscape. Nana had so many flowers. I hoped for even a quarter of the green thumb she possessed. As we got out, Granda said, "I'll pop the boot, then we'll get you settled in."

"You and Liam will be on the top floor, dear. The other rooms are all let. Is that all right?" Nana asked as we approached the front door.

"Yeah, that's perfect. I'll bet you can see for miles from the windows."

"I have you in the rose room overlooking the fields. Thought you'd like that best."

"It'll be perfect, thank you."

They helped me carry my things up to my room on the third floor of their older, yet stately manor house. Nana opened the door and soft light poured into the hallway. Four dormer windows occupied both the north and east walls. A wrought iron double bed sat between one pair, with a dresser standing between the other two. Dark stained wood covered the floor with a large pale green rug laying between the bed and the dresser. The walls were papered in a light cream color with deep burgundy floribunda-type roses scattered throughout its print. Granda set my bags on the bed, while Nana smoothed imagined wrinkles from the ivory quilted bedspread.

"Get settled, freshen up if you wish, then meet us back in the kitchen and we'll have us a cuppa before supper." Nana kissed my cheek, then followed Granda out the door, closing it softly behind her. I unpacked my things, placing them in the dresser and closet. My bathroom things were in a convenient carry case that I placed on the little table beside the door. Then I called Mom and Dad to let them know I'd made it and was, for all intents and purposes, settled in. We talked for a bit; they asked how the flight was, if there were any problems. Dad said he'd heard Liam was coming. Mom was glad he'd be there to help with the farm. Then, as it was late for them, we hung up. After that, I sent texts to both Jack and Del, letting them know I'd made it. A quick trip to the bathroom to wash up, then I changed my clothes to something a little more comfortable, and headed down to the kitchen.

Jack-
Jack dialed Delaney. "She made it; did she tell you?"
"Yeah, she texted."
"You going to miss her?" Jack guessed.
"Of course, same as you."

"Yeah, I will," he nodded to himself.

"You coming in tomorrow?"

"I'll be there."

Delaney smiled to herself after they'd hung up. Jack, she'd found over the last couple of weeks or so, had been a surprising balm to her wounded self. Though her heart hadn't been recently broken, somehow it still was. Having Bethany as her sister had seemed so natural and now that had come to an end. She felt frazzled and wounded by the realization. Jack calmed her somehow. Comforted her. Which was a boon, seeing as how they both worked for The Blues Avenue and would see each other often. Being in his presence made her warm. Not uncomfortably so. Not at all. She took a deep breath, rubbing at her lower lip, and smiled again.

CHAPTER FOUR

The Sruggle is Real

Bethany-

The first night was just us, no other guests, and for that I was happy. It was nice having my grandparents all to myself. Granda lit a fire in the brick fireplace, adding a peat briquette, and soon the homey scent of peat, wood, and spice filled the little room. "How's your ankle, Granda? You seem to be moving on it fairly well." I'd noted nothing in the way of a limp as he'd carried my bags in, nor just now as he'd moved about the parlor. Nana choked, coughing as she pounded her chest; my focus immediately shifted to her. "Nana, are you all right?"

"Yes, dear. Grand. Just swallowed wrong is all." She wiped her mouth. "Granda has his good days and his bad. Today just happened to be a good day. I'll ice it for him later and give him something if he's in pain." Granda had briefly looked like a deer caught in the headlights, but as Nana explained his condition he relaxed and leaned back in his seat, lifting his right leg onto the ottoman in front of him. Not too long after, we called it a night and headed off to bed. I fell asleep to the sound of rain as it tapped against the windowpane.

The next week seemed to fly by. We had five guests, a family of four and a lone businesswoman. Today was Friday, though, and those guests had left; new ones would arrive in the morning, and Liam would be here this evening. And today was my birthday. We were all going to Collins Bar in town to celebrate. This morning, my grandparents had presented me with a new pendant. An ornate *B* in rose gold with a tiny diamond embedded in the design. It was beautiful.

My second night in Ireland, my grandparents had taken me to Collins, where they'd introduced me to everyone. Again. I didn't know everyone who came into the pub, but I knew quite a few of them from our many trips here. Tonight, wouldn't be so much about meeting people, as it would simply be a night out and a good time. The only difference was that Liam would be there. And I wanted to look...well, I wanted to look stunning. I wanted to stun him. In a good way. No sense in denying it. I hadn't seen Liam for a couple years and the last time I had, I was already with Garrett and unavailable. My childhood crush was flaring strongly however, so now I stood in front of the closet, searching for the right outfit. I wanted him to find me attractive, but didn't want to look like I was *trying* to entice him. I wanted him to notice me, to look, well...grown up, and no longer like his faithful little shadow.

Wishing I'd packed more—I'd brought three bags as it was—I eventually settled on a dark navy A-line, knee-length dress with tiny white flowers printed on it. Pairing it with my denim jacket and a pair of tan wedge heels gave my outfit a fun and flirty look, showing off my legs. Which were my most favorite feature. Mom had her curves; my legs were my claim to fame. Wearing my new necklace, loving how it looked, I reminded myself to thank my grandparents again. My hair I left down, simply running a brush through it, and spritzed some of my favorite perfume onto my wrists, rubbing them together before heading downstairs. Before closing my door, I smelled the roses I'd received from my parents this morning, and wondered if Liam would even notice, much less respond to my new, more sophisticated look. *I really need to get a grip.*

Liam-

Liam shifted in his seat and tried to relax. The flight had been a smooth one; he'd landed close to an hour ago. Sean, his best friend from childhood, a year and half his junior, had picked him up at the airport. Sean had been born in Scotland, and had lived two doors down from the Gunn's. He and his family had moved to Ireland when Liam was ten. Despite the distance, the two had remained close. One or the other visiting to keep their friendship flourishing.

They were nearly to the pub where they were to meet everyone, and Liam shifted again, trying to settle himself. Bethany would be there. Liam found himself equal parts excited and apprehensive at seeing her. Wondering how, or if she'd changed. Would she still affect him the same as she'd always done. What if she still didn't notice him? What if he was no longer attracted to her? What if he was? Asher's warning rang in his ears. *Look after her. I'm depending on you.*

He was in a right mess, now, wasn't he? Liam ran his hands through his hair, sending the somewhat shaggy dark strands every which way. Sean glanced over, adjusted his grip on the wheel, and asked, "Something the matter, mate?"

"Nae." Liam ground his jaw and shook his head slowly. "Nae, I'm grand. Just thinking is all."

"Anything you need?"

Liam chuckled under his breath. "I need to remember that I want to live and no' get myself killed." Though Asher hadn't come out and said the words, Liam was fully aware of the warning in the message. He'd read that one loud and clear.

"Aye, that'd be brilliant, it would. Any particular reason you'd think you might be forgetting that?"

"There is."

"She have a name?" Sean shot him a look before turning back to the road.

"And who's sayin' it's a woman I'm talking aboot?"

"Well now." Sean scratched at his chin, at the stubble showing there, a gleam in his soft green eyes. "I suppose you might be referring to a lad, though if that's the case, this is the first I've heard of it, mind."

"Eejit." Liam snorted quietly. They pulled into the car park behind Collins Bar and found a spot somewhat further out. By the looks of things, it was to be a packed house.

"You planning to let yer best mate know, or will I be left in the dark?" Sean asked as he stepped from his car, his curly brown hair lifting in the mild breeze.

"No' as yet...I'm playing my cards close for the time being." Liam looked over the roof of the car at his friend. "Just keep yer eyes open and if it looks as though I'm aboot to commit suicide, I give ye permission to skelp me one."

"Fair enough. Let's head inside and see what trouble we can stir up then."

Bethany-

I became aware the instant Liam and Sean entered the bar. Not only was there a loud chorus of their names being called, but my eyes had unerringly darted to him and hadn't been able to look away. In equal measure, I was both pleased and perturbed. I still fancied myself infatuated with him. It was at that moment of realization, of course, that his intensely deep blue eyes had lifted, colliding with mine. Blushing, I tore my gaze away and silently chastised myself thoroughly for being caught staring. He was still everything. Every girlhood dream I'd had, every fantasy, Liam had firmly held the staring-role throughout. Everything I could have ever wanted in a man. And seeing him again had awoken those girlhood fantasies with a vengeance. From the corner of my eye, I studied him, allowing myself no more than that.

Liam was *maybe* an inch shorter than my dad. Both were built like some sort of Viking warlord able to swing a broadsword or an axe all day without breaking a sweat. Both had brown hair and blue eyes, though Liam's hair was so dark, it almost looked black, whereas Dad's was a somewhat lighter shade. They both had striking blue eyes, but again, Liam's were deeper, darker, while Dad's were more piercing. I didn't allow myself to look too closely at my comparison of the two of them. Dad had always been my hero, still was, but somehow Liam was there as well.

He sported a beard across his square jaw. That was new. Not one of those wispy, thin ones. No, this was a thick, full beard. He kept it well-groomed and though I'd never really been a fan of beards, I had to admit he made this one look fantastic.

Slowly, Sean and Liam made their way toward the table where we sat. Stopped frequently by various patrons, they eventually arrived beside us. My grandparents stood and gave each of them a stout hug, pounding their backs. Granda turned to me, holding out his hand, offering to lift me to my feet. As I rose, my pulse rocketing all over the place, I had to take a breath that came out all shaky while trying to calm it down. "Liam, Sean, you remember my granddaughter? Today's her birthday; wish her well. Bethany, say hello to the lads."

Sean stepped forward, took my hand, lifted it, and placed a kiss against my knuckles. "Tis a pleasure to see you again, Bethany darlin'. Happiest of birthdays to you, lass."

Smiling, I replied, "Thank you, Sean. It's great to be back, and so far, it's been a wonderful day." I turned then to Liam. "Hello, Liam."

"Happy birthday." He nodded. At first, he looked as though he might say something else, then he turned to shake hands with another person. My grandparents sat down again and I with them. Sean and Liam pulled up a couple chairs and waved the waitress over, ordering a couple more pints of the 'black stuff.'

Our reunion hadn't been quite what I'd been hoping for or expecting. I wasn't sure just *what* exactly I'd been expecting, but it was certainly not the underwhelming greeting I'd received. Something inside me sort of fell flat, like soda lacking carbonation. A balloon that had lost all its helium, sadly drifting along the floor, forgotten.

Liam-

When Liam stepped through the door of Collins, a chorus of greetings had sounded. Despite this cacophony of noise, his gaze had instantly found Bethany. It was a shock to his system seeing her again. He thought he'd been prepared for it, but still it slammed into his gut like a battering ram. It was compounded by the simple fact that her eyes had been on him, something flashing in them before she looked away. He was grateful for the delay as people stopped them frequently before he could reach her table. Then, as Tiernan helped her from the chair, and several devastating inches of a tanned, toned thigh were briefly revealed, he'd thought he was going to die. He barely managed to get his greeting out, was incapable of further speech. Profoundly thankful, he'd turned away at another call of his name. He needed to get ahold of himself before he faced her again, silently berating himself for a weak-kneed idiot.

Bethany-

Sean kept up a steady stream of conversation, asking about home, my parents, my love life. Though Liam was engaged in conversation with another patron, I noticed his shoulders seemed to tense when Sean had asked that last question, teasing me, wondering if he'd had anyone he'd need to fight off to get to know me better. I'd quietly grinned and told him, no, I wasn't seeing anyone, was recently single. Sean dropped to his knee before me, once more took my hand in his, and begged for the opportunity to help me heal my broken heart.

His antics had me laughing and he'd whooped loudly about having succeeded in doing so. Having accomplished what he'd apparently set out to do, Sean left our table then, said he was going to mingle so the other lasses wouldn't be jealous. Smiling and shaking my head, I waved him off. Various patrons, locals, friends of my grandparents stopped by to wish me well on my happy day. Some time later, my grandparents were in deep conversation with another couple at the next table over, leaving me and Liam essentially on our own. When it seemed the silence was going to win out between the two of us, I said, "So, Liam. It's been a while. What's new?"

He started at the sound of my voice and choked on his drink. Wiping his mouth, he turned those blue eyes towards me. He shook his head. "No' much, really. Taking it day by day, ye might say. And yerself?"

I shrugged, my dress slipping some, exposing part of my shoulder. "Same, I suppose." Brushing my knuckles against my chin, I said, "This is new." He stared at me, then nodded, something heavy and warm lingering in his gaze. A shiver danced across my shoulders at that heat.

Liam's gaze shifted, skimming the skin exposed by my drooping dress. He swallowed as his gaze returned to mine, then said, "Ye told Sean you're recently single. Ye doing all right from that?"

"Yeah, I am now. Wasn't at first." His regard caused me to stumble over my words. "Was...was a mess at first, but I'm much better now and looking. To put that time behind me, I mean."

"And right you are, Bethany love. He wasn't worth it, the bleedin' gobshite," Nana said as she swung back toward us. "Pardon me, pet. I ought'n to speak that way. Father, forgive me. It galls me somethin' fierce thinkin' about your heart being broken as it was."

"Ah, thanks, Nan. I'm alright now, though."

"Sure, and you are. There's a good lass." Nana patted my arm. Her eyes were getting a little glassy. "Liam, you'll be a love, and see Bethany around town, won't you? Make sure she's everything she needs while here? What with Granda's foot being gammy and such."

I couldn't help the blush that stained my cheeks, then. Nor did I wait to hear his response. Like a giant chicken, I quickly excused myself, and ran for sanctuary in the restroom.

Liam-

Liam watched her quickly walk away and swallowed his heart back where it belonged. The sway of her hips and those long, tanned legs about did him in. It was worse than he'd remembered. He still wanted her. Wanted her something fierce, and yet felt she was more out of reach than ever before. Everything inside seemed to ratchet down, to tighten. As if he was taking a firm grip to prevent himself doing something colossally stupid. Like grabbing her, tossing her over his shoulder and carrying her off. It stole his breath how badly he wanted Bethany. Made his hands tingle and his mouth dry out. Sean settled into the seat across from him, suddenly appearing from out of nowhere. "So that's the lass that has you all in knots, is it?"

"Was it that obvious?"

"Only to me, lad." Sean assured him as he took a drink. "Can't say as I blame you. If I didn't know yer sail was set in that direction, I might be tempted myself."

Liam just continued to stew in silence, trying to convince himself Bethany Fitzpatrick was entirely off limits. Problem was, he wasn't at all convincing. Not by a long shot. It didn't help that each time he looked at her he could swear he saw heated interest in her light green eyes. And the sound of his name on her lips had nearly shattered his will. He hadn't been able to speak in complete sentences. Nor did it help that her dress this evening, simple as it was, left him feeling as if he'd never seen a woman before. He could still smell her. Even in this packed room, her scent, roses and musk, came to him like a siren call, shutting his brain down. Waking his body up.

"What's the trouble, then? She's showin' she's interested. Don't tell me you've forgotten how to handle a woman?"

Liam snorted. He was so going to get killed. "Forgotten? Nae. No' by a long shot. Though, in her case, I could wish for the opposite."

"I'm not sure I'm followin' you. Yer after her, you want her. By all looks, she's got her eye on you as well. So, what's the problem, then? She's said she's single and fair game."

Liam shot him a dark exasperated look. "Ye remember who her da is?"

"I do." Sean scratched his chin in contemplation. "The Fitzpatrick's a hard man to forget."

"Aye, and her mother's no' too far off."

"Sure, and?"

"And he's fair warned me off, he has."

"He's not here, though, is he now?"

"He'll ken it. That man always seems to bloody ken everything. Has more ears to the wind than anyone I've ever met afore. It's uncanny the things he kens."

"Aye, I see yer problem. So. Yer choice is to remain in one piece and be miserable. Or experience possible heaven before dyin'?"

"That's aboot the gist of it, aye."

"I don't envy you, mate." Sean glanced over his shoulder and back. "Still, might be worth it. Guess it's something you'll need to decide. Though, I'd offer this advice: don't take too long making up yer mind. Half the blokes in here have had their eye on her. And another thing to consider: I've never known Liam Kristian Gunn to back down from a fight."

Liam clenched his jaw at that, then let his breath out in a rush as he shook his head at Sean. "No' bloody helpin', mate."

Sean just chuckled and shifted his gaze before rising and moving to another table. Liam turned to see the elderly Fitzpatricks head to another spot in the room to continue socializing. As he turned back around, he saw Bethany exit the bathroom and followed her progress, slow as it was, due to all the attention she received, as she crossed the room back to their table, to him. Everyone seemed to want to talk with the American and wish her happy. He watched, his gaze narrowing as one of the local lads, Patrick McDaniels, invited her to sit down. She glanced in his direction, not quite making eye contact, before shaking her head and continuing on. Liam loosened the fists he'd made, seeing as she was not being accosted. And wondered at her look in his general direction.

"And here's Liam, back from ol' Scotland. How long're ya here for?" Liam looked up to the woman speaking and offered a friendly smile to Bronagh. They'd known each other for years and had briefly dated, remaining friends despite not lasting as a couple.

"Ah, sure, and ye ken yourself." Liam grinned. "And ye, Bronagh, how're things?" His gaze shifted again, returning to Bethany as she moved closer still. He hoped whatever look was on his face, he didn't look like he was about to ravish her. Though, that and more was what he'd had in mind.

"Grand, thanks for asking. And who's the Yank? Don't think I've caught her name."

Liam forced his focus back to Bronagh. "That's Bethany Fitzpatrick, daughter of Asher and Kate Fitzpatrick. Ye remember them?"

"Sure, and I do." Bronagh nodded. "You've had yer eye on her this evening. Anything of interest happening there?"

"No' as yet. Though, I've given the idea some consideration."

"I suppose, her being American and what have you, and with you being Scottish, she's after you saying, *Dinna fash, Sassenach,* and all that?"

Liam heard the near silent snort just over his shoulder, and glancing in Bethany's direction, from the look on her face, gathered she'd heard Bronagh's question and had taken issue. He felt his face warm and was about to respond in her defense when Bethany took the matter into her own hands. As she'd stepped closer to him, her hip brushed against his arm, sending a jolt of heat through him, freezing him in place.

Bethany-

"Bethany's just fine, Liam. No need to call me Sassenach and all that. Though, if you were to don a kilt, I don't think I'd tell you no." Liam choked at that, beer dripping down his chin.

Bronagh blinked, then a slow grin spread across her face. "*Bollocks*, Liam. I think I might like this one."

After wiping the Guinness away, Liam looked to the both of us. "Bethany, Bronagh. Bronagh, Bethany."

Bronagh wiped her hand on her apron and then held it out. "No offense, Bethany. I was just teasing."

I hesitated a brief moment before taking hers. "None taken."

"No harm done, I hope."

"I should hope not." Something almost knowing was in her gaze and I had to fight to keep the snark from my tone.

"You'll be around for a while, then?"

"Through August." I nodded.

"I hope you enjoy your stay; don't be a stranger."

"I won't, and it was nice meeting you."

I watched her walk away, then took my seat and glanced at Liam, only to find him gazing pointedly at me. "What?" I asked.

"Ye take after yer mother, don't ye?"

"So I've been told. Why?"

"I've heard she doesna back down from a fight either."

"That wasn't a fight, Liam. And, no, I don't."

"Duly noted."

Ignoring his last comment, I let silence fall between us, wondering if she was an old girlfriend or something. It appeared there was a familiarity between them. Not liking that train of thought—Bronagh was beautiful with her dark hair and eyes, her lush figure—I took my own drink, swallowing a little too fast. I cleared my throat then looked over my shoulder, locating my grandparents. Nana caught my eye and smiled. I smiled in return, then faced forward again. Suddenly, I was exhausted and just wanted one of Nan's magical cups of tea, a warm bath, and bed. She must have seen something on my face, because a couple minutes later, she and Granda appeared at our table and asked if we were ready. Not looking at Liam, I stood and said, "I am."

"Fine then, let me gather my things and we'll be off," Nana replied.

"Think I'll stay a bit longer, there's a few more I'd like to see. I'll have Sean drop me by later," Liam told my grandmother, a smile on his face.

"You're in the blue room, you remember, top of the stairs, right across from Bethany's room."

"Grand." Liam swallowed. "That's, that's just grand. I'll be…I'll be along soon."

Nodding to him and waving to a few people, we left the bar. As Granda pulled up to the manor house, Nan asked if I'd enjoy a cuppa with them before bed. I assured her I would, but that I planned to take a bath if that was all right.

"Of course it is, dear! I'll bring your tea up right away. There's candles in the hall cupboard and towels as well."

"Thanks, Nan." I kissed them both on the cheek and made my way up to my room. Arriving there, I blew out a breath and flopped backward onto the mattress. *What a mess. What an absolute mess!* I still liked him. Still liked him a heck of a lot. And…he seemed oblivious. Story of my life lately. Seeing Liam again had sent my heart thundering and my pulse racing. As he appeared unaffected by me, I knew I'd have to get this attraction under control. Maybe it was too soon after Garrett, maybe I simply needed more time. Maybe he just wasn't interested, and I needed to not obsess over him. That was probably my most accurate thought.

Hearing Nana on the stairs, I stood and gathered my things. She'd already turned the bathroom light on and had the water running in the old-fashioned clawfoot tub. I pulled a towel from the cupboard and snagged a couple candles as well. Matches were on the counter alongside the tea. "Here you are, dear. Enjoy your bath. No need to rush, Liam'll be along after a while, the lads'll keep him out for a bit more."

"Love you, Nan. Thanks for taking me out."

"Of course, it's such a joy having you here with us, and on yer birthday, too." She kissed my cheek and closed the door, leaving me to my bath and privacy. Rummaging, I found a jar of Epsom salts under the sink and poured a scoop or two under the running water. Then I lit the candles and undressed. The heady aroma of roses filled the bathroom as I stepped into the tub. The heat of the water soon had me relaxing. As I soaked, I sipped my tea and found Liam once again on my mind.

What could be done? Anything? How did one go about attracting a man? And did I want to put myself out there like that? I'd done that for Garrett, believing he'd loved me in return. Only to find out, years later, that he hadn't. Should I act like I hardly noticed him? Get him to chase me? Or, as that seemed somewhat manipulative, should I simply let nature take its course? I didn't know, but stressing over it wasn't going to help.

I wasn't sure how long I'd stayed in the tub trying to solve all of life's problems, but the water was nearly cooled, my tea was gone, and the candles had burned low. I hadn't heard Liam return, so they must be really having a night out. Maybe he and Bronagh had hooked up after we'd left. That thought had me standing swiftly in irritation, sloshing water onto the mat. I stepped from the tub and pulled the plug, then quickly cleaned up my mess. Wrapping the fluffy towel around myself, I blew out the candles and stepped from the bathroom into the darkened hallway and immediately bumped into something, nearly losing my balance. If not for the strong arms that came around me, I'd have fallen and most likely lost my towel in the process—I hadn't tucked it, was only holding it in my grasp. As it was, I felt all the breath leave my body, as we stumbled momentarily before I found myself pressed against the wall, a warm body leaning into mine. The scent of musk and spice and something darker worked its way over me. I shivered, though not from the chill.

"Are ye all right?" Liam's voice sounded rough. He held me tightly, no room between us.

I nodded, then, unsure if he caught that in the darkness, whispered, "Yeah."

Liam's arms tightened briefly and I could have sworn I felt a pressure at my temple, a tantalizing tickle of whiskers, before he suddenly released me and stepped back. Thankfully, I'd had a firm hand on that towel.

"Sorry," I breathed. "I didn't realize you were there."

"Grand," Liam muttered, sounding almost pained. "'Night." He turned without another word and entered his room, closing the door without even looking at me. Blinking, I stood in silence for several long moments. Unsure as to what had just happened. One second, I would have sworn he'd enjoyed what had just happened—much to my chagrin, I knew I had—but then he'd stepped back as if he couldn't get away from me fast enough. I let out the breath I hadn't known I'd been holding and returned to my own room, more confused than ever.

Liam-

Liam leaned against his bedroom door, face tilted upward, hands fisted against his head, and groaned silently. As quietly as he could, he'd come up the stairs, trying not to disturb anyone, and had heard her in the bathroom. Heard the slosh of water, the rustle of fabric over damp skin, then the gurgle of the drain. Visions of her, damp skin and steam, had him near to sobbing in his agony. He'd made to rush past the door, then she'd stepped out, directly into his path. He hadn't consumed nearly enough alcohol to handle this! Hearing her door shut now, he straightened. His breath came fast, and his muscles felt jittery, as if he might fall on his short walk to the bed. Dropping face down, he growled into his pillow. He'd had her. Right there. Against the wall, against him. Nothing but his clothes and her towel separating them. He could still feel the moisture on her skin and his hands ached with need to have her in his grasp again. To touch her more, taking things further. The fragrance coming off her bathed skin had his mouth watering. Roses. Suddenly, the image of laying her back onto sheets coated with petals came to mind, and he groaned again. This was madness. *Sheer, bloody madness.* She was right there, across the hall from him. And she'd be there for the next two months. Something almost inevitable seemed to peer at him from the shadows of his mind. Reminding him of her proximity in his life, urging him not to waste this opportunity. Sheer. Bloody. Madness.

CHAPTER FIVE

Burning Embers

Bethany-

When I awoke the next morning, having no memory of having fallen asleep, the sun was shining brightly through the windows. I scrambled from bed and pulled the curtain aside. Blue skies; though farther out, dark clouds were gathering. Dressing quickly in a pair of jeans and a long-sleeved T-shirt, I pulled my hair up, keeping it off my neck and out of my face. I stepped across the hall, into the bathroom, and tried my best not to think of my encounter with Liam last night, but that was impossible. I remembered *everything* and couldn't contain the shiver of longing that coursed through me. *Darn that man, anyway!*

Shaking my head, I glared at my reflection in the mirror, then quickly brushed my teeth before padding barefoot down to the kitchen. Nana was at the stove; the smell of eggs, bacon, and yeast bread filled the room. "Good morning, Nan."

"Oh, good morning, dear. How'd you sleep? Liam didn't wake you when he came in, I trust?"

"Uh, no, he uh, he didn't wake me. I slept fine." I so did not want to discuss Liam right now. "Looks like it's going to be a lovely day out."

"This morning should be fair. Might rain this evening, though."

"When do your next guests arrive?"

"A younger couple will be stopping for a couple nights, should arrive around one I think they mentioned." Nana pulled a couple loaves from the oven. "Then a family of four are coming in this evening. They'll take the other two rooms."

"After breakfast, I'll get the beds made and then I can help you clean the house."

"That'd be grand, it would, thanks." She smiled over her shoulder. "Liam and Granda are out bringing in the cows, getting them milked. They'll be along shortly, I'm sure."

Nodding, I sat at the table. By now, I knew Nana's schedule for breakfast and helped myself to the food she'd prepared. I was just finishing my meal, sipping a second cup of tea, when the back door opened and Granda and Liam came inside, bringing with them the smell of smoke. A shiver scampered down my spine as I felt a heavy gaze settle upon me, one that fanned the embers still burning inside. It wasn't a disagreeable feeling, more a rather acute awareness. As Granda passed me, that scent of the smoke came stronger. I figured they must have been burning this morning already.

"Burned off some of those cuttings from last year," Granda said as if reading my thoughts. Leaning over, he placed a gentle kiss on my head as he sat down.

Nana poured him a cup of tea and set it before his plate. "That's evident. Good, too. More rain is coming in, I think."

"Had a bloke asking after you last night, pet." Granda smiled at me as he buttered his toast. From the corner of my eye, I noted the way Liam tensed at Granda's words.

"And who was asking after our girl?" Nan asked over her shoulder. Her hands deftly folding the bread dough, working it.

"Davy O'Connell, it was. Asked if he might come by and see the lass."

"Oh now, Davy's a nice young lad. You'll like him. Patrick McDaniels seemed to take a shine to you last night as well. Handsome lads, both. Though not as striking as our Liam, now are they?"

I glanced to Liam as he sat down, but he was focused entirely on his plate, seemingly refusing to lift his eyes. Standing, I pushed away from the table and carried my dishes to the sink to wash. "Thanks for breakfast, Nana.

Delicious as always. I'll get started on those beds now." Without waiting for acknowledgment, I quickly exited the kitchen and blew out a breath as I did. He was acting as if nothing had happened between us last night. As if he was entirely unaffected. *Fine.* If he wanted to behave that way, it was fine by me. I'd just act as if nothing had happened either. Who cares? Not me.

I had the bedding in the first room changed in record time and moved on to the second. Those embers inside had shifted from a heat full of tension to one of annoyance. I snapped the cases sharply, my emotions coming to the fore, and was just placing the pillows on the queen bed when I heard the phone ring from the kitchen. I hoped, for my grandparents' sake, this wasn't a cancellation. In the third bedroom, this one boasting both a double bed and hide-a-bed, I got busy pulling the linens out. I opened the hide-a-bed and made up that one first.

Doing so brought to mind a story Mom had told, from when she and Dad had first met. She'd been changing the sheets on a hide-a-bed and Dad, being a guest at the time, had come from the bathroom across the way. He'd been shirtless and Mom had been so distracted by him, she'd dropped the pillow and pillowcase without even being aware she'd done so. It wasn't until he'd stooped to pick them up, offering them back, that she'd realized what she'd done. Much later, Dad had admitted he'd done it on purpose just to get a reaction out of Mom. She'd apparently been acting as if she wasn't attracted to him at all. They'd always had that, though. That awareness between the two of them, the attraction.

Once again, I was struck with this pang of longing for what my parents had. For a brief moment, I let the panic and yearning overtake me. What if I never found that? What if I was alone my whole life? I didn't want that. I wanted marriage and kids. I wanted passion and intimacy. Would that never be mine? I wiped a tear from my eye and told myself to get it together. Taking a deep breath, I closed my eyes and offered up a wordless prayer, confident the One who'd made me would know the workings of my heart. Then finished making that bed and moved on to the double. Soon, that was done as well. Without being asked, I checked to see if any laundry needed folding. Sure enough, one load of towels was dried and another needed to go in the dryer. Seeing as the sun was still brightly shining, I piled the linens in the basket and took them out to the clothesline in the back yard.

From my pocket, I pulled out my earbuds and quickly slipped them in, then hit shuffle on my playlist. Soon I was silently singing along with the music as I hung the laundry on the line. Arctic Monkeys' song, *Do I Wanna Know,* played and I couldn't help but move to the rhythm.

Liam-

Liam stopped at the door, his hand on the latch, and peered through the glass. The sun shone down on her blond hair, turning it golden there atop her head. Her skin gleamed making him yearn with the need to touch her. He watched as her tall, lithe figure swayed to some tune only she could hear and had to swallow the knot in his throat. He'd never seen anything so sultry, so sensual in his life. Everything about her made him come alive. He'd had mere glimpses of this when she'd been younger. Seeing the realization of those earlier glimpses tightened his throat. She was a living flame and he wanted to be consumed by her. His mouth watered and he ground his jaw in frustration. He'd come looking for Bethany, intending to fetch her for her grandmother. Now, feeling weakened, knowing he wasn't strong enough to keep his hands off her, knowing he wanted nothing more than to claim her in the only way he knew how—with hands, body, and tongue—he turned away from the temptation and didn't allow himself to look back. Liam found Callie in the front room, dust rag in hand. Like a coward, he told her he'd been unable to locate her granddaughter, but would continue looking—maybe she'd gone for a quick walk—before heading out the front door and into the lane.

Jack-

Jack kept one eye on the group of riders, and one eye on Delaney where she led from the front. He'd caught himself doing that a lot lately. Watching her. Lately, he seemed to always have his eyes on her. Couldn't seem to help it. He'd always thought both she and Bethany were beautiful, but in a more detached sort of way. Especially in Bethany's case. Somehow, now, it felt different. _He_ felt different. His reactions were different. And not necessarily unwanted. Now, he tended to envision taking Del's hand. Pulling her close. Tasting that mouth he couldn't seem to stop focusing on. What had changed? And when? And what would she think of this change?

Bethany-

Gravel crunched from the front of the house, alerting us that guests had arrived. I slipped off the stool where I'd been perched, watching Nana as she cooked. She expertly tapped the spoon against the stock pot to knock any drippings back into the mix before setting it on the counter, then turned the heat down. I followed her into the front room just as Granda opened the door to greet the family. "Hello, and welcome!" Granda said as he waved them inside.

The younger couple had already arrived and had gone to Collins for supper. This family of four, the parents and their twin teenage daughters, would be joining us here at the house.

"I trust your drive was grand?" Nana asked after introductions were made. Brian and Michelle Miller were the parents; they looked to be in their late forties. The twins were sixteen and named Haley and Harper. "This is my granddaughter, Bethany. She's from the States as well. She'll show you to your rooms. Then if you're hungry, supper will be served when you're ready."

Once they were all settled in, I had them follow me to the dining room. Nana had the table ready and showed us all where to sit. It ended up that Liam and I were beside each other, with Nana to my left and the family across from us, and Granda sat at the head. I did my level best to not allow Liam's proximity to bother me, but I was *aware* of him. So aware. Though at least eight inches separated us, I could feel the heat coming off his body. Caressing along mine. I distracted myself with the antics of the teens, both of whom had focused on Liam as soon as they'd set eyes on him. I didn't blame them. The man was definitely a sight for sore eyes.

A steady stream of conversation flowed around us as we ate. I learned the Miller family were from Pennsylvania, and when they heard we had a dude ranch in Wyoming, they excitedly exclaimed they would have to visit there at some point soon. We were just finishing supper, Nana had gone to the kitchen for the pie she'd made earlier, when there was a knock at the door.

"Now, who could that be?" Granda wondered, starting to rise.

"I've go' it, Tiernan." Liam pushed his chair back. Haley and Harper offered a silent sigh as he left the room.

Liam-

Liam opened the door and stopped, momentarily at a loss. "All right, Liam?" said Patrick McDaniels from the step.

"Patrick," Liam said, recovering quickly. "What can I do for ye?"

"Is Bethany to home, then? Tiernan said I might call on her."

Liam was tempted to close and lock the door and simply leave the other man standing there. He was also tempted to slam his fist into Patrick's freshly-shaved jaw. But this was not his house, and Bethany was not his woman. He settled for a dark glare that Patrick missed entirely. "We were just sitting down for dessert, Patrick."

"Oh, that sounds lovely, it does."

Callie came into the hall to see what kept Liam. "Is it yourself, Patrick McDaniels? Come inside, lad. What's the craic?"

"Mrs. Fitzpatrick." Patrick removed his cap as he stepped into the entryway. "I was hoping to see Bethany."

"Sure, and you'll join us for a cuppa and pie, then?" Callie said, a warm smile on her face. "Liam, grab an extra plate for Patrick."

Liam silently ground his teeth, sincerely wishing he'd have just punched the man and saved himself the headache. There was no way he'd be able to sit through watching the lad make eyes at the woman Liam wanted.

Bethany-

"Bethany, young Patrick's come to call on you. He'll join us for dessert, then you can take a nice stroll around outside," Nana announced as she returned to the dining room. I vaguely remembered Patrick from the other evening at Collins; he was one of the gentlemen who'd asked me to join them at their table. Patrick was around my age, I was guessing. Maybe a couple years older. He had short blond hair and grey eyes. He wasn't as tall or well-built as Liam, but he wasn't unattractive either. I smiled at him, feeling only a little awkward, considering the guests that my grandparents were currently entertaining. And Liam...I wondered what he thought about this new development. Was he bothered? Did he care?

Patrick smiled warmly as his gaze met mine; *at least he's happy enough to see me.* I refused to let my eyes seek out Liam, and instead, returned Patrick's smile.

We finished our pie, then Patrick asked if I'd like to take a stroll around outside. Agreeing, we stood, and I told Nan I'd wash the dishes when I returned. Liam stood, his chair sliding noisily backward. "I've some things to finish outside before we turn in." He headed for the door without another word. Patrick sent him a quizzical look before returning his gaze to mine. "Shall we?" he asked with one hand at my lower back, the other indicating the door. We stepped outside, and I breathed in the cool evening air. "How long are you here for, Bethany?"

We started down the walkway to the front gate. "Through August."

"Where is it you live in the States?"

"Wyoming." At his puzzled look, I continued, "It's just south of Montana, which shares a border with Canada."

He nodded. "Oh, right, then. And what keeps you busy there? What is your employment, I mean?"

"My family and I run a dude ranch." His once more clouded expression had me explaining, "A dude ranch is one that offers a cowboy experience to people who aren't accustomed to living in the country. The name comes from the Old West term of dude, which was someone who lived in the city. Cowboys would call them dudes."

"I definitely qualify as a dude." He chuckled self-consciously, then added, "Maybe I'll have to come visit you on your ranch and get the full experience."

"You'd be welcome." We'd meandered around the front of the house and were circling around to the back, coming near the barn, when we heard a loud thump from inside. Patrick looked to me, but my gaze was on the barn itself. Glancing to my companion, I steered us in that direction and came to a stop as we stepped inside. Liam stood with his back to us, his hands seemed to be clenched in front of him. "Liam?" I asked.

It took him a moment to acknowledge us. When he turned around, he had his right hand cradled in his left. "Bollocks, Liam!" Patrick exclaimed as we noted the blood on his knuckles. "What happened?"

"Nothing. Smashed it is all." He flexed the hand in question, a dark look in his gaze as it settled on Patrick. "I'm fine."

"You should be more careful." Patrick offered over his shoulder as we turned to leave.

"Aye. Ye do the same, Patrick McDaniels." Liam was in motion then, moving swiftly past us, headed toward the house. I watched in stunned silence, not entirely certain what had just happened. It appeared as though Liam had punched a wall. *But why would he have done that?*

"Did he seem off to you?" Patrick puzzled aloud.

"Liam?" I asked, still staring after him. "I'm not sure, why?"

"Is there anything between the two of you?" His manner somehow seemed careful now.

I snorted silently. "Not that I'm aware of. Again, why?"

"Just a thought I was having, I suppose."

I really didn't want to talk about Liam or anything that was or wasn't happening between us. "Would you care to walk on?"

"I would." We walked another slow loop around the house, eventually stopping at the bench in the front, settling there. Nana brought out some tea and joined us, the twins soon following after. It was a nice evening. I liked Patrick McDaniels. With his sandy blond hair and grey eyes, he wasn't hard to look at, at all. He made me smile a lot, too. His humor coming to the fore often throughout the evening. The twins seemed to enjoy his company and flirted shamelessly. He took it good-naturedly, laughing off most of what they said. At one point, Harper and Haley suggested a planned trip to our ranch where Patrick would meet them there. Mentally, I shook my head at their antics. All in all, it was a nice, relaxing evening. Though, of course my heart wasn't fully committed to it. No, it was off wherever Liam had disappeared to, wondering what had happened earlier and why Patrick had felt the need to inquire about anything going on between us.

Soon, Brian and Michelle called their daughters in for bed. Nana excused herself, said she was going in as well. Patrick and I stood. The sun had set, now just a muted shade of purple on the horizon. I turned to him. "Thank you for coming over. I enjoyed this."

"As did I. Might I visit another time, do you think?"

"Please do." Patrick leaned forward, hesitated, then brushed soft lips against my cheek. Pulling back, he offered me a small grin before turning for his car. Taking a deep breath, I waved to him as he pulled away, then went inside. Remembering the dishes I'd promised to wash, I made my way to the kitchen. Nana was already at it, her hands deep in sudsy water. "Nana, I said I'd get those."

"Oh, I know, dear. You can help me dry and put them away." Snagging a clean towel from the drawer, I did as she'd suggested. After several minutes of quiet work, Nana said, "That Patrick's a nice lad, now isn't he?"

"He is," I agreed. Hearing something, or maybe not hearing something in my voice, she turned to me, questions evident in her gaze. "He is nice, Nana. And I will most likely see him again."

"I hear a but."

"But," I nodded, drying the silverware now, "I'm just not feeling *it.*"

"It," she said. "You mean that special spark?"

"Yeah. That's what I'm not feeling. Patrick is handsome and charming, and kind, and, and maybe I'm just not ready yet. I don't know."

"Give it time, love. Take each day as it's been given. There's no need to go borrowin' trouble."

I finished with the dishes on the mat and got those put away, then helped Nana prepare the dough for tomorrow's meal. "Think I'll head to bed now. Love you."

"Love you, too, pet. We're so glad you're here."

"So am I. Sorry it took so long for me to come."

"Bah. You're here and that's what matters."

"Goodnight." I headed upstairs, pausing at my room, my gaze was drawn to the light peeking out from under Liam's door. Briefly, I considered knocking, just to ask how his hand was. Chickening out, I grabbed my bathroom bag, finished with my nighttime toiletries, and closed myself in my room before I could reconsider my earlier thoughts.

Liam-

Liam heard her come upstairs. Heard her rustling around in the bathroom, then silence. He gritted his teeth and flexed his fingers. Patrick's face would have been a sight softer than the wall Liam had punched. Patrick...was a nice lad. Liam might have liked him had the man not gone and made eyes at Bethany. Now, Liam wanted to pummel him. He'd have to watch himself. If not, he'd be making declarations to the lass and then where would he be with her father. Six feet under probably. *Ah*, he thought, with deep longing, remembering the feel of her under his hands as he'd pressed her against the wall, *what a way to go.*

CHAPTER SIX

The Color Green

Bethany-

My grandparents' guests had left, the Millers promising to come see me soon in Wyoming. Patrick had visited again last night and stayed until dark. We'd sat out on the front bench, sipping tea, and talking. I'd learned he was a delivery driver for one of the local stores. I hadn't seen Liam all day, though, and wondered where he'd been. Trying, unsuccessfully, to convince my heart to let my dreams of Liam and me go, but my heart was a stubborn organ.

Delaney texted, saying her mom was pretty upset. Apparently, Garrett had left for Southern California. I wondered if he was truly planning to join the Navy. My heart...wasn't bothered by the news. I think somewhere in the back of my mind, I'd known he'd always intended to go. Regardless, he wasn't my concern anymore. My heart did go out to his mother, however, and I prayed the turmoil and heartache would be healed in that family.

More guests were arriving later this afternoon, and I looked forward to meeting them. Meanwhile, Granda had requested my help for the day. The barn, he'd said, was in need of a new coat of paint while the weather held. Dressed in a pair of Granda's old coveralls, I made my way out to the barn, pausing as I neared the structure, noting Liam standing there as well. My heart picked up at the sight of him; why couldn't I be as uncaring about him as I was towards Garrett. Granda was pointing out the paint, the brushes and the areas that needed a touch up. "Those rougher spots will need a quick sanding afore you paint them," he explained as I approached. "Sure, and here's the lass. Even in me old dungarees you're a fetching thing, pet."

Smiling, I kissed his weathered cheek. "Thanks, Granda."

"Liam," Granda nudged him with a friendly elbow, "wouldn't you agree our Bethany's a fetching sight this morning?"

From the moment I'd walked up, Liam's blue eyes had slowly perused me. I wasn't sure if Granda had noticed and thought to alert Liam he was aware of the look, or simply commenting in general. "Aye, Tiernan, that she is."

Blushing at those words, I turned my attention to the barn, trying to ignore the way Liam's gaze felt like a physical touch. "Liam'll get you squared away, lass. I'm going to rest this ankle now."

After he'd left, I asked, "So, what's the game plan?" When Liam didn't immediately answer, I turned to him. His blue eyes met and held mine, and I couldn't decipher what I saw in his gaze, but the longer he looked, the warmer I became. When the silence continued, I raised my brows.

"The west side will need the most work," he eventually responded in slow, measured words. "But there're areas all around that ye'll note need a quick sanding and new paint."

"Any particular place you'd like me to start?"

He seemed to consider for a moment, the corners of his mouth softening ever so little, then said, "As it's the west side with the most need, and the weather's good for it, I figure we'd do that one first. I'll sand, if ye'd like, then ye can follow along behind me, painting the area."

Doing my best to ignore the heated response my body seemed inclined to have each time I was near him, I turned away. The large barn door faced the south; the painting supplies were right outside the doorway. I headed towards them and began gathering what I could. Liam soon joined me and we got to work. He'd sand a section, then I'd run a dry brush over it to remove any grit before using another brush to paint. The color in the cans was that same lovely shade of green as before. Darker than grass, lighter than pine. In point, the color was beautiful. As was all of Ireland, in my opinion. We soon developed a companionable rhythm, working in silence, and before I knew it, we had over half the west side done.

Kate-

"Your mother has them painting the barn." Kate hung up with her mother-in-law and tucked the phone in her pocket. She leaned against the porch post, waiting patiently for her husband to reach her. A light breeze blew, carrying the scent of pines and evergreens. Crickets chirped, creating a symphony under the starlit sky, and she smiled as he approached, returning from the barn.

"Oh, does she?" Asher came slowly up the steps until he was one below her. His hands rose to rest at her hips, gripping lightly.

"She does; I'm hopeful. I've always liked Liam." At his quiet snort, she added, "And so do you."

"Is it too soon, though? I don't want her hurt again." His thumbs swiped back and forth in gentle motions.

"Nor do I. We aren't matchmaking; we're simply putting them in a position for nature to take its course."

"So long as that course doesn't get out of hand."

"We've raised her right. And Liam's trustworthy."

Asher shook his head. "Like me, he's not innocent."

"The Lord saw us through. We just need to trust they'll make the right choices."

Asher pulled Kate closer until they were flush. Brushing the hair from her neck, he pressed his mouth to the skin there. "We always struggled with it. The attraction. The need." He bit her neck as if to say, *point proven.*

"I wouldn't say desire was ever an issue for us." Kate's breath caught in her throat as she leaned into his touch; her eyes rolling back before fluttering closed.

"No. It wasn't." Asher kissed her mouth. Slow and full of intent. "Come inside with me." Heat flashed through Kate as she let her husband lead her into the house.

Bethany-

I was just painting over the latest section he'd sanded, when Liam suddenly spoke, "Patrick McDaniels seems a might taken wi' ye."

"Does he?" I carefully brushed a strand of hair from my face, trying to avoid any of the green paint currently staining my fingers from transferring.

"Ye haven't noticed him coming around, then?" Liam began vigorously sanding the next section, his focus seemingly intent on the work in front of him.

"I've noticed he's been here. Why?" That strand of hair was still running loose around my face, irritating me.

"Are ye favoring the lad, then?"

"What if I am?" That came out way more salty than I'd intended.

"Are ye?" A wealth of *something* lay his words.

"He's nice enough." I shrugged, fighting the blush threatening to blossom across my face, still trying to tame my flyaway hair. "I'm getting to know him, I suppose."

"Mmm...I suppose." He turned suddenly, stepping closer. Reaching out, he took hold of that wayward strand of hair, carefully tucking it behind my ear, his fingers lightly trailing down my neck. My heart clean stopped in my chest. Stepping back, he said, "Looked as though ye were struggling a might."

"Thanks," I breathed, my heart now furiously racing. He turned back to the barn, and started sanding again. I watched him a few moments, trying to understand what had just happened. His actions had seemed natural. Natural, and yet intimate. Like when he'd held me, preventing me from falling in the hallway. Before pushing away from me. Things with Liam seemed hot, then cold. Forth, then back. *Why did everything have to be so confusing?* In something of a daze, my gaze upon the man before me, I touched my ear, my neck. Lightly trailing my fingers where his had been, before realizing with a start, I'd just touched myself with my painted fingers. "Ah, crap." Grumbling under my breath, I tried wiping my neck and ear with the rag from my pocket.

Liam looked back, his gaze lighting in humor. "Oi, ye're smearing it. Best to leave it for the moment and get it later."

"Thanks," I hissed, stuffing the rag back into my pocket.

"Sure." He grinned, turning back to his work as he started whistling. Not a tune I recognized, but a catchy one all the same. One I found myself mentally humming along with. We continued our work, finishing the west side, then the south, the north, and finally the east. As we were gathering our supplies, I heard the back door open and glanced over my shoulder, expecting to see Granda coming to inspect our work. Instead, it was Patrick, flowers in hand. His friendly grey eyes travelled over me, lighting on the green paint smeared on my skin and the over-sized dungarees. A smile split his face.

"Sure, and yer a sight for sore eyes, Bethany." As he stepped closer, his smile grew. "Even with the paint."

Chuckling, I said, "Thanks."

Liam had stiffened at the sound of Patrick's voice, muttering darkly under his breath. "Patrick," he nodded by way of greeting, even as he moved past me to put the painting supplies away.

"Liam," Patrick replied, his grey eyes briefly trailing after Liam before returning to me. He offered me the bouquet he'd brought and I noted the pinkish purple blooms of a foxglove along with some white daisies.

"Thank you," I said, taking them. "They're lovely."

"And *you* more so." His compliment brought heat to my face. Liam returned from the barn, heading towards the house, sparing me a glance as he went. "Ye'll want to get that paint removed afore it sets in, lest ye're after yer skin permanently stained green."

Looking to Patrick, I blushed. "I tried to keep the paint on the barn, but, well, here I am."

"No worries. I only stopped by to give you these and to see your smiling face. I've a delivery or two to make before I'm through for the day. One is a might farther away. It'll take me longer to finish with it, so I won't make it by later."

"Thank you. That's...that was very thoughtful."

He gave me a long look. Something, some emotion seemed to swirl in his grey eyes. Inhaling, he said, "Bethany, you have to know...I like you. I'd like to get to know you better, and I'm of a mind to date you, if you'll have me?" I took a breath, preparing to respond, not sure exactly what I'd say, when he continued, "I know you're recently single and may need more time, but *I'm* here. I'd like to be here when you're ready. At the least, please consider that."

Nodding at him, I said, "I will. And thank you."

Stepping closer, his cologne, or maybe it was aftershave, tickled enticingly as he placed a gentle kiss on my cheek. "I'd best be going. It'll be later before I'm home otherwise." Patrick turned, making his way around the house to the front. I watched him go and tried to decide what my heart was doing. Patrick was a nice young man. Seemingly an honest worker. He was considerate. And attractive. And thoughtful. Yet my heart wasn't pulled towards him. Maybe I did need more time. Maybe I wasn't ready. I didn't want to lead him on or give him false hope, and knew I'd have to decide soon. Sighing, I headed inside to find a vase for the flowers. Nana had one waiting on the counter for me.

"Such a nice, thoughtful lad is Patrick." She nodded at the bouquet. "You go on, get cleaned up. I'll settle these in water, then we'll have us a cuppa before supper."

"Thanks, Nana." I set the bouquet down then headed up for the shower. Nearing the bathroom, I heard water running and figured Liam must already be in there. Entering my room, I quickly unzipped the coveralls, making sure any paint on them was dry before dropping them to the floor. Under them I'd worn a pair of knit shorts and an over-sized T-shirt, so it wasn't like I was undressing, not really. Pulling clean clothes from the wardrobe, I heard the bathroom door open and upon turning, forgot how to breathe. We'd been here before. Only our roles were now reversed. He wore nothing but steam and a towel. Moisture dripped from his hair, trailing down the strong column of his neck, over the sculpted plane of his chest, through the dark hairs that curled there, scattering my thoughts to the wind.

Liam-

Time stood still. He'd figured she'd still be outside with Patrick, the thought of it near to driving him mad. Now, seeing her standing there, mere feet away, desire slammed into him. Desire to stove in Patrick's face, desire to throw Bethany over his shoulder like some reiver of old. Opening the bathroom door, distracted by his unkind thoughts towards the other man, he'd come to a dead stop as he spied her across the hall. Somewhere in the back of his mind, he knew he should move, should retreat directly to his room, but her eyes were on him. Searing him as her gaze travelled. He watched her throat bob and fought himself not to go to her. Knowing if he did, it'd take an act of the Almighty to get him to stop. Not that he'd take her against her will. Of course not. The idea alone made him sick. But no, no that wouldn't be necessary. Not with the looks she was currently giving him, making his body respond. His body...that was only covered in a mere scrap of cotton. Awareness struck him, his hands shifting, holding his soiled clothing from earlier tighter, attempting to cover more of himself. He forced himself to move then, to turn away from her, to go to his room and close the door.

Bethany-

My heart restarted after his door had closed softly behind him, and I reflected that it probably wasn't exactly healthy for me to be having these kinds of heart issues. Arrythmia, I think medical professionals called it. I wouldn't seek help for it, though. No, that wouldn't go so well. The doctor would ask what I was doing when my heart began having issues and my response would be, *Looking over Liam Kristian Gunn, that's all.* The doctor would then ask, *And how long has this been going on?* I'd be forced to respond, *Since I first laid eyes on him when I was a little girl.* There was no way under Heaven I was admitting that out loud.

Reminding myself that Nana was waiting, I headed for that much-needed shower. Some twenty minutes later, clean from all traces of green paint, I stepped from the bathroom now clothed in a pair of soft knit pants and T-shirt. Liam's door was still closed, though all I heard was silence. When I entered the kitchen, Nana had the tea steeping beside a plate of some kind of spice cake that smelled delectable. She poured our cups as I sat down. "Smells lovely, Nan."

"Thanks, pet. New recipe I received from a woman I met down the pub last month. She swore it was a family favorite." I took a bite and my eyes nearly rolled out the back of my skull. It was that good. Like a cinnamon roll, but with a moist, cake-like form and texture. Absolutely delicious. As we sat, enjoying the light repast, Nana said, "The barn looks lovely. You and Liam did a grand job of it."

"Thanks, we were happy to do it."

"The two of you work well together." I wasn't sure how to respond to that so just took another sip of tea. After a moment longer, Nana said, "Patrick seems rather smitten with you."

"Liam said the same thing earlier."

"We've certainly seen more of him these last couple of weeks than we ever have."

"Hmm."

"Are you not fond of him?" She sipped at her tea, her eyes warm and gentle.

"He's nice, Nana. I do think he's nice. And he's attractive. And thoughtful and considerate."

"You're still not feeling *it*."

"I just don't know. I don't know if I'm ready yet for another relationship."

"There's no rush, pet. Take your time, get to know him. Looks as though he intends to be around either way."

"He said as much." I nodded, taking another bite of that cake.

"Did he now?"

"He said he wanted to date me, if and when I was ready and that he'd be here, whenever that was."

"Sounds reasonable."

"It does. I just don't want to lead him on or give him false hope."

"Take it one day at a time. Maybe it'll be Patrick that turns your heart around, maybe not. Just enjoy the moment."

Feeling better about the situation, I finished my tea, then helped her get supper ready. Their new guests were a set of newlyweds and a businessman from Dublin travelling to Cork. The newlyweds would stay three days, the businessman for a week as he met with numerous contacts in the area. The businessman, it turned out, wasn't arriving until later in the evening, so that first night, it was just the newlyweds—Brian and Theresa—from London, and us. Liam didn't appear for dinner and when I broke down and asked about him, Nan said Sean had taken him down to Collins.

Brian and Theresa were around their mid-thirties, I guessed. We were their third stop on their way around Ireland before heading home. He worked for the railroad there and she worked for a hotel. They were a quiet couple, seemingly preferring their own company to that of others. Not that

I blamed them; they were on their honeymoon, after all. Their first stop, they'd said, had been to Ashford Castle for two nights. I thought that was pretty romantic. Visiting a castle was definitely on my bucket list. I didn't meet the other guest until the following morning.

Jack-

Jack studied Delaney as she groomed her last horse. Studied her form, the way the light hit her, the way her body moved. Graceful, almost like a dance. He felt the heat rising in himself and was at a loss as to how to defeat it.

"Got a text from Bethany." Delaney led the gelding to his stall.

"She seems to be doing better." He swallowed, even as he tracked her movements.

"I told her to send more pictures; it's so beautiful there."

His eyes travelled over her again. "Yeah, beautiful." Unconsciously, Jack had moved toward her, following, trailing. When Delaney shut the tack room light off, she turned and found Jack right behind her. Startled, she took a step backward, and he reached out, stopping her. His hands snagging at her waist, holding her steady. Delaney blinked, surprised. Then she saw the look in his eyes, and heat curled in her middle. Jack gave her time to resist. To object. His grip tightened. He held still for a heartbeat, then tugged her forward.

"Oh, thank God," Delaney whispered, rising on her toes, sliding her arms around his neck. Jack groaned as his mouth touched hers. His arms slid further around her, pulling her flush with him. He'd heard her comment, heard the heat in it. Felt her response to him. And rejoiced.

Bethany-

The weather had changed overnight, bringing wind and some rain, waking me a couple times with the voracity of the storm. I hoped it hadn't damaged the paint job on the barn. When I woke the next morning, it was to fog pressing against the windows. The house was chilly, and I shivered as I came down the stairs, looking for something warm to drink. Nana was already in the kitchen, working on breakfast. Granda was bending to peer inside the fireplace, stacking the kindling to get a flame going. Nana said she'd asked Liam to bring more firewood in, and would I see if he needed a hand. Stepping onto the back patio, my breath clouding the air in front of me, I looked for him. Next to the door, I found about six split logs, but no sign of Liam. Hearing a solid *thunk* come from around the side of the house, I headed in that direction. Liam was chopping more wood for the fire, and for a moment, I allowed myself to simply watch him. Watched the way the muscles in his back and shoulders moved as he lifted that blade, slamming it down into the log before him.

It wasn't lost on me that my body seemed to have no hesitation at all when it came to Liam. My heart didn't seem to have any issue with him either. The only hang up appeared to be Liam himself. That *he* seemed to have some hesitations over *me*. It took me a moment to note that the sounds of him chopping wood had gone silent. That he was now facing me, those mesmerizing blue eyes resting on me. It was the look in those eyes that often threw me off balance. Heat, such heat in his gaze, and yet...yet he kept his distance. "Something ye need, lass?" His voice, deep and pleasing as it was, caused me to jump.

"Wood," I mumbled, shaking my head, trying to refocus myself. "Logs, um, for the fire." Before continuing, I paused, then muttered under my breath in what I hoped was clearer speech. "Nana asked me to see if you needed help bringing in more wood for the fireplace."

"Is that all ye need?"

"What...what do you mean?"

He stared at me a moment longer, seemingly trying to resolve something in his mind. He shook his head, a slow, careful movement, then said, "There're some logs near the door; if ye'd grab those, I'll bring these."

It was on the tip of my tongue to say something, to mention the elephant in the room, instead, I turned, making my way to the back door. I loaded my arms with the wood there and reached for the door handle. It opened before I touched it. "Allow me." Came a pleasant voice. Looking up, I saw a man standing at the back door. I estimated him to be about six feet tall, maybe more. His hair was brown, clipped short. His eyes hazel. "You must be Bethany from the States." He held the door open for me. "Your grandparents have been telling me about you."

"Hello," I smiled, "and thanks." I stepped into the kitchen, glad for the heat. Moving beyond to where Granda was waiting, I set the logs down and dusted myself off before turning back to the gentleman. "I'm sorry, I didn't catch your name."

Before he could respond, the door to the dining room opened and Nana came in. "Have you met Bethany then, Eamonn?"

"We were just getting there, Mrs. Fitzpatrick."

"Callie, please. And my husband is Tiernan."

"It's a pleasure." Eamonn's hazel eyes drifted back in my direction just as Liam came in, his arms full of wood. Eamonn, I decided, reminded me a little of Jensen Ackles, from the show *Supernatural*. I'd define his dress as ruggedly urban. He appeared to be around Liam's age, maybe a couple years older. Liam stood from depositing the wood in the bin beside the fireplace, dusting his hands off. With his hazel eyes still upon me, Eamonn said, "And you must be Liam." His gaze flashed to Liam and back.

"Ye'd be correct." Liam, I noted, didn't offer a hand in greeting. Instead, he'd stood tall, shoulders back, hooking his thumbs in his pockets. Waiting.

Eamonn looked to him. "You handle an axe well."

"I handle many things well."

"I'm sure you do," Eamonn mused seemingly to himself.

"Eamonn's here from Dublin; he'll be staying a week. I'll not be cooking supper tomorrow, Eamonn, as we're supping down to Collins. I hope that's agreeable to you."

"That's fine with me. I'll be in and out with business contacts. Though, I'll be sure to make time to accompany you all tomorrow evening." He checked his watch. "I'll be headed out myself now. It was a pleasure to meet you all, and I appreciate you having me." Eamonn's gaze lingered on me before he reached for a coat laid across the back of one of the chairs. His gaze sat heavy on me as he parted with, "I'll be seeing you."

After he'd left, Liam muttered, "Bugger me." Granda coughed some, though I wasn't sure if it was from what Liam had said, or from the fire he'd just lit.

"Oh, he seems a nice enough lad," Nana said. Liam didn't respond, his mouth tightened into a solid line.

"Aye, he did. Seemed a might taken with you, pet." Granda gave me a knowing look. Unsure how to respond, I simply offered something of a wan smile.

"Don't tease her. Now, Bethany, be a dear and run up to the market for me?"

"Sure, Nan. What do you need?" She wrote her list down. It was just a couple items. I should be able to fit it all on the bicycle. After I'd had my tea, I'd headed up to change. When I came back down, Liam was gone and I didn't see him again until the following day.

CHAPTER SEVEN
Stormy Weather

Bethany-

Morning dawned bright and clear, not a trace of the rain and clouds remained. I helped Nana with the linens after the newlyweds left. As it was such a beautiful day, I hung the bedding and towels out in the yard. With it being so sunny out, my jeans were soon too warm from my exertions so back inside I went, deciding to change. Just as I reached the stairs, Nana stepped into the hall from the kitchen. "Oh, there you are, Bethany. I wonder if you'd do us a favor?"

"Of course, anything."

"Tommy, down the lane, has a horse not feeling quite right, and he's got a cow in labor and can't tend to the horse. Might you be able to take a look at it for him?"

"Sure, I could do that. Can't promise I'll be able to fix the horse, but I'll take a look at any rate."

"Sure, and that's fine, dear. I'll have Liam go with you to show you which place is his and to lend a hand if you're in need of anything."

"Oh." I blinked. "Okay, then. I'm uh...I'm going to run up and change really quick. It's sort of warm out."

"Rain will be coming, dear..."

"I'll bring a sweatshirt."

It took me just a few minutes to change; I was downstairs in record time, eager to be off. I missed my horses back home and longed simply to be around one. Liam and Nana waited at the back door. "Liam says the roads are pretty wet, might want to wear the Wellies."

I swallowed my annoyance that Liam couldn't tell me that himself, but smiled at Nana and held up my old pair of tennis shoes. "These are fine for me; the rain doesn't bother me. I'm used to it." Once I had them on, I kissed her cheek, then was out the door. *Let Liam stew over that.* I slowed as I reached the gate, allowing him to step in front of me, and with a silent lift of his arm, indicated the direction we needed to go.

Liam-

Liam ground his teeth in frustration as they walked and had an irritated heart to heart with the Almighty. *And how, Lord, is this fair? Dangling her in front of me like this. I'm a man, no' a machine. I can't help what I feel for her. I can't help the longing she brings out in me. If this is some sort of test of me mettle, I fear I'm only doomed to failure.*

They'd arrived at Tommy's place; little Sarah, Tommy's youngest and not quite ten, came out to greet them and led them to the barn for the horse in question. Liam performed the introductions, but remained silent thereafter, afraid he'd say something to give himself away. Lord knew, he was doing his level best to ignore the fire she lit inside him. He watched her closely though, eye intent on her movements and that of the horse, as Bethany stepped into the stall. Alert and ready in case the animal reacted viciously out of fear or pain.

The golden-brown gelding, some sort of draft cross, held his left front hoof off the ground, the toe barely touching down. Bethany spoke soothingly to the animal and once he'd lowered his head and nudged her in the chest, she put a hand to his neck and slid it along his shoulder, then slowly down to the leg in question. She felt along the knee and cannon bone, then around the ankle. Continuing her thorough examination, she lifted the hoof and perused inside with tender fingers.

"Is Bernard going to be okay?" Sarah asked as she watched from beside Liam, taking his big hand in hers. It strongly reminded him of when Bethany had been so young, how she'd clung to his hands, confident he'd see her safe.

Bethany glanced back, a smile spreading as she noted how the little girl had attached herself to Liam. "Yes, I think he most-likely will."

"Can you help him, then?"

"I believe so; his foot seems a little sore. Sarah dear, where's your tack room? Where the medicines and hoof pick might be?"

"Back here." Sarah dropped Liam's hand and led Bethany to a room at the back of the barn, pulling the string for the overhead light. Liam watched from his position outside Bernard's stall as Bethany quickly looked through the supplies available. In the little cooler under the window, she pulled out a bottle of something and shook it up. Deciding against the use of that, she put it back and turned to Sarah. "I wonder if you might help me?"

"O'course."

"I need a large bowl, or bucket preferably, of really warm water and salt; regular table salt is fine. About a cup's worth. Can you get that for me?"

"I will, right away." Sarah scampered off to do as she was bid, and Bethany grabbed a hoof pick and a rag and headed back to the stall. She passed Liam, not pausing to spare him a glance and once more moved up to the gelding. "All right, Mister, you hold still now. This is going to hurt, and for that, I'm sorry. Liam, could you hold his head, please?"

Without responding, Liam moved to the horse's head. Bethany made sure he had a firm grip on the halter before turning back to her job. She lifted the hoof and using the pick, gently cleaned it out. Once clean, she used the rag and pressed inside the hoof itself.

"What's wrong wi' him?" Liam finally asked, curiosity overwhelming his resolve.

"He's got an abscess and it needs to drain." Bernard jerked his head and attempted to move as she continued to press down. She moved with the horse, continuing to talk soothingly to it.

"Any luck?" Liam asked after several long moments. He was trying to distract himself from the fact that she was right there, bent over in front of him. He honestly wanted to cry; he was that frustrated.

"It's coming along. Should be almost drained. Then I'll soke his foot in the salt water; that'll help to draw more of the infection out. I'll dry and wrap it, and we should be good to go."

Bethany-

The rain caught us unprepared, spitting down as Granda would say. I'd finished with Bernard and had wrapped his hoof in hopes that would keep dirt out of it long enough to allow healthy healing. We'd said goodbye to Sarah, and I'd told her to have her dad call later if he had any questions. Being around Liam had given me a raw, needy feeling. The heated looks, the close proximity. It was all driving me somewhat insane. Patrick didn't make me feel this way. Not even Eamonn had, though, like Granda had suggested, he had been giving me lingering, interested looks. If I was being honest, not even Garrett had affected me the way Liam did. Though, he seemingly wanted nothing to do with me apparently. Which, I was forced to admit was a major bummer, because I was coming to realize that no matter how much I tried not to feel this way, I wanted *plenty* to do with him.

Squinting up at the sky, I rolled my eyes at the thick cloud cover. Of course, it was raining. Of course it was. When leaving Tommy's, I'd turned in the opposite direction of my grandparents' place, uncaring right then if Liam followed me, or not. I wasn't ready to return yet and wanted to explore, wanted to see more of Ireland at my own pace. Needing to sort myself and these persistent feelings out along the way.

Thunder rumbled loudly overhead, once more drawing my gaze upward. Correction, the rain had caught *me* unprepared. My companion wore a rubber jacket and Wellies. Stubbornly, I'd opted for a favored pair of cut-off denim shorts, a soft grey T-shirt, and an old pair of tennis shoes. Because I'd been warm. I'd been warned the weather could and would change quite frequently in the spring. But, come *on*, it had been so sunny and warm earlier, I hadn't been able to resist my clothing choices. And I didn't regret my decision, not even now.

We'd been trudging down an overgrown lane, I wasn't sure just where we were, and had probably gotten us lost with my random meandering here and there. Stopping frequently, I'd wanted to see and touch everything. My phone was constantly clicking as I took picture after picture, looking for all the world like a tourist. I simply wanted to send images back to Del and Jack, to share all of this with them. The desire in me to touch Ireland in whatever measure I could attain, to pick it up, feel it, smell it was strong and I gave in, thoroughly enjoying myself as I went. Allowing myself this welcome distraction. And each time I did, with each new delight I discovered, my companion would sigh and grit his teeth. I could *hear* those blue eyes of his roll inside his head.

At any rate, the wind had picked up first. Then the rain had come. Just a light mist, then a mild drizzle. That would have been fine, but then the deluge hit. And it was a literal deluge. My hair was plastered to my skull. My clothing plastered to my body. Even the lightweight sweatshirt I'd had tied around my waist and slipped on when the wind had picked up was plastered to me. My shoes were soaked, making awkward noises as we walked. Soon, the roadway was nothing so much as a muddy pond. And the rain was so heavy I could barely see through it. The fierce wind wasn't helping us out any either. The shivering had started about five minutes ago. Try as I might to keep my teeth clenched tightly, so as not to alert my guide, he saw. And swore long and colorful.

***

Liam-

Liam ground his teeth, near to weeping he was so raw. *Lord,* this woman, *have mercy.* Her clothing was plastered to her, leaving his imagination running in high gear. All the things he wanted to do to her, with her. He trembled with need, with strain, desperately trying to hold himself in check. Hearing her father's warning in his head.

It had started with her outfit. Cotton and denim. Nothing fancy. Yet, she'd looked so bloody bonnie in them. Those legs that went on and on, so perfectly displayed. The thin cotton softly molding to her figure. All of it driving him mad. Then, as she dealt with the horse. His heart had swelled as he'd watched her. Seeing her way with the animal in pain. How she'd calmed the horse. With soft, sure words and touch. And now, as her wet clothing left him ragged with wanting. Such a longing she evoked in him. Such a longing.

She was shivering, goosebumps rose on her skin. Skin he wanted to warm, to soothe, to touch. Taste. Walsh's old lean-to was ahead, he knew. They could shelter there until the storm slackened. Though, as he turned to her, to direct her in the shed's direction, her form—shown in devastating relief—caught his eye. He should make them trudge on; he knew he should. And yet. She shivered again, crossing her arms over her chest, and he shook his head, jaw clenching in aggravation.

The devil on his shoulder suggested his kindness in seeing them out of the rain. It was, after all, caring for her wellbeing, just as her father had requested. Liam cursed that devil, even as he took Bethany's arm, angling them to the tiny barn.

Bethany-

His cursing had me gritting my teeth harder. I'd determined to just keep my head down and keep going, ignoring his impatient tirade. So, it's possible that was why I missed the lean-to off to our right. The one Liam was trying to direct us towards. It wasn't until he'd grabbed my arm and pulled me in the shelter's direction that I saw it. And jerked my arm away, snorting under my breath as I thought of the meaning of his name. Liam. It's Irish for William. And William means *Strong Protector*. I know because I looked it up. I'd done that because I was stupid. Stupidly thinking I was attracted to this, this giant, beautiful, attractive ignoramus.

Strong Protector, my hind end. *Ha!* Yeah, right. Liam wanted nothing to do with me, much less having any desire to protect me. Far from it. He did his best to avoid me at all costs. Which didn't seem to be working out so well for him now, did it? Seeing as how he ended up being the one stuck escorting me around the country at my grandmother's request. That was another thing, I fumed as I stomped through a particularly deep puddle, splashing water up my legs. I'd need to inform her that Liam simply didn't like me, and it wasn't fair to either of us for them to keep forcing me on him. I wondered when he'd started to dislike me; we'd always got on well when we were younger. What had changed for him, and when?

We made it into the shelter, and I tried to wring the water from my shirt and sweatshirt. As I dried off as best as I was able, I looked around, hoping we weren't invading some wild animal's domain. But the building seemed clean. Nothing but a couple of rakes and what looked to be old water troughs in the far corner. The shivering continued even though we were out of the wind. Liam swore again and ripped his jacket from his frame, tossing it to me. He was standing near the doorway fairly blocking it as he faced out into the storm; I stood about five feet from him, closer to the back wall.

"I d-d-don't n-need this." I shivered, holding it back out to him. The last thing I wanted was to accept charity from someone who so evidently was angry to be giving it.

"Just take the doaty thing, *hen.*" Liam's cool, growling voice made heat curl in my stomach. Not all of it from irritation. No, his voice, that growling burr, that was a different heat entirely. Mentally, I grimaced. Hen. Like I'm some sort of barnyard bird. Does he expect me to lay eggs and squawk? Because that's not happening. Hen. I'd roll my eyes if I wasn't so darned cold. Like he didn't know my name. Or just refused to use it. Which irritated me to no end. Was it so hard to just say my name?

"N-no. Th-thank you," I tried to growl back, but utterly failed from all the stuttering and shivering.

"You're soaking wet. And shivering. And...just put it on."

"Th-then you w-won't have o-one."

"Put it on, hen. Dinna be stubborn."

"B-Bethany. M-my name is Bethany, n-not bloody hen!"

"I ken fine what yer name is."

"S-Say it."

"Sure, and I've go' the bloody time for this." Liam ground out as he glanced over his shoulder at me before turning back to the doorway and the rain. His tall build began to tremble. Under his jacket he'd worn a dark T-shirt. That he filled well. Really well. Distractingly well.

"Why w-won't you s-say my name, L-Liam?" He ignored me, refused to answer, but I saw him lock down. Saw his shoulders tighten and his back become rigid as I spoke. His trembling seemed to intensify. "H-here, take i-it. I d-don't need it."

"Ye're the one shivering. Just use it."

"Y-you're shaking, too. I c-c-can s-see it."

That made him shake harder. "I'm no' cold." He snorted. "Far from it."

"Y-you are," I argued.

"Nae. I'm no'."

"I c-can see y-you!"

He swore again, which strengthened my aggravation, making me see red. So much so that I wadded up his jacket and threw it at him, hitting him in the back. His entire frame stiffened, then he turned to me, putting his face into shadows. He was silent a moment, and though I couldn't see his eyes, I felt his gaze as it settled over me. "I'm no' shiverin', because I'm no' cold. I'm shakin' wi' laughter."

"L-laughter? I don't...w-why? W-what's so f-f-funny?"

"I'm laughin' because it's better than cryin', hen."

"W-what? And w-will you st-stop *bloody* calling m-me th-that?"

"I'm laughin', *hen,* because I'm a dead man. A *dead* man." He sounded almost desperate.

"What?" My heart stopped briefly as I feared the worst. "W-what does th-that even m-mean?"

"It means that I can see me death in the verra near future. And I just dinna think I care any longer."

"A-are you sick?" Still shivering, I wrapped my arms around myself, trying to stay warm.

"Nae. Definitely no'."

"Then why would you s-say t-that?"

"I say that," he paused, then shook his head, "because of what I'm aboot to do." Something changed. Something in the tone of his voice made my knees weaken. Suddenly, I wasn't cold anymore. Far, far from it. My arms dropped to my sides. Heat curled in my stomach—I was surprised you couldn't see the steam pouring from me—and my breath...I couldn't seem to catch my breath. Liam crossed to me in two long strides. And just kept coming. Crowding me back against the shelter wall. "If I'm going to die, I'm going to bloody well make sure it's worth it."

Liam wasn't gentle as his mouth took mine, claimed it. He was thorough, however. There was such a hunger in his touch. The weight of his hands, his body, and his mouth. I've been kissed before, of course I have. But this, this was something else entirely. It was being consumed in a fire, but not burned alive. Breath after suffocating. Like I'd grabbed a livewire, the charge flowing through me, bringing me to life rather than taking it. This was a man where previously I'd only been kissed by a boy. It was night and day. And I was entirely captivated by him. My mind emptied entirely of everything that wasn't him. His mouth. The warmth, the firm gentleness of his hands. The lush scrape of his whiskers against my skin. His breath, minty and spicy. The heat of his grasp as I was gripped, my head angled, held still for him. The solid weight of his body as it shoved mine into the wall at my back.

Being completely lost to him, my arms snaked around his neck, straining to be closer. This was every dream come true. Every fantasy he'd ever stared in. *Liam was kissing me.* Not just kissing. Passionately kissing me. As if his life depended on it, as if he wanted to do this. As if he couldn't seem to help himself. I didn't want him to ever stop. Liam let his hands slide away from my face, down my side to my hips. Further still, as he reached for my thighs and lifted me, his hands slick on my wet skin, positioning himself between my legs. He didn't need to hold me for long because I locked my ankles around him.

His mouth left mine and was making its way along my throat, sending more heat racing through my body. His teeth grazed my shoulder, then came back and took a firmer grip. A soft, needy moan escaped my throat, bringing him to a halt. For one long moment we were still except for the raging breath in our lungs, then I jumped as he slammed one palm, the one not holding me against him, into the wall. With his head buried against my neck, he growled against my fevered skin, "I dinna care, Bethany. I dinna care if yer da kills me. Nor yer ma. I'd gladly die a thousand deaths to be here wi' ye."

My heart stuttered in my chest at the sound of my name on his lips, the heat, the warmth those words inspired. Then, his words hit me. "What...Liam, what do you mean? About my dad?"

He gently set me down, lowering one leg, then the other before stepping back, his eyes meeting, searching mine. "Yer da warned me off ye. Years ago. He'd caught me looking and set the boundary. Then again, a week afore I came here. He called, asked me to look after ye, said he was depending on me. And no' to let him down. I didna even ken he'd had me number."

I just looked at him shaking my head. I'd like to say I was surprised by this, but I wasn't. That was so my dad. Always protective. Always one step ahead of the game.

"But I dinna care aboot any of it. I've longed for ye for years, Bethany. And now, I've had ye where I've only dreamed of it afore, and I dinna care if he kills me. I dinna."

Reaching out, I took his shirt in my fist and tugged him forward. "While I don't want you to come to any harm, Liam, I have a confession to make to you as well. I've had a crush on you since I was about ten years old." I pulled his head down to mine and that fire between us exploded once more. It wasn't up to my dad, or my mom. This was my choice, not theirs. I appreciated their concern, I did, but I had to make my own decisions. Liam was mine.

Somehow, we ended up on the floor. He sat with his back against the wall and I sat straddling his hips. We were still now, only our hearts were racing. I leaned into his chest, one of his arms held me there; the other was bent, our fingers entwined, resting against his heart.

"Did you mean what you said?" I nuzzled against him, my nose pressing into the skin of his throat.

"Aye," his voice rumbled. "I did. I *do*."

"So do I." His arm tightened at that, and I felt his lips against my head. "What does that mean? For us, I mean?"

"Well, I guess ye could say it means yer me lass and I'm yer man. If ye like?"

"I like, Liam. I like that *very* much."

"It's glad I am to hear ye say it, because I dinna think I could give ye up. Nor do I have any intention of doing so."

"Same." I grinned.

"We do need to be going, though. Afore your grandparents wonder what's become of us." I stood from him, then offered a hand to pull him up. Grinning, he took it and was soon on his feet. The rain had subsided to a light drizzle by now, but the afternoon was waning, and the chill was beginning to seep through my wet clothing once more. Liam picked up his raincoat from where it had dropped when I'd thrown it. His mouth lifted at the corner as he offered it to me again. I opened mine to respond, but before I could utter even a sound, his finger was firm, yet gentle against my lips. "Do this, for me, please? You're wearing wet clothing that shows more than I ought to be noticin', and though it may no' have seemed so afore, I do respect ye and intend to honor ye. I'd prefer no' to test me mettle again, ye ken?"

Hearing his request in that context, I decided to do as he'd asked. Liam helped me to slip it on, then he zipped it and rolled my sleeves so my arms weren't lost. After tucking a wayward strand of hair behind my ear, he took my hand in his and we headed back to my grandparents'.

CHAPTER EIGHT
Black Eye, Warm Heart

Bethany-

Nana was waiting as we came in the back door, a knowing gleam in her eye. She refrained from comment, however, simply clucking under her breath about rain and chills and the absurd antics of youth. Whisking me upstairs, she had the bath water running in no time. "Get in, dear, before you catch yer death and yer mother kills me. I've the water on and will bring tea up shortly."

Too tired to argue, I did as I was instructed. After she'd left, I closed the door and my body was suddenly wracked with chills once more. Whether from actual cold or fatigue, I couldn't be certain; probably a combination of the two. By the time I sunk beneath the warmth of the bathwater, my teeth were rattling. Thankfully, it didn't take too long for me to begin to warm up, especially when I began considering all that had taken place this afternoon. My behavior and conduct. Liam and the fire that had sparked between us. *Omgosh, if my parents could see me now...*I was sure they'd have a few choice words to say. Best not to think about that. Things *had* become rather hot and heavy between Liam and me. Though, nothing had technically happened, other than essentially hugging and kissing. Which was all that Garrett and I had ever done. And they'd never flipped their lids over that. Actually, now that I think about it, I probably should figure out something to say. My parents would need to be told. Dad would need to be told. Told in such a way that would not cause Liam any harm. I'd have to think more on that. Besides, it was a little soon for such a step, wasn't it? We'd just admitted our long-standing feelings for each other. Better to let things progress naturally, or not, and then adjust.

Feeling better already, I stood and reached for my towel. Once dried off, I let the water from the tub, then picked up my wet clothes from where I'd set them in the sink. I wrung them out as best as I could and laid them to dry over the edge of the tub. When I opened the bathroom door, I came to a stop. Liam was leaning against the opposite wall, waiting for me. He'd already changed, I noticed. His arms were folded across his chest, one ankle crossed over the other. He remained still for a moment when he first saw me. Then, slowly, he unfolded his arms and straightened. "I wanted to check on ye, make sure ye were all right."

"I am. You?" It wasn't lost on me at all that this was the second time Liam had seen me in nothing more than a towel and that was *far* more than Garrett had ever seen.

"More than well." I blushed under his regard, then shivered as a drop of water ran down behind my ear. "Ach, here I am blabber'n on and yer still soakin' wet."

"That's all right; I'm fine."

"Go on now, lass. I'll wait for ye here. Then we'll go down; yer nan has tea waiting."

I held still for just a moment, seemingly unable to control my body, then realized I was still standing in the bathroom doorway, wrapped in a towel, and beginning to feel the chill. "Go on, lass," Liam said once more. His voice sounded a little rough. Nodding, I moved across the hallway to my room. I turned to face him again before closing the door; Liam swallowed and dipped his chin, encouraging me. Blowing out a breath, I closed the door and groaned silently to myself. *What was the matter with me?* Get ahold of yourself, Bethany!

With that pointed pep-talk out of the way, I quickly dressed in clean, dry clothes. My hair took the longest, needing to be painstakingly brushed and braided before I felt decent enough to leave my room. Liam was still waiting for me. He met my gaze and a slow smile spread across his face. An answering one lit mine.

"All right, you two. Quit moonin' about in the hall and get down here," Nan called from the bottom of the stairs. I heard a chuckle from somewhere below and wondered who had heard her. Liam tilted his head in her direction, almost as if asking, *You wanna?* He held out his hand and I took it letting him lead me to the kitchen. When we reached the bottom step, he lifted our hands and kissed the back of my knuckles.

"Nae matter what's aboot to happen in there, lass, I hope ye ken I couldna be happier."

"Same." I smiled up at him. "And do you think something's about to happen?"

"I have nae doubt summat will be said, but I'm no' worried aboot it."

Granda opened the kitchen door and peered out at us. He then held it, silently waiting for us to enter. I went to release Liam, but he tightened his grip, refusing to let go. We moved past my grandfather and found Nana already seated at the table. On it was a pot of tea, a bottle of whiskey, and four cups. Liam pulled my chair out for me and waited until I was seated before taking the seat to my right. Granda took the seat to my left, with Nana in the chair directly across from me.

"The two of you are not going to make me regret putting your rooms near each other, are you?" Granda said, speculation strong in his tone as Nana poured the tea, adding a splash of the whiskey to each cup.

"Nae, sir," Liam replied, giving my hand a gentle squeeze.

"Sure, and you'd best not," Nana said crossly, first looking Liam, then myself, directly in the eye as she dispersed the cups to each of us. "Or yer da will have my head."

"Have all our heads, he will," Granda said.

"Ach, and I wouldna do that to ye, nor to Bethany."

"It's glad I am to hear you say so."

"Nana, Granda." I smiled at Liam, then turned back to my grandparents. "We, Liam and I, we've...nothing truly happened. Other than that, we finally realized the feelings we've had for each other. I've been in love with Liam for as long as I can remember knowing him. We're not entering this lightly. Our eyes are wide open," I told them.

"Sure, and we know, lass." Nana reached across and patted my hand. "We've known for many years now and had fair given up trying to get the two of you together."

Shock settled. I felt a little as though I was falling, though I knew I was firmly seated and stationary. "You've *known?* What? How? I mean, *we* just figured it out. How did the two of you know?"

"Well, we're old, pet, not blind." That made me chuckle. Nana continued, "What's the story? Are you after telling your parents then?"

"Well, I'm certainly not keeping it a secret from them, though, we just figured this out for ourselves and are still getting used to the idea, to each other. So, I imagine it'll be talked about, but in time. Not right this moment."

"Bethany's right. Ah dinna ken, just how, or when, but her parents will be told. When the time is right."

"That sounds fair, Da. Can't ask for more than that now, can we?" Nana said to Granda.

"Aye, we bloody well can," Granda said. He gave Liam a stern look. "Just you mind who her da is. You don't want to know what that man is capable of."

"I'm well aware."

"You only *think* you're aware; if you truly *knew* you'd run and cry, mark my words."

"Perhaps. Though, I'm no' playing games here. Nor will I be scare't away from her."

"Nor I from him." I tightened my grip on Liam's hand.

"Sure, and don't make me have to have words with the two of you again."

"We won't, Granda," I assured them both.

"We'd best be going if we're to eat at Collins. Eamonn said he'd meet us there." At Nana's words, Liam and I stood, making our way up the stairs to get ready.

Tiernan-

"I think that turned out better than we expected, wouldn't you, Callie, my love?"

"I do, indeed. Though, we're not out of the woods yet. We still need to clear it all with your son."

"Oh, my son, is he now?"

"Only when he's being pig-headedly stubborn, love." Tiernan chuckled at her logic. Callie took Tiernan's hand in hers, holding it tightly, remembering her own whirlwind romance with the man at her side. "Will it work out, do you think?"

"I think we're off to a grand start, at least." Tiernan placed a tender kiss across her knuckles, lingering for a moment. "Can't ask for better than that."

"Do you think Asher will be opposed to the match?" She smiled down at him, her eyes glistening.

"Hard to say. He's quite fond of the lass; he'll do everything to keep her safe."

"Aye, he will." Sighing silently, Callie knew she'd have to be patient and simply wait.

Bethany-

Collins was crowded as they had a local band playing this evening. My grandparents and Liam and I sat in the corner, having dragged a couple of tables and a handful of chairs together, creating more seating space for our group. Eamonn was already there, standing at the bar, when we'd arrived. His hazel eyes instantly snagged on Liam's hand entwined with mine. Paying for his drink, he made his way towards us and sat across from me. "You move fast, Liam." Eamonn took a drink from his pint. "Though, you were nearly too late; I'd fair decided last night to throw my hand in the pot. Might anyway."

His tone was friendly enough, the intent behind the words had me nervous, though, unsure how Liam would react. "Liam and I have known each other for several years, Eamonn. We just came to an understanding about each other."

"Yer welcome to give it a go," Liam said, his stare direct. "Though, should the lass tell ye nae, that's the end of it."

"Fair enough." Eamonn offered Liam a grin before turning his gaze to me.

Before he could open his mouth, I said, "No. Thank you, Eamonn, but the answer is no."

"And it's my heart you've broken with those words." Eamonn pressed his hand into his chest for emphasis.

"I'm sure you'll recover." I rolled my eyes at him, then offered Liam a smile.

Eamonn looked back to Liam. "Looks as though you've won. By her words alone, I yield and relinquish the field to you. Though," he paused, looking over his shoulder towards the opposite end of the room, "you might need to have words with a certain gentleman."

Following his stare, my eyes collided with those of Patrick McDaniels. The normally open and friendly look was gone from his face. My heart skipped a beat and I felt terrible. I'd *completely* forgotten about Patrick. *How could I have done that?* And how did Eamonn even know about Patrick's feelings for me? And what was I going to say to Patrick? I knew I had to say something. Explain to him. He rose to his feet, making his way to our table. Liam stood as well, one hand resting reassuringly on my shoulder, giving it a light squeeze. "Patrick," Liam said as the other man reached us.

"I'd have words with you, Liam," Patrick stated through stiff lips. "Outside, if you will."

I pushed my chair back, fully intending to go with them. The grip Liam had on my shoulder went from tender touch to firm pressure. Glancing up, I caught the look in his eye as he leaned down, placing a gentle kiss on my forehead. "Stay, lass. We willna be long. Just need to sort out a couple things."

"But," I began.

Nana leaned over, patting my hand. "Best to let the lads talk it out, pet."

"Talk? As in words spoken, or...?" I anxiously tracked Liam's progress as he followed Patrick out the door to the parking lot.

"There's many forms of talk," Granda responded philosophically, wiping the foam from his lip as he set his glass down. "Words spoken or otherwise. Either way, it's best to let the lads sort it out. They'll be better for it."

I sighed, blowing out a breath, trying to calm my frazzled nerves.

"You act as if 'tis your first time," Eamonn said, studying me.

"My first time for what, exactly?"

"To be fought over. It's not your first, is it?" he queried, a grin teasing at his mouth.

"What kind of question is that?"

"A fair one." He scratched his chin. "Is it your first then?"

"Yes!" I exclaimed, exasperated by his continued conversation.

"I find that right shocking, I do." That grin sprang free on his face. "Lass such as yourself ought'n to have had several under her belt by now."

"Well, I haven't, nor do I wish to accumulate any more. Once is enough for me, thank you very much."

"You're welcome," Eamonn replied. As if I'd truly been thanking him instead of simply being snarky. Obviously, my sarcasm skills needed improving. Collins' door opened and Liam stepped inside, followed by Sean. I saw no sign of Patrick. They quickly made their way to our table, Liam wearing a smile on his face as Sean thumped his shoulder good-naturedly. Liam's right eye was beginning to swell; a small cut sat right above his cheekbone.

"You're hurt." I dipped a napkin in my glass of ice water.

"It's no' but a scratch. Dinna fash, lass." Liam grinned as he placed a kiss against my temple. He sat beside me, accepting the dampened napkin, dabbing at the slight trace of blood seeping from the wound.

"Let him knock you one, did you?" Granda asked, eyeing the cut under Liam's eye.

"Just the one, aye; figured as how I owed him that at least." Liam nodded.

"Oh, at least," Eamonn agreed, grinning broadly.

"And just who in the blazes are you?" Sean asked, waving a pint over from the bar.

"Sean, meet Eamonn. Eamonn, Sean. Sean is Liam's oldest friend, he is," Nana replied.

"By that look upon your face, mate, I'll go on to say I'm a guest of the Fitzpatrick's and afore the lass set me straight I'd been considering strongly on courtin' her myself."

"Stirring up quite the ruckus, aren't you?" Sean grinned at me.

"Don't start," I warned Sean, then turned to Liam. "Where's Patrick? Is he furious?"

"Nae, lass, he's no' furious." He kissed me, quick and firm. "He's just needing some time and perhaps some ice."

"Did you *hurt* him?" I gasped, my mouth still tingling.

"Well, after the first jab, I wasna after letting the lad hit me again." He grinned almost knowingly, then said again, "Dinna fash, lass. The lad's no' hurt. Least no' physically hurt. I wouldna do that. Might be a bit tender of heart, though. Best to let him work through that on his own. Patrick willna be holdin' it against ye, I promise."

"I feel bad, though; I didn't mean to hurt him." My gaze drifted to the door again. "What happened between us wasn't meant to hurt him."

"He kens that." Liam gently took my chin, pulling my eyes back to his. "And doesna fault ye for it."

"Are you sure?" My eyes pleaded with him. "Should I try to talk with him, explain?"

"You're welcome to, though I dinna ken that it'd do much good. Unless ye planned to dump me for him."

"Well, I've no plans to do that."

"It's glad I am to hear that. Best to let it lie, then." Liam squeezed my hand gently.

"When did you finally work up the courage, lad?" Sean asked Liam as his pint arrived.

"Yesterday, it was." Liam's eyes took on a dreamy gleam. "It was lashing down, and she was soaked through, and looking as lovely a thing as I've ever seen, and I just decided I'd rather die a happy man than live and be miserable."

"Took you long enough," Sean said. "Does her da know yet? How much time do you have left?"

"My dad does not know yet, and when he does, he will not hurt Liam. I'll see to that," I assured Sean.

"Who's your da, then? Some sort of tough fella, is he?" Eamonn asked.

"Ye could say that. And more," Liam replied. "He's the sort of man could take on this entire room and walk away from it. And he has connections to see to anyone else who needs it. The man is no' one to trifle with."

Eamonn studied me again. "As the lasses and myself prefer my face the way it is, mayhap it's for the best I decided to yield."

"Trust me, it's for the best," I assured him, mentally rolling my eyes.

"Well, now that's all out of the way, might we order our supper?" Nana asked. Agreeing, we waved the server over, placed our orders, then sat back and listened to the music. Some lyrics, being sung in Irish, were unknown to me, though the melody was beautiful even if I couldn't understand what was said. Liam slung an arm around my shoulder, drawing me closer, my back to his front. We listened that way until our meal was served, then listened more as we ate. Conversation flowed effortlessly, and tensions eased as we absorbed the almost festive atmosphere of Collins.

My grandparents decided to head home first. Sean said he'd see Liam and I home if we cared to stay, so we agreed to hang out a bit longer. Eamonn decided to stay with us. The band, Sons of Ireland, had a pleasant sound. Singing both contemporary and folk type songs. Some were simple instrumental pieces that encouraged patrons to dance. I enjoyed watching them, though I knew none of the steps.

Eamonn was the first of us four to leave, saying he had an early drive in the morning. We waved him off, then ordered another round. It was only my second pint of the night, so I wasn't near to tipsy, though by halfway through it I began to feel the effects of the dark beer and decided to drink more water. We stayed another half hour or so, then Liam caught my yawn and announced it was time to go.

Sean handed his keys to Liam and stood to his feet. "Take the car, mate. I've a prospect I've been eyeing all evening and plan to see if she'll take me home. I'll get it from you tomorrow."

Looking in the direction he was staring, I noted the table of three women around my age sitting against the far wall. One in particular seemed rather taken with Sean. Liam wished him luck as we rose and headed out the door. We walked hand in hand to the parking lot, and Liam followed me to my side of the vehicle. I turned, thinking he was opening my door for me, but instead, he crowded me against the door. His lips found mine easily in the dim lighting. As opposed to the last time he'd kissed me, there was nothing rushed in this act. His mouth brushed across mine; once, twice. Soft, tender kisses. Little nibbles. Deep delving explorations. His hands threaded themselves in my hair, a soft growl escaped his throat, wending its way into mine.

Everything else faded; there was only him. Only his mouth on mine. Only his hands and his body against me. Only his scent, his taste invading me. I could have stayed here forever, just soaking him in. Absorbing these, and every sensation he evoked in me.

Somebody across the lot loudly cleared their throat, bringing reality crashing back in. Liam pulled back only enough to make eye contact. "I love ye." His voice was raw, low, and full of so much emotion it made my knees weak.

Breath left my chest and I had to gasp to fill my lungs. "I love you—so much. I didn't know I could love someone like this." He kissed me once more, then stepped back as he opened the car door and assisted me inside.

Bethany-

I kissed Liam.

No doubt, my text to Delaney was like a bomb going off. She'd known of my attraction to him for years and was probably hyperventilating. Her reply was almost instantaneous.

WHAAAAT?? Details. Now.

Blushing, remembering every minute detail, I replied:

It was everything. Every dream and fantasy I've ever had fulfilled in that kiss.

Seconds later she texted:

Wowzuh. So, you're like an item now? No lingering effects from my brother?

I replied, tensing, wondering how she'd react:

No, not really. Is that bad? I mean, sometimes, I question it—how fast I seemed to have moved on with Liam. Like, am I even ready? But then...?

Her response came swiftly:

But what???

I couldn't contain my smile. I could feel it plastered across my face.

He said he loved me. And I told him the same. And I meant it. What I feel for Liam doesn't come close to what I'd felt for Garrett. Honestly, I think we had ended a long time ago, though neither of us knew it.

Her reply bubbles came up:

Whoa. That was deep. And probably true. Also, that was fast. Just you slow it down, girly.

I texted back:

I am. I will.

I must not have been very convincing, because she cautioned:

Don't do anything stupid.

I grinned, thankful for her faithful friendship.

I won't. Don't tell anyone at home yet, okay?

She promised:

Scouts honor; behave yourself.

I smiled again as we ended our chat:

I will.

CHAPTER NINE

I am My Beloved's

Bethany-

Nana was in the backyard, throwing a scratch mix to the chickens. Granda had left early, she'd said, running some milk to a couple families. I'd been standing at the back door, watching Nan through the glass, when Liam came up behind me. His arms wrapped around my front, pulling me back against him. His lips found the skin at my neck. "*Mo Gràidh,*" he whispered against my skin, causing a delicious shiver to skate its way across my shoulders.

Smiling at the sound of his voice, the cadence of the words he'd just spoken, I turned in his arms. "What does that mean? What you said."

"My beloved."

"It's beautiful. Is that Irish or Scottish?"

"Scotts Gaelic."

"You keep that up, Liam, and I may have to rethink you calling me Sassenach and all that." I took hold of his shirt, lightly tugging at the material, trying to calm my racing pulse. Pressing my face to his chest, I inhaled slowly. "You've already treated me to 'Dinna fash.' Which, I'll have you know, I thoroughly enjoyed."

"Did ye now?" He pulled my face upward, leaning down to kiss me once before pulling back. "Do tell."

"I haven't seen a single episode of Outlander." I strove for a cavalier attitude, but as the gleam in his eyes strengthened, I figured I was failing.

"Though I have read a few of the books and can understand Jamie Fraser's draw. I just never expected myself to be caught up in literally quivering over a few simple words and how they're spoken. It's like music; it's beautiful, Liam."

"Quivering ye say? I like the sound of that. Like that I can affect ye in that way." To emphasize his point, he trailed warm lips up my neck and chuckled as chills raised goosebumps in the wake of his touch. We'd somehow moved and maneuvered our way over to the counter. Liam was backed against it, his arms holding me to him. The back door opened, Nana stepping inside, carrying her basket of eggs. Startled at the sudden interruption, we pulled apart and tried not to look guilty.

"Morning, Nan." I hoped she didn't notice my blush as I moved to Liam's side.

"A good morning it appears to be." She flashed a knowing grin at us as she continued towards the sink.

"Any new guests arriving?"

"Late this afternoon; a couple of lads on holiday only staying the one night before heading on to Galway."

"Will they be in the double room?"

"They will."

"Okay, I'll get that one set up."

"They'll want the two beds. Took special care to let me know they were only mates." She chuckled at that. "Guess you never know these days."

"I'd best get myself going. Told Tiernan I'd get those stalls mucked before the evening milking." Liam kissed me as he headed out the back door for the barn. I watched him go, my heart all aflutter, admiring his form, the way he moved, the control he exuded over his body. Shaking my head, I snagged a muffin from the table where Nana had a tray full of them and got to work on preparing the room for our incoming guests.

Liam-

Liam hummed to himself as he worked, his mind on the woman he'd left in the kitchen. On the taste of her skin, her mouth. He inhaled deeply, then almost choked from the smells of the stalls. *Served him right.* Chuckling, Liam rubbed a knuckle against his chin. Ah, she was worth it. Worth it and so much more. Bethany. The dream he hadn't dared to utter. The deepest desire of his heart, she was. Mentally, he shook his head. In just a few short hours, she'd become his everything. His reason. His balance. His purpose. All his life, he'd wanted her. Had watched her grow from a toddler to a little girl, to a teen, and finally into the beautiful young woman she was now. He wanted every part of her. Wanted to share her life, her dreams. He'd follow her anywhere. Across the ocean, to the wilds of Wyoming. He just had to have her.

They hadn't talked about a future yet. He paused what he was doing, his gaze drawn to the house. He started to set his rake and shovel down, intent on discussing things now, then forced himself to hold. To wait. They'd talk, he assured himself. And soon. He could wait.

Bethany-

Close to an hour later, I was just coming down the stairs with the dirty linens Eamonn had left out for us, when there was a knock at the front door. Opening it, I found Sean, a wide satisfied grin on his face.

"Morning, Bethany darling. Liam about?"

"I take it you had a lovely evening?" I opened the door further, stepping aside to allow him entrance.

"Mmm, lovely."

"Does she have a name, or was this a one-time occurrence?"

"Erin is her name and if I can get my keys back, I plan to take her out this evening."

"Alright then, I'll just run up and grab them from Liam's room. He's out back mucking stalls." Turning, I scampered back up the stairs and retrieved Sean's keys from Liam's room where they'd sat on his nightstand. Handing them to Sean, I said, "You can tell Liam all about your date."

"I shall. You take care, lovely Bethany. Be seeing you." Keys in hand, he headed through the hall and into the kitchen, giving Nana a hug before continuing out the back to see Liam, but not before snagging one of her muffins from the table, whistling as he went. Chuckling, I made my way to the laundry room. Sean seemed to be floating somewhere in the clouds. I hoped this Erin didn't break his heart.

Shortly before three, Liam entered the kitchen. "All finished?" Nana asked as she peeled apples while I sliced them. When he didn't immediately respond, I glanced up. Liam's blue eyes were on me; the look in them seemed troubled. In fact, there was a paleness to his complexion.

"Liam?" I asked, setting the knife and apple down. "What's the matter?"

"I have to leave." Liam's voice was rough, almost raw. His gaze stayed on me. "Gran called, said Grandad had a stroke. He's in the hospital; I need to go and be wi' them."

"I'm so sorry." My heart clenched as my hand covered my mouth. "Of course, you must go. Of course. I understand. Do you need a ride to the airport?"

Liam shook his head. "Sean's coming to gi' me a lift."

"Poor Olivia. She's probably beside herself. Let me know as soon as you hear any more news, then," Nana told him, placing her palm against his cheek. Turning to me, she said, "Go on now, pet. Help Liam pack. Say your goodbyes."

I followed Liam up to his room. He moved as if in a daze. From the closet, he took two bags, then lay them on the bed. He began pulling clothing from the drawers, haphazardly folding, and stuffing them into the bags. The whole time, he was silent.

"What can I do?" I whispered. "How can I help?" Turning from his task, he faced me where I leaned against the doorjamb. Pain danced in his blue eyes, and I wanted to take it away. "What can I do?" I asked again. He dropped the clothes he was holding and strode to me. Hardly more than one long step. Gathering me close, he wrapped his arms around me, buried his face against my neck, and simply held me.

After a moment, he pulled away. "I dinna want to leave ye, Bethany. I feel as though I've just found ye. And I'm afraid all this will be for naugh' and ye'll be gone when I return."

"I won't be gone. Liam, I love you and I'll be here. Do you want me to come with you?"

"I'd love nothing more, but this wouldna be the time for it. The family, my da, ye ken, can be tough on the best of days and this will have everyone on edge. Best to wait until I can take ye when things are calm."

"I understand." I nodded. "I'm praying for Harold. Praying everything works out and he comes through this. Please, promise to keep me posted."

"I will." Liam kissed me. "I'd best shower. Sean will be here soon, and I smell rather like the wrong end of cow."

"You're not that bad."

"Bless ye for saying so, love."

"I'll finish your packing. Go shower." I let him go, then emptied his bags and refolded and repacked everything. By the time he was finished, I had the drawers and closet emptied and was just folding the last item. Hearing a noise near the door, I turned and felt desire slam through me. Intoxicating, it was. Dangerous. My mouth dried out and breath was difficult to come by. He was beautiful. I'd seen him in a towel before, but being in his room, standing beside his bed seemed to add some potent elements to the tension I felt building between us.

Evidently, Liam went without a shirt a lot, because while he wasn't tanned exactly, there was a golden hue to his skin. And obviously he stayed fit somehow. Whether by way of physical exercise, or simply the work he did, he was fit. Not like my dad was. Not with that almost weight-lifter's build, but he was cut. Solid and firm. He entirely enthralled me. A dark, heated glint shown from his blue eyes. He held still, allowing me time to look.

Clearing my throat, I said, "I should let you change. Sean will be here soon."

"Aye, ye should. And I should let ye go." He rasped, those blue eyes tracking every movement I made. "I've a mind, however, to close this door and delay my departure. Ye drive a man to distraction, woman."

"I um, I'm not the one standing in a towel. And I really should go."

Liam stepped into the room, then moved to the side, jerking his head towards the door. Somehow, we managed to keep our hands off each other as I skirted around him and out to the hallway. My back to him, I heard the long, drawn-out exhale as he closed his door. Weakly, I leaned against the wall and took a few deep breaths myself. A knock sounded from below, so I headed for the door.

"Not good news," Sean stated when I opened the door for him. His expression was somber, compared to how he'd been this morning. "Lad'll be taking it hard."

"He is, Sean. He really is." Hearing a noise behind us, we turned as Liam made his way down the stairs. "All right, then?" Sean asked him. Liam just shook his head. "Here, I'll put your bags in the boot."

Without a word, Liam handed them over. His gaze had remained steady on me. Silently, I went to him, wrapped my arms around him. Just held him, offering whatever comfort I was able, for the time I was able. Granda, having returned while we'd been upstairs, and Nana came from the kitchen to say their goodbyes. I stepped back to give them room, though Liam held my hand, almost refusing to release me. "You're all in our prayers. Don't fret, now. Everything'll be all right. Keep us posted," Nan said as she hugged Liam.

Sean had the car started, waiting. I walked Liam outside, my hand still in his. At the car, he pulled me to him, arms wrapping around me as his mouth met mine, desperation in his actions. Moments later, they were driving away. My heart ached and I prayed Harold would be all right, that he'd recover. That Liam and Olivia and the rest of the family would be comforted.

Liam-

Liam leaned his head against the rest and closed his eyes as Bethany faded from sight, the road taking them further and further apart. He knew his focus should be on his grandfather. On whether he'd survive this stroke. And if he did, how he'd be afterwards. If his grandmother was all right. What needs they would have, how to meet them. But Lord help him, he couldn't keep his thoughts off Bethany and what their future would hold.

She said she'd be there, in Ireland, waiting for him when he returned, but he couldn't shake the fear that she would disappear. That this, what they'd shared over the last several days, would all be over before it had truly started. That time would be stolen from them, that she'd leave for the States before he could return. That she'd reconsider *them*, them as a couple, once back on her ranch and see he didn't fit in her world.

Somehow, he managed his airline ticket and boarding pass. Sean had clapped him on the shoulder, telling him everything would be all right, that his grandfather would be fine, that the lass would be there, waiting. He remembered thanking his best mate, but didn't remember finding his seat. He was here, though, so he must have been functioning in some capacity. He closed his eyes again, his mind a whirlwind of thoughts, and tried to find peace to stave off the threatening panic.

Bethany-

My mind was a tempest of thought as I reentered the house. I joined Nana in the kitchen, helping her finish the pies she'd been preparing. It was the end of June, I had roughly two months left here. Two months seemed like a while, but I didn't know how long Liam would be gone. I'd told him I'd be here when he came back, but we hadn't really talked about the long term. About any plans. We'd been so caught up in the here and now. In our newfound understanding and budding relationship.

I thought about it now. Did Liam have a preference for where we'd live? Would he be opposed to the States? To coming home with me? What were his thoughts on long-distance relationships? Would he expect me to relocate here? I didn't know and now was not the time to question him about it. I'd have to wait. For now, I contented myself with a simple text, letting him know I loved him, I missed him, and would, hopefully, see him soon.

Nana was just pulling the pies from the oven when my cellphone rang. Thinking it was Liam, I answered without noting the number, but no one responded. I looked at the screen and saw a stateside number I didn't recognize. "Hello? This is Bethany, can I help you?" Silence was all I heard, though the call was still connected. I suddenly remembered Ivy, the woman I'd met on the airplane, and said, "Ivy? Hello?"

The call went dead after that. I almost dialed it when my phone rang again. Same number. "Hello?" This time, I caught what sounded like heavy rain and a staticky voice saying, "'Lo—" Then the line went dead again. I dialed the number back, but it just went to voicemail. It was Ivy; I heard her voice saying to leave a name and number and she'd call back. "Hi Ivy, sorry I missed you, must have been a bad connection. Call me if you need to; hope you're having a great time."

I waited to see if she called back, but my phone never rang. I figured I'd try her again later. For now, I just hoped she was all right and enjoying her trip.

Kate-

Kate wondered what Samuel and Tiffy were up to. It had been a couple weeks since she'd seen her friend, so she sent her a text, asking what she was doing. Moments later, Kate's phone rang. "Whatcha have in mind? I have a few hours to spare, then Samuel's taking me out to dinner," Tiffy said as Kate answered.

"Just needed some in-town time. I'm going a little stir-crazy missing my girl. Might get a pedi, run a couple errands, do some shopping. Thought you might like to join me. I could swing by and pick you up?"

"Sounds great! Give me about twenty minutes to get dressed."

"Awesome; see you shortly." Kate found her husband in the study, going over some paperwork. Though Asher no longer did work for the government, he seemed to be kept apprised of various activities, because he received these packets of papers at least once every couple of weeks or so. He looked up at her entrance, a warmth in his bright blue eyes. It never failed to make her heart race, the way he watched her. Like she was still beautiful, still everything that mattered to him. Coming around the desk, she leaned down to kiss his brow. Asher's arms swiftly snaked around her, pulling Kate onto his lap, his mouth instantly finding hers. After a moment, he pulled back, looking her swollen lips over with apparent satisfaction.

"And, what was that all about?"

"Does a man need a reason to kiss his wife?"

"A reason? No, not exactly." As he leaned forward, his mouth tickling along her neck, Kate giggled. "Okay! Okay, he doesn't need a reason." Seemingly satisfied with that response, Asher again leaned back in his chair, blue eyes gleaming as he waited. "I just came to let you know I was picking Tiffy up to do some running around in town. I should be back before dinner."

"I have a much better idea." Asher leaned forward again, nothing playful in his touch now. Only need. "A much, much better idea." Kate shuddered as his lips trailed along her neck to her shoulder. His teeth gently nipping. His voice rumbled a low groan as he pulled the collar of her shirt to the side, began unbuttoning the front. Kate's phone buzzed with an incoming text. Looking at the screen, she saw it was from Tiffy, letting her know she was ready. Sighing, Kate leaned back. Asher frowned. "You have to go?"

"I do. Otherwise, I'd stay."

"You need this, huh?"

"I really do, Ash."

"Missing our kitten?" Kate nodded, her throat closing up. "So do I, love. So do I. Go on. Go. Have fun with Tiffy. I'll see you this evening when you get home."

Kate kissed him, lingering a few moments as she rebuttoned her shirt. "I'll only be gone a few hours. Thanks for understanding."

Nodding, he let her go, then stopped her when she reached the office door, his voice full of promise. "Kate?" Stopping, she looked back at him. "When you get home, I'm finishing this. Right here, I think." There was enough heat and intent in his words that Kate nearly changed her mind. Grinning, he shook his head. "No, you go on. Have fun with Tiffy. Give her my best. And think about all I plan to do to you when you return." Taking a deep breath, Kate forced herself to exit the room. She grabbed her keys, phone, and purse and made herself walk out the door.

Some two, almost three hours later, Tiffy and Kate meandered down Sheridan Avenue, packages and beverages in hand. They'd browsed for books and picked up some new candles and hand creams. Then had gone to a local shop for some of the jam, candy, and salsa that Asher favored. They'd had their pedicures, toes now gleaming in bright red polish, as they sipped their iced coffees. Unlocking the truck, Kate placed her packages in the back seat, then climbed in and started the engine. As she and Tiffy buckled their seatbelts, Kate felt her heart stop. She stared through the windshield, trying to decide if she'd actually seen what she'd thought she'd seen.

"Kate? What's the matter?" Tiffy asked, noting the drawn, alarmed look on KatyBeth's face.

Blinking, looking closer, Kate decided she hadn't seen him. It must have been her imagination. "Nothing. Nothing; I thought I saw...someone."

Tiffy looked in the direction Katy was facing. "Who?"

"No one. Sorry. Let's get going." Feeling spooked, Katy put the truck in gear, heading for home. Needing Asher's comforting touch to calm her. Maybe it was simply her nerves, already fraught with missing her daughter, that tricked her mind into thinking she'd seen *him.* He was supposed to be in jail, though, wasn't he? He couldn't bother her anymore.

Tiffy-

Tiffy hadn't pressed Katy into delving further about what she thought she'd seen, but she could tell her friend was still rattled. They were only about a mile or two from the house now. Samuel would be waiting for her. She'd already texted him, running it by her husband, wanting to see if anything needed to be mentioned to Asher. Katy slowed the truck, allowing the one behind them to pass before the bend in the road up ahead. Suddenly, they were wrenched sideways as the other truck plowed into the driver's side, shoving them off the road. Metal screeched and groaned as it twisted and crumbled. As if in a slow-motion scene in a movie, Tiffy had watched, horrified, as Katy's head slammed into the driver-side window when the driver's door collapsed in on itself.

Later, she'd recall the look of focused hatred on the other driver's face, as he'd stared down Kate while gunning the engine, seeming intent on killing them both. Kate's truck rolled into the fencing and field as the other truck pushed it off the roadway. The horn was blaring...then everything went dark.

The Stranger-

The man stepped from his truck and made his way over to the demolished vehicle. It had landed upright. Steam and smoke poured from under the hood. Windows were shattered, the frame crumbled. From here, he could see the blood. See her there, all appearances indicating she was dead. No one else around. No one to come to her rescue. If she wasn't dead, she would be soon enough. She wouldn't survive that, the stupid uppity witch. He smiled in satisfaction. He'd waited a long time for this. His only regret was that he hadn't had the chance to have her under him. No matter. She was as good as dead, and her man would break after this. After losing her. He smiled again as he climbed into his own truck and drove away, whistling cheerfully.

Bethany-

With Liam gone, I'd been helping Granda bring the cows in and get them milked each morning. We, my parents and I, raised beef cows only, so this was a cool new experience. Liam had been gone for three days, eight hours, and thirty-seven minutes. Thirty-eight minutes, but who was counting? We'd texted a few times, as much as he'd been able. His parents, who he admitted he was not close to, mainly his dad, had arrived and it took nearly every conscious thought to keep him and his father from coming to blows. Kristian, Liam's father, was a lawyer by trade and bitterly disappointed in his only son not wishing to follow in his footsteps. Liam said Harold seemed to be improving. He was getting speech and mobility back, though he was still weak. The doctors were running tests to see what exactly was going on with him.

Liam said he missed me and felt he'd be back here by the end of the month at the latest. It wasn't that long, I told myself. Then, once he was back, we'd need to talk about future plans. About how this relationship would work.

I toed off my wellies at the backdoor and stepped inside the kitchen. The warm scent of yeast and cinnamon hit me and I smiled. "Nan, you sure have a way with baking. It always smells like heaven in here."

"Oh, go on now. Wash up, then we'll have us some tea and breakfast." After washing, as I pulled out my chair, a knock sounded at the front door. Nana reached for a towel. "Who could that be now?"

"I'll get it. You finish up here." Heading to the door, I opened it and blinked in surprise, my heart stuttering in my chest. "*Uncle Cory?* What are you doing here?" I looked past him, before turning my gaze back to him. "Where's Aunt Candi? What's going on?"

Cory stepped inside as I moved back, allowing him space. I noted the unshaved jaw, the concerned look in his eyes. "You need to come home, Bethany. I'm here to bring you home."

His words had my heart stuttering painfully, causing the room to tilt. "Where's Dad? What happened?" Panic threatened and I tried to calm my fears, tried to focus on him.

"Candi couldn't get away; she had a client deadline. I've a private jet waiting in Cork. Everyone's alive, but yes, something did happen. You know your dad always has protocols in place; this is one of them. Samuel couldn't come, nor could your dad, so he's sent me."

By this time Nana had come from the kitchen to see who was at the door. "Ma'am." Cory nodded at her. "Asher sent me to bring Bethany home. There's been an...accident. We're not sure the nature of it yet, but Kate's in the hospital. Tiffy as well."

"Cory, is Mom all right? How bad is it?" I had a hard time forming the words, as it was, they came out all wobbly.

His blue-green eyes held concern as they focused on me. "She's pretty well banged up. Both, she and Tiffy."

"How?" I shook my head, still dazed. "What happened?"

"As of yet, we don't know all the details. Katy and Tif had gone to town for the afternoon, and on the drive home were in a wreck. It looks like a hit and run. That's all we have to go by as of now. What your dad's not sure of is whether it was an honest accident, or intentional. And, if intentional, by whom. He wants you home."

Still in a daze, I packed my things, not knowing when or if I'd be back this year. How long would it take her to recover? What were her injuries? What would her recovery look like? *Would* she fully recover? Somewhere, in all my worry for my mother and Aunt Tiffy, I thought of Liam. Thought of us. Would there even be an *us*? How could there be? He lived here—not even here—we'd both only been visiting. Liam lived in Scotland. I lived in the States. Two completely different countries. Two completely different lives. My throat closed up. Tears burned my eyes. I couldn't breathe. Everything hit all at once. Just when I'd begun to think my life was taking a turn for the better. When I'd thought I'd finally found the love my parents shared, it was all being stolen away. *Why, God?*

Hearing steps in the hall, I wiped my face and swallowed, trying to calm my breathing. My door creaked as whomever it was pushed it open further. "Here now, pet. Don't fret. All will work out." Nana slipped her arms around me and the tears came again. I couldn't hold them back. She held me, murmuring sympathies, "Dry your tears, lass. Go with Cory. Your mother is a fine, strong woman. She'll recover." Pulling back, I looked at her. Nana took a handkerchief from her pocket and dried my tears. "I'll let Liam know as well. Don't fret."

"Thank you, Nana. You and Granda. I love you both and I'm so thankful for you both and the time I've had here."

"We love you as well and you're always welcome to come back. You know that. Our door is always open."

Granda waited with Cory at the bottom of the stairs. He took one look at me and pulled me in for a hug. "It'll all be all right, pet. Don't fret now. Your da will see things right."

"Okay." I nodded, then took a deep calming breath. "I know. Will you guys be all right? Do you have plenty of help? I don't know how long Liam will be gone."

"We've a minor confession to make to you, lass. Your granda was never injured. We made it up to get the two of you here," Nana said with a guilty shrug.

I couldn't help but laugh at that. "You were never injured?" My grandfather sheepishly shook his head. "I guess that's why the soreness seemed to come and go so much. *Omgosh, I love you guys so much.* Thank you."

"You're not mad, lass?" Granda asked.

"No, of course not. Of course not," I assured as I gave them both hugs, holding them close. Cory's phone buzzed. Looking at him, I asked, "Dad?"

Nodding, he said, "Yeah, he wants an update as to our status."

"Okay. I'm ready." I hugged my grandparents one more time, then helped Cory carry my bags out to the rental car. Granda followed us out, Nana coming behind a moment or two later. She handed me a wrapped paper plate. "For the road; I know how much you love my baking."

The tears came again and I blinked them away. I hated goodbyes. Hated this one so much. "Tell Liam...explain why I wasn't here. Why I had to leave. Tell him I'll call him soon and I'm sorry."

"We will, love. He'll understand." I gave them one last hug before getting in the car. Cory put it in gear and we were on our way. We passed by Collins as we left town, and I had to wipe more tears away. I would miss it here. So much. I missed my grandparents already. I missed Liam and didn't know when or *if* I'd see him again. It seemed to take no time at all for us to arrive at the airport. Then we were through Customs and boarding, and before I could properly process any of it, we were airborne.

CHAPTER TEN

Oceans Apart

Asher-

Asher carefully took Kate's hand in his, mindful of the IV and various other tubes connected to her. She'd be okay, he told himself. She'd come through this. His thumb rubbed softly back and forth over hers; he needed that contact. Needed to feel her. There was talk of moving her up to Billings, to the trauma ward there. But no concrete decisions had yet been made. What they were waiting on, he didn't know. He waited for answers. Waited to hear from Cory. Waited for Bethany to arrive. Waited for his wife, the very breath in his lungs, to wake up. He simply waited.

Thankfully, he'd been able to reach her parents; they were flying home from Greece on the fastest connection they could make. Though, it would probably take them a couple days to arrive back. He couldn't think, couldn't focus. His mind seemed fractured. Fear paralyzed him, shutting him down. This was worse, Asher knew, far worse than the time he'd been captured, held, and tortured for days. He hated this feeling of helplessness. *Hated it.* He would trade places with her in an instant. Seeing her like this was killing him.

He wanted, needed to do something to save his wife. Take some action. He needed her. Couldn't possibly live without her. Dragging in a ragged breath, he bowed his head, blinking away tears, and prayed she would heal and awaken. That God would not take away his very breath, that she would *heal* and be whole. His blue eyes opened, travelling over her sleeping form.

Noting the neat row of stitches along her left brow, the bruises shadowing her cheekbone. Her left arm was supported by pillows and held out to the side, dressings covering the stitches there. Her neck, braced. The bruising along her chest and collarbone. The ice packs against her ribs. Her right leg in a cast. She'd briefly regained consciousness the day prior, but the trauma exhaustion and pain medication had her under again. He'd been told it was normal, and all a part of the healing process. Somewhere in the back of his mind, he knew all of this, but it didn't lessen what he was feeling. The anguish, the fear.

Asher bowed his head again, offering up every prayer, every supplication he could fathom, reminding himself as he did not to be anxious, but instead to have faith. Opening his eyes once more, he blew out a breath and tried for calm. Kate's hand flinched in his own. "Kate? Love? Can you hear me?" He watched as her eyes danced behind her lids. "You're okay; I'm here. You're okay. Can you open your eyes for me?" Blue-green hazel eyes met his, and he couldn't keep the tears from pooling, from dripping down his face. "There she is." Reverently, tenderly he kissed her knuckles.

"What...what happened?" Her voice was raw, cracked.

Asher reached for the water cup beside her bed, holding the cup and straw for her to drink. "Slowly now. You were in an accident. You and Tiffy. What do you remember?"

Kate seemed to retreat inside her mind, as if trying to picture all that had happened. "Tiffy?" she asked. "Is she okay?"

"She's home now. A little banged up, some bruising, but otherwise all right. Kate, love, do you remember what happened?"

She was quiet again, then drew in a sharp breath, wincing in pain. "There was another truck. On the highway—I thought, I thought he was trying to pass me. I slowed to give him room. Instead, instead he plowed right into us." Her gaze darted to Asher's. "*Johnny.* It was Johnny Khyle. He was in town. I saw him. I thought I saw him, but then I didn't and wasn't sure. But it was Johnny Khyle. I know it was."

Every thought in Asher's head seemed to dissipate at that news. A dull roaring took its place. A roaring and fury, growing, rising, boiling over. He should have killed the man when he had the chance. He wouldn't make that mistake again. "Are you sure? You're sure it was him? Can you describe the truck?"

"Red and white. Lifted, older Chevy. Not the truck he used to drive. Older. I'm *sure;* he looked right at me and smiled. In town. He must have followed us." Kate's eyes drooped and she closed them before jerking them open again.

"It's all right, love. You can sleep. I'll be right here." Asher leaned over, kissed Kate's forehead and felt his heart clench as the exhaustion took her under again. "Thank You, Lord," he whispered. After several minutes watching his wife sleep, Asher pulled out his cellphone and dialed Samuel.

"How is she?" Samuel asked as he answered. "Did the surgery come out okay?"

"She woke up briefly. We spoke. The surgery went as expected; she just needs to heal. We'll know more then. How's Tif?"

"In pain. Worried. Getting better. She's resting right now. Did Kate say anything? Does she remember what happened?"

"She does."

"And?"

"She says it was Johnny Khyle."

"*Son of a...* You think that's right?"

"I don't doubt her. The detective called about a month and a half or so back, saying he'd served his sentence and would be released. I should have told her, warned her, but we were talking with my parents then, making arrangements for Bethany's visit. I honestly didn't think he'd be that stupid." Asher paused, clenched his jaw as he tried to tame the fury. "She said she saw him in town. He *smiled* at her. Kate thinks he followed them. She thought the truck was trying to pass her, then instead of passing, it hit them."

Samuel blew out a breath. "That makes sense..."

"What? What aren't you telling me, Sammy?"

"Tiffy said she thought she recognized the driver. When he stared at Kate as he drove his truck right into Kate's door. As if he intended to hit her, kill her. She said the look on his face would haunt her."

"*He's a dead man.*" Asher's voice held all the promise of violence about to be unleashed. "This wasn't an accident. It was attempted murder, and I will *kill* him."

"Let me call it in, Ash. Katy needs you. Bethany needs you." Asher was silent. The fury choked him, made it near impossible to speak. Samuel tried again. "Let me handle this. I want him dead as much as you do. Let me call in a favor—you're owed many of them. Keep your hands clean. I'll call it in to someone who doesn't mind getting theirs dirty."

Bethany-

Somewhere over the Atlantic, I fell asleep, only waking when we touched down at JFK to refuel. While there, I took my phone off airplane mode and was immediately inundated with incoming texts. Several were from Liam, which made my heart dance all over the place. I missed him deeply; he expressed concern and dismay over my mom's accident, and said he missed and loved me. My heart swelled with emotion, and I cradled the phone to my chest for a moment, both a smile and tears gracing my features. The most important message however, was from Dad. Mom's surgery had gone well: she was out and in recovery. When I called him, Dad said he was arranging for her transportation to the house and for in-home care, so he couldn't talk long. He ended by saying he loved me and would see me when I got there.

It was another nine hours from JFK to Cody. Then another hour to get my luggage and make it home. I was beyond exhausted by the time we reached the ranch. My eyes felt dry and strained as Uncle Cory parked his car in the driveway, then helped me pull my bags from the trunk. Dad met us at the door. "Dad!" He enveloped me in his arms, pulling me tightly against him. Being in his arms gave me the strength to push the exhaustion down. "How's Mom? How is she?"

"She's okay, all things considered. We just got home about fifteen minutes ago." He kissed my forehead, gently squeezing me again before releasing me. "Granny and Papa are here; they're with her. She's set up in a guest room for the time being. It'll be easier on her and the medical staff that come if she's here, rather than upstairs." He stopped me just inside the entryway, turning me to face him. "Your mom's tough, kitten—you need to be as well. She's banged up, can't deny that, but she's still beautiful and so strong. She'll heal from this. I'm sorry to bring you back from your trip early, but I'm glad you're here."

"It's okay, Dad—I understand. Truly, I want to be here." Dad squeezed me gently, then led me into the guest room. Seeing Mom, my strong, beautiful mother like that...it felt like my chest was collapsing. It was everything I could do to keep my emotions in check. The left side of her face was swollen, the skin shades of yellow and purple. A bandage ran the length of her brow. Her lips trembled as she saw me, causing an echo in mine. Granny and Papa were beside the bed; Granny held Mom's hand. When I came in the room, Papa cleared his throat and stepped back, giving me room.

Even as my grandparents hugged me, I couldn't take my eyes off Mom. My throat closed, and I had to swallow several times to keep the emotion out of my voice.

"I'm sorry, baby," she whispered. "I'm sorry."

Coming to her side, taking her hand carefully in mine, I said, "Why are you apologizing? This wasn't your fault—you were in an accident."

"I hate for you to see me like this." Tears filled her eyes as her chin wobbled. "I know it's hard on you. It's bad enough your dad has to, but not you, too."

"Mom, seriously." I tried to smile, though it was more grimace than anything. "That's the least of my worries. I'm just so thankful you're all right and healing. Dad said none of your injuries were life-threatening. That's a *huge* blessing."

"Your grandparents said you'd met someone there...I'm sorry you had to come back so soon."

Mentally acknowledging her attempt to divert attention, I blew out a breath and shook my head in affectionate exasperation. Then, still trying to hold my own tears back, I said, "Of course, they told you. You guys probably knew the whole time, didn't you?"

Dad gently squeezed my shoulder. "Not the whole time, kitten. We've known for the last week. Your grandmother was concerned I'd take a hard stance on the guy and thought to soften me up. Though, if I recall, I'd already given him a fair warning. He must like you a lot to risk my wrath."

"Please, Dad. Liam is a great guy and you know it. You just enjoy scaring people is all."

Dad chuckled at that. "Maybe. Still, he must think a lot of you."

"I think so. I know how I feel about him, and didn't expect to feel anything like this for a long time; I believe he feels the same for me." Mom squeezed my fingers, drawing my attention back to her. "But we don't need to talk about that right now. There are more important things going on, I think." About to ask what her status was, a knock sounded on the front door, interrupting me.

"I'll get it," Cory said from where he'd lingered by the bedroom door.

The nurse breezed in wearing a set of dark blue scrubs. I guessed his age to be somewhere in his mid to upper twenties. "Hello, I'm Ruben; I'm the nurse assigned to your at-home care." At the nurse's arrival, my grandparents excused themselves, telling Dad they were going home to change and rest as they'd been up for over twenty-four hours. Dad said he'd keep them updated. Ruben seemed friendly, yet professional as he perused Mom's medical file. After a minute or so, he looked to her and smiled. Ruben verified her identity, asking her name and date of birth, then said, "Now, it's important that you be completely honest with me. I can't help you properly if you don't. Let's start with something basic: how're you feeling, KatyBeth? What's your pain level?"

"I'm feeling all right," Mom said quietly. "Pain seems to be under control at the moment."

"On a scale of one to ten—one being no pain and ten being excruciating—where are you?"

"Probably a five, or a six."

He made a note on the tablet. "You let us know if and when the pain increases. Now, I'll check your vitals." I watched silently as he checked her temperature, blood pressure, pulse, and listened to her heart. After he'd finished with that, he checked her stitches and reapplied dressings to the surgical area. While he worked, I'd retreated towards one of the windows overlooking the mountains. I doubted he'd even seen me, focused as he was on his patient.

"How's everything look?" Dad asked, a critical eye on the nurse's ministrations.

"Everything looks normal and that's a great sign. No redness or swelling."

"What sort of things should we be watching for?" I asked, stepping away from the wall I'd been leaning against.

Ruben turned to me, a smile spreading across his face as he took me in. "Fever, swelling, redness, inordinate pain that meds aren't reaching. That sort of thing."

I nodded. "Thanks."

"No problem." Ruben looked at his tablet screen. "Looks like we've got you scheduled for a follow up with the surgeon in about a week."

"When will the stitches come out?" I asked.

"This first post-op appointment will just be to make sure that everything is going according to plan, and if it is, the staples will be removed then. The following week, the stitches will come out." Ruben turned to Mom. "And then after that, you'll be scheduled with Ortho, and I'm sure in the midst of all that, you'll be scheduled with your primary care, as well."

"All the appointments," Mom replied, an exasperated look on her face.

"It's part of the healing process." Ruben nodded.

"Oh, I'm sure it is. Do you know when I'd be able to actually begin physical therapy?"

"It just depends. You're definitely not ready to begin now. Those ribs will be sore for the next couple of weeks at best, probably longer. Then, once staples and stitches are out, you'll meet with that Ortho doctor, and he can get you on the right track." Mom blew out a breath then, wincing as she did. Ruben raised a brow and grinned at her. "See? Give your body time to heal—take care of it and it'll take care of you. Now, if you guys don't have any other questions, I think I'm done here for today. I'll be by again day after tomorrow."

"Thank you, Ruben," Mom said.

After he'd left, Dad turned to me. "He seems nice. And he seemed to like you, kitten."

"Omgosh, Dad. I'm with Liam now. And he did not."

"He smiled at you a lot."

"He smiled at everyone."

"There's smiling, and then there's *smiling*."

Mom yawned; her eyes blinking slowly a couple of times. So I ignored my father and his antics. "Mom, you need your rest. Do you need pain meds? An extra blanket?"

"Just tired is all—it hits so fast."

"That's your body healing, doing what it needs to do to repair itself." Dad pulled up a chair beside her bed and took her hand in his. At his touch, I visibly saw Mom relax and ease into sleep. Dad leaned forward, forearms resting on the bed; his gaze focused on Mom. Their love and devotion for each other sometimes took my breath away. It was such an intimate moment, the need to give them space instantly sparked. I headed for the door. "I'm going to get something to eat, you want anything?"

Dad shook his head, his eyes never leaving Mom. "Thanks, kitten. I'm good. I missed you; we both did. We're glad you're home."

"I missed you guys, too."

Leaving the room, I headed to the kitchen. Pausing near Cory, I asked, "You hungry?"

"Yeah, but I'm heading back to the hotel, grabbing my gear, then I have a flight out back to Cali that leaves around nine."

"Thanks, for everything," I told him.

"Of course. She'll be okay, your mom. She's probably one of the toughest women I know."

"Yeah, I know." I swallowed a yawn and tried to smile at him.

"You're home now, that'll cheer her up." Cory stood, gave me a quick hug, then headed out. For a moment or two, I simply stood there, my gaze unseeing as it swept the room. I'd gotten so used to being at Nana's and Granda's. Used to seeing Liam. That sensation of loss swept me again and I had to blink back tears. I had so much to be thankful for. My mom was going to be fine. She was going to heal. But the loss of Liam...of not seeing him again. That feeling was gutting me.

Taking a deep breath, I held it in until I thought my lungs would burst, then slowly let it out. Shaking my head at my own vulnerability, I grabbed my bags and carried them up to my room. I'd leave the unpacking for later. My stomach complained loudly as I entered the kitchen. My cellphone rang then, and I saw it was Liam.

"Hi," I breathed, unable to say more; emotion clogged my throat.

"Hey, how's yer ma?" His voice was full of concern.

"She's going to be all right." My mouth trembled as I sniffed, wiping at my eyes. "It'll take some time for her to heal, but she's going to be okay."

"Oh, that's grand news."

"Truly, it is," I agreed. My voice cracked. "Liam...I'm so sorry. I had to leave—you understand that, don't you?"

"There's nay need for apologies," he said firm, but gentle. "I completely understand. I'm just thankful yer mother will heal. Do they ken what happened?"

"Dad says it was a hit and run."

"*Bugger me.* Truly?"

"Yeah." My voice hardened. "Some jerk. Her truck rolled with the impact."

"Rollover accident...how bad was it?"

"Nothing life-threatening—I thank God for that." My voice cracked again. "Her left arm is broken and needed surgery for pins or something to strengthen and support the bone. Her ribs are cracked. Her right leg, below the knee, was broken as well. She's got a couple cuts that needed stitches, and lots of bruising."

Liam blew out a breath. "I'm so sorry, lass. Wish I could be there to hold ye."

"I wish you were here as well. But it is what it is, I guess." I felt hollow, frail. "I miss you. I don't know how this is going to—" Emotion choked me again, making it difficult to continue.

"Ah, dinna fash, lass. It'll itself work out."

I sniffed, wiping away more tears. "How?"

"I've nae intention of losing ye. Let's get through these next couple of weeks and we'll come up with a plan. Harold is on the mend; they've put him on some meds that seem to be working."

"That's good news." I took a deep breath, fighting for calm. "That's really good news."

"Aye, it is. Things will work out, lass; I can promise ye that."

"I love you, Liam."

"And I ye." I could hear the smile in his voice. "I won't keep ye overlong; I simply needed to hear yer voice. Needed to speak to ye myself, if ye ken that."

"I do. I *ken* that."

Liam chuckled. "I'd best let ye go. Give my best to yer ma and da."

"I will. And you do the same to your grandparents. My prayers for your granddad's continued recovery." We hung up, and I headed to the kitchen to find something to eat.

I made enough food for myself and my parents, in case they got hungry later on. After eating, I checked on them; they were both still asleep. Silently, I pulled a blanket from the bed and draped it over Dad's shoulders. They were still holding hands; my heart clenched at the sight. Blowing out a silent breath, I headed upstairs to unpack and unwind. Once my room was back to normal, clothes and bags put away, I showered, then slipped on my pajamas. My eyelids drooped and I found it difficult to keep them open. Sitting on my bed, I brushed out my hair, then set the brush on the nightstand. I remember leaning back against my pillow and closing my eyes for just a moment to rest them...the next thing I knew, it was morning.

Dad must have come up to check on me, because when I woke, I was under my blankets and my light was off. I must have been completely exhausted, because I had no memory of it. Shrugging, I sat up and kicked the blankets off, then stretched before climbing out of bed to start my day.

CHAPTER ELEVEN

Healing

Bethany-

That first week or so back home was challenging, and yet it seemed to fly by. Mom had her first post-op appointment. The surgeon, Dr. Howahkan, said Mom was healing well. No swelling or redness detected. He seemed quite pleased and had his assistant remove the staples in her arm, stating that at Mom's next appointment, they'd discuss getting her scheduled for physical therapy. Thankfully, Dad and I had been able to get her in and out of the truck without too much difficulty or pain to Mom. Later that day, my grandmother, Aunt Tiffy, and Aunt Gina came over to help me get her bathed. Well, Aunt Tiffy more watched than anything else, as she was still sore herself from their accident. Mom was nearly in tears, saying the sensation of clean hair was the best feeling she'd had in a long while.

Though I'd been gone for close to a month, it seemed to take no time to get back into the swing of daily life on the ranch. My body recognized everything by muscle-memory, but my mind had a hard time coming to terms with being back. I pined for Liam. We spoke often, or as often as we were able to. But it wasn't enough. Wasn't nearly enough. I missed *him*. Missed being with him, talking with him, touching him. I missed just having him close. Now, he was half a world away. Or maybe it was me who was away from him. Either way, I yearned for him desperately and threw myself into my work trying to stave off that loneliness.

It worked for the most part. Let's face it, there's *always* lots to be done on a ranch. I had horses to ride, cows to move, tag, and brand, not to mention just the day-to-day needs. Stalls needing cleaning, clients to contact, the feeding and watering. Thankfully, both Jack and Del had made themselves available to help me. Which was a literal Godsend, because I'd have been lost without them.

My phone buzzed with an incoming text as the three of us were riding back from one of the upper pastures. We'd moved a herd of heifers up there this morning for the grazing. Having missed my big gelding thoroughly, I might have shamelessly shed a few tears when I saw Wick again. Patting his shoulder affectionately, I checked the screen, and saw it was from Liam:

Hey lass, grand news. Harold was released from hospital today. The doctors believe they have him well in order. He'll have some physical therapy to be certain he's got full control of himself, but otherwise they think he's on the mend. I miss you. More than words can express. I love you, Liam.

Swallowing, I blinked the tears away and looked up to see both Jack and Del staring at me. "Everything all right?" Jack asked, angling his horse closer to mine.

"Yeah. That was Liam. His granddad was released today. They believe he's going to be all right."

"That's good news. Why the...?" He indicated my face.

"I just miss him, Jack."

"Are you planning to go back?" Delaney asked, coming up on the other side of Jack.

Blowing out a breath, I said, "I'd like to, but not right now, with Mom still healing."

"Things are pretty serious, then?" Jack asked with a grin. "Between you and Liam?"

"Yeah, I think so." I smiled back at him. "At least from my end they are, and I think he feels the same."

"So...you wouldn't be opposed to...me and Jack, then?" asked Del with a grin.

"*What?*" I pulled Wick to a stop and angled myself sideways in the saddle. My heart danced merrily in my chest as I studied them. Noting something there I hadn't seen before.

Delaney nudged Jack, giving him a pointed look, to which he offered a sheepish grin in my direction, and shrugged his shoulders. "You're not mad, right?"

"Are you guys for real?" My gaze darted back and forth between them. "No, I'm not mad! When did this happen? And why am I first hearing about this now?"

"It was while you were gone." Delaney took a deep breath. "I've had feelings for Jack for a long time, but always thought he was disinterested. Then we got to talking after you'd left and one thing led to another."

"Omgosh, guys; I can't believe you kept this from me. I'm thrilled for you both. Honestly. Is it serious?" I asked, putting Wick back into motion, echoing her question to me from moments before.

"We're still figuring things out," Jack said, taking Del's hand in his.

"Well, I think this is awesome. I'd say we should go celebrate, but with everything going on, and Rodeo Nites have started up again—Michele Foster called a couple days ago to ask how Mom was doing, then asked if I'd be available for a few nights in the next couple weeks."

"We both got calls from the Rodeo admin office as well. She's the new head, right? We're scheduled for Friday, Saturday, and Sunday nights next week," Delaney said.

"She is, and same. So, I guess I'll see you guys there." We'd made it back to the barn and dismounted. "Thanks for your help today. And for everything. I'm truly thankful for you both. You guys are the best."

Delaney and Jack came over and made a human sandwich out of me; he wrapped his arms around me from one side, and she from the other. "Don't you forget it. Especially if you decide to run off to Scotland, or Ireland, or wherever you go for your fella."

Chuckling, I replied, "I won't. I love you guys."

Little more than a week later, three days after Mom got her stitches out, I sat on the porch, phone to my ear as Liam and I talked. Ruben was here again, giving Mom her weekly visit and checkup. I think he'd mentioned they'd be getting her scheduled for PT while he was here as well. Liam said Harold continued to improve. His doctors had him on some medication to reduce blood clots and had him change his diet and start an exercise routine. Liam said his grandfather had had a few choice words to say about that, which made me chuckle. Liam and I talked about many things. How Mom and Dad were doing. Her healing. How my grandparents in Ireland were getting on. We talked about the ranch. How he was doing, his job, his family. But we never talked about us. About seeing each other again.

We certainly expressed how much we missed each other, but that was as close as we got to the subject. I didn't know where he was coming from, what he was thinking. Only how I was feeling and what I was thinking. No matter how much I wanted to see him again, getting away right now was simply impossible. When he'd left Ireland, he'd told me he wasn't about to lose me. He'd told me we'd figure things out. What if he'd changed his mind? What if this time apart had made him reconsider a relationship with me? I was terrified to bring it up, terrified to know, and couldn't force the words out of my mouth. They stayed trapped behind my teeth, nearly choking me. I think, with everything else that was going on, I simply didn't have the courage to face the prospect I might be losing him.

We hung up and I wiped tears from my eyes, trying to calm myself before I returned to Mom's room. "What fool has you in tears?" Turning as I closed the door behind me, I saw Ruben holding out a box of tissues as he came from the kitchen.

"No one." I took a tissue and smiled in thanks. "It wasn't like that. I just miss him is all and had to leave unexpectedly, without a proper goodbye."

"I'm too late, then?" His dark eyes searched mine.

"Too late?"

"You're spoken for?" His head dipped in my direction.

"I'm with someone; someone important to me." I hoped he still felt the same about me.

"Dang." Ruben shook his head, seemingly resigned, humor flashing in his brown eyes.

Chuckling under my breath, I tried to smile. "Thanks for the tissue. And for caring for my mom. Is everything good? Healing still going well? How about the PT, was that scheduled?"

"Everything with your mom is going well. She's a strong, determined lady. No problems there. PT was scheduled; she starts next Wednesday, I believe. Just mild stretching to keep the muscles from atrophying." He gathered his supplies, then headed towards the door before turning around and facing me. "If, uh, if anything changes with you and Mr. Whoever that lucky man is, be sure and let me know."

He didn't wait for an answer. Just shot me a grin and left. With raised brows, I turned to Mom's room and hoped no trace of emotion was left on my face. Dad sat in the chair beside Mom's bed—their hands again entwined. He was leaned forward, head on his other arm where it rested beside her on the bed, eyes closed. They both breathed evenly, though Mom's was shallower.

As silently as possible, I made to ease back out of the room, but she must have heard me. "Hey, sweetie."

"I thought you were sleeping. I didn't want to wake you."

"No, not at all. I was just resting my eyes. Ruben says everything is healing well. He did some minor stretching of my arm, more slow, controlled movements than anything. Felt good to move it, though I'm sore now."

"You want some Ibuprofen?"

"Yeah, maybe. Thanks." After getting her the pills and her water glass, Mom said, "Sit. Stay a while, I feel like I never see you."

Grinning, I turned to grab another chair. "Take this one, kitten." Dad rose to his feet. "I'm going to run up and shower while you're here."

"Take your time."

"So," Mom said after Dad left, "how're things? The horses? Did you guys get those heifers moved all right?"

"Yeah, heifers were moved without trouble. Horses are good. I'm getting back in the swing of things."

"That's good, I'm glad." She smiled at me. The bruising was mostly gone from her face and chest, just a couple yellow-tinted spots now. "And how're things with Liam? You guys talking lots?"

"I don't...I don't know how things are. And I'm afraid to ask. We both say we miss each other and we love each other, but nothing is ever said about seeing each other again."

"Give it time. He's probably trying to understand where you're coming from and wondering the same things you are. One of you will need to ask eventually."

"I know. I just have so much going on. I'm helping at the Rodeo Nites this coming weekend. Maybe I'll ask him once that's done."

"I'm sure you'll figure it out." Mom's speech was slurring just the slightest. She yawned, wincing as she did.

"You need to rest, Mom. Dad will be back shortly. I'll wait with you until he's returned."

"Sleep," she grumbled, "it's all I ever do, all I seem to be able to do. I'm just so exhausted, all the time."

"That's normal. Your body went through a lot. It takes time to heal. You have to be patient."

"I know, Dr. Daughter. When did you get to be so wise?"

"I had a great teacher." Mom grinned at that, then, seemingly against her will, her eyes closed and she was out. As I sat there, waiting for Dad to return, just watching her sleep, I prayed. For her, for her continued healing, for Liam and me. For guidance and wisdom.

Liam-

Liam leaned back in his seat, the pub noises around him providing a distracting backdrop, allowing his mind to wander from the man seated across from him. Sean wasn't fooled, however. "What's the problem, lad?" Liam narrowed his gaze, giving Sean a cursory look. "We've eaten, had us a couple rounds, and you've sat quiet, like your best mate died, and I'm sitting right here."

Chuckling, Liam reached for his pint. "Am I that obvious?"

Sean took him in, noting the strained distance in his eyes, the barely touch food, despite his earlier claims that they'd eaten. "Only if you're paying attention. Is it Harold? Thought you'd said he was on the mend?"

"He is. He's grand. At home now. They've go' him on a new diet and some medicine." He nodded more to himself. "He's grand."

"Your da, then?"

"Nae. Da and I are even doing all right, if ye ken that…"

"Then it's got to be the lass. Bethany."

"Aye." Liam swallowed his beer. "That'd be the short of it."

"Has she ended it atween you, then?" Liam sat quietly, staring into his drink, seemingly lost in thought. After a lengthy moment of silence, Sean goaded him. "Well, has she?"

"Bugger me, I dinna rightly ken. I dinna think she has, but there's been nothing said. I mean, we express feelings for each other. But she's there and can't leave any time soon, and I'm here. That's hardly any way to carry on wi' a lass, is it now?"

"Well, you know what you've got to do then?"

"An' what's that?"

"You've got to go there and claim yer lass." Sean emphasized his position with a strongly pointed finger.

"To America?"

"That's where she's at, right?" Sean's brows rose and the look in his eyes said, 'obviously.' "And you've said *she* can't come here, so that leaves *you* going there, aye?"

Liam scratched at his chin thoughtfully. "Aye."

Sean stood, tossed a few bills on the table, and said, "Ye'd best be on about your business, then."

Bethany-

Friday, the Cody Nite Rodeo went well; I ended up filling in for one of the Flag Girls. Saturday was much the same. I did an introduction run around the arena with one of the sponsor's flags, then later, helped man one of the gates. It was during a lull in the events, the mutton-bustin' was taking place, when Jack and Del found me. "Have you seen him?" Del demanded without preamble.

"Seen who?" I asked, glancing over my shoulder to her before turning once more to the sheep riders.

"My brother. He's back in town. And here."

My heart skipped a beat at that unwelcome news. Blowing out a breath, I said, "No, I haven't seen him yet. Though, thanks for the heads-up. Either way, I'm with Liam now, so it really doesn't matter about Garrett. I was bound to run into him eventually."

"Sorry, Bethany. I for sure thought he'd been planning to stay in SoCal."

I shrugged that off, then opened the gate, as the herdsman were driving the sheep out of the arena. "I'm done here for the night, how about you guys?"

"Yeah, we're both finished," Jack said, latching the gate behind the sheep once they were through. "Want to grab a bite to eat?"

"Yeah, sounds good, meet you around front, just going to let my replacement know I'm headed out before the bulls come on. You guys working tomorrow night as well?"

"We are. Jack's doing pickup work and I'm helping with Norman—I just love that bull."

"Oh, fun. I'll meet you guys around front." We waved to each other, then I headed to the back of the arena to let Jared Foster, the guy in charge, know I was taking off and would see him again tomorrow.

"Thanks for your help this weekend," Jared said, going over his clipboard before glancing back up to me. "We appreciate you filling in, especially with everything with your mom going on. How is she by the way?" I assured him she was all right and thanked him for asking, then went to find Delaney and Jack. By the time I caught up to them, they were already in line to get cheeseburgers and fries. The line was long, so we had plenty of time to chat. While we were doing so, Delaney suddenly tensed up, her gaze narrowing, even as she gave a sharp shake of her head. I figured only one person could make her respond like that, so prepared myself as I turned around.

Garrett looked good. But then, he'd always looked good. He was tanned from his time in the California sun, I assumed. As he approached, still sporting that confident swagger of his, I couldn't help but compare him with Liam and found Garrett wanting in nearly every way. Before me now, was not the man I'd previously thought him to be, but instead the boy playing at manhood that I'd never before recognized.

He smiled as he approached. "Bethany, you look amazing; I've missed you." His arms came up as he leaned forward, seemingly intent upon giving me a hug.

My hand planted in his chest, solidly pushing him away. "What are you doing, Garrett? We aren't together any longer, remember?"

"I know, I'm sorry." His voice was soft as he cajoled. "I thought I was over you, but...seeing you out there today. Seeing you ride again—like you did then, you do now—you take my breath away." In silence, I just stared at him, truly in shock by his words. Did he think I'd be interested in him again? Was he really that oblivious? "Look, Bethany, give me a chance. I'll prove it to you. I'm sorry. I know I handled things badly and was a coward. But I'm here now. Just let me be here."

I shrugged. "Here. There. Your location doesn't really matter to me anymore."

"Here with you." He angled himself closer. "Let me be here with you. Please?"

I shifted a step away. "Like I said, your location doesn't really matter to me anymore."

"Ah, c'mon. Don't be like that." He leaned down to better meet my gaze. "Give me a chance. That's all I'm asking for."

"I asked you for a chance once, remember?" I stated. "And you told me no. So, I'm not inclined to give you one now. And besides, I'm seeing someone."

"Didn't take you long, did it?" Derision filled his voice now.

"It took me longer than it should have. You aren't worth the time I wasted." I turned to Jack and Delaney, who'd remained silent through the whole exchange, waiting to see if I needed assistance. "I'm not hungry any longer, guys. Catch you later."

"Bethany, don't be like that, please." Garrett reached forward as I turned away. "Come on. We had—"

At Garrett's move, Jack stepped forward, his arm shooting out, blocking Garrett from reaching me. His voice was low, firm, and full of warning, "Out of respect for the fact you're Del's brother, I'm going to simply warn you. Leave. Her. Alone. You had your chance, and you blew it. Let it rest."

Garrett tossed Jack an angry look, almost as if he intended to take things further, then his focus snagged on something else, something behind me. He chuckled. "That's something you don't see every day. He's got some mighty big ones to be walking around here in a skirt."

At the shocked look on Del's face, I looked over my shoulder to see what or who had caught her and Garrett's attention. My heart stumbled over itself in my chest before sprinting away. My lungs locked up and I honest-to-God felt lightheaded for a moment. My mind scrambled to understand what I was seeing. Somehow, miraculously, Liam was about twenty feet away, red roses in hand, wearing a kilt, and moving purposefully in my direction. His dark blue eyes were glued to me as a smile spread across his face. His gaze shifted briefly to Garrett before returning to me. I'd forgotten how tall he was, how much taller than Garrett he was. But as I launched myself into motion, slamming into him, it all came back. His arms wrapped around me, lifted, and held me to him. My arms were around his neck and our mouths collided. It wasn't a frenzied kiss. We didn't devour each other, but there was such *emotion*.

"Ah lass, I've missed ye. I've been goin' mad wi' missin' ye." The sound of his voice in my ear, his actual voice, calling me lass, broke the dam. The tears came. "It's a'right. I'm here wi' ye now. I'll no' let ye go again. I canna face that."

He held my face in his hands, his mouth trailing across my cheeks and mouth. Liam slipped one arm—the one holding the roses—lower, circling around me. Holding me to him. With the other, he dried my tears with his thumb. I took several long breaths to calm myself. "How...when did you get here? How long are you here for? Where are you staying?"

Against my forehead, he breathed, "I'm staying at yer grandparents' place, and I'm here for as long as ye want me."

"Then you're never leaving." I hiccupped. "Because I don't think I'd survive it. Or, if you do, I'm going with you."

His arms tightened around me. Against my mouth, he said, "Where ye go, I go. It felt as though a part of me had been cut away and I was bleedin' out. It's only here wi' ye now that I can breathe again and heal that wound."

I pulled him closer and kissed him hard. "I still can't believe you're here. It's like a dream."

He kissed my nose, my cheek. "Then it's a dream we're both in, because it feels the same for me."

I became aware of the silence around us and looked up. Jack had his arms around Delaney, who was wiping tears from her eyes. Garrett stood beside them; his mouth somewhat open. Actually, there were several people standing around, taking us in. Many pointed at Liam's kilt.

"Come on, you can meet my friends." I led Liam over to Jack and Del and performed the introductions. Delaney gave Liam a hug, squealing under her breath about how happy she was he was here. Jack shook his hand, offering a hello and welcome. Liam turned expectantly to Garrett, brows raised.

"This is who you've left me for? Some dude in a skirt?" Garrett asked, disbelief and anger in his voice.

Liam cocked his head at Garrett's tone and question, the look on his face a measuring one. "It's only a skirt, lad, if you're wearing something under it."

Chuckling at that, I took Liam's hand in mine and said, "And you left me, Garrett. Let's not muddy the water on that one."

"Ignore my brother, Liam." Delaney smiled, then grabbed my other arm. "I'm no longer interested in concession cheeseburgers; let's head to The Meatery and grab us a Bison Burger. I have a feeling we're going to need some serious sustenance for this journey we're about to take."

"Journey?" I asked, allowing her to pull me along, Liam trailing after, our hands still linked.

"I want all of it. Every detail. You've been holding out on me. Plus, I just want to hear Liam talk some more. It's beautiful when he speaks...."

"I'm man enough to agree with that statement," Jack joked good-naturedly. "Just remember you're my girl and not his." Then he added, "And I'm not wearing a kilt, so don't ask."

Liam laughed. "Dinna knock it ye havna' tried it, mate."

We made it outside the main gates, heading towards the area sectioned off for rodeo workers. Stopping, as I got to my truck, I turned to Liam. "How did you get here? I mean, here at the rodeo grounds; did you drive?"

"Yer grandfather dropped me off. With a stern warning to behave my-self."

"Oh, my word." I laughed. "I'm so glad you're here. I've been miserable, and didn't know if you'd changed your mind about me, us. And like a coward, was afraid to ask. With everything going on, I just didn't have the courage to face losing you as well."

"Ye havena' lost me, lass." Liam kissed me again, just a gentle pressure of his mouth on mine. "Nor will ye."

Almost forty-five minutes later, we pulled out chairs at our table at The Meatery, having already placed our orders. "Is it actual bison we'll be eating?" Liam asked as we sat.

"It is," Jack replied.

"I though' they were extinct, nae?"

"They got pretty close, but are making a comeback. Yellowstone has a large herd and then there are ranches that raise them for meat. Canada's got a pretty decent-sized herd as well."

I couldn't stop smiling at Liam. I couldn't stop smiling, period, entirely beyond thrilled that he was here. He caught my gaze at one point, and said, "What, lass?" Causing Delaney to sigh at his pet name for me.

"You're wearing a kilt." I grinned.

"I am."

"I said you didn't have to do that."

"Ye also said ye wouldna' tell me nae, if I did." He waggled his brows at me, heat in those blue eyes.

"True." I inhaled. "If you'll note, I haven't told you no."

Liam grinned at that, then lifted my hand, kissing my knuckles. "I'd planned to take ye to Scotland wi' me, for a visit, ye ken? To take ye to a Highlan' game and had planned to wear it for ye then. As that didna' happen, I decided to wear it for ye here. Are ye pleased?"

"Very much so."

"What you said to Garrett?" Jack asked, a grin on his face. "About the kilt, were you being serious?" Our meal came then, delaying Liam's response. Once the burgers, fries, and drinks were dispersed, we waited expectantly for Liam's first taste of buffalo meat.

"*Gor!* This is grand, this is. Oh—" He quickly took another bite, making happy, little moaning noises as he did, causing us all to laugh. After that, we all dug in.

Several minutes later, as Delaney munched on her fries, she asked, "So Liam, about the kilt...?"

Grinning knowingly, Liam said, "Ye mean aboot the difference atween a kilt and a skirt? Aye, I was serious."

"Oh." Delaney blushed. "Okay then."

"Any other questions, Del?" I grinned at her embarrassment. We finished eating, finally heading out as the restaurant was closing. Liam thanked the workers behind the counter, telling them that was the best burger he'd ever eaten. In the parking lot, we said our goodbyes and made plans to meet up at the WYOld West Taproom tomorrow for dinner. While I was happy my friends and Liam seemed to get along, I really wanted him to myself for a bit, so didn't prolong our leaving.

CHAPTER TWELVE

We Were, Too

Bethany-

As Liam closed the door behind himself, after first seeing me into the truck, I breathed a sigh of relief. At the sound, his eyes met mine. Then, slowly, he leaned across, his hand rising to cup my cheek, his mouth effortlessly claiming mine. It started slow and gentle, but like a match to gasoline, quickly roared into an inferno. What had been kept tightly under wraps when we'd been around the others, was loosed.

Liam's left arm came around me, pulling me closer, even as I lunged for him. Somehow, I ended up half across the center console, my left leg shifting somehow around the steering wheel. Liam's mouth left mine, trailing along my jaw, down my neck, his teeth lightly nipping where my neck and shoulder met. A low rumble echoed from deep within his chest. Fingers soothed along my collarbone, dug themselves into my hair. My hands did their own exploration. One gripping the back of his neck and shoulder, the other inadvertently ended up at his waist, then down his hip, until suddenly I felt bare skin under my palm.

I jumped at the contact, not expecting to meet his warm skin, and we both froze. Our gazes locked, then in a knee-jerk reaction, my eyes flew down to see *what* I'd touched. His thigh. It was just his thigh, right above the knee. Nerves on display, I giggled under my breath, then pulled back. Liam released me as I tried to extricate myself from the position I was in and in doing so, my knee jammed into the horn blaring it loudly. Gasping,

I quickly shifted back into my own seat, trying to catch my breath. My eyes shot to his, then suddenly we were both laughing.

Once we'd caught our breath, I looked around the parking lot to be sure we didn't have an audience, then said, "We should probably get home."

"Aye, we should."

A thought suddenly danced through my head. "Liam, does Dad know you're here? He's not going to go all ballistic on you, is he?"

"Aye, he does. I called him last week and made the arrangements."

"He didn't have a problem with you coming?"

"Nae, no' at all. Said he'd have been disappointed if I hadna' called." He reached for my hand, wrapping mine in his and simply held it as I started the truck and headed for home. We pulled into our drive, and meandered up the long, winding driveway, then parked. There were lights on in the house, so I knew at least someone was still up.

"Um, about earlier...that was, that *was*." I exhaled, then shivered.

"Aye. I should probably apologize to ye, but I willna' as I'm no' the least bit sorry. I'd waited too long to kiss ye proper. I will promise to try and contain myself, though, from here on out."

"Ditto."

Grinning, Liam leaned closer, then swept the hair off my neck, capturing a couple wayward strands and tucking them behind my ear, causing me to shiver. "Dinna fash, lass. I've nae intention of disrespectin' ye, nor your da. I promise to be on me best behavior."

"Well, Dad's just glanced out the window, so we should probably head inside before he comes looking for us."

The evening air had cooled and crickets sang a symphony. A gentle breeze carried the scent of pine, hay, and horses. Liam took a deep breath as he stepped from the truck. His eyes closed briefly, then opened again, alive with wonder. "It's beautiful here; peaceful."

"Thanks, I think so, too." He took my hand as we made our way to the house.

Dad opened the door as we stepped onto the porch. "Hello, kitten. Liam."

"Don't start, Dad." I shot him an exasperated but affectionate look. "You know you like Liam."

"Mr. Fitzpatrick." Liam sounded calm, and from the corner of my eye, he seemed collected. "It's good to see ye again."

"Come on in, then." Dad stepped aside for us. "Your mom waited up, wanting to say hello."

"Oh, she didn't have to do that." I turned to face Dad as I spoke and was struck again with how similar they were. Liam stood near Dad as they shook hands, and Dad had no more than a scant inch on him. They were both of wide, solid frames. Both had that dark brown hair and those blue eyes. Though, Liam, in all, was a darker shade than Dad was.

Once they were finished greeting each other, Dad turned to me. "Best not keep your mom waiting any longer." Nodding, I led the way to the room she still resided in. Mom was sitting up in bed, the frame raised to support her, keeping pressure off her still healing ribs. "Mom, I'm sorry. I didn't know you were waiting up, or we'd have come back sooner."

"It's no bother." Mom smiled, then turned her gaze to Liam. "I'm happy to see you again, Liam."

Liam moved beside the bed and leaned over to carefully give Mom a hug. "It's nice to see ye again as well, Mrs. Fitzpatrick. And it's glad I am to be here."

"Oh, call me Kate, or Katy. I'm sure we'll be seeing a lot of each other in the time to come."

"Kitten," Dad sounded resigned, "your mother and I had...words, and...we've agreed that Liam could stay with us while he's here. I've already retrieved his bags from your grandparents' and moved them into the guest bedroom at the end of the hall." Dad turned to Liam. "Hope that's all right with you?"

"Oh, it's right fine, it is. And I appreciate it. Thank ye, sir."

"Don't make me regret this," Dad warned to no one in particular. Though, we all heard him loud and clear.

Hiding my grin, I turned to give Mom a hug and whispered, "Thank you," as I leaned down to her. "Get some rest. We'll see you in the morning. Love you, Mom, Dad." Turning to Liam, I said, "I'll show you to your room. Then, if you're up for it, maybe either a bonfire or a movie?"

"Either is fine; I'm simply happy to be here."

After showing Liam to his room, we headed back to the living room, then I led him on to the kitchen, so he'd have a clearer layout of the house. Liam looked around. His blue eyes touching on the dark wood flooring, the misty grey-green walls, the granite countertops. "This was the house yer mother grew up in? Seems in good shape."

"When we took it over, my parents did some upgrades, repainted and stuff, but yeah, this is the place." Liam stifled a yawn while looking around. "You still up for that movie or fire?"

Yawning again, and eyes watering, he said, "I'm game, though I canna lie and tell ye I willna fall asleep on ye."

Chuckling, I walked forward, sliding my arms around him and simply held him. He smelled good. He felt good and it was heaven to be in his arms again. "I think I'm still trying to process that you're here. You're *actually* here. In Wyoming. With me, in my house."

"I ken that, lass. And it's sorry I am that I've put ye through any doubt aboot me intentions or feelings for ye." He leaned back against the counter and pulled me with him, fitting me to his frame. "I can assure they've no' changed, other than to grow deeper, stronger."

Leaning up, I gently kissed him, then stepped back. "Go ahead and get some sleep. I'll be up by six to feed, so I might not be here when you wake. If not, I'll see you when I get back and then I'll make you breakfast."

Those dark blue eyes tracked my movements. "I ken I need sleep. I ken yer da is down that hall and probably counting down the seconds until ye've returned. But *bugger me,* I'd love nothing more than to take ye back to that room and have me way wi' ye."

Heat swamped me and I swallowed. "Oh." A door closed sharply, making me flinch.

"And there's the Good Lord saving us from unwise decisions." Liam stepped back, his eyes now twinkling with mischief. Chuckling, I bid him goodnight, then headed off for bed myself, knowing morning came quickly.

I was just pouring the coffee the following morning, having slept terribly from being far too excited knowing Liam was here, when I heard a sound behind me. Glancing over my shoulder, I spotted him as he came into the room looking as fabulous as ever. Not paying attention to what I was doing, I poured hot coffee over my hand. "*Ouch!!*" I nearly dropped the pot on the floor in my haste to set it down and tend to my injury.

Liam hurried over, taking my hand in his for inspection. "Ach, lass. Ye poor wee thing. Are ye all right?"

"Yeah, just wasn't paying attention." I chuckled, a little breathless. He looked and smelled so darned good. "I'll run it under the tap, that should help." The cold water relieved the sting somewhat, and the longer I held it until the frigid stream, the less it burned. Finally, I felt it was better and shut the water off. "This was your fault, you know?"

"How do ye figure that?" A grin played about his mouth, parting his lips.

"You distracted me."

"Ye find me distractin', do ye?" His grin spread, the look in his eyes a knowing one.

"You know I do."

Liam lifted his hands to my neck, brushing my hair away, threading his fingers into the strands, tilting my face upwards. In a low, growly rumble, he said, "It's glad I am to hear ye say so." His kiss was slow, and measured, as his mouth lingered over mine, his beard tickling deliciously. A loud clearing of someone's throat had us separating, even as I tried to catch my breath.

"Might I get some coffee for your mother and me?" Dad asked as he grimly made his way into the room.

Coughing, I said, "Yeah, sorry, Dad."

"Mmhm." Dad poured two cups, adding the creamer that Mom preferred, then with one last warning glare at the two of us, he left the room. My gaze darted to Liam's, and I laughed under my breath at his expression.

Liam's hand covered his heart, and he panted. "Me bloody life just flashed afore me eyes and yer havin' a laugh at me?"

His reaction had me chuckling again. "You know Dad wouldn't actually kill you, right?"

"Nae, I dinna bloody well ken that. I've heard enough stories aboot the man to keep me awake at night."

"And yet, here you are." A smile lingered on my face; I simply couldn't seem to help it.

"And yet...here I am, because I canna live wi'out ye." I hadn't seen him move, but suddenly he stood in front of me once more. He inhaled deep, making a satisfied sound as he did so. "Ye said ye had animals to feed this mornin', nae? Let's get them fed, then."

Asher-

"I knew I was going to regret this." Asher carefully handed Kate her coffee, then angrily took a sip of his before continuing his rant. "Just now? In the kitchen? They were making out! We haven't even had breakfast yet!" Kate silently studied her husband as he stormed around the room, humor shining in her eyes. Asher caught her looking and grumbled. "It's not funny."

"It is, actually. Babe, have you forgotten how *we* were? I can recall several rather steamy encounters that we had."

Asher stopped his pacing. He shot her a heated look. "Passion was never a problem for the two of us, was it, love?"

"No, it was not. And I don't think it will be for the two of them, either."

He rubbed a hand across his face. "But that's what I'm afraid of, and she's my little girl."

Kate studied her husband over the lip of her cup. "She'll always be your little girl, your kitten. But she's also a grown woman, and is going to have to walk her own path now."

"Doesn't mean I have to like it." Asher griped. "Or him."

Katy took a sip of her coffee, allowing the heated caffeine to hit her system, enveloping her in its warm embrace. "You like him. If you didn't, you wouldn't have allowed him to be here, nor would you have agreed to asking him to look after her while she was with your parents."

"Fat lot of good that did, huh?" Asher complained; his mouth twisted in irritation.

"Oh, I think it did. She got over the idiot and found herself a man. One who loves her and is evidently willing to risk life and limb to be with her. I couldn't have asked for better. Your parents are quite pleased with the outcome. He reminds me of someone…"

"Don't say me. He is *not* like me."

"Oh, I'd say he is." Kate grinned. "Similar in looks and in personality. I'd say our daughter is a lucky woman."

"*He's* the lucky one."

"No argument there. They're both lucky. Just like I am."

Asher set his empty mug down and prowled to her side. Carefully, he placed one hand on either side of her hips and leaned in. "*I'm* the lucky one. Still. After all these years, you are still my everything and I can't live without you. I'm forever grateful the Good Lord saw fit to let us meet." Tenderly, he kissed her, cautious as his mouth moved over hers, unwilling to cause his wife any pain or discomfort.

Bethany-

Liam and I met Jack and Del at the *WYOld West* taproom for dinner before heading to the Rodeo. The waitress brought our menus once we'd found a seat. "The Kilted Cowboy," Delaney stated. "Obviously Liam must try the Kilted Cowboy first."

Her statement had me chuckling and I wondered how long she'd been thinking about it. "And what's that then?" Liam asked as he looked over his menu.

"It's the brewery's version of a Scottish Ale," I replied and pointed to it on the menu. "It's pretty good; though, I'm not sure how it compares with a true ale made in Scotland."

"Only one way to find out." Jack flagged the waitress back to our table and we placed our orders, then went to the tap for our drinks. Once seated again, we waited expectantly as Liam tasted his Kilted Cowboy.

"Well?" Delaney asked.

Liam wiped his mouth, took another swallow, then wiped his mouth again. "No' bad. No' bad at all. Though, tis nothin' like what ye'd get in Scotland." He directed a pointed look at me. "I'm more determined than ever now to take ye there."

We ate and talked, Delaney and Jack asking random questions. I'm pretty sure, at least on Del's part, that they asked the questions just to hear Liam speak. The waitress brought us our checks and asked how we liked the meal. "Marci, you'll have to tell the big bosses that your Kilted Cowboy meets the approval of a real Scotsman," Jack told her, indicating Liam with a grin.

"Is that right? You're from Scotland?"

"Aye. And the ale was quite good. Much obliged," Liam told her.

"Well, we're glad to hear it. What's brings you to the States?"

"In short. She did." Liam placed a hand over mine, offering a warm smile.

"Our Bethany? Oh, that's so romantic. How long are you here for?"

"Until she sends me away, I reckon."

"You two are just the cutest." Marci turned to me. "How's your mom doing? Healing up, I hope?"

"She is, Marci. Thanks." I glanced at my phone for the time. "We need to go. We're working the Rodeo tonight."

After paying the tab, we headed to the rodeo grounds.

The Stranger-

The man watched as the young blond woman, flag braced in hand, raced around the arena on the horse. When first he'd seen her, he thought he'd seen a ghost. There was no way she could have survived that accident. Then, as he looked closer, he decided she wasn't the same. Too young to be *her*. Her daughter maybe? Now that would be an interesting development. What he hadn't received from the mother, he might receive from the daughter. And that would put another painful mark on the big guy, now wouldn't it?

The man chuckled to himself. He watched the young woman as she left the arena, then stood and made his way out of the stands. He circled around to the back of the bleachers and searched for the girl. Minutes later, he found her as she brushed her horse down. No one else was around. He looked about, and seeing no one near the trailer her horse was tied to, he casually made his way over. *Time for some fun,* he thought. "KatyBeth? Is that you?"

The woman spun around at the sound of his voice so close behind her. Seeing him, and no doubt guessing his age to be somewhere around her parents' ages, she most likely assumed he was someone they knew. "No, sorry. I'm Bethany. KatyBeth's my mom."

"I see." A faraway look in his eyes, he trailed a hand over the gelding's back. "And how's she doing then?"

"Mom's doing all right, all things considered. She's healing well."

The man's gaze shifted to Bethany; he stared hard at her for a moment, then nodded and said, "Be seeing you."

Liam-

Liam stepped around the trailer, drinks in hand, and instantly noted the man standing near Bethany. Quickening his pace, he caught the man's parting comment. Something about the words, or the delivery of them, bothered him. Bethany had received many admiring looks all evening and Liam had tried not to grit his teeth at each one. But something about this guy irritated him. Something in his demeanor maybe? The look on his face? Whatever it was, Liam didn't like him. If he'd been a dog, he'd have been on guard with hackles raised.

Ten years ago, after one of he and Bethany's jaunts around Kealkill, Asher had approached him with the idea of training him in self-defense. Asher had said a time may come when Liam would need to know what to do, and if he was going to be in his daughter's company, Asher'd prefer he was well-versed in the discipline. He'd started with hand-to-hand. Basic, simple moves. Breaking holds. Neutralizing an attacker. Weapons, both the use of and the defense against. He'd also learned how to spot a danger. And something about this man had him on high alert. "Who was that?" he asked, trying not to sound too harsh or even jealous. He wasn't jealous, at least, not of that guy.

Bethany-

I'd heard Liam's approach, but my gaze was still on the stranger, an odd, heightened feeling growing in my gut. Something about him, the look in his eye maybe? Something seemed off about him and put me on edge. "Hmm?" I blinked, then looked over at Liam. "What did you say?"

"I asked who the bloke was." Liam's eyes flashed over me before turning back in the man's direction.

"I'm not sure. He didn't say."

"What did he want?" Liam turned back to me, holding my cup out.

"He thought I was my mom." I accepted the drink. "It was weird, though. He seemed off somehow. Like he knows my mom enough to think I was her, but he didn't seem friendly, you know? It was just weird." Liam stared off again in the direction the man had taken.

I finished grooming Grover, then put some hay in his hay net and made sure his water bucket was filled. Right as I was finishing up, Samantha, Grover's owner, walked up. "How'd he do? You looked great on him, by the way."

"Grover was fine. He didn't give me any trouble, and the flag didn't seem to bother him at all. He might just have been having an off day. I can give it another go, if you'd like?" Samantha had called me on the way to the arena, asking if I'd ride Grover. She said he'd panicked the night before at the approach of the flag and wanted me to take a look at him.

"Of course, he was." Samantha rubbed Grover's nose, a soft smile on her face. "Yeah, maybe he was just having an off day. Well, if you think he's fine, then I guess he's fine. Thanks for doing that for me."

"Yeah, no problem. If you need me to ride him again, I could probably bring him out to the ranch and work him there. Make sure he's fully sound for you."

"I might take you up on that. Let me see how he does the rest of this week and we'll go from there."

We said goodbye, then headed around to the front to see how Delaney was doing with Norman the Bull. About fifteen people were standing in line when we arrived. "*Gor,* that's a big animal," Liam noted quietly as we walked closer. He seemed to have put the stranger out of his mind and I was glad. I didn't want anything to upset my time with Liam.

"You want to get your picture taken on him?"

"Ye can do that?"

"Sure;" I grinned, "what do you think they're all standing in line for?"

"I though' just to see him." As we looked on, two young boys, maybe around ten years old were climbing onto Norman's broad back. "He just stands there and lets them do that?" Liam's eyes were wide and intent on the goings on with the bull.

Seeing the interest on Liam's face, I nudged him. "You wanna?"

"Well now, as the wee lads have just fearlessly climbed aboard, I'll have to." I smiled at his reply, then smiled wider as Liam chuckled at the boys' antics. They'd both pulled a bull rider's pose. Hats tipped forward, one hand in the air, the other down as if to hold the flank strap, booted feet kicked forward as they leaned backward, absolutely adorable and entertaining.

I paid our fee, having Liam hold our place in line as I did. Delaney squealed in excitement as she saw us. "Omgoodness, yes! Of course, you have to get him on Norman!"

When it was our turn, I had Liam get on first to get some solo pictures, then I climbed on. He insisted I sit in front, which was fine by me as it allowed for his arms to come around me. I'm pretty sure Delaney took more pictures with my phone than she had with other people and appreciated her extra efforts on our behalf.

As Liam slipped down from Norman, I heard one of the guys standing by say, "Hey, ain't this the fella was wearing the skirt last night?"

"Kilt!" Delaney and I yelled at him, causing Liam to chuckle. We thanked Del, then, as both of us were feeling tired, Liam and I said our goodbyes and headed for home.

CHAPTER THIRTEEN

Old Wounds

Bethany-

The clock on the dash read 9:34 when we pulled up to the house. Through the open blinds, I saw Dad helping Mom onto the couch. *What is she doing out of bed? This can't be good for her ribs.* When we stepped inside, Mom looked over at us. "Don't say a word. I had to get out of that bed. I *had* to."

I glanced to Dad where he was now lighting the burner at the kitchen stove, probably making tea for Mom. Subtly, he shook his head. "Okay." I smiled at Mom. "I won't say anything."

"Good. Now, come sit down, the both of you, and tell me how tonight went. Your dad's making tea for all of us, by the way."

"Thanks." Liam and I took seats on the smaller sofa, near Mom. "I've missed that from my time in Ireland with Nana and Granda. We used to have tea practically every night."

"I can imagine. So, tell me. How'd things go?" Mom asked, then turned to Liam. "What'd you think of your first rodeo? Was it all it was cracked up to be?"

"Ach, it was. All of it." Liam shook his head in seeming wonderment. "I can hardly believe some of the things those lads do."

"He sat on Norman!" I slapped my hands down on my thighs in excitement. "We got some great pictures, too."

"Oh, fun!" Mom smiled. "I love that bull, love his long ears."

Dad brought the tea and dispersed it around. Then he leaned against the mantle, holding his mug in hand. Liam was just finishing telling Mom about the Kilted Cowboy ale when I remembered the stranger. "I ran into someone who knew you, Mom. I didn't recognize him, but he thought I was you."

"Oh yeah? Who was it?" She grinned, well-aware of our similar looks.

"That's what's weird. He never gave me his name. Just asked how you were doing. I told him pretty good, all things considered and that you were healing well. Then he said he'd see me around and walked off." Mom shot an alarmed look to Dad, her face going pale. "Mom?" At her sudden ashen appearance, I set my cup down. "Are you okay?"

"What did he look like, kitten?" Dad placed his mug on the mantle and moved close to Mom, taking her hand in his.

"Uh, white guy, probably close to your ages?" I shrugged, trying to recall the details. "Blond, with a little steel around the temples. Why?"

Dad turned to Liam. "Did you get a good look at him?"

"Aye, I saw him." Liam's voice was calm, though I thought I'd detected *something* hidden in its depths. "Though, it wasna the best as it was from a bit of a distance."

Dad pulled out his cell phone, scrolled a moment, then held it out to us. "Did he look like this?" We stood to get a better look. The photo we saw looked like a mugshot, and the man in the image was much younger than the one we'd seen, but I wasn't in any doubt that it was him, despite the cuts and bruises on the man's face.

"Yeah. That's him." I nodded, wondering at the shape the man had been in, in the photo. "Who was that, Dad? What's going on?"

"Oh, my Lord...Asher...he..." Mom looked at me, fear in her eyes, and shuddered, grimacing in pain as she did so.

Dad gently squeezed Mom's hand before setting it down. He dialed a number, then said into the phone, "I need you. Both of you. The bastard approached Bethany tonight." From the other end of the line, I heard an exclamation. Dad replied, "Yeah," then hung up.

"Will someone, please, tell me what's going on?" I glanced between my parents, exasperated as a kernel of unease began growing in my middle. Mom sat in silence, looking stricken, so I turned to my dad. "Dad!"

"In a moment, kitten." Dad leaned down to Mom and whispered something to her. Then placed a tender kiss at her temple—probably attempting to reassure or calm her—before standing upright again. He blew out a breath, then moved, agitated, pacing along the front of the couch, seemingly deep in thought, before finally coming to a stop near Liam. Slowly, Dad turned to him. Silently, he regarded Liam, then asked, his voice measured, his tone careful, "Have you continued with the training?"

Liam stared at him for a breath or two before dipping his chin ever so slightly. "Aye, I have."

"Show me." Dad struck like lightning. His movements blurring together. I'd heard stories about him, about how brutal and savage he could be. How ruthless and violent. But I'd never seen him in action. And I'd certainly had no idea that Liam knew anything like what Dad knew. He must have though, because even as Dad erupted in what appeared to be pure viciousness, Liam responded, defending himself and avoiding being struck.

An incoherent scream erupted from my throat at the suddenness of the attack. I lurched a step in their direction, hoping to somehow stop them before anyone was injured. At my approach, Dad stepped back. Liam moved between me and Dad, and after a moment or two, once he saw the threat was over, let down his guard. Immediately, I slipped around him until I was facing him. I could see he was all right, that he hadn't been hurt, but I'd needed to touch him, to hold him. After assuring myself he was okay, I spun around.

Before I could say anything, Dad spoke, "Twenty-five years ago, your mother and I put that man in prison for plotting to rape and murder her, and to murder me and your Uncle Cal as well."

Silence filled the room. I couldn't...I couldn't have heard him correctly. I shook my head in disbelief. My eyes searched those of my dad, waiting for him to...I didn't know what. Correct himself? His blue eyes stayed steady on mine. Suddenly, the room spun, and I was seeing spots. Liam's arms wrapped around me, pulling me closer. Swallowing, I managed to choke out, "*What?*"

"Close to ten years ago, on one of our trips to Ireland, I approached Liam about getting trained. You two were close; you followed each other everywhere. I knew you knew what you were doing, but still, I wanted him trained. Your and your mother's protection is *always* my top priority. If Liam was going to be around you, he needed to know how to defend you and himself. I trained him some, then gave him names, contacts of people he needed to be in touch with for further training." Dad's gaze was steady on Liam, calculating, before turning to me. "It seems he's been faithful in his endeavor." Dad paused a moment, seeming to calculate in his head before continuing, "About a week or so before you left for Ireland, I got a courtesy call from the detective who'd handled the case, letting me know Johnny Khyle was being released from prison for serving his sentence." Dad paused again, inhaling sharply before exhaling in a rush. "Your mother's accident was no accident. It was Johnny. He tried to kill her. Again."

Emotion now choked me as panic and anger began to set in. My body trembled, and I had to swallow several times to clear my throat. "Why is he still free? Why hasn't he been arrested yet for trying to kill her again?"

"Because your mother and Aunt Tiffy haven't given their statements yet to the police. I had them wait until your mom was feeling up to it." Lights flashed in the window, alerting us that someone had pulled up. Moments later, Uncle Samuel and Aunt Tiffy came inside. Tiffy immediately went to Mom.

Samuel looked at me. "Are you okay?" I nodded, assuring him that I was. He turned to Dad. "Are you sure it was him?"

"They both identified him," Dad replied, absentmindedly rubbing his knuckles. Turning back to Mom, he said, "I'm calling the detective. You guys will need to give your statements now."

An hour and a half later, lights once more flashed in the window. A few minutes later, Uncle Samuel answered the door. Detective Mercer of the Park County Sheriff's Office stepped inside. "Evening," he addressed the group gathered in my living room. I guessed him to be right about six feet tall, and probably in his sixties. His hair was more steel grey than the blond it must once have been, but his hazel eyes were sharp and friendly.

"Detective Mercer." Dad extended his hand. "Kate and Tiffy are prepared to give their statements now. My daughter and her boyfriend have additional information to provide once that's done."

Coming out of my stupor, I ascertained who might want coffee or tea, then headed to the kitchen. I got the coffee going, then filled the kettle and turned the burner on high. Feeling a presence behind me, I turned. Liam gathered me into his arms, holding me tightly. The trembling started again, and his grip tightened. Tears came and he just held me while I silently fell apart. Somehow, this was so much worse than simply thinking Mom had been in an accident. It hadn't *been* an accident. It had been attempted murder. The thought left me cold and wobbly, and so furious I could hardly contain myself.

"Breathe, lass," Liam whispered into my hair. "I've go' ye, just breathe. It'll all work out. Your da willna let anythin' happen to ye or yer ma. Ye ken that." My breath shuddered in my chest and his arms tightened. "*I* willna let anythin' happen to ye either. That bastard's as good as dead now. Yer da willna let him be."

Pulling back, I stared up at Liam. Saw the resolve in his eyes, the peace and assurance, and felt myself settle. Under his gaze, the tension in my frame began to ebb, to trickle away. I could breathe again. Standing on my toes, I dragged his face down to mine, kissing him as if my life depended on it, as if his life depended on it. I needed him. Needed to be his in a permanent and meaningful way. "Liam." I gasped against his mouth, unsure how to convey my need. He growled low in answer, surging forward, pinning me against the counter, his hands threading into my hair.

Moments later, the teapot whistled sharply, startling us, pulling us apart. Blushing, I spun away and turned the burner off, taking a moment to calm myself before getting the tea and cups ready. Liam leaned against the counter and watched as I poured the boiling water into the waiting mugs, then arranged them on the serving tray. Once the coffee was finished, I got those cups ready as well. I went to lift the tray, but he stayed me with a gentle hand before lifting and carrying it for me. Such a gentlemanly thing to do. It was a thoughtful, special gesture, not because I needed his assistance, or was unable to do this on my own. But because I *was* fully capable. He did it because he cared and that made my heart soar and settle at the same time.

Detective Mercer was just finishing with Mom when we reentered the room. Dad's eyes were on us, a resigned look in his gaze, and I wondered if he'd seen our display a moment ago. Mentally, I shrugged that away, my focus once more on my mother. After dispersing the drinks, Liam and I sat on the loveseat, and the detective turned towards us, flipping a page on his notepad. "Bethany, your father tells me you've had a run-in with Johnny. Why don't you tell me what happened?"

As succinctly as possible, I explained what took place, Liam filling in his parts as I went. The detective asked a few questions, mainly ascertaining whether we'd ever had contact with Johnny prior to today. He wrote notes down on his notepad, then quickly read over what he'd written. Standing, he said he thought he had what he'd needed, then thanked me for the coffee and thanked the rest of us for our time. Turning to Dad, he said, "Asher, I'm going to ask you to let us handle this." Dad simply stared at him, giving nothing away. Detective Mercer tried again. "Let us handle this. We'll bring him in. He'll be tried and penalized by a court of law. Now, you let us do us our job."

Dad continued his silent stare before quietly saying, "I'd suggest you find him before I do. Because if I find him, you never will."

Detective Mercer rubbed at his chin. "Now, Asher, don't say stuff like that."

"I let the law handle it once before and he was tried and served his time, then he was released and attempted to murder my wife and is now sniffing around my daughter. If the law wants him—you just find him before I do."

Mercer looked at each of us around the room, maybe hoping for someone to back him up. Hoping someone might try and side with him as he attempted to reason with my father. Seeing he'd get no help, he thanked us for our time and said he'd be in touch before heading out the door.

We remained in place and silent until we saw his headlights leaving, then Dad turned to Uncle Samuel. "Find him. Use whatever means you need to, call in whatever favors I'm owed. I want him."

"I'm already on it," Samuel replied. "I should hear something within the week."

"You let me know the moment you do."

"Ash," Mom spoke softly, drawing his gaze. "Be careful."

"Always."

"You know what I mean." She swallowed. "I need you and don't want you to end up in prison, or worse."

"I won't," Dad assured her. "But I also refuse to allow that man to get away with this or give him the opportunity to hurt either one of you again. Don't ask me to do that."

"You can't murder him, Ash," Mom whispered, her voice trembling.

"It won't be murder, or even revenge. This is about defense and ending a direct threat in the most concise manner possible. I will *not* allow him to continue to threaten my family. Full stop." Their gazes held for several long moments, then she swallowed and nodded, tears glistening in her eyes.

Dad turned to Liam, nodding in my direction. "You'll need to remain close to her. Where she goes, you go." Liam's hand came to rest on my thigh, a solid, warm weight. Dad spared a brief glance at that, then said, "Kitten, you go strapped from here on out until this is settled. I know you know how to handle yourself, but I'll breathe easier knowing Liam's around. We're a Constitutional Carry state here, Liam, so you'll be strapped as well. Have you been able to practice with a firearm at all?"

"Some, though no' as much as I'd have liked. I met wi' yer man there. He walked me through a couple drills that I've completed to his satisfaction."

"Good. I'll lend you one of mine and provide the documentation for it. You shouldn't be bothered here; however, in case something happens, you'll have it."

Aunt Tiffy stood from the couch where she'd been sitting beside Mom. "It's late; we should go." Uncle Samuel moved to her side then faced back to us, his arm around her back. He jerked his chin to Dad. "As soon as I hear, you'll know."

After they'd left, Dad helped Mom to her feet. We stood as well. I moved to begin gathering the mugs. "Bethany." Mom tried to smile at me, but it wobbled. "I love you so much."

Moving to her, I carefully hugged her. "I love you, too, Mom and don't you worry about me. Dad's got the right of this."

She sniffed and shook her head. "You have so much of him in you. Sometimes I forget that."

"I come from strong stock, and we take care of our own."

"I know. I love you. I love all of you." Gently, she brushed a hand across my cheek. "Just be careful. That's all I'll ask of you all. Just be careful."

"We will," I assured her as Dad helped her back to her room. I stood still for a moment, watching as she moved away, noting how she was getting stronger. Hearing the clink of glasses, I turned to help Liam as we cleared the dishes from the living room and carried them to the kitchen for washing. We worked in silence. Washing and drying the dishes, then wiping down the counters. I tossed the wet towels in the laundry room and returned to find Liam waiting for me. He held his arms out, inviting me in.

Moving into his embrace I said, "I don't want to be alone right now."

"I'm here for whatever ye need. For as long as ye need." Smiling, I snuggled in closer to him, wrapping my arms tighter around him.

"Let's light a fire, maybe watch a movie?" I suggested after a bit, my nose buried in his chest, just breathing him in.

"Whatever ye want, lass." Liam placed a soft kiss on the top of my head then released me. While he lit a fire in the fireplace, I searched through our movies until I found something I knew he hadn't seen yet. We then settled on the couch. I hadn't meant to fall asleep, I remember the opening credits of the movie, but the next thing I knew, it was morning. Liam was stretched out on the couch and I was cuddled between him and the back of the sofa, a blanket spread over us.

"Morning." He smiled sleepily as I lifted my head.

I blinked, groggily, then managed to croak out, "Omgoodness, I'm so sorry; I didn't mean to fall asleep on you like this."

"Dinna be—*I'm* no' sorry. I could wake like this every morning for the rest of me life." Grinning, I attempted to sit up but struggled to get the right leverage. Chuckling under his breath, Liam said, "Haud still, I'll move." He rolled to the floor landing on his knees before standing to his feet, stretching his long frame, and stealing the air from my lungs in the process. Leaning down, he pulled me to my feet but kept his hands on me to keep me steady.

Blushing under his regard, I looked to the clock on the mantle, noting it was just after six. "I should get out and feed."

"I'll come wi' ye."

"You don't have to. It won't take me long."

"I'm aware; I'd still like to help, unless ye'd rather I didna and need the space?"

"Come on, then." I took his hand and led him to the back door. "Can't have you thinking I need space."

We got the animals fed and watered, then I collected the eggs before we headed back to the house. "It's supposed to be a nice day. You want to go for a ride later?"

"Aye, I think ye may be right, and a ride sounds grand, though, it's been a time since I've been on a horse and never in one of yer western saddles."

Stopping, I looked at him. "Well, you certainly can't come to cowboy country and not ride like a cowboy. Mom taught Dad to ride—I'll teach you."

Liam-

Liam waited on the porch for Bethany, his deep blue eyes taking in everything around him. The mountains, the thick stands of evergreen, aspen, and birch. The tall, green swaying grasses. Wyoming was rugged country. Not as wet as Scotland. But still, rugged, clean. And beautiful. Somewhere in the distance, he heard cattle softly lowing. But no engines, no neighbors as far as the eye could see. A gentle breeze blew through, bringing the scent of pine, alfalfa, horse, and something sweeter he couldn't quite name. He filled his lungs, taking it all in, held it, waited a moment, then exhaled. A silence was here, a calmness, one that soothed his soul and heart. One that made him want to settle down. Though he'd never been here before, he felt this was home. Bethany stepped out beside him, her arms going around him. He held her arms to him, covering them with his own. Aye, this was home. *She* was home.

Bethany-

Almost three hours later, Liam and I walked to the barn. Wick and Rhys nickered from their stalls, greeting us in anticipation. Mom's older gelding Red was in the stall between Rhys and Wick; I paused there and scratched his head, then his shoulder as Red sidestepped closer, giving better access, making me chuckle. Though he had a touch of swayback and arthritis, he was still a beautiful and well-muscled animal. Over my shoulder, I said, "This is Mom's old gelding, Red. She trained him from a colt. I learned to ride on him."

Liam stepped beside me and Red, being the horse he was, had to do some inspection before deciding he was acceptable. Liam stood still, permitting the inquisitive snuffing before trying to pet the chestnut gelding. After a moment or two, we moved to Rhys, performing those introductions, then we moved on to Wick. My spotted gelding trotted around his stall, clearly anxious to get under saddle and ride. I pushed him away from the stall door and stepped inside, running my hands over his silver and black coat. It had been a week since I'd last thrown a leg over him and I could tell he was feeling pretty spry. Taking hold of his halter, I led him to the crossties near the tack room and fastened the ropes to his halter.

Once I had him groomed, I saddled him and grabbed a lunge line to work him in the round pen. Wick showed off by jumping around and kicking up his heels. "All right, enough of that." Turning to Liam, I said, "He's just messing around right now. He's never actually bucked with anyone in the saddle."

"If ye say so. He looks braw 'nough."

"Wick's all right. I'll ride him first, make sure he's done with the fireworks, then you can get on. How's that sound?"

"Sounds like a plan."

Once mounted, I put Wick through his paces, loping him in circles, then in figure eights until he'd worked up a decent lather before bringing him to a stop near Liam. "You ready to ride now?"

"Ach, maybe I'll just watch ye for a bit more. Seems like ye have him well 'nough in hand."

Grinning at his hesitation after Wick's antics, I said, "Tell you what, you climb on behind me. Then, once you get the hang of it, I'll hop off. How's that?"

Liam studied me and the horse for a breath or two, then exhaling, he nodded and stepped closer to us. I slipped my boot from the stirrup to leave it available for his use and leaned to the right, giving him more room and leverage. "Put your left foot in the stirrup, and grab hold of the horn and the cantle back here, then just like climbing a ladder, step up. Swing your right leg over as you do. He won't move; I've got him."

On his first try, Liam mounted correctly and was soon properly situated behind me. Wick sidestepped a little, the added weight making him nervous, but I spoke reassuringly to the Appaloosa, and he soon calmed down. Liam's arms slipped around me, pulling us closer. "You good?" I asked before letting Wick move out.

"Aye." His breath brushed my neck. "I am."

"Okay then, just hold on to me, I'll do the rest."

"I've every intention of keeping hold of ye."

His comment made me grin as I instructed Wick to walk on. We rode, just a moseying gait, in silence around the large arena for probably close to fifteen minutes before I asked Liam how he was doing. His chin rested on my shoulder, near my ear. "This is fair heavenly, it is. And I've a slight confession to make. I only feigned anxiety so ye'd offer to be right where ye are now."

Pulling Wick up, I couldn't stop the heat that rose inside as I turned in the saddle to face him. Before I could get a word out, Liam kissed me. His left arm held me tightly to him as his right hand framed my face, his mouth effortlessly claiming mine.

Asher-

"You've *got* to be kidding me." Asher stood at the kitchen sink, coffee mug in hand, staring out the window. He shook his head, looking disgruntled.

Kate slowly moved to his side—proud of the progress she was making—looking to see what had caught Asher's attention. "Oh," she murmured in surprise. "Wow, he's good."

"*Good?* How is that good?" Asher griped crossly, his eyes still on the couple outside.

"Well..." Kate grinned. "He's riding double with her. He's definitely got some smooth moves. You've got to appreciate his confidence."

To that, Asher simply snorted before grumbling, "What are they even doing?"

"Isn't it obvious?" Kate mildly nudged him with her shoulder. "She's teaching him how to ride."

Asher blinked. "Is that what we're calling it?"

"Looked that way to me."

"Yeah? Look again. Looks a far cry from teaching him how to ride to me."

"They definitely have no lack for passion," Kate agreed, even as she silently prayed they were being wise and not pushing boundaries. She remembered her own struggle to remember the boundaries she'd had when it came to Asher and what he'd made her feel, what he still made her feel.

Asher grunted, his gaze on his daughter and the Scotsman as they kissed out in the arena, *on the horse.* After a moment, he turned away, setting his now empty mug on the counter, focusing on his wife instead. "How come you didn't teach *me* to ride like that?"

Kate blushed under his regard, her lips curling at the corner, an impish light entering her green eyes. "Are you feeling neglected?"

Asher leaned down to her, framing her face between gentle hands, his lips hovering over hers. "Not even close. I'm the luckiest man alive. Never doubt that."

Kate blinked moisture from her eyes and breathed slowly to stop her mouth from trembling. "Once I'm healed, maybe you and I can go riding. Just the two of us. Like we used to do. Maybe we can ride to that spring we found and have a weekend to ourselves."

Asher brushed his mouth across hers, reminding himself to be gentle, to go slow. Kate made it hard, though. She always had. Hearing her soft moan nearly undid him. "I am *one hundred percent* on board for that." He kissed the side of her mouth, then the other side, and finally her lips, gently tugging the bottom one into his mouth for an instant. "And, as I recall, you and I had plans before the accident. With my desk." Asher wickedly grinned at her. She made that soft moaning sound again, her eyes fluttering closed, and he had to clamp down hard on the desire she sparked in him. Instead, he carefully, tenderly pulled her into his embrace and simply held her, not trusting himself for more than that.

CHAPTER FOURTEEN

Written In the Deep

Johnny-

Johnny Khyle leaned against the tiny kitchen counter in his cabover and felt the fury spike through him. And the fear. The caution. She was still alive. That stupid witch was somehow still alive. KatyBeth. He raised clenched fists to his head and cursed, his breath coming in near sobs. She was like a splinter under the skin, irritating, aggravating, giving him a fever, driving him insane. Somehow, she'd burrowed so far inside him, digging and clawing, she'd become written, scratched into the deepest part of him. He couldn't shake her.

She'd seen him that day in town. He knew he shouldn't have made contact with her, even from a distance. Knew it and yet took the risk anyway. Having her, having that sort of *effect* on her, seeing that shock and fear was the most satisfaction he'd had in ages. Seeing her frightened acknowledgment of him as a threat. He still couldn't get her out of his head, still after all these years. Ever since he'd first seen her strutting through the halls in high school, her lush figure displayed to such perfection, enticing him. He'd desired her then. Fiercely. Such a hunger she'd lit inside him. But she'd wanted nothing to do with him. Had declined his advances. He'd humbled himself for her and she'd spurned him. Rejected him. That wasn't right. Wasn't to be tolerated.

She didn't know it, but he'd almost had her once before the 'incident.' Both the one he'd gone to prison for and the most recent where she should have died. He'd come *so* close. Practice had ended early; he'd been coming from the gym and seen her crossing the nearly empty school parking lot. His truck hadn't been parked that far from hers, no more than thirty feet. He could've had her on her back and unconscious, could have had his fill and then some before anyone could have stopped him. No one else was around to see or hear. She normally hadn't parked that far out, but it had seemed as if fortune had been favoring him. He'd started towards her. Like a shark scenting blood in the water, his focus had been unerringly on her. He'd been closing in, no more than a dozen feet away, when he heard the rumble of another vehicle and looked over his shoulder. Calvin pulled up, parking his rig beside Katy's.

Calvin had shot him a hard look as he'd exited the truck—always suspicious of everything Johnny did—and moved to Katy's side. Always the faithful hound. She hadn't even noticed him, hadn't even seen Johnny, was still dismissing him. Seeing Calvin, Johnny had bent casually, picking up a piece of paper off the asphalt, nothing more than him chasing a wayward note. He held it up, waved it at Calvin, who was still staring at him. Johnny offered an ill-humored grin, then veered off to his own rig, spinning his tires before speeding out of there. Coming out of his reminiscing, Johnny took a deep breath, lowered his hands, and pondered the situation. Chances were high that her husband knew all about it. Knew he'd been near her in Cody. And chances were equally high that he was even now looking for Johnny.

There was something not right about that man. Something not quite legal. Johnny had never been able to put his finger on it, that difference. But that big man was off. Dangerous. An apex predator. He made the hackles rise on Johnny. Made him cautious. Made him feel hunted and inferior. Inferior, that was what they both made him feel. She with her refusal to acknowledge him as a man. And he for being a bigger man, a better man. Johnny hated that feeling. Hated the two of them for making him feel it.

The wind whipped past the camper, setting Johnny's nerves on edge. He couldn't stay here. Powell wasn't far enough away from Cody. He needed to go underground for a while. Disappear. He'd come back. Of course, he would. *She* was still here. And he had no intention of letting her get away. Maybe it was for the best she hadn't died. Now, at least, he had another chance at her. Another chance to make things right to his satisfaction. Another chance to make her pay for rejecting him. *And,* he grinned, *she had a daughter.* One equally as desirable. He'd have them both.

Kate-

Ruben helped Kate stretch, slowly, gently moving her arm and shoulder. "Good. Nice work, keep breathing. Don't hold your breath, breathe through it. We'll do this for two more minutes then take a break. It seems your PT is going well. You're really improving."

Asher sat at the kitchen table, going over some paperwork, where it afforded him an unrestricted view of her and her progress. Kate knew she'd come far. She could feel his eyes on her, tracking her movements. No doubt, noting the pleased look on her face at the nurse's compliment. She had every right to feel pleased in herself; she'd come a long way

"Soon, I'll be up and running around just like my old self." Kate grinned in anticipation.

"Give it time," Ruben cautioned. "You're definitely making strides, but don't rush your healing."

Kate rolled her eyes, then movement out the window caught her attention. Ruben followed her gaze, taking in Bethany and the large man on the big spotted horse as they rode by the house.

"Is that him?" Ruben asked, resigned.

"Him?" Kate replied.

"The one who stole her heart right out from under me."

Kate grinned. "That's him. Liam is his name and he's as head-over-heels for her as she is for him."

"He treat her right?" Ruben glanced over to Kate before returning his gaze out the window.

"He does."

"Guess there's nothing I can say to that. She looks happy. Hope he keeps her that way." Ruben checked his watch. "Break time's up; we'll do one more set since you paused in that last one." Kate gritted her teeth as she turned away from the window, moving back into position. Not quite five minutes later, Ruben said, "Well, that's it for today. I'll see you next week."

Asher waved him out the door, even as he kept an eye on Kate while she slowly ambled into the kitchen for another cup of tea. His cell phone buzzed, alerting him to a text. *Might have found something. Tif and I are headed over.*

He looked to Kate as she approached. "Sammy and Tif are coming over."

"Everything all right?"

Asher kept his voice level. "He said he may have found something."

Kate breathed deeply, slowly. "Just be careful, be safe."

Asher stood, making his way around the table to her side. Gently, he took the mug from her, setting it on the table. Carefully, he wrapped his arms around her, pulling her flush with him. "I will be fine. You know I can take care of myself. You know he's no match for me."

"There's something not right with him, Ash. He's unpredictable. Promise me you won't take any chances."

"I promise I will be all right, and that you and our daughter will be safe. I promise *that*."

Kate laid her head on his chest and squeezed him as tight as she was able. "I love you so much."

"I love you, too." He kissed the top of her head. "And Ruben's right, you are getting stronger. I'm impressed."

Kate chuckled as she pulled back at the sound of a vehicle. Moments later, Tiffy came in. "Hey." She smiled at them, then said to Asher, "He's waiting for you outside."

Asher glanced to the window. Samuel stood beside his SUV and catching Asher's eye, subtly jerked his chin, inviting Asher out with him. Turning back to Kate, Asher reached for her, soundly kissing her before taking his leave. "I'll be back soon."

"You'd better be."

Tiffy joined Kate in the kitchen, pouring herself a cup of tea as well. In silence, they watched as Asher slid into the passenger seat and Samuel put the vehicle in reverse. Kate turned to Tiffy. "Know anything?"

"Probably about as much as you. Samuel said he needed to talk with Ash about something, and that I should come over here and hang out."

Kate exhaled slowly and nodded. "Okay. How's your healing going?"

"I'm fine." Tiffy waved her concern away. "And you look good. Really good. Where's Bethany and Liam?"

"They left to go riding about twenty minutes ago."

"Nice. They getting serious?"

"I think so. I hope so. He's a wonderful man, reminds me quite a lot of Ash, though *he* doesn't like to hear that." She chuckled.

"I can imagine." Tiffy sipped her tea, a grin on her face.

"Have you heard from Reese lately?" Kate asked, thinking of her niece. Tiffy and Kate had several things in common. They'd married spouses who were best friends and they'd both struggled with pregnancy, resulting in them both having one child a piece. First Bethany, then the following year, Theresa, or Reese. "Does she know about the accident?"

"Yeah, we heard from her last week. She says Basic is a breeze thanks to all Samuel's and Asher's training...and no, we haven't told her. There's nothing she can do, and I don't want her distracted with worry over it."

Kate nodded, a far-away look in her eyes. Tiffy sipped her tea, her gaze on her friend, noting the signs of tension, the sallowness of her skin, the tightness around her mouth. "You should sit down. The last thing you need is to reinjure those ribs now that you're getting better." Sighing in agreement, Kate made her way to the living room and carefully sunk into the recliner. Tiffy turned to the kitchen. "What's in the fridge? I'm hungry; I'll make dinner."

Smiling at her friend's thoughtful caring, Kate said, "I'm honestly not sure. Bethany's been doing the shopping. Go ahead and look, I'm good with whatever."

Sounds of doors and cabinets opening and closing could be heard, then, "Oh hey, you guys still have several of those frozen meals Gina prepared in here. Let's see what you've got. Ooh, she made you her Chicken Alfredo. Hers is divine."

"That does sound good. Thanks, Tif."

"Of course. We're in this together, you know. Married to our warrior men; we need to support each other."

Asher-

Some forty minutes later, Samuel turned off Highway 295 a little ways north of Powell, heading west. "Word I got, he was seen out here and rumored to have a camper parked off an old access road."

"Hope you were able to narrow it down some—there's a crap ton of access roads out here," Asher stated.

"My source said he heard it was just past the mile marker after Road 9. We'll be coming up on it shortly."

Soon, they were pulling up to an older, run-down cabover camper somewhat obscured by the heavy brush surrounding it. The camper sat back under a thatch of tall pine and aspen trees. Asher and Samuel sat for a couple minutes just taking things in, studying the layout. Seeing no movement to indicate anyone was around, they got out of the Tahoe and spread out, canvasing the area.

Several minutes later, they met at the door to the camper. "There's a spot just there where a truck's been parked," Samuel stated quietly with a jerk of his chin.

"There's a generator around the back there. Cold." Asher nodded as he pulled a pistol from under his shirt. Samuel moved to the right of the door and did the same. From the left side of the door, Asher firmly knocked. Silence. He then tried the handle. Locked.

"Allow me." Samuel holstered his weapon, then stepped forward, pulling a couple tools from his pocket.

"Think you still got the touch?" Asher teased, even as his eyes continued their surveillance.

"I know I do."

"All right; I'll time you." Asher looked at his watch. "Go."

Samuel got to work. Moments later, he stepped back. "Time."

"Forty-three seconds. You're getting slow in your old age."

Chuckling, Samuel stepped to the right of the door, once more pulling his firearm. "After you."

Keeping to the left, Asher turned the knob, cautiously opening the door, swinging it wide to Samuel. When nothing happened, Samuel nodded, and Asher, holding his firearm chest height and at the ready, did a quick scan of the interior before they went in. It was a small camper, barely enough room for the two of them inside. Bed over the cab, a two-seater table and bench were off to the right. A single-basin sink, counter, and single burner stove were on the left. Asher holstered his weapon, then they looked around, opening cabinets, pulling out drawers, careful to put things back as they'd found them.

"Someone's been here. Clothes in the cupboard. Food still in the fridge, though, by the smell, that might be old," Samuel stated.

Asher studied the interior. "If you lived here and wanted to hide information, where would you look?"

Samuel let his gaze travel the tiny space, speculating as he went. He began checking the ceiling panels, then under the mattress. Meanwhile, Asher lifted the seat cushions, as well as looking under the seats in the storage area. Turning up nothing, he sat at the table and, like Samuel, thoughtfully considered every inch of the camper. Samuel eased down from the bed, careful to keep it looking as it had before. "Might not be his; could simply be bad information."

Asher nodded, still thinking, still looking. Having an idea, he felt under the table. "Bingo." He lifted the table top off the legs and turned it over. What he saw made his blood boil. Pictures were taped to the bottom. Pictures of both Kate and Bethany.

"Don't touch anything," Samuel stated, his voice firm and cautionary. "Let me get pictures first."

Breathing deeply, Asher moved back allowing Samuel access. Once Samuel was done, they put the table back. As they set the top in place, they heard a quiet clicking noise, then a near-silent beeping. "*Son of a...get out, now!*" Scrambling for the door, they jumped from the camper and hit the ground rolling. Within a breath they were up, racing away, diving behind the Tahoe. Seconds later, the cabover exploded, spewing debris and flames into the air. Asher turned to Samuel, breathing hard. "You okay?"

"Yeah." Samuel coughed. "You?"

"Just furious. Little bastard almost had us," Asher snarled. "Find him, Samuel. Your source? Could this have been a setup, or was he just lucky?"

"Anything's possible." Samuel blew out a breath. "We need to call this in."

"We need to get out of here; call it as you're driving. I'm calling Kate." Asher dialed his cell as they climbed in Samuel's rig. Kate answered on the second ring and Asher demanded, "Are you all right?"

"Yes, we're fine." Kate's voice trembled. "Why?"

"Are Bethany and Liam there?"

"They're right here."

"Let me talk with Liam." Asher hated the tremor in Kate's voice. *Hated* it. He never wanted to hear it again.

There was silence, then Liam came on the line. "Liam here."

"We found his camper and evidence he's fixating on Kate and Bethany, but he rigged the place to blow. We've reported the fire and are on our way back. You keep that pistol handy and stay at the house until I'm there."

"Bugger me," Liam breathed. "Aye, I will. Ye all right?"

"We are, and got out in time, though just."

Liam exhaled. "He willna lay a hand on them. Ye have me word."

"I know. Put Kate back on, will ya?"

Moments later, Kate was back on the phone. "Asher, what's going on? What did you find?"

"We found his camper. He had it rigged to blow—we made it out in time, but not before gathering some evidence. I'll tell you more when I get home. The fire department should be on their way. Try not to stress, love. I'll be home soon." They hung up, and Asher looked to Samuel. "We need to get moving; they could be here soon. You kept the call clean?"

"I know how to cover my tracks, Ash. My number wasn't visible."

"I know," Asher said as they reached the end of the access road. "Just double-checking—I'm on edge, is all."

"We both are. We will find him; that I can promise you."

Asher nodded silently, withdrawing into himself, allowing the hunter, the warrior to come to the fore. It had been a long, long time since he'd had to call up this part of himself. Like slipping on a worn, comfortable coat, Asher embraced the change, embraced the violence, and silently howled in anticipation, eager for the hunt, for the kill.

Bethany-

Dad and Uncle Samuel pulled up, their headlights flashing across the living room wall. We waited for them inside. We'd finished eating nearly an hour ago. The kitchen was already cleaned, and I'd been trying to remain calm so as not to stress my mom out. But I couldn't hold back my near silent breath of relief now that they were back. Dad entered first, his gaze taking us all in, lingering over me for a moment before moving on to Mom. He went to her, sat beside her on the couch, and tenderly took her in his arms. "I'm okay, love. I'm home."

Aunt Tiffy waited for Uncle Samuel near the kitchen. He embraced her, holding her close. Liam took my hand in his, raising it, his lips brushing across my knuckles before pulling me closer, knowing my emotions were threatening to get the better of me. Dad pulled away from Mom, then filled us in on what had happened. My heart stuck in my throat at the news that they'd nearly been blown up. My eyes shot to Mom, noting the paleness in her skin. Dad kept his arm around her, comforting her.

Aunt Tiffy and Uncle Samuel left shortly after that, both tired and wanting to be home and together. I understood that. As Dad stood to his feet, helping Mom to hers, announcing he was taking her to bed, I decided I needed some fresh air. "I think we're going to have a bonfire; I'm feeling a little antsy."

Dad looked to me, then Liam, then back again. "Stay close to the house and keep your guard up."

"We will, Dad. We'll just be on the patio." Liam followed me outside. I went directly to the wood pile and began gathering several split logs, then stacked them in the fire pit. After squirting on some starter fluid, I struck a match and tossed it on. The rising flames seemed to release the block on my emotions. A breath shuddered out of me. "I've never been a violent person, Liam. I'm not like my mom or my dad in that regard. At least, I never have been before. But now?" My voice shook. "Now, I'd like to find this Johnny Khyle person and do him some serious damage. Like, enough damage to make him never want to even *think* about my family again." I turned to face Liam. "Does that make me a terrible person? Does that bother you?"

Liam was standing beside one of the chairs surrounding the fire pit. His arms were crossed and he'd remained a steadfast silent presence while I worked through what was bothering me. As I finished speaking, he uncrossed his arms and came to me, stopping a hairsbreadth away. I could feel the heat from the fire on one side and heat from Liam on the other. "Nae, lass." He slipped his hands to my hips, gripping me there. "Nae, ye're no' a terrible person. For if ye are, then so am I. If the wee bastard were here right now, I'd bash him fair. And I probably wouldna' stop until he was dead. Does that make me a terrible person?"

The fire snapped and popped; the smoke a comforting aroma on the cool evening air. Logs settled sending up sparks, and nearby crickets chirped a soft lullaby. I shook my head, tears gathering in my eyes. I blinked them away and took a slow, deep breath. Liam lifted his hands to my face, thumbs under my chin, gently pushing upward, bringing my mouth closer to him. His lips brushed mine before pulling back. "There are three things I need ye to ken. First," he kissed my right cheek, letting his Scotts accent out a bit more, "ken that I love ye—verra much. Second," he kissed my left cheek, "I want to marry ye and have every intention of making that a reality." He brushed his lips against mine. Once, twice. His grip tightened as he pulled back. His voice came out low and guttural now. "And third, I willna' let ye or yer family come to harm."

I stared up into his deep blue eyes, almost mesmerized by the naked sentiment I saw there. "You want to marry me?"

"Ye ken that I do." Unable to hold back the smile, I grinned up at him. "Though, just to be clear, this is no' me askin' ye. I've summat planned, never fear on that. Just ken that it's summat I fervently desire. Ye're summat, some*one* I fervently desire."

Exhaling, I said, "When you do get around to asking...I hope you know that my answer—" He placed a finger across my mouth, forestalling any further words.

"Shhh. Keep yer answer for now. Let me wait and anticipate it, and dream of it, and hope for it."

"Okay."

Liam nodded, then pulled me close, holding me to him. Softly, he hummed a tune in my ear and slowly began to sway, moving us from side to side. "I can wait for ye. Though, it's near to killin' me—the wait is an exquisite torture." That had me chuckling and snuggling closer to him. "Ye and me, lass. I believe with all me heart, we were written in the deep dark between the stars. Ye were made for me, and I was made for ye. I willna' rush this. I want to savor each moment. I want to relish everythin' about ye, down to the last detail."

We swayed there under the stars, beside the fire, and simply breathed together, cherishing the moment. The peace. The solitude.

CHAPTER FIFTEEN

Cat and Mouse

Johnny-

Johnny crested the ridge in his old pickup, having driven nearly up to Elk Basin and was on his way back. As he cleared the tree line, he saw the thick, black smoke rising from the southwest. Almost in the general vicinity of where he'd stashed his camper. Thoughtfully, he continued driving, wondering at that smoke. About three miles from the turnoff, he was passed by forestry service fire trucks. Johnny sped up, not fast enough to draw undue notice, but faster than he'd been going.

As he neared the turn off, he kept his eyes peeled for anything out of the ordinary. Seeing nothing, he continued to his trailer. When he was close to 500 feet from his hideaway, he pulled his truck to the side of the road and turned his lights off. Where his trailer had been, was nothing more than charred rubble and flaming trees. His camper had blown up. Which meant someone had been here, had discovered his obsession. Johnny's heart slammed against his ribcage as he stared around himself, searching for the telltale size of Asher Fitzpatrick in the shadowy figures moving around the smoldering remains.

Feeling rather like a mouse being stalked by the cat, Johnny shifted into reverse, swinging the truck around. He put it in drive and floored it as he flicked his lights back on. His heart was racing. Where could he go? He had no one left here. No one to turn to for aid. No friends. His mother had passed away while he'd been locked up—another thing that stupid, uppity witch had stolen from him. And his dad had split a long time ago, worthless drunk that he was.

Texas. He'd go to Texas. Lee, his cellmate, said he had family outside Houston that would take him in. For a price. But still, it was a place to go. A place where Fitzpatrick wouldn't find him. Decision made, Johnny headed for Highway 120 and Texas.

Lucas-

On a balmy Tuesday morning in the Bayou, Lucas Espinosa, known to a select few as El Gato, lit a cigarette and cast his line out. Settling back against the piling, he adjusted his ballcap, pulling it lower on his brow. He slapped at a mosquito as he patiently waited, his keen eye on the line he tactically reeled back in. Another cast, still more careful luring. Suddenly, Lucas' line jerked hard. "Got one," he breathed as he set the hook and began to reel in the fighting fish. His phone buzzed just then, alerting him to an incoming text.

"27 years ago, your life was saved." The text read. "Your debt is being called in. Find him. Then make sure no one ever does again." A photograph and name came in next. Lucas stared at his screen, his mind racing. Only a handful of people had this number. Literally; he could count them on one hand. He hadn't heard from any of those that did in ages. Not since...not since Hollywood had pulled him from the rubble of that burning building and literally carried his near-lifeless body to safety. He'd never caught Hollywood's real name. Just remembered that he was huge and that he'd saved Lucas' life. The other man, the one covering their retreat, he only knew as The Man. Real names weren't that important. Not really. Not in the line of work these guys had been in. Shady stuff, that. Sometimes, the less you knew, the better. He was sure if he checked this number, it would already be disconnected. A burner under a bogus name.

Lucas was pulled from his thoughts as his pole gave another jerk, then went still. Reeling the line all the way in, he frowned at the empty lure. Shaking his head, he laid his pole down on the dock and opened the text again. "27 years ago." It had to be one of the two of them. Regardless, he owed them his life. And Lucas had zero qualms about what was being requested.

He stared at the image, committing it to memory, as well as the name. Then he deleted the text. Taking a deep drag on the cigarette, he considered his prey. "Well, little mouse, I don't know what you've done, but it must have been bad if they're calling in *my* debt. No need to worry, El Gato is on the hunt, and I never miss. And besides, you cost me a fish, little mouse. I don't take too kindly to that."

Bethany-

Liam stuck to me like glue all through the following week. I didn't mind; I was still feeling somewhat rattled and his steady presence settled me. We were riding up into some of the higher country, looking for strays. I rode Wick, and he was on Lincoln, one of the ranch horses. We'd just found six head of cattle and had turned them back down the mountain towards the herd, when Liam said, "Wick. What's that in reference to then? A candlewick?"

Chuckling, I replied, "No, for John Wick—the movie character."

"Aye, who's he then?"

"You don't know who John Wick is?" I turned to him, shocked.

"Canna say as I do; name's no' ringing a bell at least."

I grinned. "We'll just have to fix that then, won't we?"

"If ye say so, lass."

We finished with those cows, getting them settled in with the herd, then headed for home. A car was driving away as we rode up, and I recognized

Ruben as he waved from the driver's seat. Liam helped me finish the afternoon feeding, then we headed inside to see what I could make for dinner.

After we'd eaten, I made him sit down and watch John Wick with me. A couple times, I caught him glancing at me in a particularly violent part. When the movie was over, I looked at him expectantly.

"Earlier, ye'd mentioned that ye dinna figure yerself as a violent person, but ye named yer horse after this fella? Lass, I think ye take after yer father, and yer mother for that matter, more than ye might realize."

"Worried now?" I quirked a brow.

"No' in the least."

"Good." I smiled. "I was hoping I hadn't scared you off."

"If yer parents dinna scare me off, there's no' much chance that anythin' else will, ye ken?"

Grinning, I stood. "We'd probably best get to bed. Our first guests since the accident are due to arrive tomorrow morning. Two families. They'll stay in the cabins. You sure you're ready for this? We have a bit more going on here than Nana and Granda did."

"As I intend our connection to be that of a permanent nature, I'd best get used to it, now hadna' I?"

Taking a deep breath, I asked the question that had been on my mind for some time now. "What *are* your plans, exactly? I mean, I know and believe you that you want to marry me, but what comes after? Where would you intend to live?"

Liam took my hands in his, raising them to kiss along my knuckles. "I've told ye that me da and I have had a rough time. He always figured me for takin' after him and becoming an attorney. I tried it; I did. Just wasna' in me blood, ye ken? Working the land, working wi' me hands, that's what I've longed to do. I took every job I could find that got me outdoors. Farm work. Labor work. Anythin'.

"So, as ye have a ranch, and I dinna figure ye as one to want to quit that line of work, I figured we'd be here. Make trips back, o'course, but here is where I intended to be. Wi' ye. Always, doin' whatever wi' ye."

My breath trembled. "Will your family hate me for taking you away from them?"

He pursed his lips, then scratched at his jaw. "Ach, they might begrudge me some, but they'll come 'round. Ma kens. Aboot ye, I mean. She kens me intentions. And is happy for me. For us. Havna' told Da yet. He's a cantankerous one, to be sure, but once I tell him, Ma will help me set him straight," Liam assured me.

"If you're certain. I don't want to cause any difficulties in your family." I shook my head slowly, hating the thought of causing trouble for him.

"Ken this: yer no' causin' any difficulties. Other than trying me patience and nearly drivin' me to distraction. I've wanted ye for too long, thinkin' I'd never have ye. Now yer here, wi' me...seems all me dreams are comin' true. I couldna ask for more and that's the truth of it." Liam kissed me. A slow, gentle pressure of his mouth over mine. Those strong hands of his released mine and made their way to the back of my skull, threading through my hair, pulling me closer. I lost track of time, my only focal point Liam's touch. After some time, he pulled back, a tender look in his eye. "Yer da was just here, pokin' his head into the room. I suppose I should let ye go, afore he returns and decides to take exception to me adoration of ye."

Chuckling under my breath, I glanced to Mom's closed door, then back to Liam. "Goodnight."

"Goodnight. Sweet dreams to ye."

By noon the next day, both new families had arrived. One from California, down near the San Diego area, the other from just outside of DC. After getting them settled into their cabins, Liam and I took them on a walking tour of the ranch, going over some of the ranch amenities with them. Both families signed up for riding lessons the following day, with a planned trail ride the day after. With Liam and myself, that would be eleven riders in all, so I spent the remainder of the afternoon working through my remuda, making sure I had plenty of horses to choose from for my riders and their varying levels of experience.

The Garcias were a family of four: Joe and Mary, and their two children, twelve-year-old Robert, and fifteen-year-old Rebecca. They lived in Encinitas, just outside San Diego. Joe and Mary had been taking their children state by state each year, picking one or two things to do in each state they visited. As Wyoming was known as The Cowboy state, they'd decided that a dude ranch was just the thing.

The Zhang family were from Alexandria, Virginia, just outside of Washington DC. Han and Samantha had three children. Six-year-old Kai, ten-year-old Jimmy, and fourteen-year-old Hana. Hana was a very attentive older sister and seemed to have a patience with her younger brothers that I knew would come in handy as she continued to grow and experience more of the world. All in all, these families seemed a great addition to our clientele, and I couldn't wait to get them all on horses tomorrow. One of my favorite things is seeing the kids' excitement. It's the most precious thing.

Jack and Delaney came by later in the afternoon to help with the horses. Liam and I had rounded up twenty from the back pasture, and I'd ridden six of them by the time Del and Jack had arrived. Though Liam himself wasn't experienced with horses, he wanted to help. So, as I finished with each horse, I had him untack and groom the animal before putting it in the large arena to await the lessons tomorrow.

"You're not going to believe it, but brother dearest indicated he might see if his old summer job was still available," Delaney said as she entered the arena and selected a horse.

"Seriously?" I pulled the horse I was riding to a stop and faced her.

"As a heart attack. I told him not to even think about it, but he seemed under the impression that everything would be *cool*." Del made quotation marks around that last word as she rolled her eyes.

"I...I don't even know how to respond to that." I shook my head in bewilderment. "How can he be so dense?"

She offered an exaggerated shrug. "One too many dumps off a horse if you ask me."

Jack swung onto the dapple-grey gelding he'd picked and laughed as the horse bunny-hopped across the pen. Apparently feeling his oats, Jack swiped off his ballcap and proceeded to fan the horse, encouraging the bucking. "Such a child," I breathed at his antics.

Pulling the gelding up, Jack flashed a smile at me, apparently hearing my comment. "Am not. Just figured as he was game for it, it's best Teddy has his fit now than when someone else is on him."

"True," I said, once more putting Bear into motion. "Just make sure you work it all out of him before you head out."

"Will do, boss." Jack grinned. Rolling my eyes, I remained quiet and continued working Bear. It took us another solid two hours to get the rest of the horses ridden. Aunt Gina rang the dinner bell from the back patio, alerting us to the time. She and Uncle Cal had arrived yesterday afternoon, so he could get a head start on the farrier work. I pulled Mandy, the strawberry roan mare I'd been working to a stop, then dismounted. Liam made his way over to me. "No' sure I've said it afore, I recall that other bloke has, but yer a bonnie sight when yer ridin'."

Blushing from his simple, honest statement, I patted Mandy's neck. "Thank you."

He shot me a heated look. "I can assure ye, the pleasure's all mine."

Shaking my head, grinning, I made my way to the gate, noticing the two families that were ranged outside the fence and had been watching us. I tend to get focused on my work and simply didn't see them arrive. "You guys getting excited for tomorrow?"

After being enthusiastically assured that they were, I encouraged them to head up to the house for dinner. As they went, Liam, Jack, and Del followed me to the barn to help with the feeding and to put the tack away. Once the animals were fed, we lingered outside the barn, talking over the afternoon's events.

"Might want to give Teddy another day or so. Unless you have a seriously experienced rider." Jack draped an arm across Delaney's shoulder, tenderly tugging her closer.

"Agreed," Del said. "Though Chief, Rojo, Dean, and Sam all seemed sound."

"Did you have any problems with them?" I asked Liam.

"Nae, none. Yer horses all seem well-trained."

"That's good. Well, you guys staying for dinner; I know your mom made enough to feed an army."

"Nah, I already told them, I'm taking Del out. See you tomorrow for the lessons?"

"Sounds good. See you guys at ten."

I woke earlier than normal, wanting to get a head start on the day. Liam found me in the barn, going through the tack, making sure the saddles and bridles were all in good shape.

"Yer up a might earlier this morning. Ye worrie't on the day?" He placed a soft kiss against my temple.

"No, not worried. Just want to be prepared is all. It's been a while since I did a lesson, and I don't want to forget anything or be rusty in any way." Liam helped me with the morning feeding, then helped me catch and brush the horses we might use today. "I was thinking," I said, watching a barn cat as she stalked one of the plethora of mice we had on the place. "You should pick a horse for yourself."

"Pick a horse for meself?"

"Yeah," I nodded, "you'll need your own mount if you're going to be working here."

"Really?"

"Truly." I indicated the waiting horses. "Any that catch your fancy?"

Liam scratched his chin and gave the herd a brief once over. Suddenly he spun, catching me off guard. His arms slipped around my waist as his mouth found mine. He walked me backward until my back came up against a wall. Once there, he lifted me, hands under my thighs, holding me to him. "Aye, I've found one that catches me fancy. Catches me everything, she does."

His comment had me giggling, but it came out far too breathlessly for him to find any humor in it. After several long, enjoyable moments, he lowered my feet back to the floor. Then, placing one more kiss on my swollen lips, he pulled back, a somewhat satisfied gleam in his dark blue eyes. Taking as deep a breath as I was able, considering my still pounding heart, I said, "So, about the horse?"

Chuckling, Liam took my hand in his, then turned once more to the animals. His gaze touched each one individually, before finally landing on a tall chestnut gelding with a blaze down his face and four white socks. "How's that one?" He nodded at the horse in question.

"Lincoln?" Liam had ridden him several times before and they seemed to get along well. I'd have picked him as a mount for Liam, but hadn't mentioned it as I'd wanted Liam to choose his own. The gelding was certainly the right height for Liam's tall frame. "I think Lincoln's fine. He's a good choice. So, from here on out, while you're here, consider Lincoln your horse."

"I've never had a horse of me own afore. I dinna ken what to say. I mean, thank ye, lass. Truly."

"You're absolutely welcome." I grinned up at him, glad he was pleased.

Jack and Del pulled up as we finished brushing the horses. As they made their way to the barn, the Garcias and the Zhangs began trickling to the arena.

"Good morning," I greeted everyone, looking them over to make sure they all wore appropriate gear. "Hope you all had a great first night." I ascertained if any of them had ridden horses before, and found that of the lot, only Hana had previously had lessons. She'd ridden English, so Western would be something of a refresher course for her. They were similar practices, but their application was different.

Once I was finished determining who would ride which horse, I had Liam, Jack, and Del help me get the horses saddled, with my students watching and even assisting in the process. After that was finished, I had them lead their mounts out to the riding arena. The first thing I cover with any group is safety. The rider needs to respect the horse and understand it is an animal, not a machine. They have minds of their own, fears and confusions of their own, and we need to work with them, not against them. I was just going over mounting the horse, when I heard wheels on gravel. Glancing to the driveway, I did a doubletake and shook my head. I so didn't need this right now. Garrett couldn't have picked a worse time.

CHAPTER SIXTEEN
No Time for Trouble

Bethany-

Gritting my teeth, I watched as he swaggered up to the gate, waiting for me to come to him. I thought about simply ignoring him, but knew I'd better deal with this now before he decided to make a spectacle of himself. "Excuse me, folks; I need to take care of something real quick. Del? Jack? Could you guys take over for a bit?" Glaring at Garrett, I headed in his direction.

"Hello, gorgeous." Garrett let his eyes travel over me and I suddenly wanted to be violent. Maybe it was leftover emotion from the whole Johnny thing, but I was seeing red.

"What are you doing here, Garrett?" Anger filled my tone, then I felt a presence beside me. Liam stepped forward, reaching around me, opening the gate, forcing Garrett to step back.

"I see you finally found some pants." Irritation flashed in Garrett's eyes at Liam's approach. Liam let a smile slowly spread across his face.

"I asked you a question." I pulled Garrett's attention back to me. "We broke up. You don't work here anymore."

"Don't be like that, Bethany. Look, can we just talk? *Privately?*"

"I have nothing to say to you. I'm in the middle of a class that you're interrupting, and I don't want you here."

"I'm sorry, all right?" Garrett's voice rose with his aggravation. "Is that what you need to hear? I messed up. I thought I was over you, but I'm not. We can work things out. Just give me another chance."

Before I could respond, Liam said, "I believe she's asked ye to leave. If she has to ask again, I'm going to be cross wi' ye. And ye dinna want that, lad. It's best ye go."

"You need to shut your stupid face and freaking butt out. This is between me and my girlfriend, not some Braveheart wannabe."

"Ex, Garrett. Ex-girlfriend. Liam is who I'm with. He's my future; not you. I'm sure I don't need to show you the way off the ranch, I'm done here." I turned to walk away and felt a sharp tug on my shirt, jerking me to a stop. Almost instantaneously, I heard bone meeting flesh and spun back around to see Garrett on his butt, blood smeared on his lips. With a roar, he surged from the ground and swung at Liam. In a flurry of movements, Liam landed half a dozen more hits, sending Garrett to the ground once more. Garrett lay there, seemingly dazed, blinking his eyes, and trying to breathe.

Liam leaned over him, taking him firmly by the jaw. "That's twice I've had ye down. Dinna make me do it again. Yer sister's worrie't aboot ye already, dinna make it worse for her. I'm no' one to lay claim to a lass as if she's property. And Bethany's her own woman and can make up her own mind, but I'll tell ye this now. She's said she's mine and lad, I *always* protect what's mine, ye ken? Now, get on yer feet, and leave, and dinna be botherin' her again." Liam moved back to my side, angling himself in case Garrett decided to be more stupid than he'd already been.

Silently, Garrett rolled to his knees; he spit blood onto the dirt, then climbed to his feet. Without a further look at the rest of us, he made his way to his truck and drove away. Blowing out a breath, I leaned into Liam and felt his arms come around me. "Are you all right?" I whispered against his chest.

"Aye. It's sorry I am, if that caused ye any embarrassment; I couldna' allow him to manhandle ye like that."

"No, it's fine. What happened anyway?"

"He grabbed for ye, tried to stop ye. When I moved to stop him, the bloody gobshite took a swing at me."

Shaking my head, I leaned up and kissed him. "Thank you." We turned back to my waiting class; I apologized to them, and by the grace of the Almighty, the rest of the session went without a hitch.

After the class was over and my students had left the arena, Delaney came and wrapped her arms around me. "I'm so sorry, Bethany. I don't know what's gotten into him."

"Not your fault, Del. Garrett's his own man and has to face the consequences of his own choices."

"I know, but still. I'm sorry he came here and then tried to start a fight with you and Liam."

"Well, hopefully, he's learned his lesson and that's the last I'll hear from him."

"Hopefully."

"Say, you handled yourself pretty well there," Jack said to Liam as we put the tack away.

"He was nothing," Liam assured. "Nae challenge. And besides, it's her da who trained me."

"Garrett's lucky you didn't kill him," Delaney whispered, looking a little pale.

"I wouldna have killed the lad. Though, if he hadna quit when he did, I'd have had to hurt him worse and wouldna have liked ye, nor the bairns, to have seen that."

"Bairns?" Jack questioned.

"Kids, babies, youngins'," I replied.

"Ah." Jack nodded. "Well, will you need us for the trail ride tomorrow?"

"Don't know about need, but you're welcome to join us. The more, the merrier."

"What time are you headed out?"

"The ride should start at ten and be finished by noon. Nothing too strenuous. I'm only taking them just past the Jump Off, then up to the Valley and back down. I know we've had that elk herd hanging around; thought the group might like to see them if they're about."

"Sounds good. See you then."

Lucas-

Lucas Espinosa sat in a restaurant in downtown Houston, a steak and baked potato on the plate in front of him, but his focus was on his phone rather than his food. For information, he'd turned to the Underground, knowing eventually the data on his prey would pop up. He'd been on the trail for the last two weeks, ferreting out little bits and pieces, getting a clearer picture of the man he hunted. What his routines were, what his reactions might be to any given situation. "Soon, el ratòn, soon we will meet. Then you'll squeak no more."

Momentarily, he set his phone aside and tucked into the meal. Taking his time, he pondered the man he hunted. He'd heard rumors. Rumors, he knew, tended to have some truth to them. If you knew what to look for. Word out, was that el ratòn had attacked Hollywood's wife and daughter. Had not only attacked them, but held them in continued peril. Lucas didn't hold with men so impotent in honor they'd harm those weaker than them, prey on them to make themselves feel powerful. He didn't hold with those kind of men at all. Something was defective within them. Whatever trauma from their past, they never rose above it, never recovered from it. He'd seen it before and it had always turned his stomach.

Even if it wasn't Hollywood he owed his life to, he'd have been tempted to rid the world of trash like this. Maybe the Almighty could turn this man around. Lucas didn't understand the workings of the mind of the Almighty, but he knew his own mind and heart, and felt, if the Almighty wanted this man to live, He'd have to stop El Gato Himself. Otherwise, el ratòn's days were numbered and that number was fast dwindling.

Lucas' phone vibrated with an incoming text. Picking it up, he read the information and grinned. "There you are, little mouse."

Bethany-

I pulled Wick to a stop at the Jump Off and turned to survey my riders. "Everyone doing all right?" At their answered affirmations, I said, "We're going to do some mild climbing now; I'm taking you guys into one of our upper valleys. We've had an elk herd hanging around and they tend to be there—you should be able to get some great pictures. Quick tip about hills, your horse's sense of balance is in their shoulders—so when going uphill, lean somewhat forward over those shoulders and when coming back down, settle deeper into your seat and lean back somewhat more on their hips." I demonstrated the motions I meant and had them try them out.

"Good, good. You guys are doing great. These are mountain horses. They're surefooted and know their business. When going downhill, try not to pull the reins back tight, as it tends to cut off their breath, okay?" Again, everyone nodded. I looked to Liam, who flashed me a grin designed to make me blush. Shaking my head, I said, "Let's go."

I took the lead, with the Garcia family coming in behind me, then Liam, then the younger Zhang kids, Delaney, the rest of the Zhang family, and finally Jack pulling drag. I kept our pace slow and steady, pointing out different sights, both landscape and animals. At one point, we came to a stop as a small herd of Bighorn sheep crossed our trail. Little Kai and Jimmy were nearly beside themselves. We waited until the herd had passed on and everyone had snapped a couple pictures. Han said he'd been able to get a great shot with the sheep in the background and the rest of our group in foreground. I was happy everyone was enjoying themselves.

We moved on and made it to the Valley about twenty minutes later. As we entered the tall grasses, I spied the elk herd on the north face of the meadow and brought our group to a stop, spreading out, but not getting too close. The herd, having spotted us, were on alert. With heads up, gauging whether we were friend or foe, they made a lovely picture. We stayed there for several minutes, just meandering around before heading back. At the Jump Off, we stopped to take group and individual pictures. It was beautiful there, with the ranch, the house and barns, and the mountains in the background.

As we rode into the ranch yard, headed for the barn, I spied Mom sitting on the porch. *She must be feeling a lot better.* Dad stepped out as we rode by, offering us a wave. I wondered how much she'd had to push him to allow her outside. The thought made me grin. Mom could be quite persuasive, and let's face it, Dad was a softie when it came to my mother. I spared Liam a glance as we dismounted and assisted the others in doing the same, and hoped I'd found the one who would love me the way Dad loved Mom. I thought I had, but I'd thought that before; only time would tell.

That week went by fast. I'd ended up taking the families on two more trail rides, and Rebecca and Hana assisted me, Liam, Del, and Jack to move some cows from one pasture to another. We made sure they were properly outfitted with hats, vests, and chaps, and of course took pictures for them. At the end of the week, both families enthusiastically assured us that they'd be back, and would be leaving excellent reviews. This was welcome news.

One week seemed to roll into another. Mom was getting stronger. Her cast came off and she no longer had to wear the sling. She was still somewhat weakened, but she was able to climb the stairs to her own room now. This freed up the downstairs guest rooms, and soon we were bustling with incoming guests. We had three groups of college students, interspersed with families and couples, even some singles. Summer was nearly over, and as I waved off the last group, considered all we needed to do to prepare for winter. We needed hay. Uncle Cal and Jack would need to come take shoes off the remuda in the next month. It would start to slow down as far as the guests went, but the winter preparations would kick in and there'd still be plenty to do.

I headed to the barn, wanting to get an idea as to what tack would need the most repairs, and what should just be replaced. I flicked on the tack room light and decided to start with the saddles. Liam had said he'd had a couple phone calls to make before joining me out here. He'd been a constant, always at my side. Never balking at any task given him. He'd been a partner, working alongside me no matter what. I chuckled under my breath, when I recalled last month when he'd had to help me pull those twin calves out on the range.

He'd gone quite green as he'd watched me with my hands buried in the cow's birth canal, trying to push one calf back so the other could be born. But he'd stayed. And he hadn't passed out. Man was made of steel. He was one to ride the river with, as the saying went, and I found myself eternally grateful the Lord above had chosen to place us together. I was inspecting the fifth saddle when a noise from behind had me spinning. Liam leaned against the doorjamb, thumbs hooked in his belt loops.

"You startled me; how long have you been standing there?"

His look was measured. "Long enough to make certain I was in control and no' aboot to ravish ye."

"I see." I grinned, heat staining my cheeks under his regard. "I also see you're still over there."

"Still havena' decided on tha' control."

"Hmm." I swallowed. "And what brought this on?"

"I've been like this since I first laid eyes on ye, lass. Didna' recognize it for what it was then. But I surely do now. Especially as I've had ye in my arms, had my mouth on yers, had yer body pressed to mine." He took a deep breath. "And I want that wi' ye now, that, and much, much more."

My heart raced in my chest and I felt a longing flair inside me. Potent. Demanding. "We should...we should..." I trailed off as he stepped in my direction.

"Aye, we should." He was closer now, moving closer still. "But I'm past tha' point right now. I need ye, lass." He said that last part against my neck, his voice a growl and a plea all wrapped in one. His arms were steel bars folded around me, lifting me. Somehow, I ended up perched on the saddle I'd been going over. One hand tangled in my hair, the other found its way to my thigh, lifting it, fitting it around himself. He leaned into me, over me, claiming every part of me. Every part of my focus and attention. In that moment, I needed him as much as he needed me. It was all-consuming. All-demanding.

My arms were around him, his neck, pulling him closer, needing him closer. Needing that contact, that touch.

"Liam," a voice said from over his shoulder, "I really, really like you, but if her father sees the two of you like this, you're going to be in a world of hurt." Like ice cold water splashing on us, we jumped, panting, hearts racing at the sound of my *mother's* voice coming from the tack room doorway.

"Omgosh, Mom!" I quickly straightened up as Liam released me. He moved away, and I righted myself as much as I was able. "What are you doing out here?"

"Well, we were looking for you two. Dad wants to go into town to eat. Get out of the house," she stated, humored warning clear in her tone. "Be glad I found you and not him."

I breathed a silent sigh of relief, knowing this was as much scolding as she planned to issue, and glanced at Liam. He was faced away from us, leaning over the bench on the back wall. Hands braced along its ledge; tension clearly visible in his frame.

"I'll leave you two to calm down; when you're ready, meet us at the house." She paused as she turned to leave. "This tack room has sure seen its fair share of passion—I have *fond* memories of your dad and I and that bench..." She trailed off, a faraway look in her eyes as she smiled a secret smile.

My mouth dropped. *What?* I didn't even want to think about that statement. She shot a conspiratorial grin at me as she walked away. "I *so* didn't need to know that." I whispered, watching her disappear around the corner. I looked to Liam. "You okay?" His shoulders began to shake. "Liam?"

Straightening, he turned to me, hand over his heart, manic laughter in his voice. "She clean stopped me heart in me chest. I thought I was a dead man for sure. Then she walks away, calm as ye please, after laying tha' statement on us."

Nervous laughter bubbled up, overflowing in giggles I couldn't contain. We laughed until tears ran down our faces. Wiping his eyes, Liam said, "Yer worth it, ye ken? Dying. Being harmed for ye. Yer worth it and more."

Johnny-

Johnny Khyle sighed mentally and ground his teeth together, trying to remain calm. He'd found Lee's family, but their willingness to take him in was proving difficult. He was low on funds and the price they were demanding was greater than he currently had on him. "Look, I'll get the rest, just give me a couple days to come up with it."

"Come back when you have it. We ain't no charity house," the old woman snarled before slamming the door firmly in his face. Swearing under his breath, Johnny swung around and glared into the yard before heading for the rickety gate and out to the street where his truck was parked. He needed cash, and fast. He knew how to get it. Houston had an underbelly same as any other city. He'd find some working girls, get a little, then take the cash they were sure to have on them. And if a pimp stepped in, well, Johnny would take care of him as well. It was no skin off his back.

CHAPTER SEVENTEEN

Every Beat of my Heart

Bethany-

I saddled my last horse of the day and thought of Delany's text from earlier this morning. Garrett had left again, headed back to SoCal. I was relieved to hear this, and honestly wished him well, despite how things ended between us. The young mare waited patiently as I tightened the girth and checked the stirrups before mounting. Liam, astride Lincoln, waited for me near the gate. We'd ride out to the upper valley, check that herd of cows we took there a couple weeks back and see if they needed moving again. In four days, Delaney, Jack, Liam, and I would fly to Ireland. We'd stay with my grandparents for a few days before flying to Scotland to meet Liam's family. I was a little nervous and hoped they would approve of me. Especially his father. I knew relations between them were already tense and didn't want my presence to exasperate things.

While there, Liam planned to take us to a Highland game, and I couldn't wait for that experience. As Liam's riding skills had improved greatly, and as we had no one else with us, we made good time, allowing the horses to move swiftly, often breaking into a gallop. We reached the valley in just under forty-five minutes and pulled the horses to a stop as we looked the area over. Grass was getting low; we'd need to move them. Counting quickly, I tallied sixty-three head. "We're missing one," I said as I walked the mare into the meadow.

Liam moved Lincoln beside me as I began to meander around the small valley, looking for signs of the missing cow. Cattle can be funny critters. Most often they'll stay with the herd, but occasionally, one would get a wild hair and separate. Towards the north end, where the elk had been last month, I saw a game trail leading into the trees. Following it, I kept my eyes and ears open. After fifteen minutes, the mare suddenly became nervous, shying and not wanting to go any further. Blowing out a breath, I loosened the rifle in my saddle scabbard.

Whatever it was she was smelling, the mare was having none of it. Carefully, so as not to spook her, I dismounted. "Here, Liam, take her. I'm going to check it out."

"Bethany, lass, maybe I should go wi' ye?"

I shook my head. "Horses are spooked as it is, and I don't want to find myself walking home in the dark. Just stay with them; I'm armed." I held up the rifle in reminder. "I'll be all right."

I could see he wasn't pleased, nor reassured, but he grumbled in warning, "Ach, just be careful."

"I will. Hang tight and keep your eyes open and your sidearm ready."

Moving softly, I continued up the trail. Not much further on, maybe thirty feet or so, I caught the sickly-sweet scent of decay. "Dangit," I whispered under my breath. The stench worsened as I continued on. About thirty yards up that trail, the smell was so bad I was near to gagging, and took the bandana from around my neck, pressing it to my nose. A dozen feet or so off the trail, to the right, I found the missing cow. Or what was left of her. Looked like a cat had got her—the carcass was partially buried. Wasn't much to be done at this point. I took a screenshot of her ear tag, then did a careful search of the area, not wanting to be ambushed by the cat attempting to defend her poaching, before heading back to Liam and the horses.

Liam-

Liam swallowed his heart back down his throat and prayed that the woman who owned said organ would be safe. He waited, counting down the seconds until she returned. Every sound, every twitch of the horses, every rustle of leaves had him looking around. The silence became deafening. His nerves and patience fraying with each heartbeat she was gone. He'd considered defying her directive to stay put, guarding the horses and going after her. There was logic in what she said, as far as not wanting the horses to spook. But he couldn't get the anxious feeling out from under his skin when he remembered Asher's instruction to stay close to her at all times. What if this was that Johnny guy's plot coming to fruition? What if she was in danger and needed assistance? He'd nearly talked himself into dismounting, when he saw her coming back down the trail, and honest-to-God, felt lightheaded. Silently, he thanked the Almighty for her safe return.

Bethany-

I saw Liam's relieved exhale at my approach and told him about the carcass and my guess that it had been a mountain lion that got her. I mounted, keeping that rifle in hand and we headed back down to the herd. We got them moving and kept them going until we reached the lower pastures. By the time we reached the barn, the sun had set. Jack and Delaney were just saddling horses when we rode into the yard.

"We're here," I called to them, figuring they were headed out to look for us. "We ended up moving that herd to the lower pasture. We lost one. Cat, as far as I can tell. North of the upper valley," I said as we dismounted.

"Your dad was getting worried," Jack said.

"Sorry about that—cell service is awful up there. I'll speak with him. Your dad and the crew coming in next week will need to keep an eye on that animal, make sure it doesn't range lower."

Nodding, he said, "Go on in. Let him know you're okay. Del and I will take care of the horses."

"Thanks, guys." Liam and I headed for the house and with every breath I took, I prayed nothing would delay our upcoming trip.

Johnny-

The woman whimpered in the corner, holding a bag of ice to her lip. She glared through streaming eyes at Johnny as he slowly counted out her earnings for the night. The look on her face clearly expressed her desire that he'd die. That he'd just drop dead. Johnny Khyle pocketed the money, still short three hundred dollars, and turned to her. "You going to keep your mouth shut?"

She nodded, sniffling. He looked her over, taking in the blond hair, the short red dress that left nothing to the imagination, the bruise, even now spreading across her cheek. A woman should leave something to the imagination. *She* wasn't like this. She gave his imagination plenty of room to play, and he liked to play. He preferred the blond ones—though, he was sure this one wasn't a real blond. Not that it really mattered. This blonde wasn't actually *her,* he just liked to pretend. And he had pretended. He'd even called the woman by *her* name. Somehow, it made his excitement stronger. He looked her over again, wondering if he'd have that same euphoric feeling if he had her one last time. Maybe. Maybe not. Either way, she'd squeal as soon as he was gone, and he didn't need police sniffing after him. No, it was better to silence her now than leave that door open. He'd silence her and get more satisfaction. He'd make her beg, make believe *she* was begging him, then he'd silence her. Permanently.

"Come here," he said, standing up from the bed where he'd been sitting. "I'm not finished with you yet." He kept his voice level, barely concealing the cold, twisted nature of his soul. "Remember how to do it? Good, now don't disappoint me."

The look in his eyes caused the woman to tremble, even as she rose to do his bidding.

Bethany-

The four of us piled off the Aer Lingus jet, carry-ons in hand and made our way to customs, exhausted and yet excited all at the same time. After getting our passports stamped and we'd been cleared to proceed, we found the nearest ATM and quickly exchanged currency, then caught the next shuttle to the car rental agency. Liam had rented a car for the trip; we wouldn't all fit in Granda's little car, nor even Sean's.

Once we had our luggage stowed in the trunk, or the boot I explained to Jake and Delaney, as it was called here, we piled into the tiny SUV and were on the road to Kealkill. I was eager to see my grandparents, having missed them fiercely. Along the way, we made multiple stops because either Del or Jack saw something they just *had* to get a picture of. Each time we did, I couldn't help but smile with affection at the eager antics of my two best friends. It was a dream come true having them here with me. When Liam had first broached the subject of making a trip back, Mom and Dad had exchanged a look, making me wonder what they thought of the idea. As if he knew their upspoken concerns, Liam continued, adding that he hoped Jack and Delaney would be able to join us.

Hearing we'd not be going alone, had my parents warming to the idea. And soon, we were in full planning mode, making last minute reservations and purchasing our airline tickets. I was beyond excited, my trip having been cut short last time. Mom was doing so much better. Still not one hundred percent, but even so, she was much, much better, and improving more and more every day. We'd been able to hire a summer crew to help during those two weeks we'd be gone. Everything had moved along quickly, and now we were here!

"Sure, and here's our girl!" Nana exclaimed as we got out of the car. Her face was lit, her smile dear, and near to blinding. "Come here, pet, and give us a squeeze."

Granda reached me first, pulling me in tightly. Nana, not to be outdone, snaked her arms around me as well. I'd missed them so much and had to swallow back my emotions. After they hugged me properly, they turned to Liam and the others, giving them the same treatment. "We're eating at Collins tonight—everyone wants to see you and say hello," Nana informed us cheerily.

"Sounds good—I'm so happy to be back—how is everything?" I smiled from ear to ear, my excitement on full display. "You guys good? No more injuries, I trust?"

Granda chuckled at that. "Right as rain, pet. Right as rain."

"We've put you two back in your old rooms on the third floor; the bed in the rose room is big enough for two, and we brought another bed in the blue room for you lads. Your da was most explicit that we keep an eye on the two of you. Yer not going to make us regret that, are you?"

Del and Jack hooted in laughter at our expense, bringing heat to my cheeks. Grinning, I assured, "No, we'll be on our best behavior, I promise."

"Just you do that, or he'll never let you back." Nana smiled as we made our way inside. Everything smelled the same. Warm yeast and fresh bakery mixed with the wood polish and the cleaner Nana favored. Breathing deeply, I inhaled joy. With every beat of my heart, love and happiness pulsed through me. A portion of my brain considered the differences in my recent two visits. Last time, while I'd been happy to be here, I *had* still been dealing with a broken heart. Now, my heart was the happiest it's ever been. And the reason for that happiness, slipped his arms around my waist and pulled me closer.

Liam's lips pressed against my temple. "Well, *mostly* I plan to behave. Though, I make nae promises, mind."

Smiling, I pulled away, kissed his cheek, then lead Delaney up to our room. Hungry and eager to get to Collins, we didn't take long stowing our luggage and freshening up. The guys and my grandparents were already waiting for us near the door when we came downstairs. "Right then, ready?" Nana smiled, then we headed out to the vehicles. The pub was busy, as usual, but we still managed to find seats. As before, there seemed to be a celebratory vibe. The Irish people are a friendly lot and for the most part, made us feel welcome. Some were a little standoffish, not sure how the Americans would behave. If we'd commit any faux pas. We had such a great time though, and ended up staying well into the late evening, eating, drinking, talking, and laughing. By the time our heads hit the pillow, we were all deliriously happy and exhausted. I fell asleep faster than I'd thought possible.

Liam-

As pleased as Liam was to be back, he slept poorly. Tossing and turning all night, unable to get comfortable. It was torture knowing Bethany was just across the hall. Such a temptation, she was. In every regard. He keenly recalled the tack room and the passion that had flared up between them. Like an inferno, it had nearly consumed them. Grudgingly, he thanked the Almighty they'd been stopped in time.

He hadn't wanted to stop, though. He'd wanted every piece of her right then and there. And Bethany had wanted him. Even now, that thought undid him. Made his entire frame rigid. It had taken his breath away, how fast the flame had arisen. He'd gone to the tack room to help her sort through things, cleaning and organizing. He'd stepped into the doorway and seen her bent over that saddle and every rational thought had vacated his head. Every caution. Every notion of self-preservation. The need for her was greater than his need for air, for breath in his lungs. *She* was his need. He knew he should have turned around and walked away. Run away. But fool that he was, he'd stayed. He'd watched, fanning that flame raging inside him.

And her response to him? It had completely unraveled him. If she'd have rejected him in any way, indicated they shouldn't, he'd have stopped. He wouldn't have forced her. *Liar*, his conscience whispered. She'd started to, she'd tried and had been failing to get the words out. And he'd rushed in, taking every advantage he could. Instead of listening to her, he'd pushed forward, knowing he'd silence her words in doing so. Knowing she wanted him as much as he wanted her. Liam jerked upright in bed, glanced to where Jack still snored softly, and grit his teeth. He *ached* with need and yet, he knew he owed her an apology. He'd told her she could trust him, and then had proven that he couldn't even trust himself.

Blowing out a silent breath, he slipped from his room and took an ice-cold shower, determining to make amends as soon as Bethany woke, knowing she didn't even hold him accountable. Trusted him implicitly. He loved that woman with every fiber of his being, and despite his failure the other day, he respected her as well. Resolving to not be the gobshite he'd previously been, Liam knew he'd have to tread carefully, thoughtfully, from here on out until she was his in a permanent nature. Until he could finally have her with all the respect and honor she deserved.

Bethany-

Rain lashed against the windowpanes, bringing me from sleep, morning coming faster than I'd have preferred. It only took me a moment to place where I was. Then, I was rolling out of bed, careful not to disturb Del as she slept, excited about the day ahead. Excited to see Liam. Excited just to be *here.*

Before heading down for breakfast, I decided a shower was needed to remove the travel from my person. As I made my way to the bathroom, my gaze flashed to Liam's door and wondered if he was up yet and how he'd slept. I considered knocking but then changed my mind, not wanting to disturb the guys if they were still out. Turning from their door, I quickly showered, dressed, and headed down to the kitchen. If I wasn't mistaken, Nana had made cinnamon rolls and now my stomach was rumbling in desperation. My grandmother was just removing a pan of rolls from the oven as I entered. "Morning," I greeted her, then after she'd put the pan down, gave her a hug and kiss.

"Oh, go on with ya." She beamed at the attention, then batted me away, nodding towards the plate of rolls already on the table. "How'd you sleep? Rain didn't keep you up, I trust?"

"Slept like a babe. Didn't even hear the rain until this morning."

"Sure, and it's been brightness and sunshine these past two weeks, but the instant you arrive, a storm rolls in. Fickle weather." She tossed an irritated glance out the window, making me smile.

"I don't mind the rain, Nana. Truly. It's what makes Ireland so green. I'd be disappointed if it hadn't rained."

She smiled and patted my cheek, then nodded towards the table. The rolls were perfect. Just the right amount of fluffy-crunchy outside, warm and gooey on the inside. Kind of like Liam, I smiled to myself. As if materializing from my thoughts, Liam followed Granda into the house—so he had been up. His deep blue eyes instantly sought mine, the look in them making my stomach flutter warmly. As he moved past me to the chair on my right, the air stirred, tickling across my neck, bringing such longing, such heat.

Liam leaned in after sitting down. "Ach, lass, I need ye no' to look at me in such a way. I'm of a mind to make apologies, and those looks weaken me resolve."

"Apologize?" My brows rose. "For what?"

Liam glanced to my grandparents, then said, voice low, "We'll talk later."

Curiosity piqued, I nodded, wondering, as I took another bite, then washed it down with some tea. I was enjoying a second cup, when Jack and Del pushed into the kitchen. Delaney was *not,* by any stretch of the imagination, a morning person. Yet, her excitement over being in Ireland had her up far earlier than normal. "Please, tell me there's coffee, and omgosh, are those *cinnamon rolls?* Nana, we just met for the first time last night, but I'm in love with you already."

We all chuckled at Del's reaction and continued to snicker as she ate, her eyes nearly rolling back in euphoria as she made moaning noises and licked her fingers. When she was done, she took note of our perusal. "What?" She grinned, taking another roll. "These are divine. Heavenly. Cinnabon's got *nothing* on you."

Jack stared at her, a stupid grin on his face. "I love you so much, Del."

"Thank you, love," Nana said as she pulled more rolls from the oven. "There's no shame in a woman enjoying her food. I'd be happy to teach you the recipe, if you'd like, before you go."

"Oh, yes, please! And thank you. From the bottom of my heart, I thank you. My thighs won't thank you, nor my butt, but *I,* in my heart of hearts, thank you."

"Oh, go on with ya." Nana smiled at her antics. We lingered around the table a bit longer, just talking. Then, as we noted the rain looked as though it was letting up some, decided to dress and head out for some exploring.

Living in Wyoming, we never get to see the ocean, so for the day, we stayed close to Bantry Bay, finding little inlets and beaches to explore. The rain came and went as we rambled along the beautiful green countryside, and still, we relished in it all. We walked the long, sandy stretches of Ballyrisode Beach, in Toormore, and explored the rocky, bolder-like formations scattered along Saunders' Rocks Beach. Scouring the pockets of sand we found, looking for shells and trapped sea life. We even found some unmarked areas that we had to nearly hike into, that may or may not have been off limits to us.

A little after two, somewhat wet and soaking from our beachy jaunts, we stopped in Castletownbere and had a heavenly bowl of clam chowder at Murphy's. The little restaurant sat down near the docks, just across from Sacred Heart Church. Jonathan, who we learned was the owner of the establishment, came over and introduced himself, checking on our meal. Asking if we'd enjoyed it or not. I got the impression he was a normally friendly person, and one who took pride in his work. We assured him his food was delicious. Once we'd eaten and warmed up some, after thanking our host, we headed back out for more exploring. As it was after three already, we made Castletownbere our last stop for the day, before heading back to my grandparents' place.

Seafood seemed to be the theme for the day, as Nana had steak and lobster pie with fresh baked bread waiting for us when we returned. After warming up with quick showers or a simple change into dry clothes, we tucked in. Conversation flowed around Nana's little table, as we ate and laughed some more, sharing our adventures through pictures and animated retellings. We finished off the night around the fireplace sipping tea with whiskey, simply breathing and being there in the moment. With the rising of the sun, we—even Delaney—were up and ready for the day.

We branched out further, first driving north, bypassing many beautiful sights that had Delaney almost beside herself, so that Jack could see the John Wayne statue in Cong. The one erected to commemorate the location of where *The Quiet Man* was filmed. John Wayne stands in that iconic image holding Maureen O'Hara in his arms. Of course, we had to take reenactment photos. We spent maybe an hour there, before turning in the opposite direction and going all the way into Waterford and exploring the Viking settlements and attractions. We stopped at Reginald's Tower and did our best to find the alleged cannonball still stuck within its wall. We never did find it, but we did take some great pictures there. One unexpected thing we found, just outside Christchurch Cathedral, was a monument to 9-11, complete with a small piece from the Towers. Emotion choked us all as we read the accompanying text explaining its intent. I hadn't been alive when the attack had happened, but my parents had made sure I was well-aware of what had taken place.

Leisurely, we made our way back to Kealkill, stopping in Cork to explore along the Merchants Quay, then swung up to Blarney Castle so Delaney could kiss the Stone. She said she knew kissing the Blarney Stone was the *tourist* thing to do, but didn't care. She was in Ireland, by golly, and she was kissing that stone. And hoped, as legend claimed, doing so would gift her with eloquence of speech. We chuckled over her tenacity, but didn't feel she lacked in that department at all.

After that, we stopped at the Drombeg Stone Circle just outside Glandore. Walking the fuchsia-lined path to the megalithic stone circle, we took in the fresh, almost rejuvenating air. Originally, there were seventeen stones, but only thirteen remained now. Standing amid them, we could see the ocean in the distance, and found it to be an interesting, beautiful place. We were definitely glad we'd taken the time to stop.

The next morning we were flying to Scotland, so early on we called it a night. I wasn't nearly as forlorn as I'd been the last time I'd left my grandparents, knowing we'd be stopping here again for three nights before flying home. I wondered, as I fell asleep, listening to the soft rain on the roof, how Liam's family would like me. How I would like them. Even though I was happier than I'd ever been, I couldn't help but wonder if this trip wouldn't turn out to be our make it or break it event. Only time would tell, still I couldn't help the thoughts from rising.

CHAPTER EIGHTEEN

Mo Ghràidh

Bethany-

We landed in Inverness around three-thirty in the afternoon. After retrieving our luggage, Liam secured our rental car and we headed north to the town of Drumsmittal, on the Black Isle. His grandparents, Harold and Olivia, lived there on a couple acres. On the drive over, Liam shared that at one point, his grandparents' farm had been much, much larger—not as big as ours—but over the years, as their only child sought employment off the farm, they'd sold most of it off. Now, Christmas trees were grown around them and Harold and Olivia could enjoy the land without having to work it.

Liam explained that his parents lived here as well, though his dad, Kristian, kept an apartment, or flat as they're called, in Inverness, and came home only on the weekends. I wouldn't meet him for another couple days, at least. Iona, Liam's mother, would come over this evening to join us for dinner. We pulled up to what Liam referred to as a bungalow, but looked more like a smaller manor house, to me.

Ivy climbed the grey brick exterior, meandering in seemingly random pathways over the face of the house. Lights shone from within the front mullioned windows, and as we stepped from the car, the front door opened. A woman, tall, slender, warm, and somehow stately all at once, stepped out to greet us. She reminded me so much of a feminine Liam, that I found it obvious where he'd inherited his looks from. Silver was just beginning to encroach at the temples of her still-lustrous dark hair. "Liam, my love!" She smiled as she came down the steps.

"Seanmhair," Liam said as he pulled her into a warm hug. "I've missed ye. Come meet Bethany."

Olivia turned her warm gaze upon me as her smile widened. "I feel as though I know ye already, Bethany. Yer grandmother has told me so much about ye."

"It's very nice to meet you, Mrs. Gunn."

"Call me Olivia, or Gran, if ye'd prefer." Liam continued introducing everyone as we gathered our luggage. We followed her into the house and Olivia explained that Harold, her husband, was still feeling poorly, but would hopefully meet us later. Then she instructed Liam to show us to our rooms. Delaney and I were in a large room towards the back of the house, overlooking the Christmas tree fields. Misty mountains peeked over the treetops in the distance, bringing a satisfied smile to my face at their beauty. Liam had the room across the hall, and Jack the one next to his, closer to the staircase. A spacious bathroom was next to our room. A wide window, with a cushioned bench seat sat at the opposite end of the hall, at the head of the stairs, looking out over the driveway. We'd be here for just over a week, with one brief two-night stay at an Airbnb a little farther north of here. Liam was taking us to see the area the Gunn clan had come from, as well as to a Highland Game.

Olivia was a fine chef. She'd made seasoned lambchops with potatoes, and had picked up a couple fresh loaves of French bread. When Iona arrived, she'd brought three bottles of wine that paired well with the meal. I had to wonder how often they got together like this, or if they simply both had similar great taste.

Any concerns I'd had over meeting Liam's mother were nearly instantly laid to rest. Iona was shorter than I was, probably close to my mother's height, maybe a little shorter. She had cropped blond hair and hazel eyes. She made me feel thoroughly welcome, exclaiming how pleased she was to see her son so happy. She'd gone on to say that she'd worried he'd never settle down. We'd talked and laughed well into the evening, then after probably close to the dozenth time Liam had caught me yawning, he decided we should call it a night.

Delaney and Jack had gone up to bed before Liam and I had—we'd stayed to help Olivia clean up and put dinner away—plus, it would solve bathroom congestion with four adults attempting to use the same one at the same time. At the top of the stairs, Liam stopped, then took a seat on the bench there. I studied him for a moment before sitting beside him.

"Me mother likes ye." Liam smiled against my knuckles.

"I'm glad; I like her as well. And your grandmother. They're both gems, truly."

"If, God forbid, we were ever to break up, I think she'd throw me to the curb and adopt ye." His statement had me chuckling under my breath. "I love the sound of that, yer laughter. I love it. Love ye. And I'm beyond glad yer here wi' me."

"I'm beyond glad to be here with you. Seeing this. Experiencing it. It's magical somehow."

"Sure, and it's grand to have ye saying so." He stood, pulling me to my feet and slid his arms around me, dragging me closer. "I should let ye go to bed, but I dinna want to be releasing ye. No' yet."

Tucking my head into his shoulder, I breathed against him. "I don't want you to release me, Liam. I want you to hold me forever—I'm not rushing you, simply stating the truth."

"Ah lass, yer killing me." He pressed his lips against my temple. Inhaled, holding still. My head tilted upwards and like a magnet to metal, his mouth found mine. Soft, tentative, controlled explorations; his lips moving across mine, then deeper. Slower. Until my entire frame was trembling with want. With need. Liam walked me backwards until my back hit the wall, then he crowded in closer. One leg wedged itself between mine as his mouth lifted before, trailing slowly down my neck to where it met my shoulder. There, he applied his teeth. A soft drag across the skin, then returning to take a firmer grip.

"Ehem. EHEM!" Del said loudly from behind Liam. "Yeah, you guys need to pull it together some. Jack and I are here as chaperones, and you're making me work extra hard." She tried again. "Don't make me go get Jack, or worse, Olivia."

At the sound of her voice, we'd snapped out of our passionate interlude. Becoming aware of our surroundings and our actions. "Bloody, everlasting...that's *two* apologies I'm owing ye now." Liam shifted away, putting a tiny amount of distance between us. He shook his head, self-directed aggravation in his eyes. Sighing, he said, "Best get to bed, afore ye make me forget meself again, and I determine to ravish ye further in me grandmother's house." He stepped farther back, allowing me space, though he kept one hand at my waist until he was certain I was steady on my feet.

My gaze shot to Del, then shifted back to Liam. "Goodnight," I whispered, then moved past Del to our room.

"'Night, lass. Sweet dreams."

We closed our bedroom door and Delaney said, "Wowzuh. You two have it bad. It's a good thing I have a small bladder. Who knows what might have happened if I hadn't come along. Speaking of, you stay put while I go pee. And NO visitors. I'll be right back."

I couldn't help the smile that hit my face, though, in all honesty, I was relieved she'd come along when she had. Changing quickly, I waited for her to return, then went to brush my teeth. The light under Liam's door had me blushing, but Del had left our bedroom door open, so I stayed away from his room. Ten minutes later, we were both in bed, lights out.

I took her hand in mine and squeezed it. "Thank you, Del. You're the best."

"I know." I heard the grin in her voice, even as she yawned. "Sweet dreams."

Lucas-

Lucas pulled a drag from his cigarette as he perused the newspaper. Five unexplained deaths of working girls over the last two weeks. All of them blond. He'd be willing to wager a large sum that the prey he sought was, in fact, preying on his own victims.

Now, more than ever, Lucas wanted to find his target. He had three leads come up this week. The first of which he'd see to shortly. It was the reason he was here, at this park, keeping an eye on the construction crew across the street. They were installing drywall on a newly remodeled building in the downtown area. One of the crew was rumored to have recently been in touch with a fellow that was seemingly new in town. A fellow who'd been seen talking with prostitutes.

The crew would be calling it a day soon, just as they had for the last three days at this same time. Lucas intended to get his information from the crew member one way or another. If this lead panned out, he'd continue along this trail; if not, he'd shift gears, going back over the information, picking up from where he'd previously left off.

Good, they were closing up shop now. Lucas put out his cigarette and folded his paper. The man in question moved off to an older, dark blue sedan. Lucas watched him from the driver's seat of the car he drove, then pulled into traffic, keeping an unobtrusive distance from the vehicle he trailed. Maybe he'd finally get some answers.

Two hours later, back in his hotel room, Lucas scratched the name off his list. This wasn't the lead he was after. He'd followed the man to a dive, a local watering hole. Lucas had taken the seat beside him at the bar, then proclaimed he'd finally done it; he'd divorced the hag. His announcement had the men on either side of him thumping his back in commiseration. They'd each bought him a drink and he'd done the same back. Didn't take long to figure out the stranger his mark was seen speaking to, was in fact, his cousin from Florida come to visit for nearly the same reason Lucas had given. *This was not his target.* The next name was an older woman who lived on the outskirts of town. It was rumored a stranger had been seen off and on hanging around her rundown house over the last week or so.

Bethany-

We woke early and drove south, through Inverness, then east to Culloden Field. There, we spent the next two and a half almost three hours meandering through the area, trying our best to absorb the impact and the history. Walking through the fields, reading the names and dates, strongly brought to mind our own Revolutionary War. Though the outcomes were different, I could empathize with the Scots and their plight at the time. Americans may not have had as long a history as some other countries, but those who formed our nation came from lands that did, and in doing so, brought those histories to our shores. If I wasn't mistaken, many Scots had fought in the Revolutionary War, so maybe they got their victory, after all, though not on the soil they'd have preferred.

From there, we drove west to Loch Ness and Urquhart Castle, where we spent the rest of the day hiking and taking in the sights. We bought souvenirs and snapped pictures, having such a lovely time. The following day, we ventured into Inverness itself, visiting the castle, the Cathedral, and doing more shopping. Liam's dad Kristian was supposed to come to the house tonight to see us before we left in the morning for our drive north to Wick and the Highland Games.

I dressed with care for dinner, wearing a new outfit, one Liam had never seen. The fluttery wrap dress had a soft V-neck and was a purple so dark it almost looked black in some lights, making my eyes seem extra green. The color, texture, and cut somehow magically combined, giving me a new awareness of myself, of the woman's body I possessed. My confidence soared, knowing how Liam would react. The guys were already downstairs, so Delaney and I, once dressed, headed down to join them. I listened for new voices, but everything seemed quiet.

When I entered the large study where everyone was to gather, Liam was faced away from me, looking out the window. His shoulders seemed stiff somehow and I wondered if everything was all right. He didn't immediately turn when I came in, so I made my way to his side. My eyes travelled over his profile, noting, through his beard, the tightening of his jaw, the tension around his mouth. "Liam?" I asked softly. "What's the matter?"

Turning from the window, Liam paused in his movements as he saw me. Those deep blue eyes of his slowly travelled south, then north again, taking me in, taking a slow, deep breath as he did. "Lord ha' mercy. Lass," he growled low, his voiced almost pained, "ye fair stopped me heart. I canna fathom what I've done to please the Almighty, but I'm forever thankful He saw fit to give ye to me." He took my hand and raised it to his lips, pressing them against my skin, lightly nipping with his teeth.

I blushed under his regard, my pulse picking up speed. Shaking my head at my own susceptibility, I said, "Now *that's* a compliment. But I'm not sidetracked, nor have I forgotten how you were just moments ago. What's the matter?"

Liam chuckled under his breath, then pressed a kiss against my forehead. "Me esteemed father canna make it to meet ye this evening. He's decided to stay in Inverness, as he's work to do."

"That's okay, I understand work; I do. I can meet him another time, right?"

"He's no' actually busy. He's a feckless coward is what he is."

I heard the heat in his words, and the pain as well. Silently sighing, I stepped closer and wrapped my arms around him. "Your dad will come around, eventually. I'm not offended. I'm here for you, not him. Don't let this ruin our evening, please."

"I love ye." His arms tightened, then he sighed. "Yer right. It's gone from me mind. Let's go in for dinner, as Gran will be wondering what's become of us."

Iona did not end up joining us that evening either; she'd called and given her regards, saying she'd had a headache and simply wished to lie down. I hoped her absence didn't have anything to do with her husband not coming. Regardless, we spent another wonderful evening with Olivia, talking, laughing, and reminiscing. We shared the pictures of the day's outing with her and suggested we have pictures taken with her on our return.

We left the Black Isle with the rising of the sun, headed north on the A9 for Wick. Liam had secured us an Airbnb on the outskirts of town. The drive itself only takes a little over two hours, but of course, we had to stop many times along the way. The North Sea was a beautiful backdrop as we meandered up the coastline. Just like home, Scotland offered a wild, rugged beauty, though it was a different beauty, a different ruggedness.

We arrived at the little two-bedroom bungalow just after noon. We unloaded the car and freshened up, then decided to walk around for a while to stretch our legs before heading to town for dinner. Tomorrow was the Highland Games, and we had an hour's drive to reach the site, so we didn't stay out too late. Like Ireland, the food and conversation, the people were wonderful and welcoming. We had a great time, Liam having to be our guide, as we tried to comprehend the local lingo and customs. Back at the little house, we utilized the tiny firepit on the back patio and sipped on a late-night whisky. Liam found a stack of peat briquettes and added a couple to the flames. A rare treat, I was told, as peat burning was becoming frowned upon and most likely soon would be outlawed.

"So, this is the land your family, or clan, or whatever came from, huh? Did you grow up here?" Delaney asked. She was reclined against Jack, her back to his front, his arms around her.

"Nae." Liam shook his head. "The Gunn Clan is from these parts, but me family left here a couple generations back. Nae, I grew up around Inverness."

"Clan Gunn. Tell me about them. What kind of people were they?" Jack asked, taking a sip from his glass.

"Clans, ye ken, they're no' like what ye might think of as family in the singular sense. It's more like a big group of families. And then ye might have those of another family name, who joined wi' that Clan to be a part of that family. Most of it had to do wi' protection of land and people. The Gunn's originated from the Vikings when they settled here."

"That's cool. Makes sense, I guess," Jack replied.

"Don't all clans have mottos, or sayings, or something?" Delaney asked. "What's yours?"

"*Aut pax aut Bellum.* 'Tis Latin. Means, Either peace or war."

"Having seen you move, I'd say it's fitting." Jack chuckled.

Liam caught me yawning, his eyes crinkled affectionately as he looked down at me. We decided to head in as the fire had burned low, and I waited while he doused the embers. It had grown chilly as the sun had sunk low in the sky, though I hadn't been aware of it at the time. I noticed it now, though, and wrapped my arms around myself as we went inside.

Shivering, I turned on the kitchen sink to rinse our cups and heard the door click as Liam locked it. Del and Jack were either in their rooms, or the bathroom; I could hear noises down the hall. Then, I wasn't shivering or hearing them any longer. Liam had moved behind me, his arms pulling me close, one hand splayed across my stomach, the other lifting my hair out of the way as his mouth found my neck. "*Gor,*" he growled against my skin. "I love this spot right here. Love the sounds ye make when I pay it attention." My breath hitched as his teeth took hold, his lips following soothing any sting. His nose skimmed along my shoulder now, teeth continuing their assault in gentle bites. "I've been tellin' meself to behave, ye ken? But woman, ye make it so difficult." His hand threaded, then tightened in my hair, the other pulling me further back, further into him. "And then I remember yer da, and I remind meself, again, that I love ye and must wait if I want to live to share a future wi' ye." With those words, he inhaled long and slow as he pulled back, stepping away, putting space between us.

I took a deep breath to calm my racing heart, then turned to face him. "Thank you." At the look upon his face, I continued, "For respecting me. For not pushing me...pushing this."

"Anything for ye, lass. Anything." I smiled through another yawn, and he said, "Off to bed, wi' ye now. We've a long day ahead of us. I love ye."

"I love you, too."

The Old Woman-

The old woman glared at the man as he left. What'd he want? Snoopin' around, asking questions he'd no right to. Up to no good is what he was. No-account bounty hunter, most-like. Asking after that fella was here a couple weeks back.

She'd known then the man saying he knew her son was trouble, and sure enough, here he was bringing more trouble along, now wasn't he? If he ever showed his face here again, she'd send him packing, just as she had this fella.

She watched as the stranger strode down the street to the nondescript sedan parked across the way. Moments later, he drove past her house as he left the neighborhood. At the sight of his leaving, she breathed a breath of relief. Something about the man had set off her warning bells. Cautioning her to be aware. She locked her deadbolt, something she hadn't done in a long while. Couldn't be too careful, though.

CHAPTER NINETEEN
Battle Cry

Bethany-

It was the pipes we heard first. They're a sound one is not likely to ever forget. Hauntingly beautiful, graceful, and demanding of one's attention. I've heard bagpipe recordings before, but hearing them in person is a whole other experience. We arrived just after the opening ceremonies had begun, and as we stepped out of the rental car, the pipes began and something in my soul rose to their call.

Liam and I both paused, almost mesmerized by the sound. Delaney nudged my shoulder to get us moving again. "Hurry, guys, I want to see this."

"Well, we can definitely hear it from out here," Jack teased as he took her hand, leading the way to the main entrance.

As we walked, my heart pounded along to the rhythm of the pipes. After paying our entrance fee, we meandered through the grounds of Halkirk Farms, stopping at various booths selling their wares. Some were Scandinavian themed, but most were Scottish. In one, Liam bought me a tam beret in the Gunn colors. "Bonnie," he breathed as he settled it on my head. Of course, Delaney had to have one as well, which had Jack rolling his eyes, even as he grinned and paid for her item. Proudly, we wore them as we continued through the festivities, craning our necks, trying to take everything in. Liam had worn his kilt, as he'd promised, so, between that and my tam beret, I felt we looked, if not perfectly matched, at least well-suited to the festivities. We tasted foods and drinks, and watched the caber toss and hammer throw. We saw a tug-of-war competition and marveled at the strength portrayed there. We saw Highland dancers and heard the Calling of the Clans, cheering the loudest for Clan Gunn when that name was called. And then, as the afternoon began wearing down, the pipers once more took center stage, playing, and bringing the event to a close.

We stayed, listening to the music, even as the crowd began to disburse. We stood somewhat to the left of where the pipers were gathered. I breathed slowly, deeply, wanting to savor it, take it all in, hold it, and keep it forever in my heart. The beauty, the majesty of it all. Scripture seems to favor harps, but I think God would have a piper or two as well. Liam had remained close throughout the day. An arm around my waist, across my shoulders, at my hip, or simply holding my hand. As we listened to the music, he stood behind me, arms holding me tightly to him, his chin resting on my shoulder. The pipers began a slower, somehow fuller melody and I felt Liam's chest expand as he inhaled. He pressed a soft kiss against my neck, loosened his grip, and stepped around to the front of me. Those beautiful, deep blue eyes gazed into mine, warming me from the inside out.

With a look I couldn't quite decipher, he raised a hand and gently swiped a thumb under my eye, smoothing away tears I hadn't known had been falling. He then took my hands in his and lifted them, kissing first my fingertips, then my knuckles. "Ye're the most beautiful thing in the world to me, ye ken; and I love ye, lass." Still holding my hands, he stepped back, dropping to one knee, his kilt hitching dangerously high; my heart stuttered, squeezed, then took off like a bird trapped inside a cage. "Bethany Calista Fitzpatrick, would ye do me the greatest honor ever bestowed upon a man, and consent to be me wife?"

Everything around us seemed to pause, almost as though holding its collective breath. The pipes faded to soft background music. The activities of those around us slowed, quieted. I heard Delaney's startled exclamation, and from my peripheral saw her reach for Jack, clutching at him.

Liam let go of me, lifting and holding his hands out, as if in supplication. In his grasp sat a small wooden box. In the box was a ring. My eyes shot back to his as I tried to breathe. I'd had this answer prepared; already knew what my answer was, but couldn't get it out. Instead, I trembled and swallowed, still trying to find my lungs, my voice. In a panic to get the right reaction conveyed to him, I simply nodded, my eyes filling with unshed tears.

"Aye?" The quiver in his voice had my emotions surging. My voice still locked away, I nodded again. With shaking hands, Liam slipped the ring on my finger, then surged to his feet, taking me in his arms.

Reminiscent of a battle cry of old, noise rushed back in as cheering, clapping, and shouting suddenly roared all around us. With their loudly proclaimed congratulations, I finally found my voice. "*Yes!* Yes, Liam Kristian Gunn, yes, I will marry you!"

Liam spun me about before kissing me in a triumphant display of satisfied sentiment. Then, as my feet touched down, he pressed his mouth to my forehead. "Ye've made me the happiest of men—I willna let ye take it back, ye ken?"

"I don't want it back. I just want you." We were almost tackled as Delaney and Jack surrounded us, wrapping their arms around us both, dancing about.

"Congratulations!! I am SO excited!" Delaney squealed. "Oh, I want to see the ring." I lifted my hand so she could see the simple, graceful design. A teardrop shaped stone nestled in filigreed leaves of rose gold, mounted on a simple band of the same color.

Many of those around us stopped to pump Liam's hand, or pound his back, and wish us well. Eventually, we made it back to the car. He started the engine, then turned to me. "Afore ye begin to fret, I've yer parents' blessing." Tears fell fresh at that. "Ach, yer no' supposed to be cryin' now. Have I no' made ye happy, then?"

"These are happy tears," I whispered past the lump in my throat. "The happiest tears to have ever fallen, I can assure you."

"It's glad I am to hear ye say it."

"Well, you ken, you've made *me* glad, right?"

He lifted my hand to his mouth, kissing my palm. "I love ye. I'll never stop lovin' ye and showing ye. No' ever."

Kate-

"Did he say *when* he planned to do it?" Kate asked as she readied herself for bed. "I'm terrified I'll say something and give the surprise away."

"If all goes well, he said it should be at the Games."

"Are you just *dying?* I feel like I'm about to come out of my skin in anticipation. He'll have her call, won't he? You told him to?"

"Yes, love, I did. And no, I'm not as antsy as you seem to be. Though, I recall a time not that terribly long ago, when *I* had to swallow my heart back with each breath as I waited for *your* answer."

Kate blushed at that and grinned. She was better. Not fully healed, not quite. But her ribs were healed. Healed enough for what she had in mind, at least. Her leg and shoulder were still a little sore, but that was to be expected. They'd just have to be careful. Asher could be *very* gentle when he set his mind to it. She looked herself over in the mirror, trying not to look too closely at the fine lines she couldn't help but notice. Kate shifted her gaze to her nightgown, one she'd had Candi order in for her. It was midnight blue—Ash's favorite color—and satin, with spaghetti straps. The two-inch band of lace came to just above her knees. She thought he'd like it; she wanted there to be no mistaking her intent. Blowing out a breath, she turned from the mirror and shut off the bathroom light.

Asher was leaned back against the headboard, his reading glasses on, and a book open on his lap, when she shut the light off. He'd glanced up at the sound, then looked back to his book and froze. Kate stayed motionless by the bathroom door, waiting, her heart pounding out a tempo. Slowly, Asher looked up again, the book forgotten, the pages closing as it slipped from his grasp to the floor. From where she stood, Kate watched as her husband's eyes travelled over her, darkening, warming as they went.

Those blue eyes shot to hers, a desperate question burning in their depths. Breathless, she nodded. Asher inhaled, a long, drawn-out breath, his eyes never leaving hers. Carefully, he rose from the bed and made his way to her. "Are you sure? I'm in no rush, and I need you to be absolutely sure, Kate. I want you," he growled into her hair as he slid his arms around her, "make no mistake, but not unless you are one hundred percent ready."

"I love you, and I miss my husband." She breathed against his chest as he tenderly pulled her flush with him. Then, just to be certain he understood, she said, "I'm sure. You'll just have to be gentle, okay?"

Asher shook as he brought himself under control. He trailed his mouth along the curve of her neck, then slowly, he bent and lifted her carefully into his arms. "Oh, wife, I can be *very* gentle. I will bring new meaning to the word."

Lucas-

Lucas watched as the large man made his way hurriedly down the sidewalk, away from the old woman's house. Just as he'd hoped his little mouse would react. Lucas had known the man would eventually return here, having planted the seed of distrust in the woman's head when he spoke with her the other day. Letting her confirm to him that the mouse he hunted was known to her, was expected to return at some point. All he'd had to do was wait.

Lucas could have ended him easily. A quick shot to the back of the head would do the trick, and Lucas was certainly able to accomplish that. But he knew he was expected to act in such a way to avoid involving in-depth investigations. No, he'd have to be patient. It couldn't be simple; it had to be well thought out. He'd wait a little longer, study his prey more. Find a better solution.

Lucas watched as the mouse looked over his shoulder, spooked, eyes roving around, searching for danger. The man climbed into an older Chevy pickup and gunned the engine, tearing down the street. Lucas remained still as the truck passed him, nothing more than a dark-skinned man asleep at the wheel; probably sleeping off another bender.

Once the Chevy turned the corner, Lucas started his car and his pursuit. He trailed behind the man, staying several cars back, letting him out of sight every-so-often. Then Lucas would take a side street and meet the truck again. Time and time again, he played with his mouse. Waiting, plotting, curious to see how his prey would respond to this turn of events.

Johnny-

Johnny slammed in fists against his steering wheel, cursing under his breath. *Stupid hag!* He should have killed her. Lecturing him about bringing the law down on them. What was she spouting off about anyhow? As he thought about her words, her accusations, he got a chill, like someone had doused him in ice cold water.

Someone had told her he'd been offing prostitutes. But who? He looked in his mirrors and took another left turn. Then a right, then another left, driving aimlessly, not sure where he'd go. Houston seemed to have dried up on resources for him. He'd have to go somewhere else. He had over two thousand dollars on him now; those hookers must have known what they were about with that kind of cash. Too bad they wouldn't be around to continue that work. He figured someone would be sorry about that. Grinning, he took the freeway entrance and headed south, thinking he'd head below the border. Mexico was a big country; he could disappear there and never be found. Not until he came up with a new plan to end that witch's existence.

Bethany-

"Hey," I said to my mom on speakerphone as she answered her cell.

"Gah! Tell me all about it! You said yes, right? *Right?*"

"I did, Mom. I told him yes."

"She cried, Kate!" Liam offered from beside me. We sat around the little firepit on the tiny deck at our bungalow in Wick.

"Happy tears only, Mom. Happy tears," I assured her.

"Congratulations, guys. I'm so happy for you. Send me a picture of the ring; I want to see it." I quickly did as she requested and waited for her to get it. "Oh, Bethany, baby, it's *beautiful!* Well done, Liam!"

"Thanks, I think so." I beamed and couldn't stop staring at the ring. At the beauty of it. The meaning.

"Have you guys set a date yet?" Mom asked.

"No, we haven't even talked about that yet. We'll have to get to it soon, though. Probably after we get home."

"Well, if he's anything like your dad, he'll be all for a fast wedding." From the background, I heard Dad's rumbled, "He'd better not be rushing it." Mom just laughed at that. "Ignore him. Your dad's happy for you guys as well; he just has to act tough."

"Oh, I know." I smiled and Mom yawned. "How're you feeling? Healing still going well? Any more word on that jerk?"

"Healing is fine," Mom assured. "I feel good. Your dad has been taking great care of me."

I heard Dad say something about extra gentle care and something about the *way* he said it made me not want to know any more. "Okay, well. I love you guys and will see you in less than a week. Goodnight."

When I ended the call, there was complete silence around me, then Jack snorted, and Delaney shouted with laughter. "Omgosh, that is *way* more than I ever wanted to know about your parents!" Jack sniggered.

"Super romantic, though." Delaney smiled dreamily. "After all this time, they still have it for each other." Liam took my hand in his, tracing along my knuckles, swirling his fingertip around the ring. He kissed my hand, such heated promise in his eyes that I blushed. And then yawned. Seeing that, he announced it was bedtime as we'd be getting an early start on the day. Delaney agreed, saying there were a few places she wanted to stop on the way back to the Black Isle.

Bethany-

We arrived back at Harold and Olivia's just before noon. A brisk breeze blew and the sun shifted between the cloud layers, making beautiful designs on the driveway and house. The door was opened by an elderly gentleman who I took to be Harold; he must have been feeling better. When we were last here, we hadn't met him as he'd been feeling under the weather.

I studied him as we made our approach. His grey eyes were gentle and there was a sort of peacefulness around his mouth. He and Olivia were close to the same height, though he may have had half an inch on her. He smiled, and I saw Liam in that smile. The sight tugged at my heart.

"Seanair, feelin' better, then?" Liam took his hand, carefully pulling him in, gently patting his back. "It's glad I am to see ye up and aboot."

"I'm right as rain, lad. No' but a wee sniffle, an yer Gran, bless her soul, had me wrapped up and in bed. Was no arguin' wi' her, ye ken." Harold pounded Liam's back to emphasize his health, then turned his gaze to me. "Now, introduce me to the lass. I've been in a right fit, havin' missed the opportunity last time."

"Granda, meet Bethany...me betrothed." Such satisfaction in his voice as Liam lifted our enjoined hands, kissing my knuckles, showing off that beautiful ring.

"*Betrothed?*" Harold exclaimed, joy lighting up his features. "Olivia, my dove, come quick! Our Liam's engaged!"

We heard Olivia's startled, happy exclamation from somewhere in the house. Somehow, we managed to get inside and set our luggage down before continuing the felicitations. Olivia hugged us close, tears falling. "Oh, I'm so happy for ye! Truly, ye've made me the happiest."

Jack and Delaney carried our bags up to our rooms, then joined us back in the living room. Harold was just asking, "Now, yer da knows, aye? There'll no' be any danger to our lad from the Fitzpatrick?"

"Liam's in no danger from my dad," I assured them.

"Seanair, I asked the man first, ye ken, and received his blessing. I would-na' have asked her wi'out it."

"Ye've a stubborn-streak a mile wide, lad. I'm concerned for ye, is all."

"Bless ye for carin'." Liam rolled his eyes good-naturedly.

"This calls for a celebration," Olivia affectionately said as she leaned over, kissing the top of Harold's head. "I'll ring over to your son and invite them, though ye may need to add your two-pence to convince him to come."

Harold grumbled, a disgruntled look flashing across his face. "Oh, *my* son, is he now? Ye tell him I said to be here, or he'll be hearin' from me direct." Harold turned to Liam. "And that's where yer stubbornness comes from, lad."

Liam chuckled under his breath, then tucked me in closer to him on the sofa. Absently, he drew shapes on my back and shoulder. I lifted my head to see him better. "You're not worried about your dad coming, are you? I'm sure everything will be fine."

"With Granda here and alert, Da will behave himself for the most part. It's the rest of it I'm concerned over. I dinna want him hecklin' ye."

"I'm not afraid of him or his opinion of me. You love me and that's all that matters. Truly, don't let him bother you." I said this to reassure him, but inside, I knew the parts of me that took after my parents were readying for battle. I prayed it wouldn't come to that, but would protect Liam from his father's barbs should they make an appearance.

Five hours later, the doorbell rang. Olivia answered it and was soon ushering Iona, and a man I took to be Kristian into the room where we were gathered around the fireplace. He looked like a younger, fiercer version of Harold. He was taller than Harold, though not as tall as his own son by several inches. Iona made her way directly to Liam and I. "Let me see it." Liam had risen at their arrival, pulling me up with him, no doubt preferring to greet his father on his feet. He lifted my hand to show his mother. Tears glistened in her eyes for us. She hugged me tightly and then her son as well. "I'm so happy for ye both. So very happy."

"Da," Liam said, extending his hand as his father moved closer to where we stood. Kristian clasped it, gripping firmly, then released it quickly. I saw him flexing his hand, no doubt trying to get blood flow circulating after Liam's tight grip. The thought made me mentally grin; Liam did have strong, capable hands.

"It's good to see ye, lad." Kristian patted his son's shoulder. "You look well."

"Da, meet Bethany. My betrothed."

Kristian turned his grey eyes to mine, his expression unreadable. "Fitzpatrick's daughter, no?"

"Asher and Kate are my parents, yes. I'm pleased to meet you." I offered him my hand, aware he'd not offered his to me first.

"American," he said lightly grasping mine before letting it go.

"Yes."

"Some sort of rancher, if I remember? A worker of the land, or some such thing. Though, your father had some little fame in the cinemas, I recall."

"A little," I agreed, ignoring the slight. "Cattle ranchers, yes. In Wyoming."

"And, how's he, the Fitzpatrick to feel about you moving here? Not much living to make at ranching, I expect."

Liam startled at the comment, and I saw the muscle flex in his jaw. "Actually, Da, I plan to move there. The Fitzpatricks have a thriving ranch and business, and I plan to help them in the running of it."

"Ranching. *Bah.* Can't last for long. It'll dry up eventually. What kind of life is that? How are you to take care of a wife, start a family, if ye've no work, no employment? No, lad, it's best for you both if you give up this childish dream, and come to work for me. You've the credentials for it and the mind. You'd be a success."

Before Liam could reply, I tightened my grip on his hand, forestalling any harsh comments. "I hope you don't mind, Mr. Gunn, but with my dad's...connections, I did some research. Ranching and horse training can be quite the successful endeavor. In fact, I could, on my own, without help from my parents, buy out your company. Three times over. I'd say that makes ranching quite lucrative, no?"

Behind us, I heard coughing, even as Liam smothered his own humor. Kristian flushed, then swallowed. He inhaled to speak, but Liam beat him to it, softly saying, "Ye have a care as to how ye speak wi' her, aye." Kristian snapped his mouth shut, then nodded before stepping away. Liam watched him go, then turned to me, pulling me tight as he kissed my forehead. "I love ye so much."

"Ye handled that well," Iona murmured as she reached for me, gently squeezing my arm. "Don't fret; he'll come 'round. The man's a stubborn one, though he's no' entirely daft."

Olivia called us into the dining room for supper. Soon food and conversation flowed. Kristian spoke rarely and only when spoken to, but I could see the speculation in his gaze. I prayed he truly would come around and that he'd bestow his blessing on us, finding peace in his son's decisions. Doing so would put Liam's heart at rest.

CHAPTER TWENTY

Love this Way

Kate-

"Kate, *love,* be rational."

"I am being rational." Kate placed a hand against her husband's cheek. She loved him to distraction, loved him with her heart, mind, and body. She'd do anything for him, but she needed her horses. Needed to see them, touch them, smell them. "I'm getting stronger every day. I haven't had to use the cane in well over a week. I'm just walking out to the barn. I need to see Red and Rhys."

"I get that you want to see them, but let me carry you, at least."

Kate chuckled, shaking her head. "I love that you love me, the *way* that you love me. That you want to protect me. Take care of me. It touches deep, but babe, I need to do this. Walk *with* me. I promise to take it easy. I'm not planning to ride. I promise I won't even ask about riding until Ruben says I'm cleared for it."

Asher rolled his eyes and inhaled deeply, holding it before exhaling in a rush. Knowing he was beat, he shook his head, then carefully pulled his wife close. His arms snaked around her, tenderly bringing her flush with him. Against her forehead, he said, "I love you." In a shameless, deviant, last-ditch attempt, he trailed his mouth to her ear, then her neck, knowing how sensitive she was there. Slowly, he backed her until she came up against the patio door. He pressed her there, holding her with his body. His mouth moved to hers, moved slowly over hers.

Kate's arms reached up, grasping his hair, dragging him down to her even as she rose to meet him. He deepened the kiss then, gratified to hear the sound she made deep in her throat. "We should take this to the bedroom, love. I've a need to be extraordinarily gentle with my wife again and no wish to be interrupted." He nipped her lip lightly for emphasis.

"I agree." Kate gasped, her eyes half-closed, nearly drunk on his ministrations. "After I see the horses."

Asher chuckled weakly, pressing his forehead to hers. "You kill me, woman. You really do."

"As you do to me, as you well know."

"But not enough to distract you from this course of action, apparently."

"No, but I'll be thinking of it the whole way there and back." Kate kissed him, then pulled back. "Nice try, though."

"I nearly had you."

"You nearly did."

"I guess I can wait." Asher took her hand in his and opened the patio door. "Let's go see the horses."

Kate breathed deeply, her soul quieting, as she inhaled the scent of horses and hay. Asher opened the big door and stood by to make sure she didn't stumble as she entered the barn. He watched as she flicked on the overhead light, illuminating the interior. Red and Rhys whinnied at the sight of her. Red struck against his stall door, impatient and reaching for her with his nose.

Kate sniffed, trying to hold her emotions in check, but there was no stopping the tears from falling as her older horse shoved his head into her chest, trying to get as close as he could. She scratched his face and ears; Red knickered softly as she did, lipping at her. He struck the stall door again, so Kate undid the latch and let the big red gelding out. Asher stepped closer, putting a hand on his shoulder. "Easy, buddy, she's still healing."

Kate ducked under the horse's head, pressing her face into Red's neck. Pulling back, she looked the gelding over and wiped her eyes. "He doesn't look bad; I thought he'd look worse from neglect."

"I've been trying to come out once a week to brush him. I think he only let me because I smelled of you."

"*Ash*...thank you." Kate wiped her eyes again. "You really are the best, you know?"

"I love you. It's that simple, and yet, there's nothing simple about what I feel. From the first, it never has been." Asher trailed gentle fingers, tucking her hair behind her ear. "Now, what d'you say to brushing this guy?"

Kate nodded and turned, leading Red to the tack room. Thirty minutes later, she relatched the stall door and said goodnight to her old gelding. She stopped at Wick's stall and petted him before moving on to Rhys's stall, giving her new riding horse some love as well. Then, she let her husband lead her back to the house, her soul more healed from the time spent with her horses.

"Thank you," she whispered as Asher turned on their shower. He turned to look at her, to look her over.

"The heat should feel good on those muscles I'm sure are complaining. Though, you are stronger, I'll admit. You lasted longer than I'd anticipated."

"I can definitely feel it, but I don't think I overdid it. And I desperately needed that."

"I know. That's the *only* reason I agreed to it." Kate smiled at that, aware of the truth in his words. Then she let her husband undress her and minister to her in other ways she needed.

Johnny-

In San Diego, California, Johnny sold his Chevy for fifteen hundred dollars cash. Continuing his MO from his time in Houston, he limited his kills to one hooker every couple of weeks. Not wanting to attract undue attention. He'd lucked out in finding women with drugs on them. Obviously, they'd overdosed. That they seemed to be missing whatever cash they'd had on them was beside the point. When he had over five thousand, he bought an airline ticket to Cancun. He showed his forged documents, thankful he'd had the foresight to have some made the previous year, just in case. Once in Cancun, he found a teenager running a shuttle business out of his older Toyota pickup. He paid the kid to buy him a couple pairs of pants and shirts, then paid him again to take him to Punta Allen. The tiny town sat nearly at the end of a long, winding dirt track on a narrow strip of peninsula. After arriving, it didn't take him overly long to find accommodations. An elderly woman rented him a shed out behind her little store in trade for his agreeing to do handyman work. It irked him to no end to be in the position he found himself. For a moment, he considered just killing her. Problem was, he'd just arrived and needed to lie low for a while. The woman could always have an accident at a later date.

For now, he was far away from Wyoming and anyone who might be looking for him. No, he'd stay here a few months and plan his next move. He'd put some more money aside and when he came back to the states, he'd finish what he'd started. Who knew, maybe when he did, he'd have enough to hire some decent help to get the job done, and done right. Take out the big guy first, then move on to the wife and daughter.

Bethany-

Jack had the brilliant notion to be Captain Jack Sparrow, so when we left Scotland, we took the ferry across to Ireland. All was well, until, as we left the port, Jack discovered he was horribly susceptible to seasickness. The experience quite thoroughly ended all his thoughts of being the rascally pirate, even for the tiniest moment. Poor guy spent the entire two-plus hours of the crossing heaving his guts over the side. He was so miserable, I didn't even have the heart to tease him. After docking, and while Liam arranged for a rental car to take us to my grandparents' place, Delaney and I kept Jack company, sitting on a bench outside so he could get the cool breeze and fresh air on his face. I bought him a bottle of water and some crackers, hoping it would settle his stomach. Once he looked a little less green, we loaded into the rental car and started driving. Thankfully, it wasn't raining, because we ended up needing to leave the windows down for poor Jack.

We arrived back in Kealkill just after five in the evening. Nana and Granda must have been watching for us, because they met us at the door, having it open in welcome before we even reached the steps. Liam and I hadn't shared anything with them over the phone, wanting to tell them our good news in person. Someone must have let slip, though, because Nana's eyes, lit up like Christmas, were focused on my left hand as we approached. She clapped, nearly bouncing on her toes, as she pulled us both in for hugs. "Ye've made me so happy! I couldn't be more thrilled for you both."

We stood for a moment on the stoop, exchanging pleasantries, then Jack groaned quietly from behind us. Nana took one look at him and was suddenly issuing orders. Everyone was sorted and luggage was carried inside. Delaney, as directed, took Jack up to the bathroom, where he'd shower to freshen up and hopefully feel better before laying down to rest. Nana said she'd make Jack her ginger tea, claiming it would make him *right as rain.*

Liam did as he was told and carried our bags up to our rooms, saying he'd join me momentarily in the parlor with Granda. Meanwhile, Nana headed for the kitchen to ready the teapot. "Oh, her ginger tea will set him right up. No doubt about that," Granda said as we took our seats. "Now, tell me. How was Scotland? Did you have fun?"

"I did. Absolutely, I did. It's so beautiful. I loved everything about it. The heather blooming, and the *pipes!* The people, the land, the food, and the music—I loved it all."

"Oh, I wondered how you'd like the pipes." Granda smiled warmly. "Some folk find them atrocious, if you can imagine?"

"Oh, no; the bagpipes are beautiful."

"And Harold and Olivia? How'd you get along with them?"

"They're wonderful." I sighed, warming from my memory of them. "Loving, kind, caring, and gracious people. Truly wonderful hosts."

"And Iona?"

"She's wonderful, too, and made me feel quite welcome."

"It's glad I am to hear it, pet." Granda smiled, his eyes crinkling, then his face dimmed somewhat. "And how was Kristian?"

Before I could answer, Liam returned, explaining, "Da was...Da. And that's the short of it." He sat beside me, draping a comforting arm around me, pulling me in close to his side. "But Bethany handled him well enough."

Liam-

"Kristian had words for the lass?"

Tiernan's voice had hardened ever so slightly, and Liam caught a glimpse of Asher in the older man, then shrugged it off as he replied, "He tried having a go, but she put him in his place fast enough. Was right proud of her, I was."

"Ah, there's my pet. You do my heart good, you do." Tiernan smiled at his granddaughter. "Kristian will come 'round. He's a stiff-necked git at times, but not entirely daft. I imagine he's still sore over that stramash with Ash from some years back."

"*Da tried havin' a go at the Fitzpatrick?*" Liam lurched forward in his seat. "*Gor,* the man must have been bleedin' daft."

"T'was over a lass they'd both fancied as young lads," Nana replied as she reentered the room and took a seat beside her husband. "They were here on holiday, the lot of them, and they'd had a might too much to drink, and, well, one thing led to another." She nodded in Liam's direction. "Words were spoken. Fists went a'flyin'. And yer da ended up tail over teakettle."

"The man's bloody lucky to be alive." Liam breathed, shaking his head in exasperation as he settled back beside Bethany. It wasn't lost on him that had his father been seriously injured by Asher, Liam himself might never have been born, might never have met Bethany. The thought turned his stomach. He breathed deeply to settle it. Seeming to sense his inner turmoil, Bethany took his hand, squeezing it. "I'm a'right, lass."

"Are you?"

"I am," he assured her. "T'was a bit of a shock is all. Dinna fash aboot it."

"Funny, I was going to say the same to you. I'm not worried; I've told you that."

"I ken it. And I'm no', the news had me thinking is all."

Bethany squeezed his hand again, offering him a soft smile. Liam leaned towards her, inhaling the fragrance of her skin as he kissed her temple, thinking he was the luckiest man alive.

Bethany-

With a glance at the clock over the mantle, Nana stood and announced supper was ready. She instructed we should wash up and let Jack and Del know. Nan's tea seemed to have done the job, as when Liam checked on him, Jack said he was hungry and feeling less green around the gills. Delaney, I found sleeping on her bed in our room. I almost didn't wake her, but I knew she loved Nan's cooking and would be hungry later. I shook her with a gentle hand on her shoulder. Blinking, she came to and sat up, then scrambled from the bed at the news food was available. The four of us met in the warm kitchen, inhaling the scent of the roast Granda was slicing.

We said grace, then Nana poured the wine, and we tucked in, talking, and sharing, and simply enjoying each other's company. My grandparents wanted to hear the details of Liam's proposal, well, more Nana than Granda. So, we spent some time talking about that day and how magical it was. With a warm, delicious meal filling my belly, and the wine soothing its way through me, I found myself yawning not long into the evening. I wasn't the only one, though. My companions seemed in the same boat as I, each in turn stifling their own expressions of exhaustion.

After the fourth time, Nan shook her head and lovingly admonished us to head to bed. We thanked her for a wonderful dinner, then helped her to clean up before heading upstairs. Delaney called first dibs on the bathroom, and I claimed second, letting the guys figure out which order they'd go. I retrieved my bathroom bag and waited in the doorway for her to be finished. Liam joined me, apparently having won the pecking order over Jack.

He dropped his bag to the side of the door and slid his arms around me, pulling me to him. At first, he simply held me. After a long minute or two, he slid his hands down my back, finding my hips, where he gripped me, fingertips gently digging in. He made a growling sort of noise deep in his throat and trailed his mouth along my neck to the junction of my shoulder, finding his favorite spot. I trembled and gripped his arms, my breath catching in my throat.

Delaney opened the door. "Omgosh, *seriously?*"

We pulled apart, and Liam stepped back, giving me room, a feral look in his eyes. I glared good-naturedly at Del, unable to keep the heat from my face, even as I fought a grin. "Shut up."

She snickered as she made her way past me. "I'll just leave our door open, you know, for safety's sake. So you two won't fall into temptation again."

Liam chuckled darkly as he leaned against the wall beside mine and Del's door. I shot them both a look, then entered the bathroom. True to her word, Delaney had left our door open. She sat cross-legged on the bed when I came in, Liam having given me a chaste kiss as I passed him. "You can go ahead and close the door now, Bethany. Unless you planned to sleep in those clothes. I wouldn't judge you if you did, but you might be more comfortable if you changed. With the door closed." As I closed the door, I heard the woosh from the pillow she hurled at me, and lifted my arm just in time to block her soft missile. "Oh my gosh, you two! Every time I turn around, you guys are making out. I can't leave you alone for a minute."

"We weren't making out," I argued as I tossed her pillow back and moved to the dresser for my pajamas.

"Uh, what else would you call it? Your hands all over each other, lips locked, panting."

"We weren't panting either." I pulled my shirt on and turned on the bedside lamp.

"Close enough."

"You mean to tell me that you and Jack are perfect angels and never kiss?" My brow was raised, lips pursed.

"Of course not, but we're not talking about me and Jack, now are we? And my parents didn't ask you to chaperone us, while your parents *did*."

I laughed at that. "Whatever. We haven't crossed any lines. Our hands have stayed in neutral zones."

She narrowed her eyes. "You'd better keep it that way."

"We are."

I shut the lamp off and laid down, pulling the blankets up and getting comfortable. We were silent for a bit, and I wondered if she'd fallen asleep, when she asked, "Have you guys set a date yet?"

"No, not yet. We haven't even talked about it. I figured we'd talk once we get home."

"Good idea. The sooner the better, with the way you two are." We both giggled at that.

We woke early the next morning as we planned to go horseback riding. Liam said he wanted to show us how trail rides were conducted here versus back at home. We were all game for it. Thankfully, Jack was feeling much better and back to his usual self. We arrived at the stables and I felt my excitement soar. Our trail guides were a husband-and-wife team in their forties, I was guessing. Nora Rose and Conor. They ascertained our experience and got us fitted out, and soon we were on the trail. Hacking it was called here, not horseback riding. Liam was steady in his seat, whereas I found myself struggling just the slightest, trying to find my rhythm on the horse. Delaney did better than me, having taken a season or two of Dressage, so she was at least familiar with this style of riding. Jack, bless him, was about the same as me. Despite all, we had a great time. Nora and Conor took us through the Hollyhill woodlands, where we rode through heather, fuchsia, and gorse.

As we cleared a stand of Scots Pine, Jack looked over. "Can you imagine trying to sort cattle in these?"

Glancing down to the saddle he'd indicated, I grinned and shook my head.

"You work with cattle, do ya?" Nora asked, bringing her mount beside mine.

"Yeah. My family and I own a cattle ranch in the states."

"Oh, lovely. Where at?"

"Wyoming. South of Montana, which is south of the Canadian border."

"Oh, I've heard of Montana, I have. Rugged country, no?"

"It is. Wyoming is as well. Beautiful, though. Rugged and beautiful. Have you ever been to the States?"

"No, we haven't been on holiday for the last several years. We're keen to go, though. It'd be nice to get away. Just for a while, mind you. I do love our life here."

"I hear you." I nodded. "While I'm enjoying myself tremendously, I do miss home. You guys'd be welcome to join us sometime. We could take you on one of our western rides."

"Like a true cowboy? In the pictures? Oh, we'd love that, we would," Conor spoke up, excitement in his voice.

"I'll get your contact numbers when we're done with this ride, and if you ever get to the States, look us up. We'd love to have you."

The ride lasted a couple hours, and by the time we were through, we'd added a million more pictures, it seemed, to our collection. Elated, though exhausted, we thanked our guides again and remembered to exchange numbers before heading back to my grandparents' house. Nan and Granda wanted to eat out again tonight, so we showered and cleaned up, then headed for Collins'.

The pub was more crowded than I'd ever seen it before and it took us a bit to locate seats, this time finding them off to the left of the bar. Sean was in town, so he met us there. When he arrived, he gave a shrill yell gaining the room's attention. He grabbed Liam, arms going around him as he spun his best friend about, crowing his congratulations on our betrothal. Sean set him down then took Liam's face in his hands and planted a fierce kiss to his mouth, before pounding his back enthusiastically. Sean then turned to me, giving me the same treatment, though more sedately. I thought Delaney and Jake were going to fall out of their seats, they were laughing so hard at his antics.

Liam and I received loud congratulations from the other patrons. Not long into the evening, I caught sight of Patrick on the other side of the room, a young dark-haired woman with him. They seemed happy and quite into each other. Liam and I exchanged a look and I felt warmth rise in me, relieved Patrick seemed healed from any previous injury my relationship with Liam had caused him.

Sometime later, music began playing and soon couples were taking to the floor. I marveled at the steps and somehow wasn't surprised at all when Delaney pulled Jack to his feet, making him attempt the complicated movements with her. Liam and I watched for a moment or two, clapping along with the room. Next thing I knew, he was standing and pulling me into the action as well. Granda and Nan whooped and cheered, encouraging us.

We danced and laughed well into the night. It was only when I saw Nana nodding at Granda, saw as they gathered their coats and wraps, that I realized how late it had become. Returning to the table, we helped clean our mess up, taking out dirty dishes to the counter. Liam snagged a wash rag and wiped the tabletop down. Then waving to everyone, we took our leave and made our way home.

CHAPTER TWENTY-ONE
Moving Mountains

Bethany-

The lot of us had awoken somewhat later than normal, due, I was sure, to our late-night celebrations. With some consternation, I realized we only had another day here, so after breakfast, Delaney asked Nana to show her how to make those cinnamon rolls. Then, Jack, Del, Liam, and I headed down to The Cove beach access. We'd agreed over coffee that a walk would clear our minds and as Wyoming was short on oceanfront property, had decided a walk on the beach would be best. The four of us meandered north along the sand, and as Jack and Del disappeared around a bend, Liam pulled me to a stop.

Silently, I gazed up at him, inquiring on his intentions. Grinning briefly, he pulled me close, slipping his arms around me. "I simply needed a wee moment alone wi' ye." Nodding in understanding and agreement, I pressed closer to him, happy to hear the gratified rumbling noise he made. Liam lifted his head, seemingly looking around, then tugged me into the tall grasses, where he dropped to his back, pulling me down with him.

I shrieked in surprised laughter at his quick movements, but the sound was cut off as his mouth covered mine. The kiss was not an urgent demonstration, but more a contented one. A happy, satisfied one. After a bit he simply tucked my head under his chin and sighed. "I love ye. I hope ye ken I love ye."

"I do, Liam," I assured him. "I do. And I hope you know I feel the same about you."

"I canna describe how those words make me feel. What they, what ye do to the organ pounding in me chest. Ye steal me breath, ye do." He held me like that for several long minutes, then after some time, he sat us up, positioning me between his legs with my back to his front. He rested his head on my shoulder. I reached for his hands, entwinning our fingers. After he raised my left hand, his thumb rubbing along my ring finger. Liam placed a soft kiss against my neck and inhaled slowly, deeply. "Have ye thought at all about a date? Are ye after a long engagement? A short one?"

"I just want to marry you, Liam. Other than that, I don't exactly have any expectations."

"Oh, thank the Good Lord," he breathed.

His heartfelt response had me chuckling, and as I did, his arms tightened, holding me snuggly to him. "I guess we do need to talk about it, though. I know people will begin asking, have already asked. Do you have any preferences?"

Liam kissed my neck again, then said, "Me only preference is *soon*. Have mercy on me and make it soon. I'm holding on by a thread, fightin' no' to ravish ye at will. Make it soon, lass, and save me."

"Can't have you suffering now, can I?" His words, as honest and as raw as they were, lit a flame inside. "All right. How soon do you think we could do this? I've always liked the idea of a fall wedding. Speaking of, *where* would we get married? Who are the *must haves* on your guest list?"

Liam moved, rising fluidly to his feet, then offered a hand to pull me up. He took my face in his hands and kissed me. "Let's find the others and head back to the house. We've plans to make."

Jack and Delaney were already on their way back to us, feeling we'd had enough alone time. Soon, we were back at my grandparents' place, all gathered around Nana's kitchen table. She'd brewed tea and set a tray of the rolls she and Delaney'd made earlier out for us. With pens and paper, we began our planning. We started with who we wanted in our wedding party.

Delaney, of course, would be my maid of honor, and Liam said he'd ask Sean if he'd be his best man. After a bit, we settled on Jack as a groomsman, and I decided to ask my cousin Reese—who would graduate boot camp soon—if she could be a bridesmaid. Next, we went over the must-have names of those we wanted to be there and a part of our special day.

That lead to the understanding that having the wedding at our ranch would probably be best as we had more room to host everyone, not to mention space for the ceremony as well. I checked the time and saw it was close to seven in the morning state-side. I figured Aunt Candi and Uncle Cory'd be up, so dialed her number. After she'd made my mom's wedding dress, her name had taken off as a boutique designer, making no more than half a dozen dresses in a year. I hoped she'd have time to fit me in.

"I wondered when I'd be hearing from you," Aunt Candi affectionately said as she answered. "Congratulations! We're so happy for you."

"Thank you! How'd you hear about it?"

"Your mother of course. She'd called me a month or two back, wanting to give me a heads-up that if all went right, you'd be needing a dress."

"Bless her, of course she did." I sighed. "How'd she even manage that? She's been recovering from an injury for heaven's sake."

"Bethany. This is your mother we're talking about."

"True," I agreed.

"I'll need your measurements. I can email you instructions on the proper way. Have Delaney help you. And I'll need your preferences as far as design."

"Okay, yeah, I can get that for you. And I don't mean to rush you, but we're looking at a fall wedding. End of September, first of October, in that timeframe. Is that impossible?"

"Challenging, yes. Impossible, no. Get me what I need, and I'll have this done for you."

"You're the best, Aunt Candi. I love you."

"Love you, too," she said, affection strong in her voice. "Congratulations, again."

Not wasting time, my next phone call was to the ranch, wanting to make sure we weren't booked. Dad said there were a couple bookings at the very beginning of October, so we settled on the weekend after. Within the hour, Aunt Candi had sent me the link to her video showing how to do proper measurements. Nana had her measuring tape, so with Delaney's help we got those down and sent to her. Being the romantic I am—and ever hopeful—I'd, years ago, created a Pinterest board with wedding ideas. Delaney and I perused it now, and after some time and notes jotted down, I came up with a couple dress ideas. I was thinking an empire waist with an off the shoulder bodice. I wanted it understated and white with green accents.

Pushing back from the table, I stood to stretch, then moved to the sink for a glass of water. Liam and Jack had stepped out for a bit to help Granda with the afternoon milking, and I watched as they made their way back to the house now. My eyes lingered on Liam, taking pleasure in the way he moved, feeling my pulse kick up a notch. The presence he had, the mastery he exuded over his own body. I took a deep breath as they entered the kitchen. He caught my eye and moved to my side.

To distract myself from the direction my thoughts had been heading, I asked a question that had been lingering in the back of my mind. "Will your dad be a problem, do you think? Will he come, or will getting him there be like trying to move mountains?"

Liam turned thoughtful for a moment, then kissed my brow, and said he wasn't concerned.

"Harold will have his head if he doesn't; mark my words, lad," Granda stated. "He'll be there."

"What's on yer mind?" Liam asked quietly.

"I want him to come, I do. I just don't want this to cause any further discord between you two. I want peace and harmony. I want *you* happy."

"I ken ye do. And, deep down, the man ken's it as well. Tiernan is probably right. Grandfather will have his head if Da doesn't show up, or if he makes a stramash out of the occasion." He kissed my forehead, his mouth lingering as he said, "And ye put me heart all aflutter caring as ye do."

Grinning through my heated face, I said, "I think I have a dress idea figured out. And...I have a favor to ask of you."

"Go on...?"

"I don't know if you have plans for what you wanted to wear, but I was hoping I could talk you into, well, into wearing your kilt for the wedding."

"Ye want me to wear me kilt?"

"I do."

"Are ye sure?"

"If you don't want to, then I understand. But I'd like nothing more if you did."

"I'd love to. And I will. O'course, I will. I just thought ye'd have wanted more the traditional, or cowboy look is all."

"I have plans for a combination of both our worlds, but truly, I want you in your kilt."

"Ye can have me in me kilt then, lass."

The amount of promise in his statement sent heat to my cheeks again, had my breath catching, my pulse rocketing. "I love you, Liam. So much."

Lucas-

Lucas chewed the blade of grass between his teeth as he kept an eye on Johnny. The little mouse scurried around the tiny town, doing one odd job, then another. He fixed a fence, repaired a well, hauled water, tended sheep. Probably more physical labor than he'd done his entire life. El Gato leaned against the wall of the pueblo cantina and considered his prey. If he didn't know better, he'd think the little mouse was storing up. Johnny was putting money aside, that much was obvious. But for what purpose? He was making friendly with the people here. Getting to know some of the powerful people, doing them favors.

He was careful, was El Ratoncito. He was being very careful. Lucas decided the mouse was planning something. He'd seen the man go fishing several times. Wasn't much good at it as he only came back with a single spotted trout, the one time. Lucas considered befriending him. Taking the mouse on a fishing trip, a one-way trip where no one would ever hear from the man again. It wouldn't be difficult to make him disappear. It could be fast. The mouse would lose his hands, the faster to bleed out and prevent an attempt at swimming. He'd keep his feet; something was needed to weigh him down. It wouldn't be long before sharks and other fishes came to finish the man off. There wouldn't be much left to identify him, Lucas would see to that.

Another thought entertained his mind. Another path. There were guerrilla factions in the area. He'd seen them come and go, for the most part leaving this tiny hamlet alone. What if *they* took him out. There'd be no suspicion cast on any of those that needed to stay out of it. He pondered how to maneuver the pieces of this puzzle, to make them all fit as needed. It would take some doing, more so than the one-way fishing trip, but the outcome would be better. *Now, how to direct the action...*

Bethany-

We arrived back at the ranch, with work waiting. We had cows to move, calves to brand, fencing to fix, trails to repair. And in the midst of all that, we still had clients coming in. Guests that were coming or going. Horses that needed training. Riding lessons. So much to do. Not to mention, a wedding to plan.

I'd sent Aunt Candi as much information as I could. Including the Gunn colors to give her a reference for the green I wanted used. Delaney and Reese would wear dresses in shades of green to compliment the color I'd chosen. Liam would wear his kilt in traditional dress with a fly plaid off his shoulder. Sean and Jack would wear western gear, jeans, boots, and vest, with a Gunn plaid tie. Things were coming together. I checked the time, noting my next client should be arriving soon.

A lady was having trouble with a new horse. He apparently was quite nervous and reactive, shying and snorting at seemingly everything, despite the amount of groundwork she'd already done with him. I was going to spend some time with him and see what I could do for her. Hearing wheels on gravel, I stepped out of the barn to the sight of a truck and trailer pulling up. As I moved to the truck, Liam came from the house, having gone in to grab another cup of coffee. I secretly smiled, thinking of his newly-acquired love of the caffeinated beverage.

The woman was in her thirties, I was guessing. Brown hair, brown eyes. She smiled as she stuck her hand out in greeting. "Bethany? Hi, I'm Jules Baker, I have the gelding needing some help."

"Hello, Jules." I shook her hand. "Tell me about him." We'd moved to the back of the trailer and she lowered the ramp. Her gelding was a chestnut overo, and I could instantly see what she meant. He held his head high, nostrils distended as he blew loudly. A sheen of sweat was visible on his withers and the backs of his legs. She stepped inside, then led him out. The paint danced around, snorting and whale-eying everything around him.

I asked Jules to walk her horse to the corral and followed behind, noting the way the horse moved to the pressure she applied, and how she responded to his actions. Once he was in the small pen, she turned to me. "What do you think?"

"I'll tell you in a moment." I stepped past her and entered the corral. "What's his name?"

"Rocky."

"Well, Rocky, let's see what you've got." I moved towards him, talking softly, keeping my hands down. He snorted and trotted away, constantly moving to keep distance between us. "Has he been under saddle yet?"

"Yes, he had thirty days with a trainer up in Billings. I moved from there to here and have tried to carry on where the trainer left off, but I don't think I'm getting anywhere with him."

"Fair enough." I nodded, my eyes still on the brown and white horse. "I'd like him for at least thirty days, and we'll see how we go from there. I can start on him tomorrow, if that works?"

"Yes, it does. Thank you. Like I said, you came highly recommended."

"I appreciate that."

"You think you'll have any luck with him?"

"I do. He's not mean. He's not looking to fight. He's just scared. He's not confident and needs to learn how to be confident. I think I can help with that."

She wiped at gathering tears. "It makes me relieved to hear that."

"I can make no promises as to the outcome, please, understand that, but I will give him my best attempt. I'll be in touch this next weekend to give you an update."

I shook her hand again, then waved as she drove off. Liam had been a silent presence while Jules and I had talked. Now, he moved closer and slipped his arms around me. "Seems a might touchy, no?" He indicated the horse with a jerk of his chin.

"He's definitely a project, but I think I can work with him."

"Have a care now, lass. Ye've go' me heart in yer hands here."

"I will. I promise." He kissed my temple, inhaling deeply, tightening his arms.

I started work with Rocky the following morning. Moving him through all the groundwork exercises I knew. He complied for the most part, but there was this constant flinch, and tightening up he'd do. After having him for close to a week, I decided to saddle him. He took the tacking well enough, though he snorted through all of it as if he'd never seen a bridle or saddle before. I rode him in the big arena with Liam, Jack, and Del looking on. He moved well with leg pressure, but he kept his head high, no give. Tension was plain in his form. I could feel it under me. Like a pressure cooker about to burst. My mother was known to have ridden some ranker animals, but I kind of liked to avoid the necessity if I could.

After about thirty minutes in the saddle, I brought Rocky to a stop and dismounted, then waved Jack over. "You want to lay him down?" he asked as he approached.

"I think I'm going to have to." I shot a glance towards Liam, then looked to Jack again. "Grab me a rope, will you? Cotton, and make sure it's long enough." Jack loped off and while he was gone, I put the rope halter back on Rocky and removed his bridle.

"What's the plan?" Liam called from his spot on the fence.

I tightened my ballcap and stretched, knowing what was more than likely about to happen. "I'm going to try something with him. He needs to learn that we're not here to hurt him. I need him to trust me, to trust people." I looked in Liam's direction as Jack made his way back to me. "No matter what happens, Liam, I want you to stay there, okay?" He shot me a look with a ton of meaning behind it. I nodded, then turned back to the horse.

Liam-

Liam swallowed his heart back, not even sure yet what had caused it to lurch upwards in the first place. He simply knew something was about to happen. Bethany removed the spurs from her boots and handed them to Jack, who moved towards the fence, with a quiet reminder for her to be careful. Rigidly, Liam sat on the fence and fought with himself not to go to her. Not to just toss her over his shoulder and take her away from any real or perceived threats.

Bethany hooked the stirrup on the saddle horn, then looped one end of the rope around the gelding's left foreleg. She gently tossed the other end over the horse's back. Liam watched closely as she lifted the foreleg, tucking it up toward the gelding's stomach. Then she reached, taking the end of the rope dangling down and brought it up between the horse's belly and bent leg. Next, she fed the lead rope attached to the halter back between his front legs and up over his back from the right side.

He watched as she took a deep breath, and rolled her shoulders, positioned herself, then began applying pressure on the ropes, talking to the horse the entire time. The gelding reared, struggling, hopping around, trying to rid himself of the ropes and gain his freedom. Liam felt lightheaded as he watched her move with the animal, avoiding being trampled or kicked. It took some time, he wasn't sure of how much, but close to thirty minutes, he'd guess, before she got that gelding on the ground. Both she and the horse were sweating and breathing hard. Though Liam had been stationary for the duration, sweat dripped down his temples, and his lungs felt shredded.

Bethany moved slowly to the horse, speaking softly, encouraging the animal to respond as she wished. As she closed on him, was reaching out a hand for him, the gelding lunged upwards, coming off the ground. She blew out a breath and tried again. Three more times she got him on the ground. On the fourth try she was able to touch him for longer than a moment. Silently, he watched as she leaned over the animal, practically laying on him. She stroked him everywhere. Starting at his head, down his neck, across the shoulder, to the stomach, the hips. She leaned further, feeling down his legs. All the while continuing to speak to the horse. Bethany loosened and removed the rope from the gelding's leg. Then she slid the rope from between his front legs, draping it over the horse's neck, and unhooked the stirrup from the saddle horn.

Liam wasn't sure what her intent was, but when she carefully swung a leg over the inert animal, he thought his heart would stop, and breathed to no one in particular, "Bleedin' everlasting...she's no'?"

"She is," Delaney stated quietly, her gaze firmly on the activity in the ring.

"She's done this a million times, Liam; she knows what she's doing. It's actually quite beautiful what she's able to accomplish with horses. Mind-boggling, really," Jack said, never taking his eyes off Bethany and the horse.

Liam blew out a breath and shook out his hands; they'd begun cramping from his tight grip on the wood. Gripping it to keep himself in place like she'd requested. The horse moved. He lifted his head, then dropped it back to the soil. Bethany petted him, stroking in long, firm, comforting touches. The gelding tried again, this time succeeding as he climbed to his feet with her somehow magically in the saddle. Jack was right, it was beautiful. One of the most beautiful moments he'd ever seen. With one exception, the moment she'd agreed to be his wife.

The painted gelding stood, his head lowered, and waited for Bethany to guide him. She let him sit, waiting, on what Liam wasn't sure. Then, when he saw the gelding work his lips, almost like the horse was mumbling to himself or something, Bethany gently and firmly encouraged the horse to move. She rode him around the arena, making several laps. Then did figure-eights with him before bringing him to a stop in the center of the ring.

Bethany dismounted and gave the horse a once-over, running her hands along his coat. Feeling for heat or swelling, maybe? Once satisfied, she led the gelding in their direction. Liam felt a presence at his side, and looking down, found Asher at the rail beside him. "You look a little pale, Liam. You might want to climb down before you pass out."

"Yeah. Yeah, that's a right good idea, it is. If only I could get me legs to cooperate."

"It takes some getting used to," Asher agreed. "I've aged ten years at least each time I've seen Kate take a troubled horse." Liam nodded, then slipped to the ground, more falling and managing to land on his feet, than a controlled movement. Asher looked him over, then said quietly, "Go around the barn to be sick. No one needs to witness you like that. Trust me; I've been there, done that a time or two."

Liam again nodded, then trembling, made his way to the other side of the barn, near the corrals, and vomited.

CHAPTER TWENTY-TWO
What the Heart Wants

Bethany-

"I'm going to work with him some first, then I'll have you join me, alright?" I explained to Jules several days later when I'd set up a time for her to come see the progress her horse was making. Jules nodded and watched from beside Liam outside the pen.

Every day since that first one, I'd taken Rocky through the trust discipline. Laying him down, getting him to relax, to trust, to be confident. I'd had Jack help on the second day. Wanting Rocky to get used to another person. Then I had Liam come in. It seemed he went easier with Liam. Was calmer. Might have been Liam's usage of the soft, endearing Scots Gaelic language he spoke. I know the sound of it tended to gentle me easily enough.

Once I had Rocky on the ground, I had Jules come into the arena with me. She was nervous and breathing fast. "Take a deep breath and calm yourself," I quietly instructed. "You need to be confident if you want him to trust in you." I indicated her horse. "Look at him. Talk to him. He's lying there, waiting to see what will happen, willing to trust in you." Jules nodded, blinking the moisture from her eyes, then spoke to her horse. Softly at first, then with more confidence. The paint's ears swiveled in her direction. "Good. Now, I want you to move to him, just here. Keep talking. Now touch him. Touch him firm, so he knows it's you and not something out to get him."

I walked her through it, instructing her how to mount while he was down. How to prepare for him to rise at her command. When that command came and Rocky surged to his feet, Jules sat in the saddle, tears streaming down her face. Once they were settled, I had her ride him around the pen, just working with her horse. Bonding with him. When, after an hour, and Jules had dismounted, her face was shining. It was times like these that I felt I'd truly achieved something. That I'd done some good in this world and had accomplished something worthwhile and lasting. And offered up every praise I could, so thankful for the opportunity.

I ended up keeping Rocky for another week, but had Jules come out several times after to take part in his work. When it was all said and done, she was able to catch him, lead him, saddle, and ride him without any issues. I made sure to instruct her to continue working with him. Jules hugged me before leaving. "I'm emotional, I know. It's just, I lost my husband last year and bought this horse to keep me going. And I was struggling and couldn't seem to find my footing. You truly have no idea how...lifesaving this is. *Thank you.* Thank you for all of this."

My heart clenched at the emotion in her voice, the lessening strain on her face, and I said a sincere, quick prayer that she would be okay in the future. That strong, capable people would come into her life to continue encouraging her. That *she* would be strong. "It was my pleasure. Truly. Thank you for trusting in me. Now, go enjoy your horse." Jules put her arms around Rocky, pressing her face into his neck, trying to hide the tears that continued to fall. "What are your plans for him?"

"Trail riding mostly." She pulled back, wiping her eyes as she did, and kept scratching him, almost like she couldn't seem to help herself. I completely understood the sentiment.

"There's a few groups that do trail rides around here, you should check them out. It'd be good for both of you."

"I will, and thank you, again."

Waving her off, feeling a satisfied bubble of warmth around me, I turned to Liam. "What?" I asked at the look on his face.

Liam thoughtfully scratched at his beard, then pulled me to him. "I love ye. That's all. Just ken that I love ye."

Harold-

Close to three weeks later, Harold picked up the phone and dialed his son. "'Lo, Da," Kristian said as he answered, sounding distracted and somewhat resigned.

"Kristian," Harold said, mentally praying for a peaceful outcome as he confronted his only child on a touchy matter. "By now ye should have received the invitation to your son's nuptials."

"Aye, we did. Just three days past. And?"

"And yer goin', Son."

"Am I, now?" Kristian scoffed under his breath.

"Aye, ye are. Ye'll no' be shamin' yer ma, nor me, nor the lad." Harold fought to keep the growl out of his voice. Taking another deep breath, he calmed himself and went on. "Ye've no notion as to how fortunate ye are." Kristian remained silent. "Ye've a *man* for a son, and a right good one, too. And he's fetched himself a braw lass to stand beside him. Ye'll honor that."

When Kristian didn't bother to respond, Harold let the iron in his voice out some. "Ye'll go, and ye'll be respectful, and that's the end of it. You'll go, or I'll have nothin' more to do wi' ye. And ye'll have brought that shame down on the family. Do ye hear me, lad?"

Kristian finally spoke, his voice rough, "Aye, I hear ye."

"Gi' our best to Iona. And let Liam know ye'll be there."

"Ye can be sure of it," Kristian bit out, then hung up.

Harold ended the call and looked to his bride of nearly sixty years. "I've done what I could."

"I ken it. And it breaks my heart to know the measures ye've had to take." Olivia came to her husband, putting her arms around him, pressing her lips to his temple. She could feel his heart pounding in his chest and prayed he wouldn't have another episode. "Have ye taken' yer pills yet, my love?"

"I have, dinna fash now." Harold patted her arm and offered a warm grin. "I'm fair a'right, I am. The lad's as stubborn as they come."

"He is that, make no mistake."

"Takes after me, I suppose?" Harold chuckled darkly.

"Takes after us both, though he seems a wee more thick-headed than either of us ever were."

"Truer words. I'll check with Liam in a week or so, gi' our son time to no' be an obstinate eejit." He kissed the back of her knuckles, lingering there for a moment. "Pray he doesna force my hand, love."

Bethany-

When I opened the email, I blinked. And read everything again slowly and carefully. When we'd done our invitations, we'd mailed hard copies, but due to the time constraint, and in the spirit of efficiency, I'd sent an email version to our guests as well. Along with our phone numbers to rsvp by text. Hesitating, I hovered the cursor over the email from Liam's father. I swallowed my heart back and clicked on it. Then exhaled in an emotional rush. *They were coming.* Both he and Iona would make it. My heart swelled at this news, and I went to find Liam.

He was in the barn brushing Lincoln after their ride. Something I was thoroughly pleased he was now confident enough to accomplish on his own. Without hesitation, I threw my arms around him from the back, pressing my face between his shoulders. "They're coming! They're coming, they're coming, they're coming! I wasn't sure if they would, but I've been praying and praying about it, and they. Are. Coming!"

Liam turned in my arms, chuckling at my enthusiasm, hugging me closer. "Who's that, lass?"

"Your parents. Your dad emailed this morning. He said they were coming. Both he and your mom. Liam, this is wonderful!"

"Da said they'd come? Truly?" His expression was somehow both hopeful and disbelieving.

"Unless he's lying." I shrugged, squeezing him with excitement. "His email was from his office, so I don't think your mom would be using that one. And he clearly indicated they were both coming."

Liam blinked, his mouth lifting slightly as he swallowed back his emotions; it took him a long moment or two to get himself under control. "Lass," he kissed my temple. "I'm afraid to hope what this might mean. I dinna want him to ruin this."

"I don't want him to ruin it either. But, Liam, even if he made a scene and caused a ruckus, our day, our relationship, our *marriage* would not be ruined. Now, he'd get his butt handed to him by pretty much near everyone coming and that'd be on him, but we'd still get married. I'm just glad that he *is* coming. That means the door isn't closed, at least. There's hope."

Liam framed my face in his hands and rested his forehead against mine. "How'd I ever get so fortunate as to have gained yer heart, yer faith, yer love? It steals the air from me lungs, it does."

"I've questioned my fortune in that regard as well. You're my everything, Liam. Everything my heart has ever wanted, and I can't wait to spend the rest of our lives together."

Liam kissed me then, his hands threading into my hair, pulling me to him. It was a slow burn of a kiss. A stoking of flames. My arms held him tighter, my hands gripping, searching. Somehow, I found myself backed up to a wall, Liam pressing me into its surface. He loved me, he truly did, because even with desire burning so hot between us, he slowed the kiss, eased up on the pressure of his mouth on mine. His body still held me immobile, though he'd eased up on that pressure as well. He kissed gently, sweetly, then breathed against my mouth, "I love ye, I love ye, I love ye. Ye have me heart, all of it."

I smiled. "That's all I want. Forever."

Lincoln nickered and shifted in the crossties, apparently feeling neglected. Liam chuckled and pulled back. "Sorry, lad. Ye should ken by now, that I canna stop meself when the lass is aboot, now can I?"

"I'd doubt myself and be a touch disappointed if you did." I grinned mischievously.

Liam lifted my hand, then nipped at my knuckles. "Canna have ye thinkin' that, lass. I'll just have to have me mouth and hands ye as often as I'm able, then."

I blushed at that. "I certainly hope so."

Liam gave me a weighted, heated look. "On wi' ye now, or I'll never get this poor lad taken care of."

"Am I distracting you?" I walked my fingers up his arm and across his shoulders.

"Ye ken that ye are." His blue eyes held steady on mine. So much meaning and intent in his gaze. "Ye're all I can think aboot."

"Ditto." I breathed as I backed away and headed for the barn entrance. Knowing we both had things to finish and would get nothing accomplished if we continued to be a mutual distraction.

Asher-

Asher stepped off the ladder and wiped the sweat from his brow. He, Calvin, and Samuel were building a wedding arch in the meadow between the Big House and his in-laws' place. It had been Kate's idea to have one built rather than rented. She figured it would be yet another income generator for the ranch. He moved back several paces and studied the structure, eyeing the rough-cut timbers, making sure everything was level and secure.

"It's coming along," Calvin stated, tossing each of them a bottle of water from the cooler Jackson had brought out earlier. "I think she'll be pleased with it."

Asher nodded, then inhaled deeply to stave off the sudden rush of emotion threatening him. His throat closed up and the backs of his eyes burned. Like her mother, Kate had struggled with pregnancy. Both getting pregnant and keeping the baby. She'd miscarried twice before Bethany, and now his only living child, his daughter, was on the verge of marriage. Of becoming someone's wife. As happy as he was for his daughter, and he was truly happy for her and pleased by her choice in life-mate, it hit him in the gut at the oddest of times. Asher swallowed and cleared his throat.

Silently, Samuel gripped his shoulder, squeezing before releasing. Samuel and Asher didn't share blood, but Asher couldn't imagine being closer to his friend, or loving him more if the man had been his blood brother. Samuel always got him. Always had. Was always a silent, force-to-be-reckoned-with at his side. Asher cleared his throat again and nodded in gratitude. Hearing an engine, they turned to see a patrol car slowly approaching. Asher glanced to Samuel, who with the barest motion shook his head.

The detective exited his vehicle and approached the men. "Asher," he said by way of greeting, as he held a hand out.

Asher took it, gripping firmly before releasing the other man. "Detective Mercer."

The detective surveyed their work, an open, friendly look on his face. "Planning a wedding, I hear?"

"My daughter's."

"Congratulations."

"Thank you." Asher waited for him to state his reason for coming.

"I'm sure you're wondering why I'm here." Asher remained silent, simply waiting. "Well, I just wanted to check in; see if you've heard any further from Johnny Khyle?"

"I have not."

"You've had no contact with him, at all?"

"The last contact I had with him," Asher replied, "was twenty-plus years ago with my fist in his face."

"Uh-huh. And nothing beyond that?"

"I just told you that I didn't." Asher studied the officer. "Let me guess, you can't find him?"

"We've been looking, far and wide, but so far have come up empty." Mercer gave Asher a measuring look. "It's like he's just disappeared from the face of the earth."

Asher gave a near-silent snort. "That'd be a real shame, now, wouldn't it?"

"Is he dead?" the detective asked point blank. "Did you kill him?"

Maybe it was the lingering emotion from moments earlier, but Asher was done. He let the full weight of his considerable stare rest heavily on Mercer. His voice level, measured. "I think we're done here. I'm sure I don't need to show you the way off my property."

"You said we should find him before you. That if you found him, we never would."

"Charge me with something, or get off my property. Now." Asher turned his back on the officer, dismissal evident in every line of his body. He moved back to the work at hand. The detective looked to both Calvin and Samuel, gauging whether either might assist him somehow. Instead, he found a solid wall of obstinance.

Cursing under his breath, the detective turned to go. Asher glanced over his shoulder as he heard the car leave. He had nothing against Mercer. Nothing at all. In fact, Mercer seemed a decent man. His only problem, as Asher saw it, was that he was bound by the law and the oath he'd taken to uphold it. Asher was bound by no such thing, other than his oath to protect, love, and defend his wife and daughter. And he refused to stand by and allow them to be harmed. Never again. He caught the calculating look in Calvin's gaze and wondered what the man intended to do.

Facing him, Asher waited. He could see the wheels turning, the thoughts flying. Twice, Calvin opened his mouth to speak. Samuel beat him to it, "For your own peace of mind, let it go, Cal. Don't speculate. Don't wonder. Just let it go."

Calvin looked between Asher and Samuel. He looked back towards the Big House. To what, and *who* waited there. Inhaling deeply, he ground his jaw for a moment, then said, "Self-defense?" Asher just stared at him, waiting. Calvin studied him in return, then, seemingly more to himself than them he nodded and stated quietly, "Self-defense."

Lucas-

Lucas adjusted the lens, his finger working the shutter button. For the last two and a half weeks, he'd been compiling the *evidence* he'd need to set the ball in motion on his target. He'd chosen several of the principal characters in the various cartels working in the area. Making it look as though they were being investigated. The pictures were the last thing he'd needed to acquire.

Three days later, he carefully entered the mouse's room, after seeing the man off on one of his jaunts around the town. This time, driving a herd of goats into the foothills. Studying the room thoroughly, Lucas took note of each and every detail. Noting the tension to the bed clothes, the placement of the chair, the drawers on the bureau, the third one from the top that stuck out a quarter inch on the left side, the rug on the floor with the crease seven inches from the center. Making sure to leave no trace as to his presence in the room, Lucas hid the camera, a half dozen incriminating photos, and a roll of undeveloped film under the floorboard he'd been secretly working on for the last week. It was under the man's bed, up against the wall. Sitting back on his haunches, Lucas studied the room again, making sure everything was in its place, that nothing seemed disturbed.

Satisfied, Lucas slipped from the room as silently and swiftly as he'd entered it. He waited for darkness, then doused himself in cheap liquor, taking several long swallows for authentic measure, and made his way to the cantina on the outskirts of town where he knew the members of the cartel he was about to rile hung out. He mussed his hair and scrubbed dirt on his clothing and exposed skin, being sure to include fresh goat excrement in his carefully planned out farce.

Singing to himself, Lucas stumbled into the lit room and belched. Swaying in place, he blinked, squinting at the light. Three men sat against the wall at a table. A fourth was behind the bar, while a fifth softly played a guitar in the opposite corner. Lucas tripped going to the bar, then slapped a hand on it to stop himself from falling. "Cerveza," he muttered. The bartender shook his head, his mouth angled in disgust, but slid a bottle in Lucas' direction.

"Malo o corrupto," Lucas slurred, wiping his mouth. "He's abad man, tomando...fotos." Lucas got quiet for a bit, feigning ignorance of the attention from the men he was currently hooking. Letting them evaluate him. He sipped at his beer, breathing deeply. "Whus-he doin', then? Always sneakin' about, taking...pictures. I don'like 'im."

One of the men from the table got up and moved in Lucas' direction. He wore a thin mustache and had a scar through his lips. "Who's that, señor? The bad man...the one you don't like. What's he done?"

Lucas wobbled as he turned to the man. He blinked, then looked scar-face over and let his eyes go round. "You...he'staking picturesof," *hiccup,* "you. Areyou famous?"

"I'm no one, señor," Scar-face grinned. "Now, who's been taking my picture, eh?"

Lucas breathed heavy on the man, getting close to him, then mumbled, "Thuhbadman."

The man turned his face away from Lucas to the men at the table. One nodded at him. Resigned, the man turned back to Lucas. "Señor, I asked you a question. Who's this man?"

"Are you famous?" Lucas slurred, spittle coming from his mouth.

The man's nostrils flared in irritation, then he drilled Lucas in the stomach, dropping him to the floor. "I told you, señor, I'm no one. I want to know about the man with the camera, the one taking pictures."

Lucas wheezed from the ground, tears streaming down his face. The scarred man hoisted him to his feet, then punched his stomach again. "Are you deaf, or just drunk? I want the name!"

Lucas gasped, "No, m'not. I can proveit. Ican prove it." He told them where to look, claiming he saw the man taking the pictures, saw him hiding the camera under his bed. "I was looking for cerveza. Creepin' 'round, yousee." He shrugged, eyes rolling some. "An' I saw'im."

"Where, señor?"

"The, thehousebythestore. The one b'hind thestore. I saw'im. Look under," *hiccup*, "the bed."

"Watch him," the man seemingly in charge directed at the guitar player, who immediately put his instrument down and stood. Then the other three turned to go. The one in charge, stopped in the doorway and faced back. "If he's lying, kill him. If not, buy him a beer and let him go."

Guitar player nodded, then leaned against the bar, his gaze on Lucas. The bartender polished a glass and they waited. Mentally, Lucas grinned. Everything was going according to plan.

CHAPTER TWENTY-THREE
Reckoning

Iona-

"You'll need to be ready to go on the ninth," Kristian informed Iona one evening as he sat down at the table for dinner. "I've made all the arrangements."

"Go?" she asked, bewildered. "Go where?"

"The lad's getting married, is he not?" Iona stared at her husband. Tears pooled in the corners of her eyes, and her lip trembled. Her breath stuttered in her chest. "Ah, now don't you be cryin'."

Iona let the tears fall and stood, coming around the table, wrapping her arms around Kristian. "Oh, bless you. I'd *hoped*. I'd prayed. Ye've made me *so* happy. We're really going?"

Kristian shrugged under the weight of her emotions. "I've said we are. No reason for ye to be carryin' on for."

Overjoyed and overwhelmed, Iona kissed him, silencing his words. At first, Kristian held still, then he kissed her back. Light, tender, then with more. More force, more passion. "Bloody everlasting...woman, if I'd known ye'd respond in such a way, I'd have done this sooner."

Coyly, Iona looked at him as she took her seat. "Maybe ye've simply forgotten, love, but *we* used to be quite passionate."

"I remember." Kristian swallowed. "I bloody well remember."

"It's good that you do, love. For I'd hate to shock you later this evening." Iona put enough insinuation in her statement, in her gaze to have Kristian squirming in his seat, fervently praying dinner would be over soon. Iona knew she had her in-laws to thank for this. Inwardly, she blessed them both, and prayed this would be a fresh start for she and Kristian. She'd missed him. Missed the man he used to be. The one who'd been passionately in love with her. She wondered where they'd gone off the tracks, but was hopeful they were well on their way to getting back on.

Johnny-

Johnny returned from his latest job, tending the noisy, useless animals. He'd like to put a bullet in each of their brains. He hated goats. Hated their stupid cries. Hated their smell. But seeing as how his landlord had run out of work for him and was threatening to toss him out, he'd been desperate. Besides, the old man was paying him decent to babysit them. With derision, Johnny thought he'd like to put a bullet in the old man's brain, too. Maybe another week or two, then he could move on. He had nearly ten thousand saved. He could hire...well, maybe not anyone topnotch, but someone. Anyone really who could help him.

He'd been careful while here, staying out of sight of the guerilla fighters, the cartel members that came to town every so often. Johnny stopped beside the well and lit the cigarette, a new habit he'd taken up since being here. As he smoked, Johnny thought of _her_. Of all he wanted to do to her. And her daughter. When he got back to the States, he'd begin looking again. He'd find a way to end them, once and for all. _Who knows?_ He thought with a grin. _If the daughter proved worthy, maybe he'd bring her down here. Have his way with her for a good long while._ Women go missing all the time. An idea came to him, then. The cartel, the fighters. What if _they_ aided him? Sure, he'd have to share his spoils, but that was better than never having her in the first place. He could offer them the money he'd saved and the usage of the women. So long as he got to be a part of it. He imagined it, how it'd all play out, a dreamy look coming into his eyes.

His stomach complained loudly, so Johnny hauled a bucket from the well and doused himself with water to rinse away the cloying scent of animal. Then he unwrapped the tamale he'd purchased from the old woman this morning and he made his way back to his shack. He opened his door and clicked on the light, the cornmeal tamale in his mouth, and came to a stop.

Three men were in his room. By the looks of things, they'd given the place a once over. Only the table and chairs were right-side up. Two men flanked the one seated at the table. A camera, a roll of film, and black and white photos lay in front of him. "Buenos Noches, señor." The seated man grinned at him with hard, cold eyes. "Come in. Sit. We have much to discuss, you and I."

Johnny nodded, then bolted out the door. His heart beat a furious pace in his chest as he raced into the night. Gunshots exploded behind him and a wicked blow kicked his legs out from under him, throwing him to the dirt. Spitting sand from his mouth, Johnny grunted in pain and crawled forward, dragging his leg behind him, desperate to get away, to hide. Who were they? What did they want? They couldn't be from Asher, could they? How could they have found him?

One of the men, the one with a scar slicing through his lip was suddenly leaning over him, pistol pointed in Johnny's face. The scar-faced man chuckled. "El Jefe...he has questions. Why're you running? You guilty of something, gringo?" The scar-faced man dragged Johnny to his feet and marched him back to the shack.

Kate-

Three and a half weeks before the wedding, Kate answered the front door, laughing at something Asher had called from their bedroom. He'd come inside a few minutes ago, planning to shower before taking her out to dinner. They were supposed to meet Liam and Bethany at the restaurant to go over final wedding preparations. Kate blinked at the officer on her porch. "May I help you?" Her heart clenched, recognizing him from when she'd given her statement.

Asher must have heard something in her voice, because he swiftly made his way down the stairs. Kate glanced over her shoulder at the creek of that third step. Her eyes flared at the way he was dressed, or undressed, depending on how you viewed it. Asher was barefoot. He still wore pants, though they were undone, but no shirt. Lord help her, he was beautiful. Even under these circumstances, and after nearly twenty-six years of marriage, she still found herself devastated by him.

"Mrs. Fitzpatrick, Asher." Detective Mercer touched two fingers to the brim of his hat. "Have you got a minute?"

Asher-

Kate looked to him, seemingly content to let Asher lead in this situation. He held his gaze solidly on the officer, calculating, weighing. After a moment, Asher nodded, then slipped an arm around Kate's waist, sidestepping them to allow the officer entry.

The detective moved inside with some familiarity, veering left into the living room. He looked about, his eyes taking everything in before turning around. In silence, he scrutinized them, then said, "We've had an APB out on Johnny Khyle since taking your statement, ma'am. It went nationwide. We even sent it across the borders, not wanting to leave any stones unturned. Last week, we caught a lead. A rural police station in Mexico, down near the gulf, contacted me. I returned yesterday, having gone there to verify the story." He held up a manila envelope.

"Will he be coming back here to stand trial?" Kate's voice was low but controlled. Her breathing had sped up, however, and Asher tightened his arm around her, comforting her.

"I'm afraid that won't be possible, ma'am."

"Why not?" she demanded, her voice now sharp with suppressed emotion. Asher's hand now moved in slow circles on her back.

Mercer met Asher's gaze, studying him, letting the silence build before turning back to Kate. "Johnny Khyle is dead."

"You have proof?" Asher finally spoke, calling on all his extensive training, unwilling that *any* emotion show. The detective stared a hole in Asher and slowly waved the envelope, then after a brief hesitation, handed it over. Taking it, Asher moved away from Kate, wanting to see whatever was inside before she did. Without blinking an eye, he read the story told in black and white, studying each photograph. The pictures were detailed. The man had suffered. Though nothing showed on the outside, on the inside Asher felt the rioting emotional tumult surging through him. Relief, satisfaction, and regret. Relief, strong and swift—it was over. The man would no longer be a threat to his family. Satisfaction, sweet and blistering—a reckoning a long time coming was finally fulfilled. Regret, potent and honest—at the waste the man had made of himself, the waste of his life and potential. Regret that he, Asher, hadn't been able to see to Johnny himself.

Asher placed the pictures back in the envelope and turned to his wife, hating the paleness of her skin, the tightening around her eyes and mouth. "It's him," he answered the unspoken question in her eyes. Kate exhaled, her breath shaky. She looked at the envelope, staring hard at it. Asher shook his head when she met his gaze again as he approached her. "It isn't pretty, love. Just know that he is dead, and you and Bethany are safe."

Kate swallowed, then nodded, and as Asher pulled her into his arms, she buried her face in his chest, attempting to control her trembling. Over her head, Asher asked, "What happened? Do you know?"

Detective Mercer accepted the envelope back from Asher. "From what we've been able to piece together, it looks as though he had a run-in with the cartel. How he got on the wrong side of them is anyone's guess. Though we questioned many, no one of course, heard or saw anything. We have reason to believe Mr. Khyle was involved in several murders in the Houston area, as well as San Diego. DNA will be used to see if he's a match to those, and if he is, at least we can bring closure to those cases." He indicated the envelope. "I thought you'd want to know."

"Appreciated." Asher nodded.

The officer tapped the edge of the envelope against his palm, looking for all the world like he wanted to say something more. In the end, he simply nodded back and bid them a goodnight. Asher closed the door after him, locking it, before turning to his wife. Kate burst into tears. He lifted her in his arms and carried her up to their room where he held her as she fell apart.

Samuel-

Samuel found Tiffy curled in the big chair by the front window, a book in hand. He stood still for a moment, content to simply watch her. His dark eyes travelled over her form, lighting on her still beautiful, still lush red hair. The lowering sun came through the pane setting her hair on fire, making a halo around her—like an angel. She was *his* angel. Tiffy must have heard something, because she looked up from her book, her grey eyes crinkling at the sight of him. "What are you doing?" she asked, self-consciously.

"Watching you, what else?" Samuel rubbed at his chin and mouth with a knuckle.

She smiled, then noted something, some look in his eyes. "What's wrong?"

"Ash asked me to stop by on my way home."

"And?"

Samuel came to her, kneeling at her feet. He took her hands in his. "Johnny Khyle was found murdered south of the border. They think it was a cartel hit."

Tiffy blinked. She opened her mouth, then closed it, before finally saying, "I, I can't say that I'm sorry to hear that."

"I can't say that either."

"How'd Kate take the news?"

"She was pretty shook up, Ash said."

"I can imagine." Tiffy looked at her husband and felt her heart was close to bursting with her love for him. Taking a deep breath, she asked, "Should I go over there, do you think?"

Samuel shook his head slowly, heat building in his eyes. Standing, he pulled her to her feet. "Kate has Ash; she'll be fine. *I* need you. Here. With me." Tiffy nodded, well on-board with the ideas forming in his intent. She lifted on her toes to kiss along his jaw and wrap her arms around his neck, pulling them closer, tighter.

Samuel growled his approval low in his throat. She'd always been able to bring out the tiger in him, and had always managed somehow to tame the beast. Smoothly, he moved them, sliding into swaying, dancing steps as he led her to their room.

Bethany-

"What happened, Dad?" I asked when he met us in the kitchen and I didn't see Mom. "Is Mom okay? She didn't fall or anything, did she?"

"She's a little shook up, but fine. She's asleep right now."

"What happened?" I asked again, feeling Liam slip an arm around me.

"The detective was here." Liam's grip tightened. "Johnny Khyle is dead. He was found murdered south of the border." My breath left me in a rush.

"He had proof?" Dad nodded. "You saw it? He showed you?"

"It was him, kitten. No doubts." I didn't know what to say. I was relieved he would no longer be able to hurt my mother or me, or anyone else for that matter, but I was also shocked. Had I wanted him dead? I'd wanted to hurt him, certainly. But did that mean I'd wanted him dead? I didn't know. Did this relief make me a terrible person? "The news was just a lot for your mother to take. I don't think she knows quite what to make of it, or how to feel."

I nodded. "Yeah. I'm sure."

My vision tunneled. As if he knew the turmoil taking place inside me, Liam pulled me into his arms, and against my temple, said, "Breathe, lass."

I blinked, looking around. Dad was gone, having taken the food we'd brought home up to my mom, I assumed; I hadn't heard him leave. With a shuddering breath, I asked, "Am I terrible for not feeling sad or anything? Because I'm *not*. I'm glad. Oh my gosh, Liam, I'm *glad* he's dead. I am terrible."

"I canna say this news makes me sad, lass. Far from it. Does that make me a terrible person?" I shook my head and against my forehead, he said, "Then ye aren't either. It's natural, I think, to feel this way." He held me like that for a while, letting me work through the turmoil inside. Offering only support and comfort, asking for nothing in return. At some point, we'd retreated to the sofa. Close to eleven, he kissed me softly after catching me yawning again. "Get some sleep, lass. Ye need the rest."

The next morning, when Mom came down in search of coffee, I poured her a cup. Before handing it to her though, I set it on the counter and hugged her. "Don't feel guilty. I can see it on your face. None of this was you or your fault. The man fully brought this outcome on himself."

"I do, though." She shuddered. "I can't help it. I feel guilty. I *had* wanted him dead. And now he is. And I think I should feel terrible about it, but I don't, I'm glad. And that's making me feel worse."

"Mom." I squeezed her tighter. "I understand. I do. I'd wanted him dead, too. And I don't know if that's wrong. Mostly, I guess, I just wanted it to stop, by *any* means necessary. But I do know that neither you, nor I, are at fault in his death. He brought that on himself."

Mom pulled back and gave me a watery grin. She took a deep breath, then patted my cheek. "I know, sweetie. I know. It'll just take me some time to get past this."

I nodded and we both moved to the table to sip our coffee. We'd been there maybe a handful of minutes, when she said, "You're right. None of this was my fault. Johnny made his own choices, and I am not responsible for them. And I am *not* going to let him ruin this time with you."

"That's the spirit." I grinned.

"Now, what'd we miss from last night? What else needs to be done?"

"I told you that Liam's parents are both coming, right?"

"You did. Speaking of, when should we begin expecting guests? And have you heard from Candi?"

"Everyone should begin arriving sometime in the next two weeks. Granda and Nana, and Harold and Olivia are flying in two days before. Iona and Kristian will arrive the day before them. And Sean gets here a week from tomorrow, and Reese the day after. Aunt Candi says the dress is coming along and she plans to be here sometime next week for final fittings.

The flowers will arrive two days before the wedding, and we spoke with Nikki and confirmed the cakes will be delivered the morning of. The photographer has confirmed as well."

"It sounds like everything is coming along. Are you getting nervous?"

"It is, and no, I'm not *nervous,* so much as I just want it to be over. I want to *be* married. I want to be with my husband. I want to start our life together."

"I remember those feelings. Your dad made it the best day of my life, next to the day you were born."

I studied her. At times it was like looking in a mirror. We were so similar, and yet we were different as well. Mom was my closest friend, my first best friend, and I loved her. Knowing her as I did, I said, "I was going to head out to the barn, get some horses groomed. I have a noon appointment coming, you want to join me?"

"I would love that, thank you."

We were on our second horse each, when I looked over at her. Peace had settled into her features, into her body from the steady, relaxing work. Silently and humbly, I thanked God and blinked the moisture from my eyes. I finished the gelding I was working on and glanced at the time. It was a quarter to twelve. My client should be arriving soon. Dad and Liam had left earlier this morning, saying they had 'guy things' to do, whatever the heck that meant. I did wonder *what* they were doing, though.

Rolling my eyes at myself, I debated getting started on another horse, when Liam stepped into the barn. There was a light in his blue eyes that made my heart speed up. Without hesitation, he walked right up, took my face in his hands, and soundly kissed me. I grinned against his mouth and said, "What's this about?"

"It's aboot the fact that ye fair drive me mad wi' longing for ye, and I couldna help meself."

"I see." I chuckled, falling in love with him still more. "And I'm glad."

He kissed me again, then stepped back, taking my hand. "Kate." He nodded to my mom. "Could I get ye two fine lasses to follow me outside for a minute of yer time? The Fitzpatrick and I have summat to show ye." I stared at him, questioning what was happening. "Ach now, lass. No questions. I promise, ye willna be sorry."

Glancing to Mom, I raised a brow as we moved outside. Behind Dad's truck was one of the horse trailers. "Oh, my goodness, what's he done now?" Mom asked under her breath. We watched as Dad opened the back and stepped inside. A few lengthy moments later, he came out leading a beautiful black colt. "*Ohhh...*" Mom's voice broke, tears spilling down her face as she took in the Friesian foal. "He didn't."

"Aye, he did," Liam told her gently. "It's possible I'm wrong, but I'm fair certain that man is in love wi' ye."

We walked over and Mom breathed, her voice full of emotion, "Why? What is this?"

"I know you've had your eye on one of these colts for some time now." Dad indicated the horse, then nodded to Mom. "You're healed. And your only child is about to be married. I thought now was a good time. Plus," his blue eyes sparkled, "I just enjoy making you happy."

Mom kissed him, then turned to the colt. "Tell me about him."

"He's from Frederik the Great's line. He's intact and is a little more than six months old."

Mom whipped her gaze to Dad. "He's from *Frederik?*" My brows rose with that news. *Wow, Dad had gone all out.* Frederik was one of the premier studs of the breed. His line was in high demand. Some people, I knew, waited years to get one of his foals.

"He is."

"Why?" she asked him again, shaking her head in wonderment.

"I've already told you. But in short...I love you. It's that simple. And that was all the reason I needed."

"I don't deserve you, Ash, but I'm so thoroughly thankful for you." Mom took the colt's lead from Dad and walked the foal around.

Dad shook his head, eyes steady on the two of them, vigilant as to their safety. "It's me that doesn't deserve you, love. Though, daily, I'll keep trying."

"We've a stall prepared for him," Liam said, and we moved in the barn's direction.

"I'd wondered about that, but thought maybe you were simply extra motivated or something." I smiled up at him, and we watched as Mom settled the colt in his stall.

"I have summat for ye as well, lass," Liam told me, taking a firmer grip on my hand. "It's no' as spectacular as that fine, young colt there, but I think ye'll like it all the same." From his pocket, he pulled out a piece of paper and handed it to me. It was a confirmation for bagpipers. Tears filled my eyes and I hastily brushed them away. "I ken how much ye liked them from our trip and this trio comes highly recommended."

"This is perfect!" I threw my arms around him and kissed him thoroughly. "Thank you. How long will we have them for?"

"As long as is needed. I figure we could talk and see how ye wanted things to go. They can be the introductory music, whatever ye prefer, lass."

My heart swelled in happiness and settled in peace at the same time. Could I love this man any more? It was hard to imagine so. A text came in—my appointment was cancelling. Engine trouble. Sighing, I hoped my client was well and got his truck figured out.

"Hey, let's go for a ride. Just the two of us?" This cancellation had freed up some time, and I couldn't picture spending it with anyone else.

CHAPTER TWENTY-FOUR

Pressure Building

Bethany-

A storm was blowing in. For days, thick, dark clouds had been amassing over the northern horizon. I could feel the pressure in the air. Taste it on my tongue. The wedding was less than a week away. Aunt Candi and Uncle Cory had arrived early last week. I'd known she was talented, but my aunt had outdone herself on my dress. It fit flawlessly. Following tradition, I didn't allow Liam to see it before I walked down the aisle to him. But I knew he was going to love it. Both Reese's and Delaney's dresses had arrived, and other than mild hemming at the bottom, fit as we'd hoped.

Tomorrow, my almost in-laws were supposed to arrive. Due in part to the wedding and in part to their imminent arrival, I'd been fiendishly cleaning, organizing, and getting everything as perfect as I felt I could make it. Liam finally pulled me to a stop, admonishing me to relax, that his family's approval was not necessary for our special day. He reminded me of my words to him, that whether his dad approved or not, or even made a scene, it wouldn't affect us or our marriage. I'd kissed him soundly for that. I'd so needed to hear that reminder, and was able to battle the pressure building within.

Now, as I stood inside the barn and glared out the door, I tried to remind myself of those timely and wise words. Thunder rumbled overhead as lightning streaked across the sky, and with it, the deluge finally hit. Lashing rain and peppering hail fell in an onslaught of furious sound. The storm raged and I decided nothing else could be done today. At least not outside, not right now. As I was double-checking to make certain everything was battened down, Liam darted into the barn.

He shook the rain from his hair and instantly found me. "What's up?" I smiled.

"Just checkin' on me lass."

"You didn't have to come out in this. I was just getting ready to head inside." Thunder boomed and with it, the rain fell heavier. "Though, from the sounds of things, I may wait a bit and let the storm move on." I glanced to the doorway. "It's really coming down out there."

Liam moved, drawing my gaze. "No' this weather, nor any other kind, will keep me from yer side, ye ken that?" He slipped his hands to my hips, fingers hooking into my beltloops, tugging me against him, igniting that ever-present ember.

More than willing, my arms slid around him, a shiver of longing skating through me. I inhaled against his chest, breathing in his scent wrapped with the scent of the rain. "You smell...absolutely...*divine* in the rain," I half-whispered against his chest. I kissed the base of his throat, even as I continued to breathe him in, and made a soft throaty sound that he answered with a growl of his own.

"*Gor*, lass. I want ye. Badly." He dipped his head, his mouth finding my neck, placing slow kiss, after slow kiss. After slow kiss. His teeth slid against my skin, took a firmer hold, then softened. Liam's breath cooled me as he dragged his nose, his lips across my neck. He breathed deeply, rumbling deep in his throat, then he kissed along the length of mine, taking slow passes, tasting until my legs felt weak and I had to cling to him to keep upright. "The tension," he growled low, "the *pressure*, at times, I feel as though I'm burnin' from the inside out. It's everything I can do to keep me hands off ye."

My arms were wrapped tight around his neck, pulling him closer. Thunder clapped loudly, causing us to jump, as it sounded like a bomb going off. Startled by the sound, we parted, gasping, then laughed. "Aye,

Lord," Liam muttered good-naturedly, scratching at his jaw. "I hear ye. I'm no' havin' her as of yet, but Ye and I ken how I want to."

Blushing, I grinned and faced the storm, wondering if we'd lose any trees and how much destruction it would cause. Lightning flashed and my gaze returned to Liam. "I hope this doesn't do too much damage out there. I was hoping to take your parents for a little ride, to show them the place. Thought maybe they'd like a western ride while they were here."

He studied me, the look in his eyes one I couldn't fathom. After a moment, in a voice barely more than a whisper, he said, "I've told ye that I love ye, but I'm thinkin'…maybe I havena been as truthful as I could be." My heart beat unsteadily as he continued, almost more to himself than to me. "Though, I canna figure how to say it better. I *love* ye. But what I feel is *more* than love. It must be. I canna put words to what's in me heart, just ken that ye have it all and then some." He'd moved closer again, his hands trailing slowly up my arms to my neck. His fingers threaded into my hair as his mouth settled over mine. "Lord, I'm rememberin'," he breathed, "I swear it." He kissed me then. A slow sliding of his lips against mine. Over mine. Trailing along my cheek, into my hair. He tilted my head and found my neck again. His grip tightening, he moved and I was pressed against him. His body a solid pressure against mine. He held me close, breathing deeply as he continued his tender assault with his mouth. My whole body trembled as longing, fierce and desperate flamed inside me. I may have whimpered; I can't be sure. He kissed me once more. Tender touches of his mouth over mine, refusing to deepen it. Then he moved to the corner of my mouth. To my nose. My forehead, where he came to rest. His breath came fast, mine answering.

We heard a call from the house and stepped apart, eyes locked. "We'd best get inside, lass. Afore I forget meself and anger the Almighty."

Flushed with heat, I nodded and clicked off the lights. Liam firmly closed the door, then hand in hand, we raced for the back door. Delaney waited for us. She took one look at me and knowingly shook her head, an impish light in her eyes.

Liam-

Liam watched her, couldn't seem to take his eyes off her. In just under five days, she'd be Mrs. Liam Gunn. Bethany Gunn. He reflected on their relationship. On his feelings for her. And had to swallow emotion back. He tracked her as she moved about the room, helping with dinner preparations. In a moment, he'd get up, go to her and help. Right now, though, he thought it best to stay seated.

He wasn't sure he'd be able to keep his hands off her. He wanted nothing more than to have her. Have all of her. He wanted it like he needed his next breath. Which is why he was still seated. He didn't trust himself. He'd proved time and again that he couldn't be trusted. Never had he given so much thought to a lass. Other than the barest minimum required to achieve the desired outcome.

Bethany, on the other hand, had him tied in knots, she did. To his surprise, he found himself content to be tied up by her. Back in the barn there, with the smell of rain and pine, horse and hay, and whatever fragrance she wore, he knew it had been a close one.

With lightning and thunder flashing and booming just outside, he'd been like the calm before the storm. He'd detected the building pressure in the air. And in himself. Finding her there, no one else around, those intoxicating scents perfuming the air, he'd had to have his hands on her. He'd never noticed before the sheer sensuality of a barely-there touch. Never taken the time to discover those wonders. Those grazing, gliding pressures. Hearing her breath, the tremble, the tremor. It had nearly undone him.

Thunder muttered loudly again, and he mentally chuckled. *Aye, Lord, I'm behavin', I am.* Liam considered her suddenly from another angle. One he should have before, and would need to pay closer attention to. Bethany was a virgin. She'd never been with a man before. Heat tore through him.

Such burning heat and longing. Then, like a dousing of ice-cold water, he reminded himself he'd never been with a virgin before. Had no experience with it. He couldn't just...take her. He'd have to make it special. Memorable. Romantic. Really stoke the flame to assuage the initial pain of it. His head filled with all the possibilities as he planned, until thunder boomed once more, bringing him to himself, reminding him of his place. Inwardly, he winced good-naturedly. Inhaling, he held on to a breath for a moment, letting his lungs become uncomfortable, before exhaling and standing to his feet.

Liam-

Liam stood motionless, fighting the tension rapidly building inside, waiting for his parents to come through the exit doors at the Cody Airport. Asher waited a couple feet away, having accompanied him. When they finally emerged, Liam studied them, detecting something...different. Not wrong, just different. A relaxed air seemed to have sprung up between them. He wondered at it but refocused, feeling his father's gaze on him. He forced himself not to fidget in any way as they approached. And redirected his gaze to mother, keeping it firmly there. "Ma." He smiled in answer to hers. "Ye look well. How was the flight?"

"Fine, fine." She kissed his cheek.

"Ma, Da, ye remember Asher Fitzpatrick, I trust? This is Bethany's father."

Asher gave Iona a gentle squeeze. "Welcome to Cody." He turned to Kristian then and offered a hand. "It's been a long time."

"Aye," Kristian replied, taking it. "It surely has."

"Well," Asher said, "let's get your luggage and we'll get you back to the ranch and settled in."

"And where's your bride-to-be?" Kristian asked Liam, looking around.

"Bethany stayed at the ranch to help with final preparations," Liam replied, admonishing himself not to take offense to every little thing his father said.

They gathered the bags Kristian and Iona had brought and were soon on the road. Asher kept up a steady stream of conversation, talking about the area, the history, the landmarks, the weather. Liam continued studying the dynamics of his parents' relationship. If he didn't know better, he'd think they were in love. He couldn't remember a time when they'd been this relaxed with each other. His father was being courteous and considerate. He'd offered Iona the front seat, taking the back. He'd even helped her into the vehicle. Something was definitely changed. And for the better, it seemed.

"Liam said you had plenty of room, but if it's a bother in any way, we can find accommodations in town," Iona offered at one point, a few minutes from the ranch.

"That won't be necessary, Iona. We have plenty of room, and then some," Asher assured her.

The vehicle slowed, coming up to the Blue Spruce trees and the Blues Avenue sign over the entrance. Liam gauged their reactions—Kristian and Iona both seemed in shock at the sheer size of the place. They gaped at the driveway itself as it seemed to go on and on. Stunned was how they looked, unable to hide their awe, as the ranch house came into view. Both of them leaning forward a little in their seats. Iona gasped under her breath, and Kristian gently squeezed her shoulder in seeming agreement with his wife. Liam wondered just what was going through his parents' minds.

Bethany-

I heard Dad's truck pull up. "Omgosh, they're here!" My heart thundered, despite numerous admonishments to remain calm and not get worked up. Wiping my hands on my jeans, I opened the front door and stepped out to greet them. Iona and Kristian were getting down from the truck when I came out. They looked all around, eyes taking everything in. Moving closer, I snagged Iona's eye and gave her a warm hug. "Hello, and welcome!"

Dad and Liam got their bags from the bed of the truck and came around to where we all stood. Awkwardly, Kristian leaned in and gave me a one-armed hug. I swallowed back any surprise that hit at his show of affection, and simply smiled. Soon, we had them moving along to the middle cabin. The grandparents, both mine and Liam's would share the largest cabin. We had Sean in Dad's old guest room, and Reese was, of course, with her parents.

"You are more than welcome to eat with us in the main house, or if you'd prefer, you can take your meals here. There should be plenty of linens in the cabinets, and dishes in the kitchen. Is there anything else you might need?" I smiled, hoping everything was to their mutual liking.

"Everything looks fine, love. Thanks for having us." Iona smiled back. Kristian jerked his gaze from the mountains out the window and nodded his agreement.

"Dinner will be ready in close to an hour. Will you be joining us in the Big House, or should I bring yours out here?"

Iona opened her mouth, then paused, looking at her husband. Picking up what she was offering, Kristian said, "We'll join ye at the Big House, thanks kindly."

With that resolved, Liam and I left them to get settled in. As we stepped into the kitchen, he pulled me close, arms wrapping around my front, bringing me close. "I love ye. Everything's fine, lass. Breathe."

I exhaled and nodded. "I love you, too, and I think you're right." Turning in his arms, I said, "Did they seem...different to you?"

"Aye, they did. I canna rightly put me finger on it, but summat's changed 'atween the two of them."

"Something good, though, I think. Don't you?"

"Aye, I do."

Bethany-

Dinner was wonderful. *Peaceful.* None of the tension I'd previously experienced. If anyone seemed even remotely anxious, it was Liam. Though his, I was sure, was more from not quite understanding the almost palpable difference in his parents. I, on the other hand, was filled with so much hope, I felt I might burst. Offering all the thanks I had to give that things seemed healed, or at the very least, healing between all parties.

We leaned back from the table, full and contented, having served our guests a true western meal. At Liam's request, I'd made a smoked brisket with cheesy potatoes. And Mom had made apple pie for later. "Did you guys get enough?" Mom asked.

"Aye, we did." Iona wiped her mouth with a napkin. "That was delicious."

"Glad you enjoyed it." I smiled. "I know you're only here for a few days, and we hope you'll come again, but we'd like to take you guys on a trail ride tomorrow. To show you more of the ranch."

"Oh, I haven't been on horseback since I was a lad," Kristian stated, seeming uncertain.

"I have faith in your ability to stay in the saddle, love." Iona smiled at him.

Kristian blushed and cleared his throat. "Aye, I reckon we can give it go."

"It's settled then. We won't be gone too long, just a couple hours, and I promise we'll take it slow. We should be back well before the grandparents arrive."

"Who all's going?" Dad asked, taking another sip from his glass.

"Us, you and Mom, Iona and Kristian, Jack and Del, and Reese and Sean both said they were hoping to go on a ride while here."

"Sean wants to go?" Liam grinned. Three nights back, when Reese had arrived and Sean had caught sight of my cousin, I'd noted the keen interest in his eyes. Saw the way they'd tracked Reese's movements. Saw the way she flushed under his attention, and also saw the look in Uncle Samuel's eyes. Liam and I had speculated well into the night about possibilities in that regard.

"He said he did." I offered a knowing grin back.

"This ought to be a right banger, it will."

"It'll be fine," I assured him.

"Will you have enough horses for all of us?" Iona wondered.

"Absolutely. I figure we'll leave between ten and eleven and should get back no later than one or two. We'll take it slow and just enjoy the ride."

Later that night, I texted Reese to let her know what time to be at the barn. She texted back shortly after and said her dad mentioned he might go. Then texted back moments later to say her mom had come to the rescue and Uncle Samuel would be staying home with her. I chuckled at the dynamics playing out there.

CHAPTER TWENTY-FIVE

The Broken Road

Bethany-

We crested the slight plateau at the Jump Off, and I pulled Wick to a stop. Though our group was good-sized, everyone seemed to be doing well. I eyed each of my riders, just to be certain. Looking for any signs of discomfort. "How's everyone doing? Everything good? Need any adjustments made?"

Everyone seemed to indicate they were all right. Kristian, Iona, and Sean were snapping pictures. "Sean," I called. "You good?"

"Right as rain. This is amazing. Beautiful." His gaze had landed on Reese as he spoke the last part. His eyes travelling over her dark brown hair, hesitating over her mouth before returning to her soft blue eyes.

Swallowing a grin, I nodded. "Right then, let's keep going, still plenty of ground to cover."

Delaney and Jack shot me knowing looks, well aware of the direction Sean's interest seemed to be focused. As I took in Reese's responses to the Irishman, I didn't think she minded his notice at all. Not if the color touching her cheeks was any indication. Liam and I took the lead as we continued on, with Iona and Kristian following, my parents after them, then Sean and Reese, with Delaney and Jack bringing up the rear.

Close to noon, we stopped again. This time for lunch in a little clearing with a small creek running through it. We made dry camp as we left the horses ground tied. Finding logs, or rocks, or just dried grass to sit on, we ate the sandwiches I'd made earlier. Dad was giving Mom a heated look, paired with a knowing grin that had me wondering, and then quickly dismissing that line of thought. Honestly, it was getting ridiculous, the way I kept getting these glimpses into their history. Steamy. That's the only way I could describe the mutual look in their eyes.

Liam brushed a hand along my arm, bringing my gaze to his. I soaked in the warmth in his eyes and shivered under his regard; we were pretty steamy, too. Kristian and Iona stood, stretching their legs as they walked a few steps away from our group. After a minute or two, I joined them, as they took in the view from between the trees.

"Is all this still the ranch?" Iona asked.

"It is. See that ridge to the far left?" At her nod I continued, mapping out the lay of our land.

"It's so big," she marveled. "I didna realize it was so big."

"It is a big ranch," I agreed, "though, we're actually small compared to some others. I love it, though."

She nodded, slipping her hand into her husband's. He turned to me, a warm, thoughtful look in his eye. "Aye, I can see that ye do. That ye both do." Briefly, his eyes landed on his son before returning to me. "It's a fine place ye have here." He was quiet a moment more. "It's a fine...*braw* lass my son has found in ye. I hope...I hope we can—" His words cut off as I hugged him, my heart bursting with happiness. Awkwardly, he patted my back. "I'm glad he has ye. I'm right glad."

Pulling back, I smiled. "I'm so glad you're both here. It just wouldn't have been the same without you. Thank you."

"No, lass," Kristian rumbled, clearing his throat. "It's you we've to thank. And we're glad to be here. Wouldna have missed it. I know...I ken we got off on a bit of rocky ground. Ah, the road was, a might broke, ye might say. But, thanks to the Almighty, it's healing. And I'm glad for all that. So very glad."

Liam-

Liam did a doubletake, not sure what to make of his future bride hugging his father like she meant it. His heart thudded heavily in his chest as he studied them. Bethany, his father, and his mother. There was a peace on their faces, in their expressions. Warmth in their eyes. He felt a similar warmth climb up through him. It wrapped around his heart, his throat, making it difficult to swallow. He felt a presence at his side and glanced over to see Sean. "Steady on, mate," Sean said quietly. "She's got him well in hand, she does."

Liam's gaze moved back to Bethany. "Aye," he whispered past the knot, "aye, she does."

"Quite the miracle-worker, yer lass is, isn't she?"

"Quite."

"Think she could work one for yer best mate?" Liam turned to his friend, now studying him. Sean scratched at his whiskers. "See, I've a mind to risk life and limb over that willowy dew drop over yonder. And as I stood by you, when you were contemplating the same course, I thought perhaps, you could maybe do the same for me."

"That's the way of it, is it?" Liam speculated. "Ye'd best be sure, mate."

"She has my heart. Has had it since I first laid eyes on the lass." He shook his head gently. "I don't want it back."

Liam shot him a look. "And is she in agreement?"

"She's not opposed to the idea." Sean scratched at his chin. "Though, like yer lass, she's after taking things slow."

"Ye've talked wi' her aboot it, then?"

"We have. I suggested exchanging numbers between the four of us in your wedding."

"Ye sly, bugger, ye." Liam grinned.

"Man's got to do what a man's got to do, mate."

"True enough," Liam said, nodding. "All right, so long as the lass is willing, Bethany and I will have yer back. Though, as ye've met her da, I suggest ye tread carefully, lad."

Sean inhaled slow, then exhaled the same. "Tread carefully...this road, the one that's led me here, with her, it's been a rocky one, no doubt about that. But I'd travel through hell and back for the lass. And I mean every word I say."

Liam studied his friend and saw the truth in his eyes, heard it in his voice, and offered a silent prayer on his behalf. He clapped Sean on the shoulder, then moved toward his bride-to-be.

Bethany-

My heart felt as though it was bursting as we rode into the ranch yard. Happiness seemed to waft through the air, like a sweet pollen, enveloping us in a gentle, comforting embrace. A cleansing breeze blew, chasing the lingering storm clouds away, bringing the fresh scent of pine with it. Mom and Dad took Kristian and Iona inside to refresh themselves after the ride. They'd leave in about an hour to pick the grandparents up from the airport. Meanwhile, Reese, Jack, Delaney, Liam, and Sean helped me with the untacking, grooming, and afternoon feeding.

"How was it?" I asked Reese. "Not too sore, are you?"

"Not too bad. Not yet, at least. I'll probably need to stretch tonight, though."

I nodded. "Definitely. How long's it been?"

"Has to have been before I left for Basic."

"And you're loving Army life?"

Reese hesitated, drawing my gaze to hers. Catching my eye, she said, "I am. I love it."

"But?" Reese was leaving something unsaid.

Blowing out a breath, she carried her saddle to the tack room. Following after with mine, I waited for her to speak. "It's different. The Military has changed so much over the last year, even since I graduated. I don't, I can't quite put my finger on it."

"You thinking of retiring all ready?"

"I don't know. Maybe?" Her eyes were out the door, resting on Sean. Watching as the Irishman laughed at something Jack said to him while they brushed their horses. "I'd thought military life was what I wanted...now I'm not so sure."

"I see."

"How did you know, Bethany?" She glanced at me, then turned to Sean again. "That Liam was *it* for you?"

"You know I've been in love with him since forever, right?"

She snorted. "I'm pretty sure I still have that drawing you did when you came back the first time, talking about Liam like he was some sort of knight-in-shining-armor."

Choking on a laugh, I gasped. "You do not!"

"I'm pretty sure I do. I may have to dig that one up." We laughed over that until my sides hurt. Once we quieted, I studied my cousin. She shrugged her shoulders. "I like him, Bethany. I can't describe it. I just really, really like him."

"That's a start, at least."

"Dad's going to be difficult. I can tell."

"Dads do tend to be dads." I sighed. "Mine warned Liam away, you know?"

"He did? Uncle Ash actually warned him away?"

"He did. I didn't know he'd done it. Liam told me later. Said he didn't care if Dad killed him, he had to be with me."

"Was that how you knew?"

I blew out a breath. "It was many things. We held such an attraction for each other. Like we almost couldn't seem to help ourselves." Reese grinned at that. "It was more than that, though. He proved over and over again that he loved me. He came all the way from Scotland to see me after Mom's crash. It was Mom who told Dad to give Liam a break."

"Aunt Kate seems to be doing all right. She's all healed up?"

"Yeah, she's good."

"Dad told me what happened." She met my gaze. "And that *he's* dead."

"He is."

"Good. I'm glad."

"Same." We heard more laughter from the barn. "As for Sean. Take your time. That's the advice I have for you. Take your time and get to know him. What I know of him, and what I've seen, he's a good guy. Solid. Loyal. Like Liam, I doubt he's innocent and all that, but still, deep down, he's a good guy. Just take your time and go slow."

Reese hugged me. "Thanks. I will. And I'm happy for you."

"Thanks, so am I."

Liam-

Liam lay back on the bed, hands clasped behind his head, which was spinning slightly. Sean and Jack, idiotic mates that they were, had taken him out earlier, celebrating his last night as a free man. A free man, they'd said. *Bah,* he didn't want freedom. He wanted Bethany. Wanted her. Needed her. He'd had a couple drinks, in honor of the occasion, keeping it minimal. He'd drank in a more obligatory manner than anything else. Bethany was his future, and tomorrow he'd start that with her.

He'd had a drink in salute to the road that had brought him to this point in life. To this moment. Satisfaction filled him again. Peace. Longing. He hadn't had enough drink to drown that longing. Nowhere near enough. He'd had a drink to salute the future and the promises he would make to it. That was it, the only two drinks he'd had. It was more than the event of his bachelorhood's eminent demise warranted. Liam's mouth lifted at the corners, then he looked at the time. In less than twelve hours, she'd be his. His in every way that mattered to him. His to have and to hold until at death they were parted. He wasn't even sure if he'd be parted from her then. He couldn't imagine not having her at his side. Not being with her. Even in eternity.

Mrs. Liam Gunn. Bethany Calista Gunn. He liked the sound of that. Loved it, in fact. Loved her. It stole his breath sometimes, the love he had for the woman he was marrying. He knew he needed sleep, needed rest, but he couldn't seem to shut his mind down. It was awake, he was awake, despite the drinks he'd had earlier. He couldn't relax. He was tied in knots over the woman who owned his heart. His soul. Liam didn't feel he was being blasphemous in thinking that. More, he was forever grateful to the One who had brought them together. He'd never stop being grateful. All of a sudden, he sat up and clasped his hands together. In this world, where failed relationships and divorce seemed more common than a lasting marriage, one filled with love and devotion, he didn't want to leave anything to chance.

He prayed then, asking that he never lose his desire for his wife, that he would always value and cherish her. That he would always put her before himself. That they would never fail to communicate and strive to understand. That he would be a good husband, wise, considerate, and thoughtful.

Calming himself, he lay back and breathed deeply. Inhaling, holding it for a count, exhaling for a count. Continuing until he felt more relaxed. Bethany was his future, his purpose, and he couldn't wait. It seemed the Lord took pity on him, as he lay there, his thoughts full of her, sleep crept in, claiming him at last.

Bethany-

My clock indicated the time. A little more than ten hours until I said *I do* to the man of my dreams. Why couldn't I sleep? I needed to sleep. My heart refused to relax, though. For some insane reason, I thought of Garrett. Thoughts of how I'd imagined he and I at this moment. Maybe it was always Liam. Maybe my heart had recognized what the mind had refused to see. I was now, and had been, always in love with Liam. I prayed again for Garrett, that his heart and mind would be healed and that he'd find peace and purpose. Then I prayed for Liam and I. For our marriage, that it would be strong, that we would remain faithful and devoted to each other.

I couldn't wait. I was ready. And so very excited. Too excited to sleep, and eager, incredibly eager to start my life with Liam. Sitting up, I clicked on the lamp, my eyes taking in all the boxes packed with my things. My luggage sat, ready for our trip to Australia. Somehow, magically, Liam had found a way to go on a ride with The Man himself, from Snowy River. I hadn't even known that was possible and was beyond excited for the opportunity. I'd get to ride with Jim Craig, or rather Tom Burlinson. *Holy crap, how was this even possible?* As I climbed from bed, wanting to double-check what I had packed, I heard a tap on my door. Mom poked her head in. "Saw your light. Everything okay?"

I blushed. "Yeah. Just wound up. Can't sleep."

Mom smiled. "I was the same." She paused, then continued, "I...If you had any questions...if you are wondering about any part of it. I mean, what to expect. I'm here."

"Thanks, Mom. I think I know. Aunt Tiffy told Reese at one point, and Reese told me. I think I understand at least the basics."

Mom shook her head. "Of course, she did. Well, is there anything else you might need? Any questions at all?"

Sighing, I sat back down on my bed, abandoning my luggage, knowing everything was already correctly packed. "Like, I've seen horses breed. I know what has to happen. I guess it's the not knowing exactly *how* it will happen that has me wondering. Like, how do we get to *that* point?"

Mom hesitated, then sat beside me. "I knew, that night I knew how much I wanted your dad. Yes, there was a lingering...fear, I guess, of the unknown. But he was, he was so careful. So thoughtful. I can't imagine Liam not being the same with you."

"I know. I know he will be. I'm not worried about that. It's more..." I shrugged, shaking my head.

"Will it hurt and how much?"

"Yeah," I breathed.

Mom offered a soft smile. "Because your dad was so thorough and so careful, the pain was miniscule. Over before I'd hardly had time to register it. Everything else was so..."

"I don't need to know." I grinned. "Truly."

Laughing silently, Mom hugged me. "It truly was, though. It will be as beautiful for you as well. I cannot imagine Liam doing anything other than making it perfect."

"Thanks, Mom."

"Of course. Your dad and I love you. We're so happy for you, so proud, and so excited for your future. We love you both."

Swallowing past the lump in my throat, I hugged her. "We love you, too. And I'm so thankful for you. I don't have enough words to express my thanks to you guys for all you've done for me."

Mom stood, moving for the door. "Get some sleep. Tomorrow will be a big day."

"Goodnight, and thanks again. Love you." Mom shut the door softly behind her as she left. I climbed back into bed and clicked my lamp back off. Mercifully, sleep did seem to find me then.

Reese-

Close to one in the morning, Reese got a text from Sean.

Still up?

Reese replied:

Yeah. Can't sleep either?

He texted back:

Can't stop thinking of you.

Reese smiled to herself, her heart leaping in her chest. She'd dated before, nothing ever serious. Just couldn't seem to find someone to capture her heart or mind. What was it about Sean that attracted her? *Can't stop thinking of you.* His accent might have a bit to do with her growing feelings for him. She didn't think that was all, though. Sean made her feel like a woman. Made her glad to be a woman.

Can't stop thinking of you, either. Call me.

Perhaps she shouldn't have done that, but she *really* wanted to hear his voice. Her phone buzzed with an incoming call. Taking a breath, she answered, "Hi."

"It puts a smile on my face hearing you can't stop thinking of me either.

Reese grinned at that. "I'm glad I can make you smile, at least."

"You do far more than just that." Sean was quiet for a moment. "I think I'm in love with you, Theresa."

Reese inhaled, silently cautioning herself to go slow. "You don't know me well enough to know if you're in love with me or not, Sean."

He made a noise deep in his throat, then said, "Fair enough. I want to get to know you, though. At least tell me I've that chance."

He hadn't argued with her. Had just acknowledged her statement and requested an opportunity. Reese swallowed. "You definitely have that chance."

She heard the pleasure in his voice. "Are you of the same mind, then?"

"I want to get to know you as well."

Sean inhaled deeply, then asked, "Is there anyone else? Summat, or someone, besides yer da, that I need to know about? To be cautious about?"

"There's no one. I'm not seeing anyone. And haven't for close to a year now."

"Is there summat wrong with the men here? A lass such as you, and you've not had a man in close to a year?"

Reese gripped her phone and wondered if she ought to be honest with Sean. No, she decided. That news, that discussion could wait. "Maybe I'm just particular who I give my affections to."

"That turns me on, it does."

Reese laughed. "Omgosh, stop."

"It does." His voice rumbled deliciously in her ear. "I can only be honest with you."

"I appreciate the honesty. Truly."

"I'd best let you sleep. Can't wait to see you in yer dress tomorrow. You'll be a dream come to flesh."

"I'm blushing." She chuckled. "And I'm going to sleep. Goodnight, Sean."

"Sweet dreams, lass. I know mine will be sweet, as I'll be dreamin' of you."

They hung up and Reese lay back, holding the phone to her chest. Sean MacKenzie Murphy. It rolled off the tongue, his name. She smiled. She liked him. She really did. Men found her attractive, they always had. She was tall, willowy. With dark, auburn hair—a combination of her mom's red and her dad's dark brown. Men commented on her looks, her marksmanship on the range. But sooner rather than later, they drifted away. Intimidated maybe, by her ability to stand on her own two feet. Or maybe it was that they just didn't want to wait for her.

Would Sean react in the same way? Would he hover and chase, only to walk away when she didn't give him what he was truly after? Which certainly wasn't her heart. It was always only her body men ever wanted. Well, Reese was after more. And she would wait until she had more before giving herself to a man.

Rolling over, Reese snuggled into her pillow. It was in God's hands; it always was. Maybe this time, the One in control would answer her long-spoken prayer.

CHAPTER TWENTY-SIX
The Longest Walk

Bethany-

My heart raced, pounding furiously, as I struggled to breathe through my nerves. Not nerves from anxiety or fear. No, I wasn't fearful. Not in the least. I was antsy, ready. I wanted to *go*. Out front, just below the steps, the carriage my parents had hired waited, and in moments, Dad would walk me out to that carriage. And I'd make my way to my husband.

The photographer snapped pictures, capturing the moment, as Dad tried to gain control of himself. He cleared his throat and shook his head. "You're beautiful. You know that, right? And your mother and I are so darned proud of you. So thankful for you."

Leaning up on my toes, I kissed his cheek. "Thanks, Dad. I love you, guys. Who and what I am is due to you both. I will forever be grateful God chose you to be my parents."

Dad checked his watch. "Time to go, kitten."

I nodded and let him lead me out to the carriage. The driver had already delivered Mom, my new in-laws, my grandparents, and my bridesmaids to the meadow and the wedding arch. It was just Dad and I left. I settled into the seat, and Dad settled beside me, taking my hand in his. He kept swallowing. Kept clearing his throat. Blinking his eyes.

"You okay?" I asked, keeping my eyes ahead.

"Yeah. Just, just so proud of you and the man you've chosen. And no matter your last name, you'll always be my little girl, my kitten."

"You can't make me cry, Dad." I blew out a breath and dabbed at my eyes with a tissue from my pocket. *I was so thankful this dress had pockets.* Bless Aunt Candi's heart and intuition. The carriage stopped behind a stand of trees. I could see the crowd of our guests. Dad handed me down and as my feet touched the ground, I felt a peace settle over me. My heart slowed and I was able to breathe deeply. The scent of the evergreens, the eucalyptus, and roses calmed me further.

"You ready?" he queried.

"So ready."

Dad nodded at the coordinator and moments later the music played. The pipers played a piece, The Skye Boat Song, from the Outlander sound-track. I grinned to myself, thinking back to Bronagh's remark about Liam calling me *Sassenach.* Jamie Fraser had nothing on Liam Gunn, I was certain.

As the guests rose to their feet, and Dad and I paused at the entrance of the aisle, I saw Liam for the first time. My word, was he stunning—I hoped the photographer captured this image of him. The longest walk of my life was before me as I had to wait for Dad to lead me to my husband, to my heart, my life.

Liam-

Liam felt as though his heart had clean stopped in his chest, and he waited for it to restart. He couldn't find his lungs. "Steady on, mate," Sean murmured from off to his left. He blinked his eyes, trying to dislodge the moisture blocking his vision as Bethany made her way to him. A little more than thirty feet was all it was, but it seemed to take forever. She was a vision. An actual vision. And she was his. His eyes skimmed over her dress of pure white with the Gunn plaid displayed, and he felt his heart clench again. The music swelled, then silenced as Asher and Bethany reached him. He cleared his throat and wiped his eyes before stepping forward. The pastor said something. A greeting, maybe? He didn't hear, couldn't take in anything other than Bethany. She was his sole focus.

"Her mother and I do," Asher replied as he lifted Bethany's hand to Liam. Silent, he stared at it for a moment, lost in the moment, in the emotion. Then Bethany smiled at him and suddenly his hearing returned. He cleared his throat, and as he took her hand in his, he felt himself coming home. *She* was home. And he never wanted to be parted from her again.

Bethany-

The fading sunlight caught my ring as I lifted my hands, threading my fingers through Liam's hair. A stunning deep blue peaked at me through slitted lids, and a smile teased his mouth. "I love ye, Bethany Calista Gunn."

I inhaled, savoring his words. "I could listen to you say that for the rest of my life."

He moved us around the floor, swaying to the music as we danced, and I was blissfully thankful he was such a strong lead. "I intend to say that to ye for the rest of our lives, lass. I willna fail ye." He kissed me then. His mouth a light pressure over mine. His arms tightened and I gasped as he deepened the kiss. "*Gor,* I want ye. Is it no' time to leave yet?"

I clung to him, needing him. "What time is it?"

"It's time the two of you gave it a rest and let yer best mate cut in," Sean stated as he tapped Liam on the shoulder. "You've danced through three songs now and the other guests are wondering when they can join in."

Hiding a grin, I kissed Liam once more, then let Sean take his turn. "Yer beautiful, Bethany, darlin'. And you've made my best mate a very happy man. I thank you for that."

"Thank you, Sean. He's made me very happy."

"I see that. We all see it. It's happy, I am, for the both of you." He spun me out, then brought me back.

"Show off."

"I can't help I'm a superior dancer, darlin'." He spun me out again before bringing me back once more. "Now, I've a question for you. What advice can you offer me?" I blinked, unsure what he meant. "I'm after courting yer lovely cousin, I am. What should I know?"

"Ah, Reese."

"Aye, that's the one. The only one."

"My advice is to not rush things. Reese doesn't like to be rushed. Take things slowly. I offer that advice for your own safety. You know my dad is a violent, dangerous guy, right?" At Sean's nod, I continued, "Dad is more explosion, a battle axe, a broadsword. Strong violence. Brutal. Uncle Samuel is the destruction you'll never see coming. He's the blade in the dark. Tread carefully."

"She's worth it. And I already knew that. You can see it on them, feel it, that violence. I recognize it and accept it." He nodded. "It's Reese I want and no other will do."

"Tread carefully with Reese as well. She takes after her dad and it's her dad who trained her. She's a dead shot. Excellent marksmanship. She can field strip any gun with her eyes closed."

Sean blew out a breath. "Am I deranged for saying that turns me on even more?"

Chuckling, I shook my head. "Best of luck to you both. Be kind and gentle with her, Sean."

"I promise." Uncle Cal claimed his dance then. Followed by Jack, then Uncle Cory, then Uncle Samuel. While we danced, Uncle Samuel's gaze kept drifting across the floor to where Sean swayed with Reese.

"He's a good guy," I told my uncle. His dark eyes flicked down to me before returning to his target. "I believe he truly is in love with her. He's Liam's best friend; give him a chance."

Samuel sighed, a low rumble in his chest. "Best I can say is, I'll try."

"That's the spirit." He brought us to a stop as the song ended, then Dad was standing there.

"It's our dance, kitten." Sinatra's *The Way you look Tonight* began to play as Dad took my hand. We swayed and the cameras flashed. "I'm going to miss you. Miss having you around and under foot."

"I haven't been under foot for several years." I smiled up at him, then hugged him. "And I'm going to miss you, too. Though, the addition should start while we're gone. Are you sure you and Mom want to move into that? Liam and I could start there. We don't need that much space."

"Your mother and I are stepping back. You and Liam will run the ranch. Like your Granny and Papa, we might do more travelling. We're excited to see what you two do with the place. Liam's got a fair number of good ideas. You and he will hold a third of the ranch, your mother and I will hold a third, and your grandparents will hold a third. We've got it all worked out."

"Sometimes, this all feels like a dream. I pinch myself occasionally just to make sure I'm actually awake."

Dad chuckled. "Your dream is coming true, kitten. And our song is ending, and your husband would like to cut in. Typical impatient Scot." Dad winked to show he was only kidding, then kissed my forehead, and stepped back, handing me to Liam.

My husband's arms slid around me, pulling me close. "It's time, Mo Gràidh."

"Is it?" I shivered.

"It is, love. Are ye ready?"

"So incredibly very ready."

Bethany-

My heart thudded, pounded as I tried to catch my breath. Liam slid to the side, pulling my head down against his chest, where I heard his heart hammering along with mine. Sweat beaded on our skin, glistening in the glow from the dozens of candles he'd lit in the room. My limbs felt weak as I trembled; if there was a fire, I wasn't going to make it out. We lay there for several minutes. Liam trailed his fingers lightly over my skin as we caught our breath. "Are ye all right, lass?" Liam finally spoke, nuzzling my temple. He kissed me there, his breath still harsh, making me grin.

Mom had been right. This was everything. Liam had made it everything. When he'd lit the candles and laid me on the bed covered with rose petals, and he'd looked supremely satisfied and simultaneously hungry, any lingering fears were erased. He built such a fire in me, bringing me to the point of shattering, just to ease me back again, before bringing me to that point once more. Taking his time. Refusing to rush. Liam was *thorough,* so incredibly thorough.

"I didn't know it would be like that. I am *very* much all right. Better than all right. *Much* better than all right." Liam chuckled and kissed me again. "Is it always like that? No wonder people have such a hard time not doing...*that.*"

He chuckled again. "Nae, lass. 'Tisna always like that. *That* was another level entirely. I've never experienced anything even near to that afore."

"So...you enjoyed it? Enjoyed me? It...I wasn't a...a disappoint—" He rolled fast, pinning me under him. The look on his face was irritated disbelief.

"I'll stop ye right there, lass. Ye could *never* be a disappointment. Dinna ever let me hear ye suggest such a thing to me again. Ye're perfection, ye ken that?" He tightened his grip on my shoulders, then kissed me hard, deep. "Mayhap I needs must show ye again how extraordinarily un-disappointed I am. Ye fair took me breath away, ye did." His hand left my shoulder, sliding down my side, curving over my hip, reaching my thigh, grasping it firmly as he lifted, hitching it over his waist. "I need ye now, if ye're willing. I must have ye again. Now."

Spectacular. Devastating. Beautiful. Raw. Sweet. Mind-blowing. I was running out of adjectives. I had no words to describe what he did to me;

how extraordinarily beautiful he made it. How breathtakingly, masterfully he loved me. Liam left me without doubt. I no longer wondered. I knew.

Bethany-

Almost three weeks later, we pulled into the ranch driveway. I had thoroughly enjoyed our time away together and would never forget getting to meet Tom Burlinson in person, nor getting to ride out with him to the Jim Craig cabin, but I had missed home. I'd missed my family, my horses. Liam turned his deep blue gaze to me. Such heat in his eyes. Such knowing, *needful* heat. My heart and body responded eagerly, anticipating our first evening home.

As we stepped from the car, construction sounds filled the air, coming from the back of the house. The whine of electric saws and the pounding of hammers had me wondering how the new addition was coming. For the time being, Liam and I would take the smallest of the cabins, not needing much space. Plus, it was the one furthest from the main house. Mom and Dad met us on the front step. "Welcome home, newlyweds!"

I smiled as Mom hugged me tight, then Dad wrapped his arms around us both, even as he offered a firm handshake to his son-in-law. "Welcome back, kitten. Your mother has the cabin set up for you, guys. Should be everything you need in there."

"Thanks, guys." I smiled at them. "It's good to be home; I think I'm traveled out. How's everything here?"

"We're all good," Dad said. "Better now you're back. How was your trip?"

"Magical. Extraordinarily perfect." I smiled even as I blushed under my husband's regard. What this man could do to me with a simple look.

"Get settled in, then I want to hear all about your ride with Jim Craig." Mom smiled. "And I hope you took pictures."

"We've got *all* the pictures, Kate. Ye willna be disappointed," Liam assured her even as he continued his intense study of me.

"Kate, love, let's let the kids get settled in, and when they're ready for company, they can come see us." Dad must have noted Liam's line of thought. Though, it wasn't difficult to grasp. Not with the heated intent virtually pouring forth.

"But they just—" Mom started to say. Dad whispered something to her. "Oh. *Oh.* Seriously?"

"Apparently. Now, let's leave them be. I understand entirely; in fact, I remember that state quite well. If you need, I can refresh your memory." Mom gave Dad a heated look that I caught from the corner of my eye as he took her hand and led her into the house. I couldn't help the grin that flashed, then quickly faded.

Liam's voice was raw, full of need as he took my hand. "We'll get the luggage later. I need ye, now." Nodding, I let him lead me into the cabin, our temporary home. He shut the door behind us and locked it before lifting me into his arms and carrying me up the stairs. His mouth met mine in ardent, happy, desire. And though this wasn't our permanent residence, in his arms, I knew I was home in every sense of the word.

The End

Read on for a sneak peek at my latest project.

BETWEEN BLOOD AND STONE:

A Guardian Series Sneak Peek

**This snippet from Between Blood and Stone—technically the third book (standalone) in my Guardians series (Between Earth and Eden, and Between Heaven and Hell)—is NOT the final piece and most-likely will change to some extent as this is a first draft work in progress.*

***While Between Blood and Stone may have faith themes, it is NOT intended to be a Christian novel. However, it WILL be closed door.*

****The first two books in the Guardian series are NOT currently available (I am working on revisions for them and intend to re-release them late this year or early next year).*

BEFORE

The Guardian

From out of the void the King spoke and Creation took place. All that was, is, and would be was set in motion. Nothing was outside His grasp. His knowledge infinite. His power unimaginable. His forethought, purpose, and intention unknowable, even for those of us that dwelled with Him *outside* the bonds of time. When the clock struck, with the first tick, when the first moment of measured time and existence began, the entire realm shuddered. And all of Heaven took note.

We didn't know then, couldn't have fathomed the reach of that simple action...of *time* beginning. It was a ripple that turned into a tidal wave, that became a tsunami, that flooded the heavens as we knew it; the effects of which we still feel to this day. A ripple in time—the sheer weight and depth stealing the breath from our lungs.

I, and those like me, Guardians and other angelic beings, have stood witness to several of these *rippling* moments: Time's beginning, The Creation, The Fall—when the Deceiver raised his fist against the King, The incomprehensible act of the King lowering Himself to become as the humans—to be born of a woman, and thirty-three years later when He allowed Himself to be slaughtered once for all. When He rose again just three days later. To the most recent. An event just as perplexing as the rest. When Aurek, the Guardian, took his human, Jane, as wife. To live with her as *Man and Wife.*

What did it all mean? What was the purpose? I felt it then and feel it now. That shudder. That tremor. It reaches deep within my bones, going further still to my soul. To the very essence of my being. What did any of it mean? I was still mystified, entirely lacking in understanding. But just as before, I, and those of my ilk, had a job to do, a purpose to perform. We were not to question, not to assume, or ponder the mind and purpose of the King. Our purpose was to obey. Guarding, shielding our charges from the fiery attacks of the enemy was our order, even unto death. I may not comprehend what was happening in the heart and mind of the King, but I knew that no matter the cost, I would follow Him.

My human was awakening. Gifts the King had bestowed upon her were coming alive. Her spirit was sparking like a flint against stone. Knowing the distance I must maintain, I've stayed in my spiritual form, battling in this body rather than my human version. The latter being so unwieldy. So unpredictable. What would happen if I took a form like hers? If I became as she is? Would I succumb? Aurek was, *is,* a powerful Guardian. Yet he was not strong enough to withstand his human, or the ways of the heart, nor the desires of the flesh.

Why did the King make them if they are this dangerous? This volatile and unpredictable?

Is it a test? Is that what they are? *Perhaps.* Either way, I fear I will need to get closer to her, my human. The darkness circles, drawing ever closer. *It* certainly hasn't hesitated to exchange its spiritual body for an earthly form to accomplish its nefarious goals.

Why do I hesitate? I *must* not. To do so is to bring harm to my charge. To fail in my endeavor. How to approach her and not fall, not fail? How do I battle what I am uncertain of? The enemy will not hesitate. I must cement it in my mind, make it firm in heart—I will get closer, but I *will not* touch her. No matter the draw she is for me. No matter the temptation, I will be strong enough. For her sake, I must be.

The Hunter

I hovered, unseen, some distance from the circle of standing stones, quietly studying them. Desperate. Planning, and plotting. Knowing what was within the stones, what they allowed, but how to gain access to it? Hallowed ground, those stones. Gateways to what had once been my home. I and the rest of the Fallen were banned from the circles, hadn't set foot inside one in thousands of years. All for what? Because of some misunderstanding? The Morning Star had lied to us. Had told us of the King's desire to replace us with His new human creation. What else were we to think? The Morning Star was second only to the King Himself. And the King had certainly proven His regard for the human worms, even going so far as to stamp His image upon them. Setting them apart for His special purpose.

With disdain, I studied the humans. My disgust clearly written upon my face; if the humans could have seen me, that is. They walked to and fro, taking pictures with their contraptions and devices, oblivious to the holy ground they tread upon. Oblivious to the hunter contemplating their destruction. What utter uselessness. I abhorred them with an unending loathing. *Why?* Why should *they* receive the King's regard? They who don't even acknowledge Him. Who tell each other He's nothing more than a figment of their imagination. All for what? Because of choice? Because of free-will? Was it really worth it to the King? Truly? Is this chaotic, hellish existence what the King had envisioned for them? None of it made sense. It nearly drove me mad, at times, trying to sort it all out. The only thing I knew for certain was that I despised them.

Shifting, I tried to get closer to the stones. The repulsive energy like an aura around them lashed at me, burning with fiery sensation. As it always did, and had since the Fall. The pain of it drew a growl from deep inside, and I ground my teeth together, snarling softly against the burn. In pain and frustration, I shook my head, agitation a maelstrom inside me, as I was forced to move away. Suddenly, from across the expanse of time and space, a spark flashed, almost like lightning, drawing my gaze, snagging my attention from the pain, the circle, and the people there. It was the brilliance of the flash that snared my focus. The magnitude of it reminded me of the King, only slightly weaker. The thought of Him had that insufferable loathing taking another bite out of me. *What could have caused it?* And why? With one last longing look at the desire of my heart, I left the stones and began to pursue whatever it was that had momentarily lit the heavens. Perhaps whatever had caused it would be the key to returning to my former celestial home.

CHAPTER ONE

Flight

Ivy-

Twenty-one years later

Mom and Dad drove me to the airport. This would be my first time away from home by myself and we were trying to not acknowledge how difficult this was for us all. They'd already helped me get my luggage checked and get my boarding pass. Looking over my shoulder, I stood in line at the security checkpoint, then waved at them before handing over my passport and other needed items. The gentleman quickly checked those, then motioned me to the security scanner. Once through, I located my parents again, and waved once more, blinking away tears, before heading to find my gate.

How had I arrived here? Not literally, like how had I arrived in Seattle for this flight. But how had I arrived at this decision in the first place? Making a solo trip to Ireland. *Me.* Me who had never flown anywhere. Ever. Had never even traveled farther than Seattle before. *It was that moth.* It was more than the moth, though, wasn't it? Unseeing, my eyes watched the crowds of people shuffling past. Arriving in Seattle, or like me, leaving it.

Honestly, this trip had been a long time coming. Moth notwithstanding. I think my entire life had led me to this point. Finding an empty seat within eyesight of my gate, I settled as best I could into the uncomfortable chair, and tried to calm my unsettled nerves.

My mother, my birth mother, not the woman I called *Mom*, but the one who'd physically given birth to me, had surrendered me, just hours old, to the Clallam County Fire Department, District 3, in Sequim, Washington. No questions asked. No statements given. That was all I knew of the woman who had chosen to allow me life, rather than end mine at her convenience.

I didn't begrudge her the choices she'd made. That she'd given me up. That she hadn't wanted me. Heaven knew she'd had choices I'd have had no say in. For some reason though, a reason known only to she and God, she'd allowed me life. For that alone, I was grateful. I was grateful, too, that it was my *parents* who'd adopted me.

From the start, my parents had been open and honest with me about my birth and how they'd adopted me. They, too, were grateful to my birth-mother. At no time, in my last twenty-one years, had I ever doubted their love for me. That they cherished and wanted me. Not once.

Not even when the strange occurrences had begun. The premonitions, the...visions. Gifts from God, Mom had always told me. Sometimes, I wondered about that. Good typically came from the things I saw, sure; there was no doubt about that. But I always felt a little off, a little spooked by them afterward.

Poppy had been my first...vision. Poppy is my best friend. I work for she and her mother, both named Paige, though my friend went by Poppy instead. Turning Paiges, their bookstore, was located in downtown Sequim. It had been the week before first grade. I'd dreamed of this slender, blond girl with a missing front tooth. Dreamed of her for that entire week. I met her the first day of school, and we've been best friends ever since.

My granddad's heart attack had been another incident. The ambulance had arrived in time. In other instances, we'd avoided heavy traffic, or accidents. I'd even helped to locate a lost pet or two. And, I'd known beforehand on that last heart attack, that Papa wasn't going to make it.

Overhead, I heard my flight called, pulling me from my thoughts. I gathered my things and stood, getting in line with the other passengers. Once I found my seat, my carry-on stowed and I'd buckled myself in, my pulse began to ramp up again, so to divert myself, I considered once more, the path that had brought to this point.

"So," Poppy had said over the noise in the room, "you going to tell me what's been up with you lately?"

We'd finished eating and now were just waiting on our checks. "What do you mean?"

"Planning a trip, are we?" Her dark blond brows arched with her question, framing her blue eyes.

I just stared at her. Of course, she'd noticed. Of course, she had. I'd tried to be so careful to not alert anyone. I'd ordered those travel books off Amazon for crying out loud. Used my Prime account and everything. Should have known I hadn't been fooling anyone. "I don't know...maybe."

"Were you going to say anything?" I'd heard the trace of pain, or was it fear in her voice? "Or were you going to wait to tell me until you needed me to look after your pet plants?"

"It's not like that, Pop." I'd kept my voice calm.

"What's it like then?" Those blues eyes had beseeched me. "Tell me."

Our server arrived then with our checks and I'd picked up the bill for both, feeling guilty. The server, Daryl, walked away with the cash after I thanked him.

"You didn't have to do that, Ivy." There was censure in her voice. "I can pay for my own meal, you know."

"I know." I'd said as I'd stood and gathered my coat and purse. "I wanted to."

"*Stop feeling guilty.*" She'd admonished. "There's no need. And, thank you for dinner. I still want to know what's going on, though."

Taking a deep breath, I'd nodded towards the door, and we'd exited into the damp spring night. A crescent moon had been peeking through the clouds, filtering down through the budding trees along the sidewalk. We'd started meandering, the silence between us stretching until Poppy had finally prompted, "So?"

"Truly," I'd exhaled, unsure how to explain my reasoning. "I honestly don't even know if I'm going. It's...there's this pull, this almost *need* to go. I didn't say anything, to *anyone* yet, because I just don't know."

"I get that, but you went so far as to read books on travelling there. That says you're at the very least giving it some serious consideration."

"I *am* considering it. I'm just not *sure* yet." Poppy had just given an exasperated look and waited for me to continue. "I've been having these, these dreams of places there. That's what caught my attention with the books. Two of the places I'd dreamed about were in those books. It was just weird, and I wanted to know more about it."

We'd received a large shipment of travel books in at the shop, and as I'd been scanning them, entering them into our inventory, I'd looked through them. Just skimming random pages. Imagining what it was like there. My eye had snagged on that fireplace. The stone one. The one I'd been dreaming about for the last several weeks off and on. My brain had tickled, an itch I hadn't been able to reach. It was just an almost *knowing*.

"You've been dreaming about places in those books?" she'd asked, shooting me a sharp look. "What kind of dreaming are we talking about here?"

"You remember what I told you before? About getting feelings about certain things? Like, when I knew I was going to meet you and we'd be friends?"

"Premonitions, you mean?"

"Yeah," I shrugged, "and that's not all. There've been other...occurrences."

"Like what?"

"Well, like, I had a, a vision or something. I could hear and *smell* the images I was seeing. And then, there was this moth that for three days in a row, had showed up in the exact same place on my bathroom mirror."

"The vision thing is weird, I guess. But, let's face it, like you've stated, you've had them before. And, you do tend to attract wildlife of various kinds."

"Yeah, but how many times has the wildlife left an imprint in the shape of Ireland before?"

"Seriously?" she'd stopped walking and turned to me.

"Seriously."

"Ivy, maybe you shouldn't go. I just literally got chills down my spine. You know we used to tease you about your affinity for the local wildlife."

"I remember. You called me a witch." I'd chuckled then and shook my head at her.

"You know we were just teasing. Honestly. And besides, we meant you were a nice witch." Poppy had grinned back at me. "But seriously though, this is all extremely odd. Even for you." We'd walked on in silence for another half-block before Poppy continued. "Tell me more about the visions."

"Well," I'd taken a deep breath before diving into this one, knowing how it would come across, "the other morning, as I was getting dressed, I saw a man leaning up against a fireplace. He looked right at me. Then both he and the fireplace were gone. Later that same day when I got home, I opened my door and for a very brief moment, that fireplace was back and a fire crackling in it. I could *hear* it and I *smelled* it. The smoke and the burning peat. And then, I'd had this dream, I'd been standing in a stone circle and there was fog and mist all around, and then this growling started from someplace within the shadows beyond the stones. I'd tried running from whatever it was, but slipped and fell. I'd scraped my hands on one of the stones and then this...that same man was there. The one I'd seen earlier, near that fireplace. He helped me. He'd lifted me off the ground and had said I'd needed to hurry. Then he kissed—"

"He *kissed* you?"

"On the forehead only. Calm down."

"Whoa." She'd grinned and wagged her brows suggestively. "Forehead kisses are super sweet. What did he look like?"

I'd rolled my eyes at her antics. "*That* I can't remember. I've tried. Maybe this is just my over-active imagination at work here."

"Maybe. But do you honestly believe that?"

"I don't know."

"But you're still considering going?"

"I think so...I don't know. Maybe?"

We'd stopped at a bench near Washington and Bell and sat. The mist shifted through, damp and heavy as Poppy stared off across the street for a minute or two, then turned to me. "Ivy...you know I love you and always will. Have right from the start. Even with your little special gifts, shall we call them? Even with those, I still love you."

"But?" I'd asked, because I could hear one coming.

"But I'm worried about you. I'm worried about *this*. Whatever this is."

"I am, too."

"And yet you're still going."

"Pop, I think I'm meant to go."

"Meant by who, or what, though?"

Chills had skated down my spine at that. I had shaken my head, then croaked, "I don't know."

Ivy-

I don't remember the takeoff, flight, or landing. I just knew we were now in Salt Lake City. *Had I blacked out?* If I had, I would think someone might have noticed. My heart pounded in my chest. How could I have no memory of the first part of my flight? The feeling, the not knowing was terrifying. I blinked and took a deep breath, trying to calm myself.

"Hi." A female voice said. Looking up, I took in the young woman before me. She was probably around my age. She had blond hair and blue-green eyes. She wore faded blue jeans and a deep wine red flannel.

"Hello," I replied before turning back to the window, still trying to get my bearings. The terminal crew seemed to be just finishing up with their preflight activities; I watched as they drove the trucks away from the plane.

Anxiety spiking, my thoughts attacked, swarming like angry hornets. My throat felt dry and my breath became shallow. I'd never flown before this trip, and hadn't anticipated being *afraid* per se, however, it would appear fear was now on me. Especially because of the time I lost on the first portion of this flight. I took another slow, deep breath, just trying to calm my frazzled nerves. Of their own accord, my hands gripped the armrests, tightening.

"Nervous?" the woman beside me asked.

I swallowed, then nodded.

"First time flying?" she continued. Nodding was all I could manage at the moment. "There's not much to it; really, it's pretty easy. Bit of a rumble at takeoff and landing, but otherwise, it's smooth sailing. Or, flying, I guess."

"Thanks," I managed to whisper. The flight attendants began their safety speeches, explaining all that I'd need to know in case of malfunction. Tuning out everything around me, I zoned in to each and everything they had to say. Once they were finished and seated, the engines of the plane revved up and it began to move.

"Where're you headed?"

"Ireland."

"So am I!" She replied. "My name's Bethany, by the way. What part of Ireland?"

"Ivy," I said. "Ultimately, I'll land in Cork, then plan to explore around Clare, Cork, and the surrounding areas."

"Oh, nice! Are you going by yourself? Or are you meeting someone there?"

"Just me." I swallowed.

"Wow, that's awesome. Wish I'd taken the time, or been brave enough to come on my own before. I've been several times with my parents—my grandparents live just south of Kealkill in County Cork—so we visit them quite a bit. But I've never been on my own. What brings you to the Emerald Island?"

"I'm...to be quite honest, I'm not sure really. I just really wanted to come, and it seemed like a good idea...so here I am."

Conversation seemed to flow easily after that. Turns out she was from Wyoming and owned a real, working cattle ranch. I thought that was pretty cool. I've never ridden a horse, and felt a moment of whimsy at the thought of learning to ride. Bethany seemed to be such a capable young woman. She impressed me with her ability to start a conversation with a complete stranger, and her ability to simply embrace life so thoroughly. Dinner was served and once we were finished eating and everything had been cleared away, in unspoken agreement, we each turned to our own activities. She picked up a book and began reading, and I surfed the available movies and ended up picking one of the new Marvel movies. Chris Hemsworth was in it and I figured I couldn't go wrong there.

I'm not sure when I fell asleep, but I woke as the plane engines shifted sound and began to descend. Sitting up, I stretched then looked out the window. Green; everywhere I looked was green. The beauty of it took my breath away. Sequim is quite green, but these shades somehow seemed different. Different, yet stunningly beautiful. I continued staring out the window even after the plane had landed.

Bethany and I made our way through the Dublin airport, and I was glad for her continued assistance; she knew exactly where to go. We stopped at a currency exchange station to get the correct currency for the country before heading off to our gate. We were on the same connecting flight to Cork, though not beside each other on this flight. Having been through the first two flights, this one wasn't as harrowing to me. No more than thirty minutes or so.

The seatbelt light turned off and I stood to stretch. As I gathered my things from the overhead, Bethany approached. "Ivy, it was really great to meet you. Here's my number, in case you need anything, even if it's just a face you happen to know."

"Thanks so much," I said as she handed me her business card. "I appreciate that and may take you up on your offer."

"Do that. I look forward to it."

I watched as Bethany moved off, headed towards an elderly couple. Taking a deep breath, I turned from her and made my way to the baggage claim. After gathering my luggage, I headed for the loading zone at the airport to locate my Hackney driver, then sent a quick text off to my parents so they knew I'd at least arrived safely. Ryan, my driver, helped me load my bags into his car, and then we were off. Cork traffic was a bit crazy, not to mention the whole driving on the wrong side of the vehicle and roadway. Cork wasn't as big as Dublin, but it was still sizable. My anxiety ratcheted up as Ryan maneuvered through the congestion. Soon, though, we were moving into the more-scenic countryside.

ACKNOWLEDGEMENTS:

I will try to keep this short, but make no promises. Because, truly, I am thankful to and for so many and so much. To you, the readers, thank you. Thank you for reading closed door romance books and for picking this one up and giving it a chance. Seriously. Without you all, there would be no me here to write these books. My truest desire is to see them read and enjoyed, so again, THANK YOU.

Thank you to the BETA readers, for your early eyes on this story and your supremely valuable feedback. Dawn, Kym, Mary, Debi, Judi, truly, I appreciate you and the time and consideration you gave to me and this story.

To the editors, Kristin Vayden, and Ramona Mihai, thank you. Kristin, thank you for your fantastic job in helping me to see this story in a different light and helping me to take it to the next level. And to Ramona, thank you for putting the polishing touches in place. To Rachel Parker for shining a light on my writing and these characters, and for the love you've shown them.

To Jena Brignola for yet another grand slam of a cover. I thank you for having the vision and having the talent to bring it forth. Perfection. Just, thank you.

To my family, my husband, William, my boys, Aaron and Andrew, guys you mean the world to me and I will ALWAYS fight dragons for you. To my daughter, Lindsay and son-in-law, Hunter, thank you for constantly inspiring me.

To my Lord and Savior, Jesus Christ, thank You for loving me so unconditionally, thank You for Your grace and mercy, and for blessing me with this opportunity, and for the people You've brought into my life.

ABOUT THE AUTHOR:

A child of divorce and abuse, E. L. Irwin found escape in reading and writing. She's a self-described romantic-rebel who wears her heart on her sleeve and tends to shoot from the hip on subjects that matter. E.L. lives in the Pacific Northwest on a small farm with her husband, children, and four dogs. When not reading or writing romance, E.L. enjoys, riding horses, going for drives, tattoos, antique shopping, starry nights, the smell and sound of rain, a deep red wine, a smooth whisk(e)y, camping, bonfires, and hanging out with her horses, cows, chickens, ducks, and goats.

NEWSLETTER SIGNUP:

 Scan the QR Code to signup for my monthly newsletter and receive firsthand knowledge of upcoming projects, release news, and giveaways. When you sign up, you'll receive the prequel chapters for Out of the Blue, book 1 in the Blues Avenue series.

BOOKS BY E.L. Irwin:

The Blues Avenue Series:

Out of the Blue

Written in the Deep

AUTHOR NOTE:

If you've read Written, or its predecessor, *Out of the Blue*, you will have "spent time" on a dude ranch. The Blues Avenue ranch is entirely fictitious however, the dude ranch experience is not. Cody is a real city in the state of Wyoming, and dude ranches are a part of the community there. The Cody Nite Rodeo is a real event. In fact, Cody is known as the Rodeo Capital of the World. Their Nite Rodeo begins around the beginning of June and runs nightly through August. When able, and for authenticity ONLY, I tried to use actual places and events for the story. My daughter and I attended the opening night a few years back and had a wonderful time, and even got to sit on the bull, Mongo—though, he's since retired, and at the time of writing this, Norman has taken his place. In addition to that rodeo experience, we were able to go on a trail ride with the crew at the Bill Cody Ranch, and **highly** encourage the experience. We had a wonderful time, and the area is ripe with history, scenery, and culture.

Two or three years before our Cody trip, my daughter and I also took a trip to Ireland. And yes, we visited a pub and had a proper pint of Guinness (having one in Ireland is truly tops), and stayed in Airbnb's. One was even a manor house in Enniskillen in County Fermanagh. Now, while Collins Bar is a real pub in County Cork, we did not visit this particular one while there. Instead, we went to one similar in the town of Ringaskiddy. Unfortunately, that one didn't work for this story setting, so I had to choose another. An Irish pub is a completely different experience from what one might find at a local bar or nightclub in the States. The true Irish pub is a meeting place; it's a gathering place for conversation, a hearty meal, and good drink. It's a family environment, and an enjoyable one at that. Murphy's restaurant in Castletownbere is another real place, and we did eat there. The clam chowder was to die for. Cong is another real town, and the John Wayne and Maureen O'Hara statue from the movie *The Quiet Man* is there. In fact, most of the places mentioned in Ireland, are real places, even that monument to September 11.

Now, Scotland, I have not visited. Yet. But I definitely plan to, and tried to do my due diligence making this as authentic to the culture and people as I could, and fervently hope I have done it justice. For instance, Edinburgh (ed-in-bur-uh), Inverness, Wick, Black Isle, Drumsmittal, these are all real places in Scotland. The farm, Halkirk, where the Highland Games was held is the actual farm for the location of this particular event, though the time of year was changed slightly for this story.

Horses, and to some extent, cattle, are something I do know, and have experience with. I never did any Eventing, other than Team Penning with a local group, but did own and ride horses. Mostly trail riding, but I did ride some that needed a firm hand and deep understanding. Problem horses were ones I tended to tangle with, and seemed to do well with. Some of the things done with horses in these books I have personally done, or have seen done by others. And cattle, well, I breed and raise them, and eat and sell them. And love them all the more for each experience they offer.

Thank you for reading this book and for your interest in life in the west and in the cultures of the fine peoples mentioned here.

GLOSSARY AND PRONUNCIATIONS:

<u>*Ranch Terms:</u>

Remuda (reh-mu-duh): a herd of horses that have been saddle-broken and are available for use on a ranch.

Gelding (gell-ding): male horse that has been castrated and cannot produce offspring.

Paint (pane-t): technically the word paint is a shortened term for the breed, American Paint Horse, but is used loosely along with pinto for a darker colored horse with white areas of color, like paint splashes, on it. Sometimes they end up more white than the darker color, and sometimes the white is almost nonexistent.

<u>*Scottish Terms:</u>

Aye (eye/I): yes, okay.

Nae (nay): no.

Ken (ken): to know or understand.

Aboot (uh-boot): about.

Lass/Lad (just as they look) girl/boy.

Dinna Fash (din-uh f-ash): don't worry.

Doaty (doh-ty): slang for stupid or ridiculous.

Bairn (bear-n): baby, infant, small child.

Braw (bra): fine, lovely, strong.

Bonnie (bon-nee): lovely, beautiful, pretty.

Wee (we): small, of little stature.

Haud (hod): hold.

Reiver (Reev-er): robber, raider, plunderer.

Kilt (is what happened to the last person who called it a skirt): a plaid patterned garment used in traditional Scottish dress.

Sassenach (sass-eh-nak): someone not from the Highlands.

Mo Gràidh (mo gry): Gaelic for my love, my dear, my darling.

Seanmhair (shen-a-ver): Gaelic for grandmother/grandma.

Seanair (shen-er): Gaelic for grandfather/grandpa.

*Irish Terms:

Skelp (skel-p): to slap or hit someone.

Boot (boo-t): the trunk of a car.

Lorry (lor-ree): truck.

Gobshite (gob-shy-t): fool, idiot, or jerk.

Eejit (ee-jit): fool, idiot, or jerk.

Wellies (well-eez): short for Wellingtons/rubber boots.

Stramash (Stray-mush): scuffle, or fight.

Craic (crack): What's the craic, meaning, "What's new?" or "How're things going?"